"You must be the most beautiful woman ever created by God," Dempsey whispered hoarsely.

"And every year of your life, Vernie, God has added to your beauty inside and out until now, at the very sight of you, my heart cries aloud in wonder."

"You are mad," Veronica replied softly, trapped in the intensity of his gaze, unable to look away from the piercing blue of his eyes.

"Am I?"

"Yes."

Her gloved hand went to Dempsey's cheek and lingered there. His hair was no longer the blond of his youth, but dark now, like honey, sparkling with gold and silver in the sunlight as it whispered down across his brow. His wide, breathlessly beautiful eyes, fringed by thick, dark lashes, blinked down at her in silent inquiry. His lips parted the slightest bit, revealing the ivory whiteness of his teeth. He had grown into a strong man, a man rich in virtue, an honorable man, she was certain. How could he have grown to be anything less than strong, honorable, virtuous? Veronica rose on tiptoe and pressed her lips gently against his.

"I am mad as well," she whispered when their lips parted.

Books by Judith A. Lansdowne

JUST IN TIME

MY FAIR QUIGGLEY

THE MYSTERY KISS

SHALL WE DANCE?

JUST IN TIME

Judith A. Lansdowne

ZEBRA BOOKS
Kensington Publishing Corp.
http://www.kensingtonbooks.com

One

Shropshire, England, 1795

"Release me at once, sir! Where the deuce did you come from and what the devil is wrong with you?" Berinwick struggled mightily to free himself from the hound. He held to the corner of the door frame with his left hand and swung his right leg one way and then the other. The dog grunted. It drooled. Saliva flew. But the beast had seized the duke around the ankle and, though its teeth did not pierce the boot's leather, the dog's hold was strong enough to keep Berinwick from shaking the danged animal loose. In frustration, Berinwick raised his riding crop. He could not bring himself to whack it down across the hound's snout, however, so he whacked it against the rectory door instead. Once. Twice. Thrice. "Devil take it, answer the door, Langton!" he shouted, exasperated.

He was about to pound the riding crop against the door a fourth time when it opened abruptly and a gentleman—definitely not Langton—a somewhat older gentleman without a coat or a waistcoat, his shirtsleeves rolled up to his elbows and his gray-streaked, honey-blond hair sticking up in scattered peaks, stepped out, reached down, and seized the hound by the scruff of the neck. "Drop!" the gentleman ordered as he shook the animal—shook it much too gently, in Berinwick's view. "Drop it at once, Theophilus!"

"Drop *it?* I'm an it?"

"Do you want him to let you go or not?"

"Yes."

"Then cease quibbling over words. He does not in the least realize he has taken hold of a person. He simply thinks he has found a boot. Quite a lively boot. Theophilus, drop it this instant!"

With a growl much resembling a mutter, the hound did as he was told, whereupon the man released the scruff of the dog's neck, knelt down beside it, and took its head in his hands. He stroked the beast gently and whispered words that sounded to Berinwick suspiciously like praise.

"Oh, that's just the thing," Berinwick mumbled. "Tell him he's a good dog so he will do it again."

"I am telling him he was a good dog to drop you, lad," the gentleman replied, unperturbed. "Not that it is any of your concern what I say to him."

"Not any of my concern? After that fiend—"

"He is not a fiend. He's an elderly hound who has lost a good deal of his eyesight and a wee bit of his mind." The man rose from his knees to face Berinwick straight on. "And I am an elderly gentleman who has lost all sense of propriety," he grinned. "I beg your pardon. I ought not to be spouting excuses for my dog gnawing on your boot with you in it. I'm weary, is all. Theo would beg your pardon as well if he realized you were in the boot. I'm the Reverend Mr. Dempsey," he added, extending his hand. "And you are?"

"Berinwick."

"Berinwick? His Grace the Duke thereof?"

"Precisely."

"Well, I am pleased to make your acquaintance, your grace. Theophilus, you devil, you have just attempted to eat our benefactor."

"Rowf!" responded the hound in what Berinwick decided was a most unrepentant tone.

"Do come inside, your grace," Dempsey invited. "I regret the rectory is in turmoil. I was not expecting visitors quite so soon." Especially not you, Dempsey added silently as Berinwick stepped carefully over the hound and into the vestibule.

"I have been moving things around," the rector continued as he escorted Berinwick in the direction of the front parlor, attempting to ignore the duke's amazing youthfulness and the fact that Berinwick wore a black patch over his left eye. Whoever would have guessed the man would prove to be so young and so fierce-looking.

"However, two chairs do remain before the hearth, at least," Dempsey said, "and I believe I saw glasses somewhere about. I know I have port to fill them. You would not be opposed to a bit of port, your grace?"

When no reply to his question was forthcoming, Dempsey, who had just entered the parlor, turned to discover Berinwick standing on the threshold, scowling.

"You pushed the front of the sofa flat up against the window like that on purpose, Dempsey?" the duke queried. "How the deuce do you expect anyone to sit on the thing?"

"Well, I don't, actually. It is merely there because I—"

"And you think tables ought to be stacked one upon the other in a corner?" interrupted Berinwick.

"No, but—"

"Well, the tables certainly didn't leap there by themselves, did they? And what have your chairs been doing, Mr. Dempsey? Dancing a reel?"

Dempsey smiled at that. Actually, the chairs did look as though they had been engaged in lively exercise.

Berinwick, his fisted hands on his hips, stared around the room, perplexed. "How long have you been here?" he asked. "I mean to say, how long did it take you to destroy this parlor entirely?"

Dempsey blinked at the duke in bewilderment. "I arrived about an hour ago, your grace. And since I had to remove the holland covers from the furniture anyway, I thought I may as well—"

"What? You may as well what?"

"Move things out of the way so that I could get a better look at—"

"The carpet? I see. And, of course, you decided you were not particularly fond of the carpet, so you rolled it up and wedged it against the wall like that until you could carry it out to the burn pile, eh?"

"No. I rolled up the carpet because there was a lump beneath it and naturally I wanted to see what it was."

Berinwick's fists left his hips. He thrust his riding crop into the top of his boot, leaned a shoulder against the door frame, and crossed his arms over his chest. "You wanted to see what it was. You thought it might be the remains of the gentleman who held this position before you?"

Dempsey laughed. "No, your grace. It was not as large a lump as all that."

"What was it?"

"What was what?"

"The lump."

"Nothing really. A bit of rubbish."

"Beneath the carpet?"

The Reverend Mr. Dempsey shrugged his shoulders. "I cannot explain how it got there. Do sit down, your grace, and let me pour you a glass of port. I promise not to move another piece of furniture as long as you remain if it annoys you to see it done, but I should like the satisfaction of having welcomed you properly."

Berinwick uncrossed his arms and stalked toward one of the two chairs that were accessible near the hearth. They didn't face the hearth, he noted, as any reasonable chairs would have done. They faced each other head-on as though in the midst of some portentous discussion. Berinwick lowered himself into the least lumpy-looking of the two.

"Yes, there's the wine," Dempsey murmured, his gaze having searched the room and come to rest at the windowsill just beyond the sofa. "I knew it had to be here somewhere. I took it from the cellar to, ah, let it warm up a bit before dinner. Mr.

Langton did promise to return with my trunk and a bit of dinner. And the glasses are—beneath the sofa!"

"Beneath the sofa?" Berinwick stopped in the midst of removing his gloves and stared at the gentleman's back. "What the deuce is glassware doing beneath the sofa in the parlor?"

"I cannot say," Dempsey replied, hunkering down to retrieve two wineglasses from a set arrayed on a silver tray. "They did not begin here, I know. I cannot quite remember where they did begin. Wherever that great heathen of a hunt table was, I should think, but this is where they seem to have ended."

"I'll be deviled," murmured Berinwick.

"Aren't we all?"

"Aren't we all what?"

"Bedeviled," Dempsey replied, regaining his feet, the glasses in hand. These he set down on the sofa, then stretched over them to the windowsill where the early afternoon sunlight glinted off a dusty, open wine bottle balanced precariously near the edge of the sill. "I don't know a man who has not been bedeviled from time to time, your grace," Dempsey added as he poured the port.

Berinwick finished removing his gloves and looked about him for a place to deposit them. No free flat surface existed. Everything that was not stacked one upon the other tilted this way or that. With a sigh, the duke tucked his gloves down beside him in the chair. "Did my father," he asked as he accepted a glass of the port from Dempsey's hand, "did my father ever actually make your acquaintance, Mr. Dempsey?"

The parson took the chair opposite Berinwick and crossed one knee over the other. "Your father? No, I have never met your father, your grace."

"No, I didn't think so. Never would have offered you the living had he actually made your acquaintance. Not one for disorganization, disruption, or dithering about, my father."

"It was your father offered me this living and not you, your grace?" Dempsey's blue eyes widened in surprise.

"Just so," Berinwick replied with a nod that set his dark curls tumbling down over his brow. "Were he here now, he would likely regret it and send you packing, too. Especially if this," he motioned about the room with one hand, "is an example of the state of your mind. My father was a practical, methodical sort of man. A place for everything and everything in its place. The same for thoughts and things alike. One glance at this room and he would chase you back to wherever you came from."

"Herefordshire."

"Herefordshire. Yes."

"But *you* are not going to chase me back to Herefordshire, are you, your grace?"

"I am seriously considering it," Berinwick replied as he leaned back in the chair and sipped at his wine. "I cannot imagine why my father offered this living to someone he never met. Did he know of you through acquaintances? Are our families connected in some fashion? Did he lose a wager? And even if one or all of those things apply, why did he not extend the offer to you in person?"

"Because I was, ah, incommunicado at the time, I expect."

"Incommunicado?"

"Just so," Dempsey replied with a nod. "I was hidden away in a cave on the Kentish coast. No one knew where I was to be found except the Bishop of Hereford, and I doubt Hereford actually knew how to reach the place, much less direct your father there."

"You were hidden away in a cave?" Berinwick cocked an eyebrow in disbelief.

"Yes, but—I do beg your pardon, your grace—but the entire episode of the cave is a secret of sorts. I ought not to have mentioned it to you. I would not have done, except that you do deserve some explanation. Forget I said anything at all about it, will you not?"

Berinwick, who had just then taken another sip of the port,

which was actually quite good, almost choked on it. "Oh, certainly, Mr. Dempsey," he managed around a strangled cough. "Consider your inhabiting a Kentish cave wiped from my memory."

"I really cannot enlighten you further on the matter."

"No, of course you cannot."

"Not until the Bishop of Hereford dies. He's forbidden me to say a word about it to anyone until he's dead."

"Of course he has. Embarrassing for him, I should think, to have one of his clerics hiding away in a cave somewhere in Kent. Kent, of all places!"

"Ah, now you're being droll, your grace." Dempsey smiled and downed his entire glass of port in one long gulp.

"And while I am being droll, Mr. Dempsey—if you *are* the Reverend Mr. Dempsey—may I be so bold as to inquire what you did with Mr. Langton, who has been kind enough to attempt to look after St. Milburga's of the Wood for the past four years and more?"

"If I *am* the Reverend Mr. Dempsey? What did I *do* with Mr. Langton?" Dempsey thought surely the duke was joking and chuckled.

"I do not see the humor in my words," Berinwick said.

"No? Well, it sounds as if you suspect me of being some lunatic escaped from Bedlam who, pretending to be the Reverend Mr. Dempsey, came here, lopped off your Mr. Langton's head, and disposed of it and the rest of him in the privy."

"Let me point out to you, Mr. Dempsey, that I expected Langton to be here," Berinwick replied, "and he is not. I did not expect you to be here, yet most assuredly, you are."

"I arrived before my letter, did I?" Dempsey queried, smiling. "No wonder you looked so startled to see me at the door. I promise you, your grace, I have not murdered your caretaker. I sent him to the village with his dog cart—actually, to pick up my trunk, which I chose not to carry on my shoulder all the way from the inn. Your Mr. Langton will return alive, I promise you."

"We'll see," Berinwick drawled.

A silence arose between them, then, as the cleric studied Berinwick through puzzled morning-blue eyes brimming with curiosity. Berinwick studied him back, suspiciously, through one eye as black as midnight. From beneath the black patch which covered the duke's other eye, thready scars wandered hither and thither, stark and distracting against the bronze surface of what must once have been a perfectly handsome face. Though now it must send a bit of a shiver up people's spines, Dempsey thought with considerable pity for the young man.

Dempsey had not been prepared for those scars or the patch or anything at all about the gentleman who sat opposite him. He had expected to deal with the Berinwick who had written to him. He wondered if this Berinwick knew the first thing about the letter his father had sent, but then he thought not. It had not sounded in the least as if the late duke had confided the particular knowledge contained in that letter to anyone, not even his heir.

I delayed too long in coming, Dempsey thought, twirling his empty wineglass in his hand, attempting to ignore the sullen study Berinwick's one eye was making of him. I ought to have come at once. I told the bishop so. But would he listen? No. I must finish up my work in Kent before I came here. And I could hardly make Hereford privy to what was in Berinwick's letter aside from the offered position. To confide in Hereford about Glyndwr's cup would have proved an enormous mistake. As it is, the bishop merely thinks me tired of mucking about and eager to settle down and become a respectable preacher at last.

"I did write to inform you of my arrival, your grace," Dempsey said, breaking the silence. "Well, to inform your father of it. Sent him a letter by the post the day I departed Herefordshire."

"How did you get from the Kentish coast to Herefordshire?"

"I drove."

"Oh? You came out of your cave and the bishop blessed you for it with a curricle?"

"Precisely."

"And you drove the curricle here as well?"

"No. Not here. Theophilus and I came by the mail."

"You carried that hound with you in a mail coach?"

"Atop it, your grace. Atop it. And since no one appeared at the inn to meet us, we walked here. That's why I abandoned my trunk and had to send Langton to fetch it. I did advise your father that it would be some months before I could take up this living and—"

"And he saw no problem with that," inserted Berinwick. "Mother and I saw no problem with it either when he told us you would be delayed. Six months, a year, no difference, actually. There has not been a rector at St. Milburga's of the Wood in more than twenty years, after all."

"Twenty years? No wonder the place looks the way it does," mumbled Dempsey, causing Berinwick's right eyebrow to tilt ominously.

"I have lost an eye, Mr. Dempsey. I have not lost my ears."

"I said that aloud? I do apologize, your grace. No, on second thought, I do not apologize. This rectory is liveable, I will give you that. But the church is a disaster. Have you gazed at its north tower of late? It is about to move swiftly toward the ground."

"Is it?"

"Yes. And the roof over the nave—"

"Leaks appallingly. Langton sets buckets about every time it rains. We saw no great urgency to repair it. There has not been a service held in the church since the Reverend Mr. Dight passed on."

"No services at all in the church for two decades? Where do the people—where does the congregation worship?"

"In the village square in fine weather. They stay at home and read their Bibles when the weather's foul."

"Good Lord, the poor people. And what a waste of a church."

"Actually, everyone has been rather satisfied with the arrangement up until now. None of us has been forced to pay any tithe for the longest time."

"Your grace!"

"What?"

"Am I to accept that two generations of your tenants and your villagers *enjoyed* not having a church to attend simply because they need not pay tithes?"

Berinwick nodded. "Precisely so. And myself as well. I do not mind to see you come, Dempsey, because I can well afford to pay the tithes, but there will be some hereabout who will not be overjoyed that my father bestowed this living on you."

"The Bishop of Hereford knew of this? That these people were without—without—"

"A collector of tithes?"

"Someone to turn to in times of crisis."

"Of course he knew," Berinwick replied. "He certainly knew that the Reverend Mr. Dight had departed. Even the Archbishop of Canterbury knew that. My father went so far as to go to London and say what had happened before Parliament. Up until now, the Bishop of Hereford has been sending us a series of itinerant preachers, but he has balked at recommending anyone to take the living on a permanent basis. Father did consult with him on the matter from time to time, but Hereford always had some reason why no one was available."

"I cannot imagine such a thing. Certainly, in twenty years time, there were countless gentlemen of the cloth importuning Hereford to recommend them for a living. Why would he—"

"I assume it was due to the manner in which the Reverend Mr. Dight passed on," Berinwick interrupted.

"Was it something—contagious? Some dreadful fever? I can see how the bishop might fear to expose another clergyman to something contagious."

"In a manner of speaking, it was contagious," Berinwick replied promptly. "My father ran Dight through with a rapier. He ran three other men through with that same rapier. One after the other," Berinwick added, extending his right arm as though holding a blade himself and making several short thrusts in a semicircle between them. "Shhh-wish. Shhh-wish. Shhh-wish. Shhh-wish. I expect you could call that contagious, Mr. Dempsey, if you think on it."

"Glory," murmured Dempsey. "That's why he went up to Parliament to tell the tale. He killed four men."

"Indeed. Hereford could not be convinced to send us anyone after that. No one but the itinerants who came whenever they happened to be in the area. But Hereford warned them, I think, because none of them would ever set foot inside the church."

"Your father killed Mr. Dight *in* the church?"

"While he was preaching in the pulpit. Blood splattered. Mr. Dight groaned and fell. There was a tremendous row. I remember the blood especially. But then, I was very young at the time and had never seen gentlemen skewered before. Do you know, I cannot think why the bishop should alter his mind so abruptly and honor m'father's request for a rector at long last. Perhaps Hereford is not overly concerned for your welfare, Mr. Dempsey, eh?"

Dempsey, though he attempted not to do so, chuckled low in his throat. Berinwick grinned. His single eye gleamed wickedly.

"Our new rector has arrived, Mother," Berinwick announced as he strolled into the summer parlor in Blackcastle's east wing. "His name is Dempsey and he's peculiar," he added, as he leaned down to bestow a dutiful kiss on one of the duchess's pale cheeks. "It's likely he murdered Langton. Langton is nowhere to be found."

"The new rector has arrived?" The Duchess of Berinwick abruptly set aside the embroidery in which she was engaged. "He has arrived without the least warning? I shall have to speak to Cook. We will be forced to reconsider dinner at once. I had not planned on a guest. Why did he not advise us of the date of his arrival? Of all things!"

"He says he wrote to tell us that he would arrive this morning, Mother. His letter has been delayed or it's gone astray."

"Then Mr. Langton ought to have come pounding on our door the very moment the man turned up," she murmured, rising from the chintz-covered sofa and starting toward the bell that sat on the side table beside one of the wingback chairs.

"I daresay Langton could not come pounding on the door. Did you not hear me, Mother? I believe our new rector bashed Langton in the head and buried his body beneath the parlor floor."

"I heard you, William, and I assume you are teasing me," she replied, reaching for the small, silver bell. "His name is Dempsey, you say?"

"Dempsey, yes." Berinwick crossed to her and took the bell from her hand before she could ring it. He stood, staring down at her through his one dark eye, pinning her in place. "I daresay it's a good thing he introduced himself. I should have looked a veritable simpleton, not knowing his name. I cannot think what got into Father to bestow the living on some cleric and then not tell either of us what he was called."

"Your father expected to be here himself to welcome the gentleman and to introduce him to us," the duchess replied uneasily. She detested to be stared at by her son in such a way. Her hand fluttered toward the bell he had taken from her, then fluttered away again. "I knew some Dempseys long ago," she said in a whisper. "I wonder if our new rector is somehow related to them?"

"I doubt it. There are hundreds of Dempseys in England. Thousands, perhaps. Go and sit back down, Mother. There is no need to ring for Gaines and have him send Cook to you. This particular Mr. Dempsey is not coming to dinner. At least, not this evening, he is not." Berinwick set the bell aside, took his mother's elbow, and escorted her back to the sofa. Then he crossed to the armchair nearest her and sat down in it. His spurs jangled as he stretched his long legs out before him. "I did invite the Reverend Mr. Dempsey to join us for dinner this evening but he declined."

"He declined to dine with us?" The duchess's wide brown eyes narrowed considerably. She clasped her hands in her lap and focused her gaze on them, noting the few dark speckles that had begun to mar the once-creamy silk of her skin. "William, precisely what did you say to the man to cause him to decline?"

"Nothing untoward, Madam."

"What did you do to him, then?"

"I merely held him in polite conversation, nothing more."

"Something more, I think." She peeked up at him for a moment, gazed down at her hands again, then straightened her shoulders and forced herself to meet her son's gaze head-on. "I mean to say, William, a clergyman who has been given a living does not decline to dine with his benefactor. It is not done."

"Not in general, no. But I am not the Berinwick who bestowed the living on him, Mother. He was Father's choice, not mine. Perhaps he thinks I'll take it away now that Father's dead."

"All the more reason for him to accept your invitation and ingratiate himself with you."

"Well, he didn't seem very intent on ingratiating himself with me. Perhaps he is having second thoughts about accepting the position, eh?"

"Why on earth would he have second thoughts? St. Milburga's of the Wood was once one of the most lucrative—"

"I told him about Father and Mr. Dight without actually explaining the whole of it," the duke interrupted.

"Oh, William, no! How could you? Now the man will sneak off into the night and St. Milburga's of the Wood will be rectorless for another twenty years."

"Somehow I don't believe that's going to happen," Berinwick replied, running his fingers through his hair, setting his dark, windblown curls into further disarray. "He may be having second thoughts, but I doubt he will leave us, Mother. He's quite a fellow, I think, this Reverend Mr. Dempsey."

"What do you mean by that—quite a fellow?"

"I mean he is not at all what one thinks of when one thinks of a parson. He's not some obsequious little toad. No, and he's not built like a dancing master with a face like a prune, either. He's bold for a parson, if you ask me, and tall and strong-looking as well. Old, of course, but I expect you and Hannah will think him handsome. And he does have a certain appealing nonchalance about him. I expect 'nonchalance' is the word I mean."

"Whom will I think handsome?" asked Berinwick's younger sister entering the room with a whisper of wide skirts.

"The new rector," Berinwick replied. "What the deuce are you wearing, Hannah?"

Lady Hannah glared at her brother with all the disdain her fourteen years could provide. "It's the gown I am to wear for my birthday celebration, if you must know, Will. It arrived this afternoon and I thought to don it and see how it looks."

"Well, go up and take it off. Of all things, Hannah. Father has been in his grave a mere nine months and here you are flouncing about in white lawn striped with cherry red."

"William!" the duchess exclaimed, and then gazed away from him at once, holding out a hand to Hannah, silently begging the girl to leave off the discussion and sit quietly beside her.

"She has no business to be strutting about in such a gown, Mother," Berinwick growled. "We're in mourning. Anyone would think Hannah doesn't care a whit that Father's dead."

"I do care!" Lady Hannah protested vehemently, spinning down beside her mother. "I care just as much as you do, Will. I loved Papa very much."

"Which is why you are parading about in that concoction without a thought as to how you dishonor his memory by it?"

"William, that is quite enough," the duchess declared quietly, staring down at her hands. "Hannah has merely donned a new gown to see how it looks. Nothing more. It is only natural for a young lady to wish to try on a new gown," she added, forcing her gaze to meet her son's once again. "It is lovely, Hannah," the duchess added, giving her daughter's hand a pat while attempting to convey a plea for silence to her son with merely a look. "It's perfectly lovely. But you will change into the brown silk for dinner, will you not?"

"Yes, Mama."

The gown isn't lovely at all, Berinwick thought, bewildered by both his mother's words and the look she gave him. It's a dreadful gown. Perhaps on some other young lady—on an older young lady—it might be fetching, but—why on earth did Mother not protest when Hannah selected the thing?

Well, I know perfectly well why she did not, he told himself with an inward sigh. She chose not to protest because she knew that it would make Hannah happy to have it and that it could do Hannah no harm.

With quiet sympathy, Berinwick recalled the years before Hannah, the times when he had been summoned home from school to make the acquaintance of a new baby sister or brother, and the equal number of times he had returned to Blackcastle to attend the funerals of those same infants. He remembered too well the stoic, silent pain that his mother and father had endured with each tragic loss, the horrific well of sadness from which they had been forced to raise themselves time after time. Until Hannah. Until chubby, cheerful little Hannah had decided to thrive and grow into this bit of sunshine that continually warmed his mother's heart.

"I beg your pardon, Hannah," he murmured, fiddling with one of the buttons on his coat. "I was wrong to speak to you so. I did not stop to think how it must feel to be just out of the schoolroom and abruptly condemned to dark colors and people murmuring condolences and not much else. Certainly you wished to don the gown. It gives you hope of a more joyous time to come."

Dempsey stood, hands on hips, in the center of the dining room floor. He had returned the parlor to its former faded splendor and now it was the dining room that resembled a nest made by a muddled rat—its furniture stacked haphazardly about the room, its carpet rolled up against the far wall.

"Drat," Dempsey mumbled. "Blasted rectory would be the ideal place to stow it. Likely it was built with that purpose in mind. But there's not the least hint of the hiding place. Perhaps it's in the study or the kitchen or the cellar."

The cellar? Dempsey thought for a moment. He had spent merely a moment or two in the cellar because he'd noted nothing at all significant there. It had proved a dismal old root cellar with a series of empty shelves and one dusty bottle of port. Nothing more. It occurred to him now how very odd it was for someone to have abandoned a single bottle of port in a rectory's root cellar—to remove all the foodstuffs and yet leave behind a bottle of wine. "I do hope it wasn't poisoned," he murmured, a mischievous gleam rising to his eyes. "Not at all a good idea to send my benefactor home to drop dead from a bit of bad port. Of course, if it was poisoned, I'll drop dead right along with him."

Dempsey took his hands from his hips and went to unroll the dining room carpet, sending it back across the floor. Then he set about replacing the sideboards, the table, and the chairs. The muscles in his shoulders and arms rippled, his flat stomach stretched tight as he moved piece after heavy piece of furniture. His shirt grew damp with perspiration, but he ignored it. The caretaker would return soon, bringing with him not merely Dempsey's trunk, but hopefully a meatpie or two, courtesy of Mrs. Langton.

Dempsey had decided, having conferred with Langton, to hire the caretaker's wife to prepare him three meals a day. He'd also allowed himself to be talked into paying Langton's eldest daughter a small wage to keep the rectory neat and clean. Both women would accompany Langton from their cottage in Barren Wycche each morning and return home with him each evening, thus making themselves of use during the daylight hours and allowing Dempsey his privacy once night descended.

"Which is a situation devoutly to be wished," Dempsey mumbled, jiggling the last of the massive sideboards into place. "Especially now, when the Berinwick I expected is not the Berinwick I have." He brushed wet strands of silver and honey-blond hair from his brow and sighed. His back ached and he had two rooms on the ground floor yet to search. "Tomorrow evening," he murmured, leaning back against the sideboard and gazing around the dining room. "Berinwick did not think to do it in all these years, then went off and died instead of lingering about to help with it. It can wait until tomorrow. Theophilus!" he called, rolling down his shirtsleeves, snatching his coat from the cricket table in the corridor where he had tossed it shortly after his arrival, and strolling toward the front door of the rectory. "Theophilus, m'boy, time for a walk! If we're lucky," he added as he stepped outside and leaned down to give the hound's head a hearty pat. "If we are very lucky, Theophilus, Langton will deliver my trunk and leave again while we're off gadding about and neither one of us will be forced to be sociable until he arrives with his wife and daughter tomorrow."

The Duchess of Berinwick set her fork aside. "I find I am not at all hungry," she said. "It comes of dining later than usual. You will excuse me, William, Hannah. I cannot face another bite. I think I shall take advantage of the lingering twilight and stroll the park for a while."

"But Mother," Hannah protested, "Cook has made all your favorites."

"Yes, and presented them delightfully, too. You will tell her I said as much, Hannah."

"Yes, Mama."

"One of the footmen will accompany you, Mother," Berinwick declared from the head of the table. "Harold, relinquish that serving dish to John and escort her grace—"

"No, no, no," the duchess interrupted. "Harold, maintain the serving dish and your position. I have no need for an escort, nor do I wish for one."

"But Madam," Berinwick protested, gaining his feet quickly as his mother stood.

The Duchess of Berinwick forced her shoulders back and raised her chin the least bit. She could be an imposing figure of a woman when she made the attempt—the mature round-ness of her figure and the chubbiness of her cheeks notwithstanding. And she intended to be imposing now be-cause she needed, for the space of an hour or so, to be alone. "No, William, I will not take Harold from his duties, nor will I consent to be accompanied by one of the grooms. I have wandered Blackcastle land for years without escort. I cannot conceive what has gotten into you since your papa's death, thinking that I must be accompanied everywhere. I have not abruptly become an addlepated, infirm old woman simply be-cause your father is no longer with us."

"Of course you have not, but—"

"William is merely concerned for your safety, Mama," Hannah inserted. "He fears you will be pounced upon by the dogs of Little Mynd Moor. Not that any of them has appeared anywhere near Blackcastle for a century. Or that you will be torn to bits by a pack of foxes. We do have foxes. Mad Jack imported millions of them for the hunt this past season. They are everywhere."

"That's true," Berinwick agreed, studying his mother with a keen eye as he crumpled his napkin in his left hand. "Mad Jack has got us overrun with foxes. Our farmers have been wishing him at the devil since November. I only fear that you will turn an ankle or catch your gown in some thicket, Mother. And then, you know, you will be thankful for Harold's presence."

"I am always thankful for Harold's presence," the duchess replied with a hint of a smile for the young footman, "but this evening I should like to be alone. I will attempt not to turn an ankle and I will stay far from any thickets. Now, finish your dinner and mind your manners while I'm gone."

Hannah giggled at those familiar orders which had met her ears in the schoolroom for as long as she could remember. But Berinwick smiled not at all as his mother turned and left the room. He stared after her with the oddest expression on his face. "Set the dish aside, Harold," he commanded when she was out of earshot, "and go after her. Stay far back, but keep her in your sight."

"Certainly, your grace," the footman replied, passing the serving dish he held to the footman stationed behind Lady Hannah's chair.

"Oh, Jules, why did you not leap from the coach when it looked to overturn?" the duchess whispered as she came to a halt at the top of Thrwick Hill where the land swirled down toward Little Mynd Moor through Grydwynn Wood. In the distance she could just make out the Stiperstones, ghostlike in the twilight. But they were solid, those rugged mountains. Not ghostlike at all, really. They were just as solid as her husband had been, and she had often thought Julian Thorne would last forever, just like the Stiperstones.

She pulled her cloak more tightly around her and swiped a tear from the corner of her eye with one gloved finger. Though she realized the ache in her heart was settling at last into a rather dull sort of emptiness, she wondered if it would ever completely depart from her. She thought not. She thought it would linger until she died herself, just as the pain she carried for William and for her lost sons and daughters lingered.

"Only see what you have done, Jules," she said softly. "You have left me here to deal with Will alone. How can I? Where will I find the strength to do it? Who is there to make me strong? Why did you not make me strong before you left me here without you?"

In an oak nearby, an owl ruffled its feathers and called to the awakening night. At the edge of the wood a rabbit scampered into a deadfall. As the twilight deepened, the wraith of a half-moon appeared on the horizon. Somewhere, out on the moor, the duchess heard a dog bay and another and another. They were sad, savage creatures, the dogs of Little Mynd Moor. Centuries ago a mad Thorne of Barren Wycche had driven his pack from Blackcastle into the wilderness to die of the winter and starvation, but the dogs had not died. To this very day the pack lingered on, sometimes great in number, sometimes few, just as the Thornes of Barren Wycche—from whose loins sprang each Berinwick of Blackcastle—just as the Thornes lingered on.

Lingered on until now, the duchess thought as she dashed another tear from her eye. There has always been the prospect of another Berinwick and another, until now. But now, there is only William, and when he dies, the title of Berinwick will die with him and the Thorne name as well. "And it is my fault," she whispered. "All my fault."

On the branch of the oak, the owl spread its wings, called once more, and took flight, disturbing her thoughts, forcing her to return her attention to the place where she stood and to the life going on around her. She saw the darkness descending, the moon rising in the sky, and heard from somewhere nearby an odd, snuffling sound. She turned slowly, beginning a small circle to see what she could see. At the base of the hill, in shadow, a man stood, immobile, staring up at her. Harold, she thought, recognizing the footman's tall, lean figure and his proud stance. William has countermanded my express orders and sent the poor man after me. Which he has every right to do, she reminded herself. He is the Duke of Berinwick now, and I merely the dowager duchess. William is in command and I am but one of his insignificant charges.

As she continued her circle, the snuffling reached her ears again, and with it a rattling of leaves and the hushed whisper of waving grasses. She focused her gaze in the direction of the noise and in a moment the cause of the snuffling reached the base of the oak. Nose to the ground, tail curling high into the air, a hound came around the tree, up the remainder of the hill and directly toward her. Thinking, for one brief moment, that it was one of the legendary dogs from Little Mynd Moor, she began to call out for Harold. But his name died on her lips as a high, loud whistle slashed the air, followed by a harried voice. "Theo! Theophilus! Where the devil are you?"

This was followed by the snapping of twigs, a loud "Ouch! Dang it!" and the unmistakable sound of booted feet attempting to detach themselves from the vines that populated the edge of the wood and gloried in twisting themselves around unwary ankles.

The Duchess of Berinwick smiled. "So, you are not one of the pack from Little Mynd Moor," she said to the hound as it snuffled its way relentlessly toward her.

The hound registered her words and bumped its snout into one of her stout walking shoes at one and the same time. It lifted its head in surprise, sat back on its haunches, and peered nearsightedly up at her. "Rowf," it said, in pleasantly surprised greeting.

"Rowf to you as well, sir," the duchess replied, bending down to pat the hound's head. "You are Theophilus, I assume."

"Rrrrruph," Theophilus acknowledged, raising a forepaw which the duchess, thoroughly surprised, caught in her hand and shook. Her smile widened. "My, what a rogue you are, offering your paw to a lady you have never met. I do believe I am pleased to make your acquaintance."

"Your grace?"

The duchess turned to see the footman just gaining the top of the hill.

"I heard a whistle and a man's voice, your grace. And then I saw the hound approach you. I thought you might require my aid."

"Thank you, Harold," the duchess replied, dropping Theophilus's paw and standing straight again. "I do not believe I have anything to fear from this fellow, but his owner is even now crashing through the underbrush in our direction, so you may remain beside me. Yes, there he is, just fighting his way between the twin elms. Oh, dear, he is not looking up this way. Go to him, Harold, and say I have his missing hound beside me."

"Yes, your grace," the footman replied, taking but a moment more to satisfy himself that the dog was no danger to his duchess. "No threat there," he murmured to himself as he started down the side of the hill in the stranger's direction. "Dog be a hunered years old if it be a day."

The hound, ignoring Harold's coming and going completely, reached up, took the duchess's gloved hand softly in its mouth, and tugged.

"What? Am I not so much as to take note of your master's arrival?"

"Rar-rowf."

"No? *You* are to occupy my full attention?"

"Woof."

"What a fine, funny fellow you are," she said, kneeling to take his broad head in her hands and ruffle his ears. This resulted in Theophilus's tongue lolling happily out the side of his mouth and elicited a series of satisfied grunts from him as well. Then his long tongue reached up and licked her cheek.

"You old rascal," said a somewhat breathless voice above them. "Stealing kisses from a lady as though you have had the upbringing of a chimney sweep!"

A large hand reached down and offered the duchess support in rising. "I apologize, your grace, for that rapscallion," the gentleman continued. "I apologize for myself as well. I know we have neither of us the right to tramp all over Blackcastle lands."

"Your grace, this be the new rector," Harold said tentatively, not knowing whether it fell properly on his shoulders to introduce the two or not, though the gentleman had urged him to do it on their hike up the hill. "The Reverend Mr. Dempsey, be his name. Mr. Dempsey," the footman continued, when the duchess did not protest his audacity, "this be her grace, the Duchess of Berinwick."

The duchess peered at the rector through the thickening darkness. She blinked her wide, brown eyes at him. Blinked again. She raised one gloved hand to his cheek and turned his face more fully into what remained of the twilight. "Richard?" she asked softly, hesitantly. "Richard Dempsey? Can it possibly be you?"

Two

"You cannot bring yourself to believe that I grew up to be a parson, that's what it is, Veronica," Dempsey said as he strolled beside her toward Blackcastle with her arm tucked neatly away in his while Harold and Theophilus wandered on before them. "Oh-oh."

"Oh-oh, what?" her grace asked.

"Oh-oh, I called you Veronica. That will not do at all. I must accustom myself to thinking of you as 'your grace' from this point onward. It will take me some time to do it, however, because I always think of you as Veronica. You must be patient with me."

"You always think of me as Veronica? I doubt that, Mr. Dempsey. Truly I do."

"Well, perhaps that is a bit of a fib."

"I should think so."

"Truth be told, I always think of you as the Vivacious Vernie of Arrandell."

"Richard Dempsey!"

"I know. I know. Your cheeks are very likely growing red as apples right this moment, but—"

"Yes, they are. Especially since the thing I doubted was that you had given me one thought in the past thirty-some years."

"I beg your pardon? Not think of you?" Dempsey drew to a halt and gazed at her, amazed. "I thought of you for years afterward. I was madly in love with you, your grace. I wished your mother at the devil and hoped to personally kick your stepfather into Hades right after her when they returned and took you from us."

"For shame! Such words from a clergyman. And such nonsense! You could not possibly have been in love with me, Richard Dempsey. Not truly. You were merely a child." She urged him forward again through the simple expedient of tugging on his arm.

"We gave each other leave to use our Christian names," Dempsey declared, thoroughly amazed at the memories that had come rushing back to him the very moment he had recognized her. He thought at this moment that he remembered clearly every moment in time that they had shared together. "You gave me a kiss on the cheek. I gave you my *frog,*" Dempsey said with great emphasis accompanied by a mischievous grin. "A fellow does not part with the frog he has captured with his own two hands—his very own frog who has been his dearest and constant companion for a year and more—a fellow does not part with such a treasure as *that* unless his heart is compromised."

The Duchess of Berinwick giggled. The sound startled her so much that her free hand went immediately to cover her lips.

"No, do not," Dempsey said at once. "It's such a lovely sound. Do not hush it. Walpool."

"What?"

"His name was Walpool. My frog."

"Oh, of course. And you will be delighted to know that I kept him for an entire year. There was a little serving boy in my stepfather's house in London—Jemmy—whom I sent to catch flies for Wally."

"Walpool survived for merely a year after I gave him to you?"

"I should think that he survived a goodly number of years, but not with us. My stepfather could not abide him longer and sent him to the country."

"I suspect that your stepfather merely told you that he sent the frog to the country to keep you from crying after he broke poor Wally's neck."

"Richard!"

"I never did trust your stepfather, not from the first."

"He was very kind to Mama and to me."

"Yes, but he took you off to London. I never once guessed," Dempsey added with a shake of his head.

"Guessed what?"

"That you became the Duchess of Berinwick, Veronica. No one ever said as much to me."

"It was in all the newspapers."

"When?"

"Twenty-nine years ago." Veronica laughed this time—no mere giggle. "You must have been all of twelve by then."

"I was thirteen, thank you very much, and my mind was overflowing with ambitions. None of them, however, sufficient to force me to read the society columns in my father's London newspapers. Will you look at that?" he said, pausing in his stride. "It is compelling enough from a distance, your grace, but as near as this, your home is astonishing."

"Especially when the twilight is all but gone," Veronica agreed. "I have always loved Blackcastle with its windows aglow. It is a stark, intimidating pile of stones in the daylight, but its welcome and warmth increase immensely as the night descends. You will come inside and have a cup of tea while Harold fetches a lantern for you, Richard. You cannot possibly return to St. Milburga's without a lantern to light your way. The moon sheds but a paltry glow tonight and it will be full dark in moments now. And you *will* call me Veronica, at least when we are alone together. And I will call you Richard as I was accustomed to do."

"I thank you for the offer of a light to guide my way, and I thank you more for the restored privilege of using your given name, Veronica, but I will not enter Blackcastle tonight, I think," he replied, giving her hand a gentle pat. "I will simply wait in the turnaround while your man fetches the lantern for me."

"Never!"

"But, Veronica, I am not dressed for paying anyone a call, much less the inhabitants of Blackcastle."

"Bosh! As if I care for that."

"You will care for it do you see me in full light. I expect I am the most disheveled gentleman on the face of the earth at the moment. And I have Theophilus with me. He will set up the most distressing howls outside your door do I disappear through it. It took a good hour of accompanying him in and out of the rectory, proving to him that all was well with me inside the place, before he would consent to remain outside on the rectory doorstep today."

"Then you will come to us tomorrow," the duchess declared, releasing her hand from the crook of his arm as they halted in the semicircle at the upper end of the drive before Blackcastle's main entrance. She turned to him, took both of his hands into hers, and gazed wistfully up into his eyes.

At least Dempsey thought it was a wistful gaze, a gaze filled with memories of more innocent times. Her face shone pale but happy in the light from the flambeaux that burned beside the great double doors and along the turnaround where they stood. Dempsey's heart lurched just a bit with his own memories as he smiled down at her.

"We generally dine at half-past five," she said. "But I shall move dinner back to whatever time you name. Harold," she added, not once shifting her gaze from Dempsey, "go around to the stables and fetch Mr. Dempsey a lantern so he may walk safely home."

"Yes, your grace," the footman replied and departed at once.

"What time will prove best for you, Richard?" she asked. "Six? Quarter past?"

"Rowf!" Theophilus exclaimed before Dempsey could say anything at all, and then the hound seized the hem of her grace's cloak in its teeth and tugged gently.

Dempsey laughed. "Theo wishes to be included in your invitation, I believe."

"Do you, sweet thing?" Veronica asked, freeing Dempsey

from the soft scrutiny of her gaze to bestow a gracious glance on Theophilus. "Well then, you shall be included."

"No, Veronica, you cannot wish to have a nearsighted hound raise a ruckus outside your door for an entire evening. Truly, he will drive you mad, and I dare not leave him to his own devices as yet. I expect I must decline to dine here at Blackcastle for a week or more."

"That's all you know," Veronica replied. "Theophilus will not raise a ruckus outside my door. He will come inside my door, into the dining room where he will lie at your feet if that is what must happen for you to say yes to my invitation and present yourself here tomorrow evening. It will not be the first time a dog has lain at someone's feet during dinner at Blackcastle. Men and dogs dined together in the Great Hall regularly once. It was considered most unexceptional."

"Centuries ago," Dempsey said, smiling.

"It seems like centuries since I have had the happiness of gazing upon your beautiful face, Richard," the duchess replied, one hand going to touch his cheek. "A face so beautiful that even an absence of thirty years and more could not make me forget the gentle angles and planes of it. The face of an angel. Come to us tomorrow," she whispered. "Come merely to please me."

"Veronica Longwood has grown up to become the Duchess of Berinwick," Dempsey murmured as, lantern in hand and a lead contributed by one of the Berinwick stablehands fastened around Theophilus's neck, he strolled slowly along the road from Blackcastle to St. Milburga's of the Wood. It was a cloudy night. The half-moon shone fitfully and was not to be depended upon. Dempsey was thankful for both the lantern and the road. "Can you imagine, Theophilus, the two of us attempting to make our way back through that wood? Well, you likely could do it, did you scent a hare bound in the precise direction, but I have no doubt I would end by drowning in the underbrush with brambles biting hungrily at every inch of me." Dempsey smiled to himself. He could not seem to cease smiling this evening. "I am inclined to allow you to run free more often, Theo. I will, too, if each time you do, you flush out such a sweet, pretty little bird as you have this evening."

"Aroof," Theophilus agreed, long tail wagging.

"I wonder if Berinwick knew when he wrote to me that his duchess and I had been children together? Might she have mentioned my name to him? No, of course she did not. I'll wager that Veronica never gave me a thought once she entered Society. I was a mere child, after all. Certainly she did not realize that I was the Dempsey to whom her husband offered this living. I could tell that by the honest surprise on her face when she recognized me. Glory, but she is still as beautiful as she was at fourteen, Theo. Not in quite the same way, of course. She is older and rounder in places than I remember. But there is something about both alterations that I find most enhancing. Well, of course I do. I am older myself. I have had the opportunity to observe a goodly number of ladies in all these years and so I have acquired certain preferences. I wonder if I would have accepted Berinwick's offer did I realize he was the gentleman who had married Veronica?"

The road between Blackcastle and the Church of St. Milburga's of the Wood was earthen, narrow, and bermless. It meandered along, wandering hither and thither, winding first one way and then another as though laid down by some Roman soldier unsteadily weaving his way home from a victory celebration. It darted past hedgerow-bounded fields and around a number of trees. It skirted Grydwynn Wood, crossed a low ridge from which Dempsey might have looked out and seen the lovely hill called Little Mynd in the distance and the moors surrounding it—if it had been daylight, if he had been interested in the view. But it was not daylight and he was not interested in the view and all he could actually see was a bit of the road before him, the tops of field grasses, and tree limbs edged faintly with moonglow.

Of course, I would have accepted Berinwick's offer, even if I did realize that Berinwick was Veronica's husband, he decided as he trudged onward. Certainly, I would have accepted the position. How could I not have done? The gentleman practically begged me to take up the living. It was the most seductive, intriguing offer anyone has ever made me. And for such an offer to come from him, from a gentleman whose work I have so admired—I could not have refused it, not even did he boast that his duchess was the former Miss Veronica Longwood, whose loss devastated me all those years ago.

"Besides, Veronica did not actually break my heart," he whispered to the night. "I was only eight years old when she left. A fellow's heart cannot become truly entangled with a young lady's and ripped from his breast when she leaves him—not at such an age as that."

But to think that the Duke of Berinwick, with whom I share so many interests, should marry her, he mused. It seems highly unlikely. And yet, why should he not have coveted Veronica by the time she reached a marriageable age? Every gentleman in London with eyes in his head and a heart in his breast must have longed to marry Veronica Longwood when she made her comeout. Why, then, does it seem like such a miracle that she is here now, that she is the Duchess of Berinwick, that she should be so unexpectedly—widowed?

"I wish we had come sooner, Theophilus," he muttered then, abruptly angry with himself. "Had we come sooner, Veronica's husband would be alive and he and I might have established more than a working relationship. We might have become good friends. And then when he did die—when he did—she might have turned to me in her sorrow and—Great heavens! What am I saying? What am I thinking? Before tonight, I have not spoken to Veronica in almost thirty-five years! She has grown. I have grown. Beyond a doubt, we have grown far, far apart."

Dempsey was so involved in his one-sided conversation that he failed to notice the hound begin to lag behind. He was nearly jerked from his feet when Theophilus sat down on his haunches, pulling the lead tight between them.

"What the devil?" Dempsey murmured. "Theophilus?" He

turned to see the hound's nose in the air, his ears back and his teeth bared. A low growl rumbled in the dog's throat. Dempsey lifted the lantern to shoulder height and made a slow, small circle. Seeing nothing at all unusual, he knelt down beside the dog. "What is it, old boy? What do you smell, eh? Not a hare from the look of you. Not a fox, either, or you'd be attempting to pull me off in pursuit of it."

For a full minute Dempsey knelt, stroking the hound's head, listening to the songs of the night. And then, mixed in among the owls, the rabbits, the dormice, and the hawks, all scurrying and fluttering, squeaking, and screeching about, he heard something that did not belong—a discordant note that set the tiny hairs at the back of his neck to prickling.

"What the deuce was he doing wandering about in Grydwynn Wood?" Berinwick queried, beginning to pace the room.

"You actually know him, Mama, from years ago?" Hannah asked, her face beaming while her brother scowled. "How do you know him? Was he one of your beaux, like Papa?"

The duchess, installed in a wingback chair in the smallest of the Blackcastle drawing rooms, smiled softly to herself. "He was wandering about the woods in search of his hound, William. The poor old thing put its nose to the ground and charged off and Mr. Dempsey was forced to charge off in pursuit of it. He cannot see well, you know—the dog, not Mr. Dempsey—and Mr. Dempsey feared it would lose itself and wander off onto the moor."

"I should think if it followed its nose to Blackcastle, it could follow its nose home again," muttered Berinwick.

"William, of all things! You are fond of your horses. Allow Mr. Dempsey to be fond of his hound. He has only the one."

"I do not like to have some parson we don't know from Adam make free of our land whenever the mood strikes him, Mother."

"Oh, pooh," Hannah said, taking her brother's wrist and drawing him to a halt beside the comfortable old armchair in which she sat. "In a month or two you *will* know Mr. Dempsey from Adam and you will not mind at all. You know that's true, Will. Certainly Mr. Dempsey could not allow his dog to run off alone in a place so very strange to it. *Was* Mr. Dempsey one of your beaux, Mama?"

The duchess smiled all the more at that particular question. "Mr. Dempsey was a beau of mine long before I ever saw your father's face, long before I even knew what a beau was. We were children together. He was a nice little boy and I think he has grown into a fine sort of gentleman. I was happy to see him again. And tomorrow, he has promised to join us for dinner."

"Which we will all likely regret," Berinwick stated, sitting down on the arm of Hannah's chair since she would not release the hold she had taken on his wrist.

"Why will we regret it?" Hannah asked.

"I thought you rather liked the gentleman when you met him this afternoon, William," the duchess said.

"I did. I do. In a manner of speaking. But having a parson to dinner—"

"Have you ever dined with a parson in your life, William?" his mother asked, discovering a vague ache in her stomach at the realization that she did not know, that she had not the least idea with what sort of gentlemen her son preferred to dine with and what sort he generally avoided.

"Never, and I am not looking forward to it, either. Oh, I know we shall be forced to do it, Madam, but I was hoping for a bit more time to accustom myself to the thought."

"The thought of what?"

"The thought of someone praying over every course as it finds its way to the table—blessing the pheasant, thanking God for the creamed peas. I will likely starve to death in the midst of it all and Hannah will go off into such gales of mirth that she will be forced to leave the room. You, of course, will go after her, thus abandoning me to the company of a man I wish to strangle. There will be no one but Gaines and the footmen to keep me from doing it, either. And they will not, you know."

"If you have already starved to death, you will not be able to strangle the man," Hannah pointed out helpfully as the duchess stared at her son, wondering if he actually intended to be humorous, unable to believe that he did.

"Hush, Theo," Dempsey whispered. "I hear it, old fellow. It's close. Coming closer." Hurriedly, Dempsey shortened Theophilus's lead and shuttered the lantern. Then he gained his feet, took the lantern in one hand and tugged the hound off the road with the other. The two of them stepped as quietly as possible into the intense darkness beneath the trees. Certain that not so much as a flicker of starlight was likely to reach them and betray their presence, Dempsey set the shuttered lantern aside, sat down beside the old dog, and began to gentle it. The wailing he had heard, faintly at first, was progressively increasing. Dempsey wrapped his arms around Theophilus and rubbed at the hound's long ears, hoping to dull the sound for the animal, hoping to keep Theo from baying and disclosing their presence.

For a moment the wailing ceased. Then it began again, an odd, fluctuating sound like a soul in torment, but only sporadically in torment. Apparently this tortured soul had need to pause and catch its breath. It approached on Dempsey's right, and now the parson could hear clearly that it was accompanied by an odd clanking and a muffled thudding very much like the beating of a man's heart. Dempsey strained to see through the darkness without being seen himself, but there was nothing visible as yet. Nothing. And then the muffled thudding rose up around him, engulfing him. The clanking seemed to be inside his skull and the wailing soared above his head. Theophilus shuddered in Dempsey's arms and attempted to hide himself inside the parson's coat as less than three feet from where they hid a monstrous curiosity emerged from the cover of the trees. It took the form of a man—a man fashioned of haze and hoar frost. It groaned and wailed, then charged onto the road astride a horse more spirit than substance, a ghostly horse that shed bits of itself onto the roadbed as it galloped. Tatters of ancient armor, the whitish-gray of the mist itself, bounced and trembled about the figure as it urged the spirit horse up the road—up the road in the direction of St. Milburga's of the Wood.

Dempsey watched it disappear around a bend. Then he unshuttered one side of the lantern, gently pried Theophilus from the shelter of his coat, and spoke softly to the hound. "You heard, but you did not see, Theo. It was quite a vision," he whispered. "After my conversation with the young Berinwick today, I would be inclined to say it was the Reverend Mr. Dight searching for his soul, but I expect it was not. I expect from the armor it was wearing that it was Owain Glyndwr. You'll remember him, Theophilus. I've spoken to you about him any number of times since I received Berinwick's letter."

In response to this news, Theophilus stuffed his head back inside Dempsey's coat.

"Come now, Theo. There's no reason to hide," Dempsey chuckled. "Glyndwr was the last true Prince of Wales, you know, not some barbarian. And just because he led the Welsh rebellion against the English domination, it doesn't mean he will harm you. Why, I doubt he cares one way or another if you are a Welsh hound or an English hound." Dempsey attempted to pry the old dog's head from inside his coat, but the poor beast fought against him and trembled so badly that he did not insist. He continued to speak to the hound in gentle tones, patting his flank instead.

"It is incredible, don't you think, Theo, that the late Duke of Berinwick should write to us about Owain Glyndwr and now Glyndwr's ghost appears before us? And on our first evening here, too. Though why the old fellow should ride through the wood, neck-or-nothing, bemoaning his fate, I cannot think. What he ought to do is sneak about very quietly, searching for his little cup so he can rise again."

Theophilus, cajoled by Dempsey's conversational tone, brought his head out of the parson's coat and peered questioningly up at the man.

"That's better," Dempsey grinned. "What a fine, smart dog you are. Much more intelligent than that ghost. It was a rousing good tale Berinwick told us in his letter, was it not? I read it to you. You were all agog with it, old boy. Come now, Theophilus. It's all right. I doubt this particular Owain Glyndwr will come riding back at us. One appearance a night is all he can summon up and still remain a mystery, I should think."

Sensing the hound's courage begin to return, Dempsey reached for the lantern and unshuttered the other side, allowing a wide path of golden light to shine before them. Together he and Theophilus made their way back onto the road and continued their journey toward St. Milburga's in the spirit horse's wake. Theophilus, growing bolder with each step, put his nose back to the ground and began to snuffle again. Then he paused and sneezed.

"Bless you," Dempsey responded instinctively.

Theophilus snuffled some more and sneezed again.

With the cock of an eyebrow and a curious gleam mounting to his eyes, Dempsey paused. He dropped to one knee and studied the road before him in the lantern light. He put a finger to the ground, then to his tongue. "Shades of Hansel and Gretel," he mumbled. "No, no, that is not a good analogy at all. They used bread crumbs, and used them to find their way home again. And their plan didn't work, besides. This is flour and I intend to use it to follow our ghost to wherever he's bound, and my plan will likely work. Must practice my analogies, Theo. Now that I am going to be a real preacher, I shall find myself in need of one or two appropriate analogies for my sermons, I should think."

The Duchess of Berinwick held her breath as her son sat down at the pianoforte. He had declined to touch the instrument since his father's death, and though the often plaintive quality of his music added to the burden Veronica carried deep in her heart, the absence of his music had proved a subtle torture as well. *Does he truly intend to play this evening?*

she wondered. Why? What is it that moves him to do so after all this time?

And then Berinwick's long, lean fingers stroked the keys. His mother inhaled deeply. Her heart stuttered. A melody—fluid, haunting, as beautiful as Little Mynd Moor beneath a full moon—flowed through the drawing room, filled it with mist, with longing, with a melancholy acceptance and a solid, imperturbable courage.

Tears rose unbidden to Veronica's eyes as she listened. Her bottom lip trembled. She watched him as he played and wondered how such incredible beauty could emanate from her poor, disfigured son. She wondered how it could reach out to touch her so intimately, to touch Hannah so sweetly, to touch all in Blackcastle, each with a subtle, secret, solitary nuance. The maids and the fireboys even now paused at their tasks, she knew. Gaines was setting aside his silver polish. The footmen were gathering at the base of the staircase in the Great Hall. Cook and her helpers were climbing the steps of the servants' staircase to listen. From the rafters to the cellars, the true voice of this remarkable Berinwick, this Berinwick to whom *she* had given birth, this last of the Berinwicks, beckoned all to share in the anguish and the courage of his soul.

When he ceased to play, all of Blackcastle lay silent around him. He sat, motionless, his one eye staring beyond the drawing room at something his mother could not see, though Veronica attempted to see it, willed herself to see it with all her heart. Then he stood and turned to her. "I have ledgers to peruse," he said. "I beg you will excuse me, Madam." Before she could reply he had departed the room.

"Shall I read to you, Mama?" Hannah asked after a moment. "We have not finished *Paradise Lost.*"

Veronica nodded. *Paradise Lost,* she thought. Paradise stolen, rather. Paradise stolen from William and never to be regained by him. Paradise gone so far from my son that he cannot imagine what the word itself means, and all because of my selfishness.

"I love it when Will plays," Hannah said quietly, returning

with the volume in which their place was marked and settling herself comfortably on the couch. "But he will never write down the notes for me. If he would only write them down, perhaps I could learn to play his songs. And someday when I am married, I might teach my children to play them as well. And they could go on to teach Will's music to children of their own. We might keep him with us forever, Mama, that way. Then when he is gone from us, he would seem to be with us still."

"You could never learn to play Will's music, Hannah," the duchess replied. "There is more to your brother's music than mere notes on a page."

"Yes, I know," Hannah sighed, "but having the notes would be a start, don't you think?"

With Theophilus at his side every step of the way, Dempsey paced around the entire outside of the rectory at St. Milburga's before entering through the kitchen door. He lit several candles and a whale oil lamp in the kitchen, then went back out to the pump to fill a dish with water for the hound. He stepped out a second time, in the midst of eating a meat-pie Langton had left for him, when he thought he heard a muffled footstep. And a third time when a howling reached his ears. "Someone's dog has flushed a deer and is giving chase, I expect," he muttered to himself as he reentered the kitchen. "Nothing more than that. Certainly not the return of Owain Glyndwr. At least Langton has come and gone and I needn't deal with polite conversation tonight. I am growing old, Theo, just as you are. I would not have lost our ghost's trail else, nor would I find myself growing so on edge over the episode."

He left the dog behind him in the kitchen once more, feasting on a meatpie of its own, and, candlestick in hand, he rambled through every ground-floor room of the rectory looking for evidence of flour dust. Then he climbed the stairs. He checked the largest of the bedchambers first. His trunk lay there, unopened, at the foot of the bed. He knelt to check the lock on it. No one had tampered with the thing. His relief at that expressed itself in a soft sigh.

But then, why would anyone think to look inside a parson's trunk? he asked himself in silence. What would they think to steal? Prayer books? I am being foolish. That deuced spectre has prodded my imagination to such heights that I am no longer thinking rationally. Why should the wretched ghost appear before me or come to wander about in my rectory? he wondered, gaining his feet and stepping out into the corridor, determined to inspect the remainder of the rooms and the attic as well, regardless of whether it was a rational thing to do or not. Why would anyone waste such effort on a mere preacher, and a newly arrived one at that? Certainly no one can know why I have truly come. No, nor can I be considered a threat to anyone. Unless I was not the personage intended to view the mighty Welshman. . . .

Dempsey halted abruptly. "I was *not* the person intended to view Glyndwr!" he exclaimed softly and whistled through his teeth. There was no reason for me to see him, none at all, he thought. Unless someone has guessed that I am not here for the precise purpose I claim. No. Who would guess that? Even Hereford believes that I wish to possess a living of my own at last. Of course, had he actually read the elder Berinwick's letter, the bishop would have divined the truth of it. But the seal was unbroken when Hereford sent it on to me. Hereford did not open it and read it, nor did anyone else in his office. And even if some person here might suspect what Berinwick had written to someone about the cup, how would they know that I was the someone to whom he wrote? Yes, and how would they know that I had departed the rectory this evening to walk with Theophilus? That I was trudging along the road between Blackcastle and St. Milburga's? I did not expect to be on that particular road tonight myself. No one knew of it. Well, Veronica knew, but certainly she had no part in the extraordinary vision that came riding from that wood.

Dempsey said her name aloud, softly, "Veronica," and he

smiled. Why do I even bother to think of some lunatic dipped in flour pretending to be a dead Welshman when I might think of Veronica Longwood? he wondered as the memory of the dowager duchess gazing at him in the twilight, smiling a surprised welcome, rose to the forefront of his mind. I never thought to see Veronica Longwood again. And yet here she is, as beautiful, as gentle, as kind as ever. How thoroughly I loved her once. Dempsey's smile widened. How thoroughly I could come to love her again, he thought. If she were to provide me with the least encouragement, how truly and thoroughly I believe I could come to love her again.

Berinwick, seated behind the enormous mahogany desk in his father's study, looked up from the ledger entries he was reviewing at the sound of his sister's slippered tread. "Yes?" he asked, as she paused on the threshold. "What is it, Hannah?"

"Mama has gone up to her chambers."

"And?"

"And I should like to know . . ."

Berinwick waited for her to complete the sentence. When she did not, he frowned and closed the ledger completely, resting his elbows on its cover and his chin on his folded hands. "You should like to know what, Hannah? You have my full attention. Ask away."

"I should like to know why Papa bestowed the living of St. Milburga's of the Wood on this Reverend Mr. Dempsey, Will," she said in a great rush, her hands twitching nervously at the folds of her brown silk skirt.

"Yes, so would I," Berinwick agreed quietly, his one dark eye studying his sister, the scars that seared the skin around his patch, stark in the candlelight.

"I mean to say, Will, St. Milburga's of the Wood has been without a rector practically forever, has it not? Why did Papa suddenly decide that it ought to have one? And why decide on a gentleman who knew Mama when she was a child?"

"I doubt Father had the vaguest idea that Dempsey and Mother were children together, Hannah." Berinwick reached out and picked up the inkpot from the center of the desk. He turned it about, thoughtfully, in his hands. "Father would have told Mother the parson's name and made some reference to his background else. He did neither. He merely told her that he had at last managed to bestow the living on some fellow. Told me the same. Never did mention the man's name."

"Perhaps he intended to surprise Mama?"

"Why?"

"I don't know. I cannot think why, unless . . ." Hannah stepped into the room and crossed the burgundy carpeting to the chair in front of her father's desk. She could not think of it as her brother's desk as yet. She knew that Will did not think of it as such, either. She placed both hands on the back of the chair, her knuckles growing white from the pressure of her grip. "You do not think, Will, that Papa knew something was about to happen to him and wished Mama to have someone—some gentleman who cared for her—to stand beside her in her time of sorrow?"

"Father? Invite one of Mother's old flames to Blackcastle knowingly? To comfort her because he knew he would die? Of all the romantic rubbish I have ever heard," Berinwick replied, noting the grip his sister had on the chairback and finding himself considerably disturbed by it.

"It is *not* romantic rubbish."

"It is, Hannah. Father and Thistledown and the two footmen were all killed when the drag overturned coming around the bend at the far end of St. Milburga's graveyard. It's a treacherous curve and always has been. Do you mean to say that Father expected that to happen?"

"Well, no. Not precisely," Hannah replied.

"No, of course he did not expect it."

"I was thinking more that perhaps Papa was ill, you know, and intended Mama to have this Reverend Mr. Dempsey to comfort her should the illness—should it—carry him off."

Berinwick stood, walked around the desk, removed his

sister's hands from the back of the chair, and held them, rubbing the backs gently with his thumbs. "What is it that frightens you, Hannah? Tell me."

"Nothing. I only—I cannot bear to think of Papa ill and none of us realizing."

"Father was not ill."

"Are you certain, Will?"

"Positive. He was never ill a day in his life, Hannah," Berinwick assured her. "He left for Ludlow in high spirits. He was on the box with four in hand and Thistledown beside him when he departed Blackcastle. No gentleman feeling the least bit ill would mount to the box of a drag and take it on himself to handle a four horse-hitch over such roads as these. He would risk everyone's life in the process if he did, including the life of any other driver he might encounter along the way. Father certainly would not take such a risk as that. Not our father. Not with Thistledown there to drive for him. You may place your faith in that, Hannah. And as for Dempsey being someone who cares for Mother—she and he have not so much as set eyes on each other since they were children. You heard her say as much. What would make Father think that Dempsey could bring her any more comfort than Mrs. Hepplewaithe, who is Mother's best friend and spent two months with us after Father's funeral doing precisely that, comforting her?"

"But then why is the Reverend Mr. Dempsey here, Will? Papa cannot truly have wished to put a rector back in charge at St. Milburga's. The church has been neglected forever. Why, it is rotting away bit by bit, year by year. And as far as I know, Papa did never set foot in it."

"He did set foot in the church before you were born."

"He did?"

"Yes. He killed the Reverend Mr. Dight in that church."

"Oh!" Hannah gasped. One hand tugged free of her brother's grasp and went to her lips. Her eyes opened wide and she fixed a most astounded gaze on her brother. "William," she said breathlessly, "you do not think that

Papa invited the Reverend Mr. Dempsey here, that he convinced the man to accept the living, because he wished to kill him, too?"

"No. I don't think that at all." Berinwick placed an arm around his sister's shoulders and urged her toward the door. "Go up to bed, Hannah," he said quietly. "Your mind is overflowing with Gothic tales told by a lunatic. Think of this. Even if, for some unfathomable reason, Father did invite Dempsey here to run him through, it is nothing to cause you the least worry now. Father is dead and I have never heard of Mr. Dempsey before in my life. Father did not confide any secrets about the man to me and order me to run him through should he become unable to do it himself. He said nothing to me about the man except that some parson would be coming to take charge of the church sooner or later. Your Mr. Dempsey is not, by any stretch of the imagination, in danger of losing his life at the hands of a Berinwick. Besides, Father did not just take it into his head to kill the Reverend Mr. Dight. The Reverend Mr. Dight had done something most nefarious and—"

"What?" Hannah asked, as the two stepped out into the corridor. "What did the Reverend Mr. Dight do?"

"Never mind. It will only give you bad dreams. Go to bed, Hannah, and think of better times to come, eh? Think of your birthday celebration and how you will look in your new gown. I've decided that we will put off the harvest home until your birthday. Then we will invite all of Blackcastle and Barren Wycche to celebrate with us. We will be out of mourning, then. I'll hire musicians from Ludlow or Shrewsbury or London. From wherever you like. You'll be able to dance at last, Hannah. Think of dancing with Miss Tofar's brother or one of her cousins, or my friend, Elliot, who may come to visit us if we're lucky. The moon will be full in the night sky. Violins will play as one young man after another leads you down the floor. It will prove a glorious night, I promise. And it is much more worth dwelling upon than these odd misgivings you're having about Father and Mr. Dempsey."

Berinwick bent stiffly and kissed his sister's cheek. It was a token of affection so unlike him that all he had urged Hannah to think of slipped right out of her head to be replaced by a rapidly beating heart and the most dire suspicions.

The Duchess of Berinwick extinguished her lamp, slipped between the sheets, and pulled the counterpane up to her chin. She shivered a bit, not because the bed was cold, but because the familiar warmth of her husband was absent.

"Will I ever be warm again?" she whispered into the darkness. "Surely, one grows accustomed to sleeping alone sooner or later."

A week after her husband's burial, Veronica had insisted on removing herself from the master bedchambers at Blackcastle, giving them over to her son. She had chosen this lovely suite of rooms in the south wing, which was quite as far from her old rooms as she could get, and as far from her children as she could get as well. Had there been a dower house on the property, she would have moved into that, but none of the Dukes of Berinwick had ever built one. Perhaps because Blackcastle itself was so large and sprawling that the addition of a dower house had seemed most unnecessary.

I never understood about a dower house before now, Veronica thought to herself as she waited for sleep to come. I always supposed it to be a cruel and hateful thing to send a widow from her home at her husband's death. But as much as I have come to love Blackcastle, everything within these walls—everything—makes my heart ache for Julian's presence, for his arms to be around me, for his lips to brush against my ear. Even these rooms and this sweet little canopied bed remind me of him. I remember when we purchased this bed in London. How excited we were because the Queen herself was coming to visit us. I remember how the workmen painted and papered and paneled this entire wing for the occasion and how Jules urged them on.

"And how you introduced each and every one of those

workmen to Her Majesty and the princesses, you rascal,"
she said softly. "Oh, what a thing to do, Jules! The workmen were so petrified and the Queen and her girls so utterly
flabbergasted. I expect she told the King all about it. I am
certain she did."

Why could William not have been here then? the duchess
wondered. What did I say or do, precisely, to keep him away?
And why did you never stand up against me, Jules, oppose me
in it and say that William must be present? You did never do
such wonderfully silly things when William was at home. I
doubt he ever did see that smile in your eyes—that mischievous sparkle that I loved so much. No. He feared you and
respected you. He honored you and he honors your memory
now. But he did never know the part of you that was a rascal,
the part of you that made me laugh and love you.

We must be proud of William, Jules. He has taken the responsibilities of the Berinwick dukedom on his broad, young
shoulders willingly and capably. But he remembers you only
as the stern, frowning personage who would not allow him to
hide away here at Blackcastle, who demanded that he attend
Harrow and Cambridge. Oh, Jules, we sent him out to face a
world, you and I, filled with schoolboys who mocked him
cruelly and ceaselessly. We taught him courage in the doing
of it and determination and independence as well. But we did
never teach him joy or silliness or love.

"We ought to have taught him joy and silliness and love,"
Veronica whispered. "But I could not bring myself to do it
and you would do nothing against my will. I was weak and
selfish and you never once insisted that I become strong and
unselfish. And now, though I attempt every day to gather my
courage about me for William's sake, it is a thoroughly useless exercise. Because I do not know how to begin to teach
William about things like love and laughter, Jules. Not at so
late a date as this. I haven't the faintest notion where to begin.
He mimicks Hannah in his humor. He feigns joy. He pretends
to silliness. But no mischievous sparkle ever rises into
William's eyes, as it once did into yours.

"No! I must say it correctly!" she told herself sternly. "No sparkle ever rises into William's *eye*. Into William's one, dark, utterly bewildering eye. Into that eye whose glare could make the Prince of Wales shiver in his shoes and, if rumor is to be believed, has done precisely that any number of times."

Three

Dempsey awakened with the dawn. He stepped out of the rectory into the light of a rising sun and with Theophilus at his heels he strolled to the church. He studied the building thoughtfully, rubbing at his freshly shaved chin. Then he stepped from the cobbled churchyard into the narrow road and followed it around to the side of the building. Theophilus snuffled along beside him and released a minuscule bay as they halted.

"Yes, indeed," Dempsey agreed, hunkering down beside the hound. "I cannot think how we lost the trail last evening, but the dew has formed the flour into tiny clumps now, Theo. It will not make you sneeze anymore, but it's a sight easier to see. Apparently our spirit Welshman on his spirit steed traveled the road this far and then turned into our cemetery."

Dempsey stood again, opened the wrought iron gate, and entered the graveyard. All sight of the flour trail disappeared here where the tall grass, apparently as neglected as the church itself, had not been tended for years. The grass stood thick and high over and around the graves. But the spirit horse had made a path through it nonetheless, bending and breaking the grass as it passed. In silence, Dempsey followed in its wake. Apparently the Welshman's horse had leaped several gravestones and made directly for the far end of the cemetery where it had jumped the low iron fence, cut across a harrowing bend in the lane, and gone off into the wood on the other side.

"Well, I cannot make heads or tails of it," Dempsey muttered to himself, staring off in the direction the horse and rider had taken. "If the vision of Owain Glyndwr was *not* intended for my eyes, why should it come past the rectory and the church and through the cemetery? Who could be expected to see it besides myself? Mr. Langton? Could it be Langton someone wishes to frighten? He was here last evening. He delivered my trunk while we were off on our walk, Theo. I wonder if Mr. Langton knows anything at all about our Owain Glyndwr?"

When Dempsey returned to the rectory, Harvey Langton's dog cart was tied to the hitching post before the establishment. From the rear of the rectory came the sound of a carpet being beaten to within an inch of its weave, and smoke was rising from one of the three chimneys.

"Ah, there you are, Mr. Dempsey," Langton greeted, opening the door to the parson. "Come inside, do. My Eulie has the oven heated and water on the boil, but she cannot guess what you would like for your breakfast."

"Did you bring anything with you for breakfast, Langton?"

"Indeed, sir. Brought a bit of this and a bit of that from home, Eulie did. Says she will take the cart into Barren Wycche later and purchase whatever staples you lack. I told her you lack everything. Well, you must. No one has actually resided in the rectory for ever so long. Merely myself, some nights, when the fog was too thick to think of driving home. Eulie will see you are provided for, Mr. Dempsey, and sufficiently so, or I don't know the good woman I married from the Stiperstone Strangler. Good morning to you, Theophilus," Langton added, bending to give the hound's head a pat. "And what a fine day it is for a new beginning."

"The Stiperstone Strangler?" Dempsey queried as he and Theophilus followed Langton into the rectory.

"You don't wish to know, Mr. Dempsey. Besides, that was years and years ago. I was a child when he first came to fame."

"He would not be dead now and ride about in perfectly ancient armor on a veritable spirit of a horse, wailing like a soul in torment?"

"Riding a veritable spirit of a horse? Ancient armor? Wailing like a soul in torment? No, that would be the ghost of

Owain Glyndwr. You do not mean to tell me that you have actually seen the ghost of Owain Glyndwr, Mr. Dempsey?"

The abruptly frightened look on Langton's countenance caused Dempsey to reconsider discussing with this gentleman the vision he'd seen the evening before. "No, I don't mean to tell you that I have actually seen such a thing, Langton. I merely wondered who the Stiperstone Strangler might be."

"Oh, he be a great hulk of a man with hands as big around as frying pans. But he does not visit this county any longer, Mr. Dempsey, unless there are naughty children to be dealt with." The fear disappeared from Langton's face as quickly as it had appeared and the man laughed as they turned from the corridor into the kitchen. Dempsey noted it was a pleasant, honest laugh—the laugh of a man in whom a fellow could place his trust if it ever came to that. For a moment, Dempsey wondered if the time would ever come when he would have to place his faith in a man like Langton, a gentleman little more than a stranger. He hoped not.

Veronica placed the freshly laundered quilt tenderly over the woman and tucked it in securely at the sides. Then she sat down on the edge of the bed and brushed a strand of blond hair from Widow Thistledown's brow. "You must rest, Henrietta," she said quietly. "You will never recover fully if you do not rest. Both I and Mr. Grafton have told you the same thing over and over again. And yet, what did I find when I arrived this morning but you seated on the back step, attempting to pluck a chicken. I expect it was you who chased it down and took the axe to it, was it not? That was too much in itself. And then what must you do but set yourself to plucking. No wonder you fainted when you stood to greet me."

"Is that what I did, your grace?" asked the woman beneath the quilt. "Fainted?"

"Dead away," Veronica replied. "Most elegantly, too, if I may be permitted to say so. You fainted, my dear, just as though you were some grand London lady in the midst of a ball. All you lacked was a painted fan to drop as you fell. I admit I was most impressed by the style of it, Henrietta, but I do not wish to see you do it ever again. Do you hear me?"

"Yes, your grace. I be sorry, your grace. It were merely—"

"It is merely that you will not do as you are told," the duchess interrupted.

"But I cannot lie about and do nothin' at all from sunrise to sunset. There be Millie and little Charlie to look after. I have been tryin' to rest, I have, but the children must be fed and the cottage cleaned. I cannot bear filth, I cannot. And I did not be plannin' to pluck the chicken. It were Meg was to pluck the chicken, but the poor child screamed the most frightful scream and ran off before it even came time to do it."

"She did?"

"Oh, yes, your grace. The very instant the bird took to dashing about the yard headless, Meg took to screaming and dashed off up the road. Frightened the poor girl near to death to see it. She's not come back yet—has she?"

"I have not seen Meg, Millie, or Charlie, Henrietta. Did they all run off at the sight of tonight's dinner running about dead?"

"Millie and little Charlie went off with his grace a short time ago. I thought you knew. Came and got them, the duke did. Said as he required their assistance with something. Took them both up on his horse and off he rode."

So, Veronica thought, I am not alone in fretting over Mrs. Thistledown's health. Apparently William worries about her as well. Well, he must. Why else would he come and carry her little ones off with him but to allow her time to rest and recover? He has not the least notion what to do with children, and he cannot actually require their aid. What a puzzle he is. He would have me believe that he blames Mr. Thistledown's ineptitude as a coachman for the accident that killed Julian, and yet he bestowed a pension on Mrs. Thistledown almost immediately afterward. And he gave her this little cottage rent-free for all of her years. And provided her with extra chickens and a fresh cow. And he sends his gardeners to help her with the planting and the picking. I cannot believe he would do any of these things if he actually believed that Thistledown had caused his father's death. Or would he? He's my son. I ought to know what he would do. I ought to know him thoroughly but—I do not.

"Your Meg has likely run all the way to Blackcastle by now and is begging Mrs. Bigham to be allowed to take up one position or another," Veronica said into the mounting silence her thoughts had brought about. "It is likely she thinks that providing you and the children with earned monies will prove the best thing she can do—especially since the chicken convinced her that she is not fashioned for housewifery. I remember when first I saw a chicken run about with its head cut off," she added, her eyes shining with humor. "I was perfectly flabbergasted by it."

"You never witnessed such a thing, your grace?"

"Oh, yes. When I lived in Arrandell with my guardian while my mama went to Greece and Italy and Sweden. It was not unusual for my guardian's wife to send her sons out to kill a chicken or two."

"But she never asked such a thing of you, your grace, surely?"

"No, but I was curious to see how it was done and her youngest son, Richard, invited me to—well, never mind. I will send Meg home at once, Henrietta." Veronica paused for a moment's thought. "I do believe I will ask Martha to accompany her," she said. "Yes, indeed. Martha was naught but thirteen when her mama and papa died and she was thrust into responsibility for her brothers and sisters. She will remember how difficult it was and will be most kind to Meg. But she will still teach the girl how to pluck a chicken correctly while you rest."

"But if Meg wishes to obtain a position at Blackcastle—"

"Someday we will find one for her, Henrietta, but not while you are ill," Veronica declared. "Meg is needed here. You cannot rest as you ought without your eldest daughter to assist you in caring for the cottage, the farm, and the younger children."

Berinwick lifted the children down to the ground in an open space between the old barn and the approaching tree line at the far end of the length of Hatter's field. It bothered him that Hatter's field lay fallow this year after the cruel weather and the grim harvest of the year past, but there was nothing to be done about it now. "Charlie," he said, handing his horse's reins to the boy. "Take Penn over and tie her to a tree."

"Any tree in perticular, Duke?"

"A thin tree."

"Why a thin one?"

"Because I want her to be able to step around a bit once you tie her to it, Charlie. If you tie her to a fat tree it will use up all the reins."

"Oh." The five-year-old took the reins Berinwick handed him and skipped merrily off to do as he was told. The mare followed just as compliantly as Berinwick hoped she would. He had ridden Penn this morning precisely because she was docile around children, even skipping ones, and she dealt good-naturedly with them. At least his grooms had told him that she was docile and that she dealt well with little ones. Penn was Hannah's horse. Berinwick had never before taken her out. Wondering at the patience the old mare had already shown with two urchins perched on her broad back wiggling and giggling, Berinwick kept his gaze on the boy and Penn to be certain that the little fellow could manage a knot and that Penn did not pull free from him as he hitched her to the sapling. As this task was being admirably accomplished, Millie silently reached up and grasped as many of the duke's gloved fingers in her tiny hand as she could manage. Berinwick scowled down at her the instant he felt her touch.

Innocent blue eyes stared back up at him and served to

soften his scowl a bit, though it did not disappear completely. The six-year-old's grip tightened.

"Are you afraid of something, Millie?" Berinwick queried.

"No, yer grace."

"Then why have you taken possession of my hand?"

"Don't I be allowed to hold yer hand?"

"Not unless you are frightened of something and require my hand to give you courage, no. I am a duke, Millie. You are a coachman's daughter. Such things are not done."

"Perhaps I be a tiny bit frighted," Millie replied softly.

"Truly? Well, I expect you may hold to my hand for a bit, then. What is it that frightens you?"

"That ol' barn. We be not going in that barn, be we?"

"Of course not," Berinwick replied. "We are simply going to stand here and stare at the thing for the rest of the day."

"We are?"

"No. I was merely jesting. Of course we are going into the barn, Millie. Why should we not?"

"Because a haunt lives in there."

"A haunt? Lives in that particular barn?"

"Uh-huh. Ma told us so."

"When did she tell you so?"

"I don't recollect."

"A long time ago?"

"Uh-uh. Not very long ago at all. She seed it, Ma did."

"The haunt?"

"Uh-huh."

Berinwick could not believe his ears. Why the devil would the Widow Thistledown tell her little ones that the Hatter's field barn was haunted? Because she wished to be certain that they would not run out into the field to play in the old building? But why should they not play in it? There had been nothing to store in it last year, and this year it would remain empty as well.

The field lies fallow. The barn stands empty. There is nothing the children can harm and nothing to harm them, he thought, puzzled. Except the foxes, he remembered abruptly.

Perhaps Mrs. Thistledown is afraid to have Millie and Charlie wander about in the field because of Mad Jack's foxes. But foxes are like to turn and dash off long before children ever catch sight of them.

"Ho!" Charlie cried, prancing up before Berinwick and Millie, a wide smile on his round little face. "I tied a excellent knot, Duke. Penn willn't be able to wander off now. Not at all."

"Very good," Berinwick replied with a curt nod.

"His grace means to go inside the barn," Millie informed her brother in a serious tone.

"Inside of it?"

"Yes," Berinwick replied. "Inside of it."

"Didn't you not tell him about the haunt, Millie? There be a haunt lives in that barn, Duke. My ma says so."

"I told him," Millie declared as Charlie reached up and took hold of Berinwick's other hand, "but he don't believe me, I think."

"Do not tell me that you believe in such things as haunts, Charlie?" Berinwick asked.

"Uh-huh."

Now two sets of innocent blue eyes stared up at him and two tiny hands clutched his fingers tightly. Berinwick, unsettled by their grasping of his hands but unwilling to betray it, berated himself for a fool. He ought not to have invited these tow-haired urchins to join him this morning. He had planned to bring them here for a week and more, merely to give Mrs. Thistledown a bit of peace. But the more he considered it now, the more he wondered why he thought he could ever manage such a thing. He knew nothing about children. He had been off at school and university, riding about London and exploring the countryside, for most of Hannah's young life. And when he *had* spent time with her, his mother had always been nearby to keep the child properly entertained.

"There are no such things as haunts," he said gruffly. "Your mother likely saw a branch waving in the breeze, or the shadow of a cloud crossing the sun."

"Who told you there ain't no such things as haunts?" Charlie asked, increasing his hold on Berinwick's hand by taking it in both of his. "Yer ma?"

"No one told me. I merely know it to be the case."

"But how do you know?" Millie asked.

Berinwick paused, wondering what would be best to say. "I know because I'm a duke," he declared at last. "Dukes know a great deal more about everything than commoners like your mother."

"Oh," the children replied simultaneously.

"So, are we going in then? Millie? Charlie?"

Two blond heads nodded hesitantly.

Berinwick took one long step toward the barn. Millie, not wishing to release the strong hand to which she clung, took three hasty, shorter steps. Charlie, not wishing to free the hand he held, either, took five. Bit by bit, somewhat lopsidedly, the trio made their way to the open door of the barn.

"I hear something," Millie exclaimed in a husky whisper just as Berinwick was about to step inside.

"B-breathing," Charlie stuttered around a bit of panic lodged in his throat.

"An' snuffling," whispered Millie.

"Haunts do not breathe," Berinwick declared from a good three feet above them. "And they do not snuffle, either."

"What do they do?" Millie rocked back on her heels, keeping her balance only because of the death grip she now had on Berinwick's hand.

"They moan."

"I hear moaning!" Charlie proclaimed. "Run!"

Before Berinwick could say another word, the children spun him around one hundred and eighty degrees by the simple expedient of circling him without letting go of his hands and began to tug him back toward his horse. Had he not been a bit off balance, they would not have managed to move him the two steps they did, but he had been a bit off balance, and he did lurch slightly forward.

"Come on, Duke! Run!" Charlie insisted urgently as Berinwick regained his balance and brought them all to a halt. "The haunt'll get us if we don't run!"

"You run then. Go on. Run and hide behind Penn, the both of you. I am not running," Berinwick grumbled.

"You got to run," cried Millie. "Haunts be terrible things. They eat people!"

"They do not," Berinwick protested.

"How do you know they don't?" Millie asked, her eyes wide, her little hands tugging at his fingers.

"I'm a duke. I know all about these things."

"Why would you know things about haunts if there ain't no haunts?" Charlie squeaked, tugging as hard as he could on Berinwick's hand but failing to make him take another step. "If there ain't such things as haunts like you said, then there ain't nothin' to know about 'em. An' you just said they moan an' they don't eat people."

"I only meant that if there were haunts, it's likely they would moan and not snuffle. And even though they do not exist, if they did exist, they would not eat people. I will tell you again that there are no such things as haunts, but you need not believe me. Off with you, then," Berinwick said grumpily, shaking his hands in the air gently in an attempt to dislodge the handclutchers. "If you do not believe me and think a haunt lives in that barn and is going to eat you up, run right over there by Penn. Doubtless, she will protect you."

"An' let you go in there all by your own self?" Millie's eyes widened and they shamed the blue of the sky as they did.

"Not never," Charlie declared, glancing fearfully around Berinwick at the opening to the barn.

"Uh-uh," Millie concurred. "You be our duke and we be 'sponsible for you."

"Jus' so," Charlie agreed. "An' we be bound to stand by you to the death, just like our pa standed by your pa."

Mrs. Eulie Langton proved to be a cheerful woman with a wide smile that revealed three missing teeth, an ample bosom, and a waist distinguishable only because the strings of her apron were tied around it. "We are that pleased to have you with us, Reverend Dempsey," she said as she poured the new rector a second cup of black tea. "Mr. Langton and I have been praying for a new rector for months and months."

"Have you?" Dempsey asked. "And to think his grace would have me believe that my parishioners would be perfectly happy to muddle along without me."

"No! Did he say that? His grace?"

"Words to that effect," Dempsey replied. "Come inside and sit down, Mr. Langton, and join me in a cup of tea," he called as he noted Langton's lean, slope-shouldered form passing by outside the kitchen door. "There is nothing must be done that will not wait while we have a cup of tea. You as well, Mrs. Langton. Abandon the washing up, pour yourself a cup of this fine beverage, and join me here at the table."

"I would be honored," Mrs. Langton replied, going at once to fetch teacups for herself and her husband. "And Mr. Langton would be honored as well."

"Yes, I am honored," Langton acknowledged as he stepped inside the kitchen, his hands freshly washed at the pump. "Cease dithering about, Eulie, m'dear, and be seated," he urged his wife, pulling out one of the chairs at the kitchen table and settling her into it. He poured the tea for his wife and some for himself, added two dollops of cream to each cup, and, setting the teapot aside, sat down. "Eulie and I have been hoping for an opportunity to speak plain to you, Mr. Dempsey," he said, "though we never did think it would come so soon, did we, Eulie? No, we did not. Thought it might prove weeks or months before we knew you well enough."

"Oh, Mr. Langton, ought we? So soon?" asked Mrs. Langton.

"Indeed, m'dear. I admit I did have doubts about what sort of a parson we might expect, but I have not one doubt now. Not a one. No groveling little toad, our Mr. Dempsey. No, and not a man to pale must he abruptly confront the extraordinary or run screeching into the house should some horror suddenly descend upon him."

"How do you know that?" Dempsey queried, a smile twitching at his lips. Beneath the kitchen table Theophilus stood up, turned in a circle, and lay back down with a sigh.

"By looking at you," Langton replied. "And speaking to you. A sniveling little music teacher you are not, Mr. Dempsey. I have always prided myself on being a fine judge of a man's character and I judge you to be honorable, courageous, and not likely to run from even the most horrendous threat."

"Likely your judgment was influenced by my taking the name of Berinwick in vain yesterday when I stepped inside the north church tower, eh?"

"A bit. And the words you uttered when you entered the nave. I was impressed by them, Mr. Dempsey, emerging from the mouth of a preacher like they did. But it's the look in your eyes, and the way you walk and the manner in which you treat those around you that makes me think you are to be trusted with the knowledge. Eulie and I have a difficulty, you see," Langton continued, resting his elbows on the tabletop, his teacup disappearing into the two large hands he wrapped around it. "All in Blackcastle and Barren Wycche may well have a difficulty soon if something is not done. And so, Mrs. Langton and I have been praying for you to come and for you to be precisely the sort of fellow you have turned out to be."

"Indeed." Mrs. Langton nodded enthusiastically, accepting at once her husband's assessment of Dempsey's character. "Praying for months and months, we have been, for a strong preacher, a fearless preacher, a preacher with courage."

"Why?" Dempsey asked.

"Because we are in grave danger, Mr. Dempsey," Langton answered before Mrs. Langton could. "All of us."

"All of us?" Dempsey cocked a disbelieving eyebrow.

"Aye, Mr. Dempsey, it be true," Mrs. Langton said. "The duke and the duchess and Lady Hannah, and myself and my dearest Mr. Langton. And once Mr. Langton says what he must, quite likely you as well. They know everything, they do, the haunts."

Dempsey leaned back in his chair, crossed his arms across his chest, and gazed from one to the other. "Precisely what haunts are we speaking of?" he asked quietly. "Because, generally, I don't believe in ghosts and such."

"No, nor does his grace, which is why it has fallen to Mr. Langton, Thomas Hasty, and Harold Belowes to keep watch over the lad and the duchess and Lady Hannah," Mrs. Langton replied. "And a proper difficult job that has turned out to be."

"Proper difficult," confirmed Langton with a curt nod. "Nearly impossible. Especially when it comes to the duke."

"It *is* the Duke of Berinwick, you speak of, eh? The fierce young gentleman who stalked into the rectory yesterday afternoon and came near to sending me packing?"

"Did he? Stalked in? Almost sent you packing? Indeed, that would be him," Langton nodded.

"That particular duke, Mr. Langton, did not impress me as a gentleman who would require anyone's protection."

"No, he does not impress anyone as a gentleman who requires protection," Mrs. Langton said, "but he does all the same."

"Well, we believe he does, Eulie and me," Langton said. "We be not certain that the duke's to be murdered. We only be certain that his father was."

"Berinwick's father was murdered?" Dempsey stared at Langton in amazement. "Does the young Berinwick know it?"

"I have attempted to tell him so any number of times, but he will not believe it," Langton replied. "Thinks his father's death was an accident. His mama and Lady Hannah think the same."

"But you believe differently, Mr. Langton? You and this Harold Belowes and Thomas Hasty?"

"And me," Mrs. Langton added as her hand began to tremble on the teacup. "I believe, Mr. Dempsey."

"And I *know* it was murder," Langton replied, his eyes narrowing in anger. "Coming around the bend at the far end of the graveyard, the old duke's coach was when it left the road and overturned. Killed them all—Thistledown, the two footmen, Jeffries and Gulliver, and the duke himself. I saw it happen, I did, and it were no accident. That coach was made to overturn."

"Made to overturn? How the deuce does one make a coach overturn?" Dempsey queried.

"I will tell you how," Langton began. "I were walking home through the cemetery, I were. It were past dusk, the mist be rising and me on foot because my dog cart had broke an axle. I was directly behind the church when first I heard the duke's drag coming along the lane. Coming at a spanking pace, it were, and I thought to myself that he must be driving like a madman so as to be home for Lady Hannah's birthday."

"It were Lady Hannah's birthday that very next day," Mrs. Langton explained. "Never a year when her pa did not make a special occasion of her birthday."

"No. You could depend on it," Langton agreed. "No matter what he must set aside, no matter where he happened to be the night before, come the thirty-first of October, the Duke of Berinwick would be certain to be at Blackcastle to celebrate Lady Hannah's birthday. Which is why I was not surprised to hear a coach in the lane and in a great hurry at that. I paused to watch him go by, I did. And it was then I saw that villain rise up out of the mist before me. Rose straight up out of the ground, he did, and urged that devil's steed under him toward the bend."

There was fear in Langton's eyes as he related the tale. Dempsey took note of it.

"I called out and ran after him, but I tripped over a headstone and fell. I heard horses and men screaming, heard the coach roll over and over, creaking and cracking apart as it did so. When at last I managed to gain my feet, there the villain sat, in the middle of the lane. Laughing he were. Great bellows of laughter. And then he turned slowly in his saddle and pointed his finger at me, as if to say that he knew who I was and I were to beware. Turned my blood to ice, he did, and then he rode off beyond that poor broken coach and those poor broken men and disappeared."

"Who?" Dempsey asked in a whisper.

"Glyndwr, Mr. Dempsey. The ghost of Owain Glyndwr."

Berinwick, with Millie and Charlie so close beside him that a cat's whisker would not fit between his breeches and their bodies, stepped into the barn. "There, you see?" he said. "No haunts. No ghosts, no spirits, nothing but a smattering of wheat lying about here and there, a broken plow, and a perfectly useless trunk."

"What was it that moaned then?" asked Charlie, looking carefully about without leaving Berinwick's side.

"And what was it breathed and snuffled?" added Millie.

"The wind moaned through the cracks in those old boards," Berinwick replied. "And I daresay it was the three of us you heard breathing, Millie. And what snuffled was, well, what snuffled was the reason I brought you here in the first place. This barn has been mistakenly inhabited, you see."

"Inhabited?"

"Yes indeed, by a most confused interloper. And I require your aid to remove the trespasser to a more hospitable situation. Ah, just as I thought. There it is now."

"Where?" asked Millie and Charlie together, looking excitedly around.

"There, in the far corner."

"It's very dark over there, Duke," Charlie murmured, squinching his eyes in an attempt to see through the shadows better. "I don't see nothin'."

"I do," Millie announced. "It be a hedgehog! It does be a hedgehog, don't it, your grace?"

"Precisely so, Millie. And it ought not be living in this old barn. Hedgehogs were never intended to live in barns."

"They wasn't?" Charlie squinched his eyes even more. He dearly wanted to see a hedgehog. "Why is it here then?"

"I expect with all the bits of wheat and leaves lying about, the barn seemed a likely place for it to spend the winter, but it's far from winter now. It built an elegant nest behind those boards there," Berinwick replied as he placed one hand on Charlie's shoulder and another on Millie's and urged them forward. "Take merely one step at a time, mind, or you will frighten the devil out of the thing."

"We wouldn't want to do that," Millie whispered.

"No, never," Charlie agreed in as soft a voice as he could manage. "I see it," he said after two more steps. "I see it, Duke! I see it!"

"Yes, yes, but not quite so loud, Charlie. It has taken me a week and more to gentle her enough to let us move her today."

"She's a girl?" asked Millie.

"I believe so. And she has done some harm to her right front foot somewhere along the way because it's shorter than the rest."

"How do you know?" Charlie queried.

"How do I know what?"

"That one foot is shorter."

"Because I watched her walk and I could see, Charlie."

"She's not walking now."

"No, she be sniffing at us," Millie giggled. "How funny she be with her nose in the air like that."

Slowly, carefully, and keeping the children as quiet as anyone could expect to keep them, Berinwick approached the bristly little animal. When he came to within three feet of it, he knelt down on the wooden floor, bringing his charges to a halt, one on each side of him. "Kneel down," he ordered. "Slowly. And quietly, Charlie."

"I are bein' quiet," Charlie protested as he lowered himself to the barn floor. "Oh, look, Millie. She ain't runnin' away."

"Hedgehogs do not," Berinwick explained softly. "They roll up into a ball when they are frightened rather than attempting to escape. But we do not want her to roll up into a ball, either."

"Why not?" Millie asked, her gaze fastened on the little brown-and-gray creature.

"Because we want to pick her up and she will be prickly all over if she rolls into a ball."

"You got gloves on, Duke," Charlie pointed out. "She willn't prickle you through yer gloves."

"She might," Berinwick murmured. "Hello there, Miss Quillbristle. You remember me, do you not? I have brought Millie and Charlie just as I promised."

"Her name be Miss Quillbristle?" Millie giggled behind her hand as Berinwick reached into the pocket of his hunting jacket.

Charlie's eyes widened as Berinwick pulled his hand back out and opened it, palm up. "Yer ma lets you keep worms in yer pocket?"

"Only because I am a duke, Charlie," Berinwick replied. "Here you are, Miss Quillbristle. A bit of a nuncheon for you."

The wet little nose rose higher into the air and as Millie and Charlie held their breath, the hedgehog, recognizing Berinwick's scent as well as the alluring aroma of worms, trundled lopsidedly toward them.

"When we catch her," Charlie whispered, "what be we goin' to do with her?"

"We are going to take her to your cottage, Charlie," Berinwick explained, "and set her loose to wander through your kitchen garden and your flower garden. She'll eat the slugs and caterpillars and all the things that eat your plants. We'll help her make a little nest of leaves and twigs beneath the woodpile or in the tiny hedgerow near the roses. But you and Millie must remember to put water down for her every evening. Can you remember to do that?"

"Yes," the children replied simultaneously as Miss Quillbristle climbed up to seize a worm from Berinwick's gloved hand. "We willn't forget. Not never."

Veronica brought her horse to a halt along the road and gazed thoughtfully up at the clear blue sky.

"Is there something you require, your grace?" asked her groom as he drew up beside her.

"No, Tom. I was merely thinking. It is not yet noon and we have already delivered Mrs. Hynde her quince jelly, made it excessively clear to Reading that the next time we discover he has beaten his wife the duke himself will escort him from Blackcastle land, peeked in on Margaret May to be certain she is actually eating the apples you delivered last week, and checked on Widow Thistledown."

"Just so, your grace."

"And there is no one else requires us at the moment?"

"No, your grace."

"Then I think I shall ride to St. Milburga's, Thomas, and pay a call on the new rector while you return to Blackcastle. You will explain to Martha that she is to accompany Meg home and help the girl to finish plucking that chicken, will you not? And she's to help the child prepare a decent dinner for the family, too. Say to Martha that we shall not expect her back at Blackcastle until half-past four. Meg is to remain at home until her mother is well."

Tom Hasty moved uneasily in his saddle. He stared down at the rutted road, then off at the trees, then down at the road again.

"Tom? What is it?"

"Pardon, your grace?"

"What is it that you oppose in such a simple plan? You did not say, 'Yes, your grace,' and take yourself off at once, you know."

"You ought not be riding about alone, your grace."

"Oh, for heaven's sake! What is it of late? I rode this land alone when you were in short pants, Thomas Hasty, and I shall ride it alone for years to come. Has my son ordered you to attach yourself to my side like an annoying burr?"

"N-no, your grace."

"Are you certain? Because if it is William's notion that I am so old and withered I am like to fall to my death from the back of a meandering old mare, then I will have words with him. I promise you, I will. And he will not order you or any-one else to remain at my side ever again."

"N-no, your grace. He didn't say anything about it. I merely—I—it is hard times, your grace, in England. Danger-ous, dire times. What with the bad weather last year and the crops doing so poorly and the large landowners enclosing the public places, and the price of corn rising, there's many a man, woman, and child feels the famine gnawing at their bel-lies. Only a month ago, McClane came upon desperate men camped close by the mere. Poor and hungry and unable to find work, they were, and angry, your grace—on their way to London to join in the rioting there."

"What a stupid choice they made, then. They ought to have remained here, not gone on to London. Have we not begun to scythe the grasses, Thomas? Indeed we have. And more men would be welcome, would they not? Indeed they would. If there are any people hungry in our midst, they need but come to Blackcastle to be filled. If people have lost their lands and their livelihoods, they need but knock at our door and work they will find aplenty."

"I know, your grace, but some of them—they have grown rough and wild and would as soon steal a bit of bread as earn it. And there are those men who—who have not—who would see a woman alone and—"

"Oh, my goodness, Tom," Veronica said, stifling the urge to laugh as the groom's cheeks betrayed tinges of red in the sunlight. "You cannot believe for one moment that any man would think to—to—attack and ravish *me?*"

"Such things h-happen, your grace, in times when unrest stirs the land and the people rise up in protest."

"Then you would do best to accompany Martha and Meg back to the Widow Thistledown's and remain there to escort Martha home again, Tom. If such desperate men are like to trespass on Blackcastle land, then it is Martha and Meg who will require your escort, not an old dowager such as I. I can-not believe a man exists who would wish to ravish the likes of me at any time in any place. But I do believe you ought to set yourself to protect Martha and Meg if what you say is true. Now, off with you. At once!"

Tom Hasty sighed, but he bowed his acquiescence, urged his horse forward, and proceeded up the road at a canter, leaving her grace to turn her own mount in the direction of the Church of St. Milburga's of the Wood.

Dempsey gave thanks for small favors as he rearranged his long legs and took another slate in hand. At least they had extra slates. At least one of the Berinwicks had thought to purchase them from the same quarry as the originals so the church roof would not look as though it had been extensively patched. He wondered which Berinwick had thought it prudent to provide for the church even to this extent—the father or the son.

Could be either one, he thought as he placed the slate, took nail and hammer in hand, and began to attach it. Both expected me. Though, this new Berinwick did not seem at all concerned with the state of the church. On the other hand, I cannot think his father much concerned, either. He is the one let it get this way in the first place. Likely he helped it to get this way, what with searching about for the cup. "Langton?" Dempsey called out. "Who purchased these slates?"

"That would be her grace, Mr. Dempsey."

Yes, Dempsey thought. Veronica would care about a church with a leaking roof.

"And *that* would be her grace," Langton added from his perch atop the peak of the roof.

"What?"

"Riding this way, Mr. Dempsey. Her grace. As fine a lady as was ever born."

"Where?"

"Just coming along the road."

Dempsey, eager for a glimpse of her, scuttled like a crab up the far side of the church roof to join Langton at the top. He had just swung one leg over the peak when a loose slate gave away beneath his foot and sent him lurching to the side. Langton reached out at once to seize Dempsey's wrist but he was too slow. The rector tumbled over the peak and began to slip and slide down the roof, searching for something to cling to every bit of the way. His left hand sent Langton's pile of slates clattering ahead of him to shatter on the cobbles below. His right hand slithered through a particularly disgusting patch of mold. His face assumed a decidedly fierce scowl.

"Is this what You intended for me all along?" he shouted in a rush, his heart beating rapidly, sweat streaming into his eyes. "To meet Veronica again after all these years and then die at her feet from a broken neck? For shame, I say!" And then his right boot heel caught on a broken slate and his left on another and one gloved hand slipped through a hole in the roof and seized hold of a solid rafter. Dempsey came to an abrupt halt, spread-eagled, three feet from the edge of eternity. "I do beg Your pardon," he whispered. "I ought not have shouted at You."

The noise of the rector's rapid descent had drawn Veronica's attention at once and, witnessing his impending doom, she had urged her mount into a run, arriving at the church just as Dempsey came to a jarring halt. "Oh, thank goodness!" she cried, staring up at him. "Mr. Dempsey, are you all right?"

"Just fine and dandy, your grace," Dempsey replied in a somewhat strangled voice as Langton made his way slowly, carefully down the roof toward him. "Never better."

It took a good ten minutes and involved the widening of an already-large hole in the roof and the combined efforts of Langton, Mrs. Langton, the eldest Langton daughter, and the duchess herself to get the parson safely down inside the church.

"Will you see what I've done?" Dempsey muttered, embarrassed and angry as his feet touched the floor of the nave. "There is not a bucket in the world large enough to catch the rainwater that will rush in through that crater. And surely we have not enough slates to cover it."

"We've slates enough to put on an entire roof if need be,"

Langton assured him, relief apparent on his face. "It is merely a hole in a roof, Mr. Dempsey. What is a hole in a roof compared to the likelihood of our new rector lying cold and stiff on the cobblestones?"

"Precisely right," the duchess agreed. "And if we have not enough slates, I will send McClane to purchase more. It is worth the price to have you alive and in one piece, Mr. Dempsey. Only think how difficult it would be to explain to the congregation that we were fortunate enough to procure a new rector at last but we allowed him to break his neck before he even read himself into the position. I should not want to face them all and tell them that, should you, Mr. Langton?"

"Never."

"No, and goodness knows if we had to get William to do it, he would make a tremendous muddle of it, Mr. Dempsey. My son would most likely have the entire congregation believing that he had pushed you off the roof himself."

Dempsey gazed at her as she took his arm to see the most delightful imp of mischief darting about in her eyes. "Come into the rectory, Mr. Dempsey," she said, urging him toward the door, "and Eulie will make us both a cup of tea."

"Indeed, I will," Mrs. Langton said, shooing her eldest daughter ahead of her. "And put a dollop of brandy in it, too."

"Brandy?" asked Mr. Dempsey.

"Oh, I beg your pardon, Mr. Dempsey. Do you not drink spirits?"

"I should be grateful for a dollop of brandy in my tea, Mrs. Langton   for medicinal purposes, of course—but we have no brandy in the house."

"Not to worry," Mrs. Langton replied. "I know where a bit may be hiding." And she hurried off ahead of them.

"I, too, know where a bit of brandy may be hiding," Veronica said as she accompanied an aching Dempsey toward the rectory.

"Where?" he asked, astounded at the manner in which the sunlight, as though unable to resist, came to shimmer around her, coaxing silver sparkles from her hair, setting her face aglow.

"In a little silver flask in one of Langton's coat pockets."

"Langton carries a flask of brandy about with him?"

"Oh, yes. All the gentlemen of Barren Wycche and Blackcastle do, Mr. Dempsey. Even Julian did. Even William does. One never knows, after all, when a bit of brandy—for medicinal purposes, of course—will prove necessary."

"You will not use this bit of an accident to cry off from dinner at Blackcastle tonight, I hope," the duchess said, seated comfortably on the sofa in the rector's parlor.

"Cry off? I think not." Dempsey, who had hurriedly donned a coat over his shirtsleeves for propriety's sake but remained without neckcloth, collar, or waistcoat, studied her intently from across the low table that separated them. "I look forward to dinner at Blackcastle, Veronica," he added, wondering why the soft smile she bestowed on him should be tinged with sadness.

Does she think of her husband? he wondered. I doubt he would have gone sliding down the church roof like a veritable simpleton. "I should like to have had the privilege of meeting your husband," he said quietly. "I expect he was a most remarkable gentleman."

"You and Julian never met?"

"Never."

"Then why . . . ?"

"Why what?"

"Why did Julian offer you—no, I mean to say—what was it brought you to Julian's attention? Why should he offer you this living, Richard, if you did never meet each other?"

"He heard of me here and there."

"Oh."

"Drink your tea, Veronica. It will grow cold."

"I *am* drinking my tea." Veronica raised the teacup to her lips and took a sip. The brandy made it quite delicious and she took another. "You ought to slide down the church roof more often," she said. "An excellent excuse for a dollop of brandy in the tea."

Dempsey chuckled low in his throat and Veronica was astounded at the shiver of pleasure his chuckle sent through her. She studied him over the rim of her teacup, her eyes wide.

"What?" Dempsey asked.

"N-nothing. You have grown up to be the most remarkable gentleman, Richard."

"Remarkable? Me? What makes you say that?"

Your beautiful face, your broad shoulders, the courage and confidence that shimmer all around you even as you sit here simply drinking tea, she thought as she studied him.

"I expect I ought to have said you have grown up to be a most remarkable parson," she replied. "Even William finds you remarkable."

"He does? Your son? I am greatly relieved."

"Why?"

"Because I thought he would tell you that I am likely the most disorganized, shatterbrained, unlikely parson he has ever set eyes upon. We did not meet under the best of circumstances."

"Nevertheless, William thinks you are remarkable. But he'll prove a veritable plague to you if you do not face up to him at every turn. He is accustomed to having his way in things whether others will agree to it or not and you . . ."

"And I?"

". . . and you, I think, are accustomed to having yours."

"Yes, indeed. You're correct there. I am an obdurate, mulish old man when it comes to things about which I feel strongly."

"An *old* man? I shall not argue with the 'obdurate' or the 'mulish,' Richard, for those two qualities you possessed even as a child, but I take leave to question the 'old.'"

"I'm forty this year. Definitely not young."

"In your prime."

"Ah, it would be nice to think so, but my prime passed me

by some time ago. 'Here I am, Richard,' it said. 'Make use of me while I exist, eh?'"

Veronica's eyes sparkled with laughter. "Is it supposed to address a man so? His prime?"

"Yes. Certainly. In just those words, too."

"And did you make use of it?"

"In a manner of speaking, I believe I did."

"How?"

"I cannot tell you how, precisely. Not at the moment." He grinned at her—the impish grin she remembered at once from childhood. "Perhaps in a year or two, when you have come to find me irreplaceable and your son is not likely to send me packing, I will reveal to you the harrowing tales of a parson in his prime. But not now. Tell me instead how you have fared as a married lady—the Duchess of Berinwick, no less. How excited you must have been to receive that offer. Though I've no doubt the duke was smitten with you from the first. Lost his heart completely, I should think."

"Yes, he did," Veronica replied with good-natured smugness. "One sultry glance from these devilishly fine eyes and Julian Thorne was mine."

"Devilishly fine eyes? He called them that?"

"Often."

"Not a poetical bone in his body, eh?"

"Not a one," Veronica said, her smile encompassing her entire countenance now. "I never did meet a truly poetical gentleman after you, Richard."

"Poetical gentleman? Me?"

"You don't remember. And I have treasured it all these years. I even went so far as to take it from my jewelry box this morning, intending to present you with it after dinner."

"What? Present me with what?" Dempsey was so unwise as to take another sip of his tea at that very moment.

"The poem you wrote me when you were seven."

Tea sprayed from between Dempsey's lips like water from a fountain. He coughed and jumped up at one and the same time. He reached hurriedly for the handkerchief in his coat pocket, mumbling his apologies as he did so. He wiped at his mouth, at the lapels of his coat, at his shirtfront, at a spot or two on the tabletop. His hair, which he'd attempted to comb with his fingers when he'd donned his coat, came tumbling down over his brow. His ears grew red. His blue eyes hid behind lowered lids to avoid meeting Veronica's gaze.

"After that, I was ruined for all others with poetical leanings," the duchess teased. "No one could match, much less exceed, your efforts in my eyes. I think you remember it now, do you not?"

"I am in the process of remembering it," Dempsey admitted, ceasing to dab at this and that and lowering himself once again into his chair. "Veronica, how could you have saved it?" he asked, his eyes meeting hers once more. "Of all things! The scribblings of a seven-year-old!"

"A precocious seven-year-old whom I had come to love with all my heart."

"Did you?"

"Oh, yes. How could I not have loved you, Richard, when the first day we met you put your arms around me and told me I was not to cry because my mama went away, when you said in the most serious tone that you would be honored to share your mama with me for as long as I required her? And then you took me—do you remember where you took me? You were only five, almost six, then, I think."

"I took you to my father's church and lured you through the little door behind the altar into the Lord's Chamber."

"The Lord's Chamber." Veronica's eyes shimmered with memories. "I have never been anywhere lovelier in all my years. Even here in Shropshire, when the sun sets over Little Mynd Moor, it does not approach the beauty of the Lord's Chamber. Do you remember how the sun spilled rainbows through the stained glass?"

"I remember."

"And how the wind whispered to us and when it rained, how the rain sizzled and breathed like a thing alive?"

"I remember."

"Oh, Richard, I have not thought of the Lord's Chamber in so very long. I wish I could see it now. I wish I could be inside of it and safe."

"Safe?" Dempsey's eyebrows lifted at the word. "Safe from what, Veronica? From whom?" Did she know? But Langton had said not. Her son did not believe his father had been murdered and had forbidden Langton to so much as mention the possibility to the duchess, Lady Hannah, or anyone else, for that matter.

"From myself," she replied softly. "From the memories of other days much less inspiring than those I spent with you. Oh, but I have made a muddle of things, Richard. Not only for myself, but for my son. I have—I have ruined William's life."

Four

Four heads around the dining room table bowed respectfully. "Heavenly Father, for this food of which we are about to partake, we are most humbly grateful. Amen," Dempsey said.

"Amen," Berinwick, Veronica, and Hannah echoed. Beneath the table, Theophilus settled his chin on Dempsey's foot and closed his eyes.

The soup, a fine mulligatawny, followed the simple prayer to the table. "I expect we ought to be most humbly grateful," Berinwick allowed gruffly, "that the present famine has not much affected Blackcastle or Barren Wycche. Our larders are not as full as they might be, but there is no panic among our people or any great hardship, either. It is far different, I understand, in the cities. Even bread is difficult to come by there for some."

Dempsey swallowed a sip of soup and nodded. "Just so, your grace. Precisely so. The war, the crop failures, the rise in taxes, all have made life extremely difficult, especially in the cities. There have been riots in Nottingham and Coventry, in Sheffield and Sussex."

"And in London," the duchess offered. "The King's coach was attacked, I understand, and people broke all the windows in Prime Minister Pitt's residence."

"Not all the windows, I think," Dempsey replied, "but a goodly number. One never knows just how much to believe between one newspaper's report and another's."

"And Kent?" Berinwick queried. "How fare they in the caves of Kent, Mr. Dempsey? Any windows broken there?"

"In the *caves* of Kent?" The duchess stared at her son in amazement.

"People actually live in caves in Kent?" Hannah asked. "And they have windows in the caves? I never heard of such a thing. You are jesting, Will."

"Well, I am jesting about the windows," Berinwick conceded, "but people do live in caves in Kent. I know of some who do."

"Some?"

"One, at least," Berinwick replied. "A clergyman, I believe he is."

"Balderdash," Hannah proclaimed. "No clergyman would even think to live in a cave. Perhaps hundreds of years ago, but today they all wish to have their own livings, a perfectly elegant rectory, enormous glebes to plant, and tithes that amount to a small fortune. You have told me so yourself, Will. They are all in search of wealth and power, even the itinerant preachers. Offer them a living and they will do anything to acquire it."

The Duchess of Berinwick cleared her throat.

"Oh!" Hannah exclaimed. "Oh, I do beg your pardon, Mr. Dempsey. I did not intend to imply that you—"

"Forgot there was a clergyman at your table, did you, my lady? Never fear," Dempsey responded, his lips twitching upward at the corners. "I doubt not that your observations are accurate in a number of cases. Not all clergymen, however, are cut from the same cloth."

"Of course not," Veronica agreed. "You must forgive Hannah's generalization. She listens when William mutters to himself. Neither of my children is well acquainted with any of the clergy. Clerics are rather a foreign breed in our neighborhood."

"So I hear," Dempsey replied. "But that is about to change."

"Is it?" Berinwick queried with an insolent cock of an eyebrow. "What makes you think that, Mr. Dempsey?"

"William!" exclaimed his mother.

"No, no, quite all right, your grace," Dempsey said with a wink in Veronica's direction. "What makes me think that, your grace, is my inherent optimism."

"Your inherent optimism?"

"Just so, that and the fact that I have taken it into my head to remain at St. Milburga's of the Wood whether I remain in possession of the living or not. I will remain until the poor church is repaired and useable again. You will discover that I am a stubborn man, your grace. Nothing can force me to deviate from a path I have firmly chosen."

"Nothing at all, Mr. Dempsey?"

"Nothing, your grace. You may withdraw the living, but I will remain to repair that church must I reside in a tent on the moor and beg for my food while I do it."

At the hands of the footmen, the empty soup plates departed and the butler poured a bit of claret into Berinwick's wineglass. The duke tasted it, nodded, and his glass was filled along with the glasses of the other three at table. Berinwick caught Dempsey's eye as he ought. Dempsey returned the gaze, smiled, and raised his glass. Berinwick raised his in response and both gentlemen drank. The ritual was repeated once more, Berinwick raising his wineglass to his mother, Dempsey to Hannah. It was a tradition in the country, this way of taking wine, the raising of glasses until all present were included. Berinwick thought it a ridiculous tradition. One ought to drink when one was thirsty and not drink when one was not. But he performed the ritual this evening out of respect for his mother, who wished so very much for the Reverend Mr. Dempsey to be favorably impressed with them. The duke had seen the hope of gaining the parson's favor reflected in his mother's eyes since three o'clock this afternoon. And though he could not resist teasing the gentleman a bit, he was determined to do his best to gain his mother the favor she sought from the fellow.

A smoked salmon arrived on the dining room threshold, accompanied by a turbot in lobster sauce and the essential cruets and side dishes. Dempsey bowed his head and prayed once again, stopping the footmen in their tracks on their way to the table. "For this bounty of the sea, Lord, we give you thanks," Dempsey intoned. "Amen."

"Amen," echoed the others.

The duchess, her eyes sparkling, motioned with one finger and the fish, with all its accompaniments, approached. When the remains departed, Gaines refreshed the claret and Berinwick instigated another round of the wine ritual. Following this, the footmen appeared with trays laden with pheasant and dove, peas, asparagus, cucumber. Once again they were halted on the threshold by Dempsey's abruptly bowed head, which was followed by three more heads bowing just as abruptly. "Oh, most gracious God," the parson prayed, "bless this charming and delightful pheasant and the sweet little doves on which we dine. We give you thanks for the peas and the asparagus and the cucumbers. Amen."

"A-amen," Hannah giggled.

"Amen," the duchess managed without a giggle, though her eyes positively flashed with good humor.

"By gawd, I *am* going to starve to death at my own table," mumbled Berinwick under his breath. Gaines, standing steadfast behind the duke's chair, was the only one to hear him. The butler waved the footmen into place with some urgency.

Three courses, three more prayers of thanksgiving, three bottles of claret and a half a bottle of burgundy later, when the fruit, the cheese, a chocolate cream, and a plum pudding edged nervously into the dining room, Mr. Dempsey began once again to bow his head. "Dearest Father," Dempsey began.

"Allow me, Dempsey," Berinwick interjected, unable to bear with blessings any longer, not even for his mother's sake. "Dearest Father, if You care at all for this parson of Yours, stuff something in his mouth now, because if I hear one more word of blessing out of him, I am going to strangle the man. Amen."

Dempsey roared into laughter. Lady Hannah was so overcome with hilarity that she hid her face behind her napkin and shook with glee. The Duchess of Berinwick's mirth chimed like tiny bells all around them. Beneath the table, Theophilus awoke, yawned, stretched, stood, and bayed.

Berinwick's glare fell on each of them in turn. He went so far as to lean down and glare under the table at Theophilus. "What? Were you in on it, too?" he asked the hound. Then he straightened up, cut a chunk of cheese, and bent back down again. "Cease baying, you wretched beast," he commanded quietly, offering the cheese to the tail-wagging hound and giving the old dog's head a pat. "Which one of you told our Reverend Mr. Dempsey about my previous comments?" he demanded, as he straightened up again. "You, Hannah?"

Hannah, still hiding behind her napkin, shook her head vehemently from side to side.

"Mother?"

"I d-did mention your fears about him praying over the pheasant and blessing the peas," the duchess admitted, wiping tears of laughter from her eyes. "But I had no idea he would actually do such a thing."

"Blame only me, your grace," Dempsey said, grinning madly. "I thought you ought to get the sort of parson you expected, for one evening at least. Do give over, Berinwick, and smile. The joke is not on you, you know. It is on a number of toadeating little preachers who want nothing more than to seem holier than everyone else and who sport their piety at every opportunity. They do actually exist, men like the preacher you imagined. I, in fact, have dined with some of them. Oh, how I wish I had thought to bid the Lord to stifle them before I did so myself! That would have given the lot of them pause, let me tell you!"

Once Berinwick, Hannah, the Reverend Mr. Dempsey, and Theophilus had all seated themselves comfortably in the drawing room after dinner, the dowager duchess lifted a timeworn scrap of paper from the cherrywood cricket table beside her chair. "My dearest daughter," she said, "has been asking unending questions about our relationship, Mr. Dempsey."

"Our relationship?" Dempsey queried.

"Yes, indeed. I did confess to knowing you in my youth."

"You did?"

"Yes, she did," murmured Berinwick. "Why do you suddenly grow pale, Mr. Dempsey?"

"Pale? I am not growing pale," Dempsey protested, his gaze fastened on the duchess and the scrap of paper she held in her hand. "Veronica, that is not—you do not actually intend to—"

"Veronica?" Berinwick was so startled by the sound of his mother's Christian name on the Reverend Mr. Dempsey's lips that he stood straight up out of his chair. The toe of his left boot connected abruptly with Theophilus's backside. The hound exploded from drowsy complacency into unbounded ferocity on the instant, attacking the boot with savage abandon.

"Blast!" Berinwick exclaimed over intimidating growls and the snap of teeth.

"Theophilus, cease and desist!" Dempsey ordered. He rose from his chair and dove for the hound, arms going around Theo's neck in an attempt to draw him away from the duke. "Stop, m'boy. His grace did not intend you an injury."

"Injury? I barely touched the beast."

"You kicked him," Dempsey pointed out.

"I nudged him. With the tip of my toe. I did not so much as realize he was there."

"Well, you ought to have realized it. He lay himself down right at your feet. Theo, stop! And you, your grace, cease wiggling your foot all about. Did you learn nothing the last time? And this time is different. He thinks you more than an empty boot, this time. He thinks you intend him harm. You are urging him to protect himself all the more by wiggling so."

"I am attempting to shake him off."

"Well, you cannot shake him off. He hasn't many teeth, but those that remain are strong and he has jaws of iron. How am I to unclamp him if you persist in your attack?"

"In *my* attack?" Berinwick glared down at the top of Dempsey's head and ceased to move at all. He stood, balanced awkwardly on his right foot as his left lingered in Theo's mouth.

Dempsey whispered to the dog. Dempsey patted the hound's head. With great determination, Dempsey placed himself directly before the animal, took Theo's jaws in his hands, and pried them apart. "Poor Theo," he said softly as he freed Berinwick's boot, then tugged the hound into his arms. "Poor old boy. The duke surrenders, Theo. It's over now. His grace will not remount his attack. I give you my word on it."

"I ought to shoot the beast," Berinwick declared. "Assaulting a duke in his own drawing room! Hannah, ring for Gaines to escort this animal from my house, and this lunatic of a parson along with the beast."

"Hannah, do not you dare," the duchess countermanded immediately. "William, do cease making such a fuss. Theophilus did not do you a bit of damage."

"No, but he attempted it. And after I fed him cheese from the dinner table, too."

"He merely thought," said Dempsey, now ruffling the dog's ears, "that you intended him harm. He does not always realize what is happening around him when he grows drowsy. He was beaten when he was a pup. Beaten most severely and put into a sack to be drowned. I expect the tip of your toe to his haunches brought it all back to him."

"Oh, poor, poor dog," Hannah murmured sympathetically.

"And you need not ring for your butler, your grace," Dempsey continued. "Theo and I will see ourselves out."

"You will do no such thing," Veronica protested.

"No, don't," Berinwick added, as Dempsey gave the hound's head a final pat, left his knees, and stood, coming almost toe-to-toe with the duke.

"I shall merely thank your mother and Lady Hannah for a lovely dinner, your grace, and then Theo and I will be gone from your sight."

"I said you need not go, Dempsey, either of you. What must

I do? Fall to my knees and beg the beast's pardon? I'm sorry I kicked him. I am sorry he was mistreated when he was a pup and I do understand his reaction. I forgive the blasted dog!"

"You do? Well. Good."

"You, however, had best have an acceptable explanation."

"For what?"

"For *what?* What the deuce do you mean by calling my mother Veronica?"

"I never . . ." Dempsey sputtered.

"You did, Richard," the duchess said with a soft smile. "You forgot yourself when you thought I intended to read your poem."

"Richard?" Berinwick glared over Dempsey's shoulder at his mother. "You will call him Richard?"

"Indeed, I think I will when I want to, William. We used each other's Christian names when we were children. It is a natural thing between us. Now sit down, both of you, please, and let us continue what has so far been a most interesting and enjoyable evening."

"Interesting and enjoyable," grumbled Berinwick, as he lowered himself back into his chair. "He prays over every course at dinner, sends Hannah into hysterical mirth, decimates my wine cellar, calls my mother Veronica as though they are intimately acquainted, and then his dog attacks me. Yes, indeed, a most interesting and enjoyable evening."

Dempsey, hearing every word clearly, guffawed.

Berinwick glowered at him.

"Enough," the duchess commanded. "William, Theophilus is curling up at your feet again. Do not spring suddenly from your chair for any reason. You have been warned. Richard, I should not laugh too loudly, because I am about to read the lovely poem you wrote for me all those years ago."

"A poem?" Hannah asked with obvious delight.

"The finest poem anyone has ever written for me," Veronica nodded. "No, do not blush, Richard. It is not in the least embarrassing. It is, in fact, lovely. And, it is perhaps the best way for my children to come to know you as you were then."

"When?" Berinwick queried, noting the red staining Dempsey's neck and rising up into his cheeks.

"When he was seven."

"And you were?"

"I do believe I was thirteen, almost fourteen. Now hush." Veronica held the scrap of paper at arm's length and squinted a bit. "Really, Richard," she said with a shake of her head, "I do hope that your handwriting has improved immensely since then."

"Read it, Mama, do," Hannah urged, her smile wide.

"Very well. *To Veronica* it is called."

"Most imaginative," Berinwick muttered.

"Will, hush!" implored Hannah.

"To Veronica," the duchess repeated.

*"You are lovely as the portrait at the top of Papa's
    stairs.*

*Your voice is cheery, gurgling like Squire Topper's
    spring.*

*Your eyes are kind and gentle and the sun glows on
    your hairs.*

When you are near, the bees forget to sting."

"The sun glows on your hairs?" Berinwick snickered.

"Mr. Dempsey was merely seven, Will," Hannah protested in the parson's defense. "No doubt it was difficult to find a rhyme for stairs. It is a fine poem, Mr. Dempsey."

"And there is more to it," the duchess said, noting that although Dempsey had slumped lower in his chair and his chin was apparently being swallowed by his neckcloth, his eyes were not only aglow with memories, but laughing up into her own.

"If ever you should need me, for certain I'll be there.

For you I will prove loyal, brave and true.

Because you are an angel with whom no one can compare,

Veronica of Arrandell, I pledge my life to you."

The dowager duchess lowered the paper and gazed in silence at Dempsey. "I have kept it all these years," she said after a long moment, "because it has always seemed to me the most innocent and honest declaration of love that I have ever heard. How my husband came to pick you, Richard, to receive the living here, I cannot guess, but he could have done me no greater kindness than to bring you back to me again."

Dempsey declined Berinwick's offer of a carriage. "I prefer to walk when I can," he said. "And I have brought a lantern with me to light my way and a lead for Theophilus so he will not run off and cause me to trespass on your land tonight, your grace."

"I expect you may trespass on Blackcastle land whenever you have a mind to do it," Berinwick replied as the two exited through the great double doors side by side, Theophilus between them. "Lock up the doors, Harold. I have a mind to stroll down to the stables and check on Triumph's hock. I shall let myself in when I return."

"Yes, your grace," the footman responded.

"I may trespass whenever I have a mind to do it?" Dempsey could not quite believe his ears.

"I expect so. I have never seen my mother smile so readily and so often as she did tonight."

"Surely that cannot be. I cannot recall a time when a smile did not linger on your mother's face. I should think she smiled readily and often before your father's death, your grace."

"Perhaps, though I cannot remember a time when her smiles lingered. But then, I was rarely home. Sent me off to school at the age of six, my father did. I have no idea what occurred at Blackcastle while I was absent. Perhaps they were very gay, Father and Mother. Hannah would know. Speaking of which, I have not heard Hannah giggle quite so uncontrollably in a goodly long time, either. I am more adept at making her angry than making her giggle. So, I have decided that you are welcome here and may make free of Blackcastle lands because you can produce giggles and smiles. Mother and Hannah are sorely in need of both, I think. I will accompany you to the end of the drive if you will have me."

"Of course we will have you, will we not, Theo?"

"Rarf," Theophilus agreed with great good will.

"Do you always speak to that hound as though he is a person?"

"Yes. Why?"

"I merely wondered. You have spent a great deal of time alone, then."

Dempsey gazed at the younger man from out the corner of his eye. "What makes you think that?"

"I learned long ago how people who address animals and objects as though they are human come to the doing of it. I have come to it myself once or twice. When there is no one else with whom to speak, one must speak to someone. And if you are alone for an extended period, it becomes habit, this humanization of animals and things. About that poem, Dempsey. You turned red as a beet when Mother read it but you did not protest."

"No. How could I? She was determined upon it and, embarrassing or not, it did bring back to me some of the happiest times of my life."

"Just so. The times when the bees forgot to sting."

They strolled on in silence beneath the branches of the elms that lined the drive until they reached the gatehouse.

"You no longer have a gatekeeper, eh?" Dempsey queried.

"Not since my great-great grandfather's time. No need for one after the gate disappeared."

"The gate disappeared?"

"I expect it was torn down," Berinwick explained, "though I never did hear the story. Father was always going to tell me about it when I grew older. Well, I have been old enough, I should think, for years now, but he never did get around to it. You can find your way to the rectory from here without difficulty, eh, Dempsey?"

"Indeed. The road is not straight, but it is the only road."

"Just so. Good evening to you then and—"

"And?"

"Be careful of the bees hereabout, Mr. Dempsey. I daresay

my mother's presence does not make bees forget to sting any longer. At least, I have not found it to be so."

I expect that gentleman has been stung innumerable times, Dempsey thought, strolling off toward St. Milburga's of the Wood, Theophilus trotting confidently along beside him. Stung by some perfectly barbarous bees, I should think. He bristles up at the least thing, like a hedgehog expecting always to be attacked.

Dempsey allowed more of Berinwick's words to echo through his mind and frowned over a number of them. He does not recall smiles lingering on his mother's face? How can that be? the parson wondered. What kind of a son does not remember with fondness his mother's smiles, does not treasure them and hold them dear? What did the old duke do? Send the boy off to school at six and not allow him home again until he was twenty-one?

No. Never. Veronica would never have permitted such a thing as that, Dempsey assured himself. Surely Berinwick's time at home was not as rare as he makes it out to be. He was simply feeling dejected for some reason. He seemed perfectly fine for most of the evening, but perhaps he required a brief period away from his mother and sister to indulge himself in remembered sorrows. Perhaps the conversation in the drawing room brought back to him memories of other, less pleasant, times and he thought I should not care one way or the other if he indulged in just a bit of self-pity. We all do indulge in it, after all. And why should I, stranger that I am, think anything at all of his doing so?

"I wonder if we will see any visions tonight, Theophilus," Dempsey murmured, his thoughts turning in another direction entirely. "I should like to have a second look at this Owain Glyndwr—especially after Langton's tale. Langton believes he saw a true ghost and that the ghost caused the elder Berinwick's death. Can you imagine that? But then, Langton did not have the advantage of your nose, Theo, to discover that the grave dust was naught but flour and the ghost merely a man playing a role. And I did not tell him, either. I ought to have told him, because he confessed at last, you know, that he saw the ghost again last evening. It was to the rectory that the villain was bound, Theo, to frighten Mr. Langton. Langton was waiting there, along with our meatpies, but he departed once he saw that ghost."

They trudged along in silence for a while, Dempsey's ears attuned to the night, listening for a wail, the clank of armor, the muffled thumping of hooves. None came.

"I did not bargain on murder when I agreed to come here, Theophilus," he said at last. "I imagined from the duke's letter that all was well and we would have a perfectly smashing time, he and I, searching out the cup."

"Rrrruph," Theophilus observed.

"Just so, old boy. Now, aside from searching out the cup, I have the man's family to protect and his church to restore. Certainly provided me with more than a mere living, the late Duke of Berinwick did. You don't think he knew all along that he and his family were in danger, Theo? You don't think that he feared to write a word of it into that letter because he thought that then I would not come? I expect it's likely, my being a clergyman and all, that he thought the mere mention of danger, blood, and guts might cause me to decline his offer."

"Rrrrrrr."

"Exactly right, Theophilus. If that were the case, the late Duke of Berinwick did not know me nearly as well as he thought he did. My reputation with antiquities may have reached his ears, but my personal reputation must have eluded him. I would have come sooner had he included the merest hint of a threat to himself and his family. Whether he and I stood a chance of recovering the cup or not, I'd have defied the Bishop of Hereford, abandoned all search for the ruby-and-diamond ring of the Tudors, and come to St. Milburga's at once."

At least I am here now, Dempsey thought as he paused along the road to listen again for the sound of wailing or the muffled hoofbeats of the spirit horse. If I could not protect the last Duke of Berinwick, at least I have the opportunity to protect this present one, and Lady Hannah and Veronica as well.

"Veronica," he whispered, "if you had been in that coach when that villain sent it careening off the road, if you had died because I delayed my arrival from Kent for so many months, I would never have forgiven myself. Never."

But she was not in that coach, he reminded himself silently. Nor does she so much as suspect that her husband's death was anything but an accident.

How lovely she looked tonight, he thought then as, hearing neither wail nor hoofbeats, he continued on his way. Her face was so pale above the black of her gown and the jet of her beads. Her eyes absolutely glowed with laughter, especially at the dining table. And her cheeks blushed the most perfect pink when she read my poem. I cannot think why she should blush so sweetly, and I turn red like a beet over the exact same thing. Although, I rather expect I should not like to hear anyone say of me, *Look how sweetly the Reverend Mr. Dempsey blushes.* No, I shouldn't like that at all. And her hair is as dark and glossy and glorious as it always was, except for a bit of silver here and there—beautiful, astounding silver! How I should like to see her curls swing long and free as they were used to do when we were young, before she put her tresses up, before she went off to London.

"What a fool I am, Theophilus," Dempsey muttered. "I gave my heart to Veronica Longwood at the age of seven and it has taken me all this time to discover that she owns it still. All these years, I could not think why no woman's form seduced me, why no woman's eyes lured me to thoughts of matrimony, why no woman's smile turned my mind to mush no matter how badly I longed for it to do so. And now, I know. Now, when it is much too late to do a blasted thing about it."

"I do think that went quite nicely, do not you, Hannah?" Veronica asked as she settled more deeply into one of the chairs before the fire. "I do believe our Reverend

Mr. Dempsey is just the gentleman for the position of rector at St. Milburga's of the Wood. A strong, stalwart man. Not some wisp of a willow who will blow this way and that at every cock of William's eyebrow."

"If you mean that Mr. Dempsey will not be bullied or coerced into anything that goes against his principles, Mama, not even by Will, I expect you are correct."

"Just so," Veronica replied. "I only hope that I am equally as correct about other things."

"What other things?"

"Hmmm? Oh, nothing. I was merely thinking what a good influence Mr. Dempsey may prove to be on your brother."

"A good influence?" Hannah pondered the words, finding them most curious. "Why do you think Will requires anyone at all to influence him, Mama?"

"You find your brother perfectly acceptable as he is?"

"Yes, Mama. Do not you?"

"No," Veronica admitted, staring into the flickering flames. "At times he seems utterly without sensibilities. He has a cold, brittle wit that can pierce one to the soul, and a most cynical outlook on people and the world in general. And he never laughs."

"He laughed this evening, Mama."

"Not truly. He merely made the sounds of laughter because he knew that was what we expected of him."

"What makes you think so?"

"I do not merely think it, Hannah, I know it. As you meet more people and grow more aware of those around you, you will learn to tell the difference between laughter that comes simply from the lips and laughter that comes from the heart."

"You do not believe that Will has a heart, do you, Mama?" Hannah asked, rising from her seat on the sofa and crossing to sit on the footstool at Veronica's feet. "No, do not give me such a look as that," she said, taking her mother's abruptly trembling hands into her own. "And do not shiver as though a goose has just walked across your grave, either, Mama. I have not lived in Blackcastle for all these fourteen years with my eyes blinded and my ears stuffed full of chicken feathers. You are afraid of Will at times, are you not? I have seen you watch him and gauge your remarks to what you judge his mood to be. Yes, and I have seen you attempt time and again to avoid being alone with him, too."

"Melodramatic balderdash," the duchess responded. "Me, afraid of your brother? Of all the things to say!" But the duchess's hands persisted in their trembling and Hannah began to massage the backs of them with her thumbs.

"It is not balderdash. It is truth," she said quietly. "But it is a very sad truth and I wish I could think of some way to convince you that you are wrong about Will. You are, you know. Very wrong. Will has a heart like everyone else. He is not a gentleman to be avoided or appeased or feared. He is kind and considerate and willing to do anything to help anyone if he can."

"Our William?"

Hannah smiled and Veronica smiled back at her.

"I know Will is gruff and he grumbles a great deal, Mama," Hannah said. "And sometimes he travels off into another world that none of us can see or hear or even imagine. And when he does that, it is perfectly daunting, too. But Will has a heart that he puts to good use often. He merely hides the softness of that heart beneath a scowling countenance and sharp words. I think we may depend upon the Reverend Mr. Dempsey to look beyond Will's perfectly outrageous outer self. The Reverend Mr. Dempsey is just Will's opposite, I believe. He is perfectly outrageous on the inside. I predict they will see through each other in time and become the very best of friends. I am certain of it."

I pray her words prove true, Veronica thought, removing her hands from Hannah's so the girl could turn on the footstool to stare into the fire. The duchess then leaned forward and placed her arms lovingly around Hannah.

"You are wrong in one thing, dearest one," she whispered, her chin resting lightly on the top of Hannah's head, her breath sending puffs of Hannah's hair billowing about. "I am not so much afraid of your brother as I am afraid for him, Hannah. I thank God for putting some thought into your papa's mind that caused him to offer Mr. Dempsey the living at St. Milburga's. You do not know the entire Mr. Dempsey as yet. You have merely met a tiny bit of him. But when you come to know him well and when you come to know me even better than you do already, perhaps you will remember and understand what I say to you tonight. I have hope I never had before, Hannah. A hope of miracles. Richard Dempsey has not changed so very much from his youth—not in his heart he has not. If anyone alive today can perform miracles, Hannah, it will prove to be Richard. And I have hope he will perform one for me if only I can gather the courage to request it of him."

"How is he doing, Tom?" Berinwick asked, stroking the horse's nose. "I intended to come check on him earlier, but we had the new rector to dinner, you know."

"Yes, your grace. It will heal nicely, I think. I was just about to clean it once again and apply more of the ointment and a fresh bandage for the night."

"I will give you a hand with him, then. I should like a better look at the wound myself. If you will remove the old dressing and clean his hock, I'll fetch the ointment from the tack room."

"The salve requires a bit more water mixed in with it, your grace," Tom Hasty called after him.

"Fine, Tom. I'll see to it."

"And a pinch or two more of the white powder," the groom added as he entered the box stall and made his way cautiously along to the young stallion's left rear leg. "Easy, Triumph, m'boy," Tom Hasty whispered, giving the horse's flank a pat. "Do not go making a fuss, eh? Not with his grace here. Believes you're the finest horse in all of England, his grace does. Wouldn't do to act like a ninny and disabuse him of his prejudice."

"Has he been acting like a ninny, Tom?" Berinwick queried, mixing the salve in a cup with a pestle as he stepped into the box. "He cannot abide the smell of this stuff, I should think. It stinks to high heaven."

Hasty grinned. "My observation as well, your grace. Makes a man's nose pucker, it does. I expect it makes Triumph's nose pucker as well. But he's a fine animal nonetheless." Hasty removed the dressing and set to washing the wound as Berinwick, still stirring the mixture, looked on.

"I cannot think how he came to get that," Berinwick said at last, setting the cup and pestle aside and kneeling to examine the horse's hock. "We were taking the gate at the bottom of the south pasture on our way home this afternoon. He was not injured before he leaped, but when he came down, he began to dance under me as though an army of ants were battling for possession of his hindquarters."

"And there were no thorns near?"

"You think a thorn did it, Tom? But that bit of skin and muscle is ripped clean away. A thorn would need to have been as big and round as a man's finger and as sharp as a razor to do that. And yet, I cannot conceive of anything that could have done it. I had not even considered a thorn until you mention it now. I looked around as long as I dared, but he was bleeding, you know, and I did not like to keep him waiting while I searched. No, go to his head, Tom. I'll apply the stuff. I expect if you do it a second time, he'll kick at you."

"Better he should kick at me than you, your grace," Hasty observed, but he did as he was told and went to stand at the stallion's head, gentling the enormous black with soft words and cooing sounds, rubbing the velvety nose slowly, tenderly. He watched as Berinwick spread the thick salve over the injury on the horse's hock, then wrapped fresh strips of linen around it and tied them carefully in place.

"I went back to look, Tom, after I brought him to the stables," Berinwick said. "I could not see a thing that would have caused such a wound. But I was not thinking of thorns. I shall ride out and have another look in the morning—with enormous thorns specifically in mind. A good thing I brought Penn home and rode Triumph to check on the haymaking, though. M'sister would never forgive me did I cause such an injury to Penn."

"I will go to the south gate in the morning, your grace," Hasty offered. "Be pleased to do it. A fresh pair of eyes, you know, might be just what is called for in the matter."

"Are you hinting that I cannot see as much with one eye as you can with two, Tom?"

"Me? Hint at such a thing as that? Never, your grace. I'm not looking to gain two black eyes and a bloody nose at your hands. Not me."

"Or a new position in another establishment, eh?" Berinwick chuckled.

"Precisely. But something might come to my attention that did not come to yours."

Berinwick nodded. "That could be. Do it then," he said as he gathered the soiled dressing, the partially emptied cup, and the pestle up into his hands, carried them to the front of the stall, and gave them to Hasty. "Get rid of these, will you, Tom? I should like to have a bit of a talk with this fellow here."

Hasty nodded, watching as Berinwick wiped his hands on his black velvet knee breeches. He smiled a bit as the duke took a carrot from his coat pocket and offered it to the black.

"You won't forget, will you, Tom? You will ride out first thing in the morning and come tell me at once if you find anything? I shall see whatever did it will never do it again," Berinwick said over his shoulder.

Thus dismissed, Tom Hasty carried the paraphernalia back to the tack room where he tucked the cup with the remaining salve into a cupboard. He then left the stable to deposit the soiled dressing in the pile of rubbish to be burned in the morning. He stood very still for a moment at the burn pile, his eyes scanning the paddock and the treeline, his ears listening for the least hint of sound that did not belong to this place and this time. There was nothing. Only the murmur of the duke's voice from inside the stable.

"Speaks to that horse as if it were human," Hasty observed to himself as he made his way to the pump to clean the pestle. "No. I take that back. Speaks to that horse with a deal more consideration than he does to most humans. Though that ain't his grace's fault. Ain't his fault at all."

A thorn, Hasty thought as he primed the pump. Now why did I think to say that? Why did I not say what I thought the moment his grace brought the animal back to the stable this afternoon?

"Because I cannot prove it to be true," he said aloud. "I cannot prove that it was lead from a long gun did that to his grace's stallion any more than Langton can prove that the ghost of Owain Glyndwr murdered his grace's pa. I wasn't there to hear the gun fire or see the shot hit. And even though Langton was there to see the ghost, there was nothing to be seen afterwards. Broken heads and broken necks. Things one would find after any such accident. No proof at all that it weren't an accident. And Harvey was sipping from his flask at the time. He admitted as much. It would not be such a strange thing for Harvey Langton to have imagined a ghost appearing before him that evening."

And things have been silent for nine long months, Hasty thought. Why should some imagined ghost rise from the grave today with a perfectly solid long gun in his hands and shoot the duke's horse? That's what his grace will ask. And what will I answer? I haven't the vaguest idea, your grace, but such it is? No, that won't do at all. I shall have to speak to Langton first thing in the morning.

Poor Langton will have palpitations of the heart when I tell him, Hasty thought as he cleaned the pestle under the slow flow of the water. But at least I am certain of one thing. Belowes and I have not been wasting our time attempting to keep watch over his grace and the duchess and Lady Hannah. It becomes more and more clear to me that Langton was not drunk and seeing visions. Whether he was made of haze and hoarfrost or blood and bone, some villain did murder the eighth Duke of Berinwick and now intends to take down the ninth. We shall have to convince his grace of it and without any more dillydallying about, too. If a man is being hunted, he has a right to know that he is.

Five

The Reverend Mr. Dempsey settled comfortably into his bed, his back against a plethora of pillows, his hands linked behind his head, and stared at nothing in particular. He was somewhat disappointed that the walk back to the rectory had not been interrupted by any ghosts wailing or even the far-off beat of muffled hooves. "Decidedly boring," he mumbled to himself. "Neither Theo nor I so much as stumbled over a rough spot in the road. What the deuce is wrong with that brick?" he added, as his gaze abruptly focused on the lower right portion of his bedchamber fireplace. He stared at the offending brick intently but there seemed no reason for him to do so. It was simply a brick like all the other bricks, and yet . . .

Dempsey rose from his bed and crossed to the fireplace. He knelt and ran the flat of his hand over the entire section where the brick that had caught his attention was embedded. "It protrudes the slightest bit from the rest," he murmured, intrigued. "The rest are even. It's not as though the entire thing is coming undone." A sense of anticipation swept over the parson. He gained his feet, hurried to his chest of drawers, and took his penknife from atop it. Returning to the offending brick, he pried at it with the short blade. It wiggled slightly. This set Dempsey to prying some more, then using the tips of his fingers in an attempt to wiggle the brick outward. When at last it came out of the fireplace into his hand, it proved to be merely a half-brick. Dempsey eagerly inserted his hand into the space it left. His hopes soared. His pulse beat increased. Could this be what he was seeking? Could this possibly be the hiding place of the Glyndwr cup? He reached in farther, up to his elbow, before his hand came into contact with something. Something small, definitely not a cup. He clasped it quickly in his palm and pulled it out.

Rising to his feet, he stared down at the thing in the flickering light of the dying coal fire. Barefoot before the hearth in his nightshirt and nightcap, Dempsey pondered the object in his palm. "What the devil is it?" he asked. He moved from before the hearth to his bedside where he held the object beneath the light of the several candles in the candelabra on his bedside table. In the increased illumination the small article took on a more distinctive shape and form. It looked a good deal like a black lion with a crown between its front paws—and something rising from the crown. Dempsey squinted, brought the piece closer to his eyes, held it farther away. "It's a griffin's head!" he exclaimed at last. "A lion holding a crown with a griffin's head rising from it! A deucedly good bit of artwork, too, for a trinket." The crown and the griffin's head did not lie flat with the figure of the lion but were offset, making the top of the piece rise a bit higher on Dempsey's palm. "What do you think it was intended for, Theophilus?" Dempsey queried.

The old hound, stretched comfortably at the foot of Dempsey's bed, blinked up at his master and yawned.

"It's certainly not Glyndwr's cup, but it appears to be old. Well, I expect it's twenty years old at least. No one has lived here for that long. Perhaps it belonged to the ill-fated Mr. Dight, Theo. Beneath all that black tarnish, I think the thing is silver. But what the deuce is it? An heirloom of some kind? It's definitely not a stickpin or a brooch," he mumbled, turning the piece over and over. "And it's highly unlikely it was ever a part of a necklace or a bracelet. Devil it, if the lion hasn't one red eye!" he exclaimed as he studied the piece. "And the griffin's head has a red eye as well! I wonder if they're rubies. Well, they're very tiny ones if they are. Not like to make anyone rich. Still, I am fairly certain the figure itself is silver. I shall attempt to polish it in the morning. Then we will see if I'm correct or not."

Dempsey returned to the hidey-hole and reached inside once more to be certain that the lion was all that it contained. Then he replaced the brick, set the lion on his bedside table, and crossed the room to the washstand to clean the soot and grime from his hand and arm. He settled again into his bed, said his prayers, and put out the candles. He leaned back against the pillows and closed his eyes. Theophilus was already asleep. The sound of the hound's snores brought a smile to Dempsey's face.

The smile widened as an image of a youthful Veronica Longwood wandered through his mind. She was picking wildflowers in the meadow near his father's rectory and placing them in her hat. Her long, dark tresses streamed behind her in a hearty breeze. Six brown-and-white-spotted puppies played around her. They tugged at the hem of her dress, scrabbled at her half-boots, jumped and rolled and scampered about in the long grass until she could resist them no longer. She set her hatful of flowers aside, sat down, and allowed them all to climb rambunctiously up into her lap. Aglow with glorious golden light from a brilliant afternoon sun, the meadow, the flowers, the puppies, and the girl shimmered mystically, magically before him. Veronica tossed her head back and began to laugh and there the image froze. Like an exquisite painting, the vision culled from Dempsey's memory hung suspended in his mind. With his eyes closed, he gazed at it, enthralled. His heart beat joyfully in his breast. His breath came lightly from between slightly parted lips. The sweet sound of Veronica Longwood's laughter sang to him of long ago and far away and in a matter of moments, the Reverend Mr. Dempsey fell happily asleep.

Veronica carefully refolded Richard Dempsey's poem and tucked it safely away in her jewelry box. Then she crossed the carpeting in her bare feet and, gathering her long, silk nightdress around her, she slipped between the sheets and turned down the lamp. For the first time in nine long months the bed was not cold. For the first time since her husband's death, no chill lingered in the bedchamber and Julian's absence did not weigh heavily on her mind.

William had accompanied Richard all the way to the front doors of Blackcastle. And then, Harold Belowes had informed her in answer to her probing, his grace had continued to accompany the parson down the drive to the road. It was most extraordinary that William had done so. He had never seen fit to accompany a guest in his house three feet into a hallway before tonight. Visitors came to Blackcastle and visitors departed, and always William would bid them farewell at the drawing room door or the morning room door, or the door of the Gold Saloon and allow Gaines to escort them through the maze of corridors, down the winding staircases into the Great Hall, where the butler would open the double doors for them and see them safely on their way. But tonight her son had dispensed with Gaines's services entirely. He had escorted the Reverend Mr. Dempsey into the hallway, through the corridors, and down the staircases himself. Harold Belowes, the only footman on duty in the Great Hall at the time, had been so surprised that he had almost forgotten to open the doors for the two men.

It is a very little thing, Veronica thought. A minor alteration in William's conduct. Certainly it is nothing to pin my hopes on. But it is *something.* "It must mean *something* that he bestirred himself to accompany Richard so far," she whispered into the darkness.

She lay very still in the canopied bed. She closed her eyes and allowed her mind to wander. In mere moments her thoughts carried her into a field of memories—a field cloaked in green and gold, orange and violet. And there, she saw her younger self in an old round gown, picking wildflowers and placing them carefully in her hat. Puppies played around her feet and once the hat was filled, she sat down to play with the tiny hounds. They all filled her with happiness—this field, these flowers, these pups. And as the puppies all scrambled up into her lap at once, she leaned back and laughed aloud with pure joy.

It was then that she saw him, seated astride a shaggy brown pony beneath the oak at the center of the field. He was watching her in silence, his lovely angel's face smiling. He was hatless and his golden curls—dappled warm brown in places by the shadows of the leaves above him—blew wildly about in the breeze. Unlike his elder brothers, Richard had not yet reached the awkward, gangly phase. His was a husky, solid little body decked out most fashionably this morning in one of Geoffrey's outgrown hunting jackets, a pair of Arthur's leather breeches, and miniature riding boots that had once belonged to John. Veronica could not see Richard's eyes at such a distance, but she imagined them as she knew them to be—wide and shining and the most disconcerting blue—bluer than the sky above.

She waved to him and he urged the pony forward as fast as it would run. "I have brought you something, Vernie!" he called enthusiastically in his child's voice as he drew near and brought the little beast to a halt. He scrambled down from the saddle and ran to her, luring barking puppies to his ankles as he came. Directly before her, he stumbled to a stop and began to search anxiously through the pockets of his hunting jacket. "It's here somewhere. I know it is. Yes, here it is!" he cried excitedly and tugged a scrap of paper from one of the pockets. With a creditable bow, Richard presented her the paper. "It's a poem, Vernie! I wrote it all by myself! It took an entire hour!"

Veronica unfolded the paper. Through ink blotches and crossed-out words, she read his rhyming lines and her heart stuttered the merest bit. "Oh, Richard," she said, rising to her knees, taking the boy into her arms and giving him a tremendous hug. "It's beautiful. It is positively the best poem I have ever read. I will keep it with me forever."

"Forever," the Duchess of Berinwick murmured in her sleep, and the most entrancing smile played across her face.

"You ought to have tried harder to convince his grace at the time," Tom Hasty said around a bite of toasted bread as he leaned against one of the cupboards in the rectory kitchen shortly after seven the following morning. "Ought to have lied to him, I expect, and told him that you saw some ordinary man, not Owain Glyndwr's ghost."

"And what would I have said when he asked what the fellow looked like, Tom?" Langton queried. "Ought I to have made up some dastardly-looking fellow? What good would that have done but likely get an innocent man hanged? It was the ghost of Owain Glyndwr I saw. You believed me. Belowes believed me. I cannot help it if his grace did not."

Tom Hasty shrugged his shoulders and then stared sheepishly at the stone floor. "To tell the truth, Harvey, I did not believe you, either—about the ghost, I mean. It was Belowes convinced me that we ought to keep an eye out whether there be such things as ghosts or not. Because the duke was dead, after all. There was no refuting that. Dead is dead."

"There was not the least thing I could point to, Tom, to support my story and make his grace believe me," Langton sighed. "You know that's true. The coach came around the bend at a considerable speed and it overturned. There was not a pistol ball or a knife or a sword involved in it. Heads and necks were broken—a natural result of an overturned coach. If I had not been there to see it, who would have known whether the ghost of Owain Glyndwr were responsible for it or not? Ned Thistledown might have misjudged the turn or dozed off and pulled back abruptly on the reins. It would have proved a perfect crime had I not been an accidental witness to it. Ghosts can do that—commit perfect crimes. They aren't solid, you know. They leave nothing solid behind them."

"Well, there was something solid involved in yesterday's attack, Harvey," Hasty replied. "If that is not lead from a long gun lying on the table before you, then you may invite me to dine on my hat for the next three evenings. It was that lead what caused the damage to Triumph's hock, just as I thought. Dug it out of the gate post in the south pasture the very first thing this morning."

"Triumph is a horse?" queried a quiet voice that belonged to neither one of the men.

Tom Hasty was so startled by the unexpected sound of the Reverend Mr. Dempsey's question that his toasted bread flew out of his hand all the way to the kitchen ceiling where it clung for a moment by glistening threads of congealing butter before it made a stunning descent, landing with a soft plop on Eulie Langton's head, just as she stepped into the kitchen through the garden door.

Mrs. Langton reached up to the top of her ruffled cap, removed the toasted bread, and stared at it. Then she stared up at the ceiling. "Thomas Hasty," she said softly, "you will climb up there and remove that spot before you depart."

"Yes, Mrs. Langton," Hasty agreed at once. "I surely will."

"And you and Mr. Langton will both apologize to the Reverend Mr. Dempsey for whatever you were doing that sent bread soaring about his kitchen like a dead pigeon in flight. Good morning, Mr. Dempsey," she added, nodding politely in his direction. She dipped the parson a bit of a curtsy, then turned with the toasted bread in hand and trundled back outside.

"Feed it to the birds, she will," Langton observed. "Good morning to you, Mr. Dempsey. This be Thomas Hasty."

"Good morning, Mr. Dempsey," Hasty said at once. "You surprised me, you did, sneaking in like that."

"I did not sneak in, Mr. Hasty," Dempsey replied, resting a shoulder against the door frame, his arms crossed across his chest. "I seldom sneak into my own kitchen. I expect you were so engrossed in your conversation with Langton that you failed to hear me arrive. *Is* Triumph a horse?"

Hasty glanced questioningly at Langton, who had risen from his chair at the kitchen table on Dempsey's appearance and was now lowering himself back into it. "You may speak freely, Tom, in front of the Reverend Mr. Dempsey," Langton replied to the unspoken query. "I have confided all in him."

"You have? Harvey Langton, you barely know this parson."

"He knows me well enough," Dempsey offered. "Men get to know each other quickly when they are pounding slates onto a church roof together in the hot sun. I'm no threat to your duke,

Mr. Hasty, I assure you of it. In fact, I am determined to join you and Mr. Langton and Mr. Belowes in protecting him and his family. I ask again. Did I hear correctly? You were speaking of a wounded hock? Triumph is a horse?"

"Aye, he's a horse," Hasty replied, leaning back against the cupboard once more. "The duke's new stallion. Fetched him home merely three weeks ago, I did, from Gurley Farm."

"And someone shot this stallion?" Dempsey left the doorway, fetched two cups, and set them on the kitchen table. Then he fetched the pot of coffee, filled them, and refilled the one sitting before Langton. "Sit down, Mr. Hasty, and join us," he urged Berinwick's head groom.

"Shot the horse yesterday afternoon," Hasty replied, accepting a place at the table and taking a cup into both hands. "I reckon whoever it was thought to shoot the duke, not the horse, though."

"Why do you think that?"

"Because the horse hasn't done anything worth shooting it for as yet."

"And the duke has?" Dempsey grinned.

"Five days out of seven his grace offends someone," Tom Hasty sighed. "That's if he's having a good week and in a dapper sort of mood."

"Offends someone seven days out of seven and twice on Saturdays and Mondays if he's having a bad week and is in a foul mood," Langton added.

Dempsey leaned back in his chair and laughed. "And this is the gentleman you have set yourselves to protect? Not that you shouldn't do so, but may I ask why you do?"

"Because for all his life, until nine months ago, he were our Baron Thorne of Barren Wycche and now he's our Duke of Berinwick," Hasty replied.

"All of the Thornes of Barren Wycche, no matter their eccentricities, have been loyal to us and ours, Mr. Dempsey, from the earliest times until this very day," inserted Langton. "We don't any of us truly take offense at the young duke's brusque manners, we don't."

"Comes by 'em honestly, he does," Hasty nodded.

"He does. And there be more important things than his manners," Langton added. "He be like all the Thornes what lived before him. Takes his responsibilities seriously, he does."

"If there is a man, woman or child within a day's ride of Blackcastle who lacks for bread, work, or monies this day, it is merely because our duke doesn't know of 'em," Hasty explained, turning his cup about in his hands, his gaze fixed on the black coffee as it swirled.

"Just so. People be losing farms and grazing rights and the use of public land everywhere because of the enclosures," Langton said, meeting Dempsey's gaze with serious eyes. "All over England people be running off to big cities for to earn their livings. But not our people. Our people stay here, they do, and thrive. Why, we got more freeholders today than fifty years ago—"

"Besides," Hasty interrupted what he thought was likely to become a lengthy monologue on Langton's part, "we actually do like the duke."

"Reason enough for me," Dempsey smiled. "Now, confide in me, Mr. Hasty. What is this about Berinwick's stallion being shot?"

Veronica, surprised but pleased, welcomed Dempsey later that morning as he stepped from behind the butler into the morning room. "You have not brought Theophilus," she observed, as the parson bowed over her extended hand.

"No, not this morning. This morning Theo remains in Mrs. Langton's charge. She is baking tarts, you see," Dempsey replied with a boyish grin. "Theophilus greatly admires tarts."

"And he will utterly beguile her into giving him one or two," Veronica replied. "I would lay a wager on that. Do be seated, Mr. Dempsey. Is there something that you especially require? Have you need of more slates for the church roof or lumber to replace some of the beams or—"

"I have come to speak to your son. He is in the north meadow, Gaines informs me."

"Yes. They are just beginning to cut the grasses there today. I expect he will return soon. Would you care for anything to eat or drink, Mr. Dempsey? Have you breakfasted?"

"If I may be allowed to await his grace's return in your company, I require nothing further, your grace."

"You may go then, Gaines," the duchess said. "Please tell his grace when he returns that Mr. Dempsey awaits him here."

"Yes, your grace," the butler replied and departed.

"Mr. McClane is supposedly in charge of the haymaking," Veronica explained, "but William is not one to surrender all decisions and responsibilities to his farm manager. He likes to oversee things himself when he can. I daresay he will not be at it more than a half-hour more. He will return once things are properly underway. I—I thought the two of you got on very well last evening, Richard," she added with a note of quiet hope in her voice that did not go unnoted by Mr. Dempsey's ears.

"Did you fear we would not?" he asked, his fingers playing with the doilies that decorated the wide arms of the chair he had taken opposite the sofa on which she sat. "I promise you, I like the lad, Veronica. He will come to like me as well. You need not fret over that. We'll muddle through these early days, the duke and I, and form a relationship to last a lifetime—even if he is as contentious as a baited bear and I as stubborn as yesterday's boiled beef."

"I realize William seems querulous at times," the duchess replied, her voice abruptly quieter, her gaze leaving Dempsey's face to stare at her hands as she folded them together in her lap. "I realize his manner is not always easy on one's nerves, Richard. But it is because of—"

"Because of what?" queried Dempsey, leaning toward her, wondering at the stiffness that had risen so abruptly to her shoulders and at the way she bowed her head. In one instant her entire demeanor had altered. Why? Because of his unguarded jest? Dempsey's stomach seemed suddenly to be digesting lead. "Veronica, what is it? I was merely jesting, you know, about your son being as contentious as a baited bear."

"No, you were not merely jesting, Richard. William *is* peevish, irritable, and ill-mannered," she replied stiffly, avoiding Dempsey's gaze. "He is so because of me."

"Oh, certainly not!" Dempsey exclaimed.

"Yes, Richard. I—I—it is all my fault that he has become the cynical, unpleasant gentleman he is. Oh, what am I doing? What am I saying? You have just come to us, Richard. You do not wish to hear me spouting such nonsense." She looked up at him and attempted a smile, but it trembled and then slipped from her face before she could save it. She stared back down at her hands on the instant. "You do not know. You cannot understand. I have no right to bother you with it."

"I should be pleased to have you bother me with it if you care to do so, Vernie," Dempsey said softly, reaching out and taking her hands into his own. She still would not meet his gaze and so he bowed his head and studied her sweet, plump fingers. "I will be pleased to listen, m'dear, and pleased to understand. But you ought not think of your son as cynical and unpleasant. Perhaps he is at times, but so are we all. I ought not have called him contentious. It was merely an attempt on my part to laugh at both myself and his grace. Actually, I found your son to be a polite and gracious host last evening."

"Yes, he was for most of the evening. I cannot think why. He is generally much less patient with guests."

"Is he?" Dempsey could not help but smile. "I must be grateful to you then, Veronica, because I expect he discovered more patience in himself on your behalf—in deference to our previous relationship."

"You believe that William was polite and gracious to you to please me?"

"Indeed. Why else but to please you, my dear?" Dempsey looked away from her hands, up at the face that she was still attempting to hide from him, and saw a silent tear hesitate at the corner of her eye, then slide down her cheek. "Your son loves you, Veronica, and wishes to please you because of it. What is there in that to bring tears to your eyes?" he asked softly.

"William does not love me," she whispered on a trembling breath.

"His grace does not love you?" The Reverend Mr. Dempsey, without letting go of the duchess's hands for one moment, transferred himself from the chair on which he sat to the place beside her on the sofa. "Veronica, what are you saying, m'dear?"

"I am s-saying, Richard, that William does not love me, nor ought he to love me. You are wrong when you conclude that he was polite and gracious to you for such a reason as that."

For the first time in all his years, the Reverend Mr. Dempsey could not think of anything at all to say. He searched his mind for some reply and could find none. Then he searched his heart. Surely, what she said could not be true. This was the sweet, kind, gentle Veronica Longwood who had brightened his youth, who had been loved by all who knew her, and who had loved all in return—and she thought her son did not love her? How could this be?

"I cannot conceive of it," he said softly into the silence that had grown up between them while he searched for words. "Veronica, everyone who knows you must come to love you. I cannot conceive of one reason why your son should not."

"You need only look at him, Richard, to know the reason outright," she replied in a shaky whisper. "You are not blind."

"You think he does not love you because of his damaged eye?"

"It is not damaged. It is altogether missing. And it is my fault that it is. All the pain William has suffered, all the scars he bears—n-not only on his face but in his m-mind and h-heart—they are my doing. All my doing."

What Dempsey wished to say, and loudly, too, was "Rubbish!" but he did not. He sat in silence beside her, quietly massaging her hands, waiting patiently for her to discover enough trust in him, enough courage in herself to continue.

* * *

"You will not hire them?" The Duke of Berinwick glared at his farm manager. "And why not, may I ask?"

"Because they are Welsh, your grace. All five of them."

"Tell me, McClane, have we no room for more hands in this field? Have we drivers for every cart and wagon? Have we men to wield each and every scythe? We cannot do with more gatherers or rickmakers?"

"We can always do with more hands, your grace. Especially in this field, this year, but—"

"And are there any of our own people unemployed at the moment and seeking labor?"

"No, your grace."

"Then you're hired," Berinwick growled at the five men gathered around them. "Put down their names, McClane, and see they are paid at the same rate as all the rest."

"They are Welshmen," McClane protested once again. "They are not to be trusted. It would be best did they move on."

The men stared at McClane in disbelief. They had traveled a goodly long way, depending on Blackcastle land to employ them if only for the space of the haymaking season. Five heads lowered in frustration, angry lips moved with silent curses. But the Duke of Berinwick himself was present and the Welshmen would not protest aloud in his presence.

"It would be best if they moved on?" Berinwick replied, loudly enough that all of the men recognized the anger in his voice. "Welshmen are not to be trusted? Are you mad, McClane? Blackcastle has never made hay without the strong shoulders and competent hands of Welshmen. If there is anyone I hesitate to trust of late, it's you. I suspect that some worm has bored into your brain and is gnawing greedily away at it, impairing your common sense. Set their names down, McClane, and put them to work, or *you* will be seeking employment before this day is out."

Berinwick waited to see that the protesting farm manager

did as he was commanded. He watched as the Welshmen joined the others in the field where they were welcomed at once and gratefully, too. He stood for a bit, gazing over the field as the haymaking progressed, glancing from time to time at the overseer beside him and wondering what it was that had gotten into McClane of late. Then he gave the farm manager an abrupt nod, mounted his horse, and turned the animal's head toward Blackcastle. As he paused at the crest of the first hill and turned in the saddle for a final look at the work proceeding below him, he wondered if he had been wise to give McClane such a severe setdown, and within earshot of the Welshmen, too.

I'm already drowning in father's notes and ledgers, his journals, and all the books about new farming techniques, he thought. What the deuce will I do if my words fester in McClane's craw and he comes storming into my office this evening and tells me to oversee the rest of the haymaking myself?

"What the devil," Berinwick muttered, turning from the sight of the field and urging his horse onward. "If he does do that, I *will* oversee the haymaking myself. It's not as though I do not know how to go about it. Damnation! How dare the man suggest that those laborers were untrustworthy simply because they're Welsh! As if we Thornes were not Welshmen ourselves when first we came to this bit of land, set our heels stubbornly in, and built Blackcastle!"

It occurred to the duke that he might ride around to the south pasture, to the gate where Triumph had been injured, but then he thought better of it. Tom Hasty had announced last evening that he intended to do just that and Berinwick had no wish to make Hasty think he lacked confidence in him. Unlike McClane, whom his father had hired barely fourteen months ago to replace David Hancock, the previous farm manager who had simply disappeared one day and had never been heard from again, Tom Hasty had been born into Berinwick service. The son of a Berinwick coachman and a Berinwick maid, Hasty had lived at Blackcastle three years longer than the new duke himself.

"And for his entire life Tom has put up with me without the least complaint," Berinwick mumbled to himself as he rode on toward the stables. "Born to be a saint, Thomas was. Well, at least he'll not have to deal with me or any Berinwick when he dies, then. I cannot think there is even one Thorne of Barren Wycche ever got into heaven."

No, he thought with a slow smile. And somehow, I cannot think that the Reverend Mr. Dempsey will have an easy time to get into heaven, either. I can hear him now, attempting to talk his way past St. Peter.

"What the devil made me think of Dempsey?" Berinwick muttered. "Is he up on the church roof pounding slates and taking my name in vain?"

"William was merely three years old," Veronica murmured so softly that Dempsey, close enough beside her that their shoulders touched, had to strain to hear her words. "He and his nurse accompanied us to London that spring. He was such a beautiful child. So sweet. So full of life.

"It was the evening of April the twenty-third, 1773. I shall never forget that date. Never, as long as I live. Julian and I were to dine at St. James's Palace by personal invitation of the King."

She ceased to speak. Her hands trembled in the parson's.

"I cannot imagine such an honor," Dempsey said, because he had to say something. He feared she would not continue if he did not say something.

"An exquisite honor," she whispered in reply, "and I had purchased a most magnificent gown for the occasion. I ought to have gone up to the nursery earlier to bid Will good night, before I had finished dressing, you know. But I was so very involved with myself and my gown and my hair, that I did not."

Veronica looked at the Reverend Mr. Dempsey then, her brown eyes filled with pain and glistening with tears. "William escaped his nurse and came toddling down the stairs to find me. To bid *me* good night. 'Mama!' he called in the most jolly voice as he came stomping into my dressing room. 'I founded you!' and he ran to me with his arms wide to give me a hug. And his fingers—his fingers were all the colors of the rainbow. It was all I could see, his fingers covered with paints. I could not have smears of paint on my magnificent gown. It would be ruined. I should not be able to attend the dinner. Julian would not attend without me. King George and Queen Charlotte would be furious. My life would be ruined. These were the thoughts that flew through my mind. Vain, selfish, stupid thoughts. As if all that mattered was myself, my gown, the dinner at St. James's Palace!"

"You were very young," Dempsey said tentatively as silence threatened to rise up between them again.

"I pushed him away!" The words burst from her on a great rush of air, crashing into the room like a great body of water that had been dammed up and was abruptly set free. "I pushed William away from me so suddenly and so firmly that he spun around and practically flew across the room. He hit the corner of the clothespress and then bounced away and into my looking glass. I have lived it over and over again, that particular night—William lying amongst shards of glass, sobbing. Myself screaming for Julian.

"I screamed and screamed until Jules came at last and picked Will up in his arms. And there was blood and gore smearing itself all over Julian's ruffled shirtfront, all over his lace cuffs, all over the fine blue silk of his waistcoat."

The Duchess of Berinwick burst into sobs. Her breath came in short gasps. She fought free of Dempsey's hold on her hands, turned to him and threw her arms around his neck, burying her face against his shoulder. "William's eye had burst open on the corner of the clothespress," she whispered, her lips touching his lapel as she spoke. "The place around the eye had been sliced into little pieces by the shards of the looking glass. My boy, my baby, was bleeding, blind, and crying in Julian's arms—all because I feared to have a bit of paint on my gown. And the paint was dry!" she said, her voice barely audible. "The paint on Will's sweet little fingers was dry!"

The Reverend Mr. Richard Dempsey's arms went around

the Duchess of Berinwick. He held her safely within them and rocked her gently, now and then rubbing her back, or reaching up to free a strand of hair from her hot, wet cheek. The shoulder of his coat, his waistcoat, his shirt grew saturated with her tears, but he did not take note of it. He did not take note of it at all.

Tom Hasty stepped up and took the horse's reins as Berinwick halted before the stables. "I missed you this morning, Tom," Berinwick said as he dismounted. "Lancaster said you had ridden over to the rectory."

Hasty nodded.

"Did you ride down to the south pasture as well?"

Hasty nodded once again.

"Did you find anything?"

"No thorns, your grace. I rode to St. Milburga's to speak to Harvey Langton for a moment or two as well."

"About thorns?"

"Yes, about Thornes," Hasty murmured, knowing the duke would not distinguish his change of meaning. "There be something important that we wish to discuss with you, your grace, me and Harvey Langton and the Reverend Mr. Dempsey. And we were wondering if you might join us for a bit of ale at the Fallen Dog this evening so we can all speak comfortably together."

Berinwick cocked an eyebrow in surprise. "Will not that give rise to a good deal of talk, Tom? You, I, Langton, and the new preacher all gathered around a table at the Fallen Dog?"

"Talk, your grace?"

"Yes. Gossip. You remember what gossip is, eh, Tom? Last time I joined you and Langton for a drink at the Fallen Dog, rumors raged through the village like some unquenchable fire. Everyone would have it that I had seduced Langton's eldest daughter and you were brokering an agreement between Langton and myself to provide for the girl should she turn out to be in the family way."

Tom Hasty nodded. "Talk," he said with a lopsided smile. "But no one in Barren Wycche actually believed a word of it, your grace. It was merely a week's entertainment for the lot of them—a game of speculation."

"What *is* her name?" Berinwick asked.

"Whose name, your grace?"

"Langton's eldest daughter."

"That would be Beth, your grace."

"She survived the rumors, did she? Langton never said."

"Survived nicely, your grace. Thought them good fun, actually. Walked around Barren Wycche like a queen that week, saying 'la-de-da' to everyone who approached her. Well, Beth be a jolly sort of girl, you know. Like her mama. Came to an understanding with Giles Pervis's boy just last month, Beth did. The two of them are going to be married as soon as the corn crop is in and sold."

"Good. I expect I will join you and Langton and Mr. Dempsey at the Fallen Dog this evening, then. Old gossip harmed no one. Most likely it's time to let some new rumors rise up."

"Likely to center on the new parson this time," Tom Hasty offered. "Be interesting to hear what gossip the villagers will concoct about him. He be inside, by the way."

"Who?"

"The Reverend Mr. Dempsey. Came to have a word with you about something other than what we mean to speak of at the Fallen Dog. He's having a word or two with her grace at the moment."

"And Hannah?"

"Lady Hannah has ridden off to pay a call on Miss Tofar. I sent Lancaster with her, your grace."

"Good. What time do we ride into the village tonight, Tom?"

"I told Mr. Langton we would meet him at a quarter past seven, your grace, if you be amenable to it."

Berinwick nodded, turned, and strolled off toward one of the side entrances of Blackcastle, his spurs jangling and his boots kicking up little puffs of dust as he crossed the stable yard. Whatever Dempsey wishes to speak with me about will wait long enough for me to change out of these clothes, he thought. Likely Mother is treasuring some time alone with the man. Probably recalling old times at the parsonage in Arrandell and all that. She would be most unhappy did I tramp into the middle of their conversation, smelling like horse and looking like a veritable dust ball. Fond of Mr. Dempsey, she is.

"Fond of *Richard*," he murmured, a rather cynical smile turning his lips upward. "Mama will call him Richard whenever she wishes. And he will call her Veronica. I can only hope that none of the staff overheard that particular declaration."

If word of that precedes us to the Fallen Dog, he thought, dashing up a staircase toward his chambers, the gossip that our little meeting stirs up tonight will involve Mr. Dempsey having come to St. Milburga's for the express purpose of marrying my mother. Our innocently shared drinks and conversation will somehow become his asking me for Mother's hand in marriage. And they will say that Hasty and Langton were there to keep me from ripping the upstart's throat out with my bare hands. The Duke of Berinwick chuckled to himself at the thought and turned down a corridor toward another short flight of steps.

"I could not bear to be near my own son," Veronica murmured, the back of her head resting against Dempsey's arm as she wiped at her tears with the parson's handkerchief. "I feared to be alone with him. I avoided William whenever I could. Each time I looked at him, his face reminded me so clearly of what I had done—what my vanity, my selfishness had done—that I could not bear the sight of him. To this day, when he appears before me—I am overwhelmed by his scars and my own guilt."

"Veronica, it was an accident," Dempsey murmured, his

strong arm around her shoulders, supporting her. "You did never intend for such a thing to happen."

"No. No. Never. But when it did happen, Richard, when it did, I could no longer bring myself to hold Will, to touch him, not even to speak to him at first. I trembled at the sound of his voice. I became like a woman carved from stone in his presence. And because Julian loved me, he made excuses for my weakness. Instead of forcing me to confront what I had done, instead of urging me to be strong, Jules as much as confined the poor child to the nursery so I need not see Will unless I specifically requested his presence. And when Will turned six, Julian sent him off to school."

Dempsey thought of so small a boy with so great and noticeable an impairment amidst a school filled with older boys and his heart lurched in his chest.

"And they were c-cruel to him, the other boys," Veronica stuttered. "Julian did never tell me so, but I overheard William beg his father to allow him to remain home and to study with tutors at Blackcastle. William was nine that year, the year my daughter, Charlotte, was born."

"And what did his grace say when the boy asked to remain at home?" Dempsey queried, wondering what he would have said himself—what he would have done.

"He told Will to learn to be a man. 'Stand up for yourself,' Jules said. 'Show the world that you're bred of guts and glory' he said. 'You're not some insignificant little twit to be cowed by looks and words. You'll be the Duke of Berinwick one day. Act like it.' Oh, how could he?" Veronica sobbed. "How could Julian have been so cold and unfeeling to his own son, to a boy who already possessed a perfectly dreadful mother and needed a father who loved him, to a boy who was suffering so very much through no fault of his own, suffering only because he came running downstairs one night to hug his mother good-bye?"

"Your husband wished to give you peace, Veronica. He knew what the sight of the boy did to you and he—"

"He treated me like some delicate flower. He demanded

nothing from me. He expected nothing of me. He did nothing but allow me to continue to indulge in my own selfish wishes until it was much too late to undo what I had done," she continued. "Julian ought to have demanded more of me, expected more of me. No. No. That's not right. That's not fair at all. I ought to have demanded more of myself. I ought to have sought courage and strength in myself on Will's behalf and on my own. But I did not and Jules could not bring himself to force me to do it. N-now my son's melancholia, his brusqueness, and his hardened heart must all be added to my original crime against him."

She turned and buried her face against Dempsey's shoulder once again, sobbing anew. He stroked her back gently with his hand. He must think of something to say. If he said nothing, Veronica would continue to believe every word she had just said. She would accept as her own every crime of which she accused herself. Every fault, every sadness, every cynical cock of an eyebrow that she saw in her son now or later, she would lay at her own feet for the rest of her life.

"What the devil are you doing?" Berinwick growled from the doorway just as Dempsey's hand moved to sweep a loosed strand of dark hair from Veronica's flushed, wet cheek. "Cease petting my mother as though she is some hound and remove your arms from around her at once or I'll cut them off."

"William, do not say such things," the duchess protested, removing her head from Dempsey's shoulder on the instant and dabbing quickly at her eyes and face with the parson's handkerchief.

"He has no business to be putting his arms around you like that, Madam. Nor do you have cause to be snuggling against his shoulder like some harlot. You are a duchess and he is a parson for gawd's sake!"

"He was merely attempting to comfort me," Veronica said,

sniffing into Dempsey's handkerchief. "I w-was speaking to him of—of Charlotte—and I—"

"Oh." Berinwick entered the room and took the chair Dempsey had long ago abandoned. "Were you crying, Mother?"

Veronica nodded.

"I'm sorry for what I said, then. You loved Charlotte the best of all of us. I beg your pardon, Dempsey. I expect you did what you ought if she was crying over Charlotte's death. Are you better now, Mother?"

The duchess nodded.

"Should you like me to call for Gaines and have him order up some tea?"

"No, thank you, William. I think not."

"Tom Hasty said you wished to have a word or two with me, Dempsey," Berinwick said then, abruptly changing the subject. "Should you like to speak with me in private?"

"Indeed, but your mother—"

"Go," the duchess commanded. "Both of you. Go speak together in the study. I will be perfectly fine in a moment and there are things I wish to accomplish before the sun sets today."

The two took leave of her, Dempsey lingering behind, gazing at her over his shoulder as he followed Berinwick from the room. "Does she cry often, your mother?" he asked as he trailed the duke down a long hallway.

"Seldom, I think. I have never seen her cry before."

"Surely, you must have done. You simply don't remember. After you lost your eye she—I do beg your pardon. I ought not to have mentioned your eye."

"Why not?"

"Well, it must have been a dreadful experience for you and I doubt you wish to recall it." Dempsey would have punched himself in the jaw if he could have done so without looking a complete lunatic. Even if he wished with all his heart to help

Veronica and her son, to start babbling on now about the duke's missing eye was a stupid idea. Obviously Veronica had not wished her son to realize they had been discussing him. Charlotte's death, she had said. He must pretend he knew a good deal about Charlotte's death and nothing at all about Berinwick's eye.

Berinwick turned into a second corridor at a right angle to the first. "M'mother might well have cried when I lost my eye," he said with a thoughtful expression on his face, "though I don't know it for a fact. No one ever said as much."

"So you don't actually remember yourself?"

"No. I don't remember anything at all about THE ACCIDENT. That's what everyone called it when I was young—if they referred to it at all. THE ACCIDENT. I have always thought of it as being writ quite large and in uppercase," Berinwick replied with a twisted grin.

"You have no idea how you came to lose your eye?" Dempsey could not believe his ears.

"No idea whatsoever. Actually, I never dared to ask. I did something childishly imprudent, I expect, and losing an eye was the result of it. In here, Dempsey. Take that chair there. Now, what is it you want to speak with me about that cannot wait until this evening at the Fallen Dog?" he asked as he seated himself in the chair behind his father's desk.

"You do intend to join us then?" Dempsey queried. "At the public house, I mean."

"Why not? Barren Wycche is a small village. It has only the one pub. If a duke wants to drink in a public house and a groom, a caretaker, and a parson have the same desire, then they all drink at the Fallen Dog. A great leveler of men, the Fallen Dog. No standing on rank and ceremony under its sign."

"I see."

"Most likely you do not, but it doesn't matter. You will learn soon enough how people go on hereabout, especially when it comes to rank. What is it that cannot wait until tonight?"

"This," Dempsey said, taking the polished silver lion from his coat pocket and placing it on the desk before Berinwick.

The duke sprang from his chair at the sight of it, spun about, and seized a rapier from the wall behind him. Before the Reverend Mr. Dempsey could comprehend what was happening, the tip of the blade rested against his coat, mere inches from his heart.

"Who are you?" Berinwick asked quietly, his lips barely moving as he spoke, his one midnight eye filled with menace. "You cannot be the Mr. Richard Dempsey my mother believes you to be. What gives you the gall to think that you can stroll into Blackcastle and place that wretched lion on my father's desktop as though it were a meaningless trinket? What lunacy makes you imagine that I will not kill you this instant, whoever you are?"

Six

Dempsey stared at the point of the rapier against his coat for a moment, then stared up at Berinwick, whose lone, dark eye glittered threateningly down at him. Daintily, with the tips of his thumb and index finger, the parson plucked the weapon's point from the region of his heart and set it aside so that it lingered in the air beside his left shoulder. "If I had known the blasted lion was going to get me killed, I would have left it in the hidey-hole where I found it," he declared. "Of all things, Berinwick! Run a man through for asking a perfectly innocent question, why don't you?"

"Do not address me as Berinwick. We are not intimates nor are we friends."

"I do beg your pardon, your grace. The sharp end of any weapon pointed at my heart tends to make me forget the niceties. Are you going to tell me what it is about that particular lion that sets you off? I, myself, have no idea why it should. I merely carried it here, hoping to discover something significant about it. There is, I take it, something significant about it. Or are you perfectly mad?"

"What hidey-hole? Where did you find it?" Berinwick countered, the rapier lingering in his hand, quite capable of returning to the region of Dempsey's heart at once if his answer should prove unsatisfactory.

"I discovered it last night behind a brick in my bedchamber fireplace."

"What the devil are you doing in that rectory?" Berinwick roared. "You are rearranging fireplace bricks now? Thinking of stacking some in one of the corners and setting your bed atop them? I did not trust you from the first, Dempsey, and I trust you less, the more I come to know you!"

"You don't trust anyone, do you?"

"Certainly, I do."

"No, you do not. Not truly. Not here at Blackcastle at any rate. There is no one has your complete confidence, no one in whom you confide your deepest thoughts and feelings and fears, not even your mother or your sister, I think."

"What the devil are you talking about?" asked Berinwick, the rapier's blade wavering in midair beside Dempsey's ear. "My deepest thoughts and feelings and fears? Why would I confide such rubbish to anyone? This is an attempt on your part to distract me from the topic at hand, I believe."

"The topic at hand?" Dempsey cocked an eyebrow as insolently as Berinwick had ever seen a man do it. "My death at your hands, do you mean, *your grace?* In your opinion, I ought not attempt to distract you from that?"

Though he made no reply to this foray, Berinwick's lips twitched the merest bit upward at one side.

"I would be a perfect fool not to attempt it, I think. And you think the same," Dempsey added accusingly. "Admit it."

"I need not admit anything," Berinwick replied. "May I remind you that I am the gentleman holding the weapon?"

"No need to remind me. I am like to be missing an ear shortly if you do not pay attention to what you're doing with it. I wish you will put the thing back on the wall where it belongs," Dempsey muttered. "It is distracting beyond belief."

"I can lower it back to your heart if you prefer."

"Thank you very much, but no. I rather think not."

Berinwick's lips twitched upward on the other side. He chuckled softly. "You truly found that lion behind a brick in a fireplace, Dempsey?"

"Behind a half-brick, yes. It rested in the space left by the missing half. A perfect hiding place—except that the brick had worked itself out a bit over the years. Not much, mind you, but enough to catch my eye."

"You've sharp eyes for an old man, then."

"I am *not* an old man," Dempsey protested as Berinwick removed the rapier from beside the parson's ear, turned, and set the weapon back in the rack on the wall behind him. "Of all the impertinent things to say."

"I was born impertinent," Berinwick replied, regaining his seat behind the desk. "Impertinent and cautious. The lion belonged to the Reverend Mr. Dight, I expect, since you discovered it in his former bedchamber. I wonder m'father didn't tear the rectory apart searching for it. Perhaps he did not care to find it. He had other proof of Dight's nefarious intentions." Berinwick took the silver lion from the desktop and studied it thoughtfully. "It's quite like the others," he added, turning the figure around and around in his hands.

"The others?"

"Two others our family has collected to date. This will be the third. Come, I'll show you."

Dempsey followed the duke back along the corridor, up five stairs, along a shorter corridor which proceeded in the opposite direction, down an enclosed and winding staircase, through what appeared to be a tunnel, and up another winding staircase, this one quite three stories high. They paused before an oaken door bound in brass. Berinwick inserted an enormous key into an equally enormous lock set into the wood, turned it, and opened the door to reveal a circular chamber into which he stepped, waving at Dempsey to follow him.

Dempsey did so and took a deep breath at what the sun, shining in through six high, narrow windows, revealed to him.

"I doubt we require the lamps today," Berinwick murmured as he turned his back on the silent, wide-eyed parson. "It will be on one of these shelves. Yes, here it is."

The duke lifted what appeared to be a delicately formed silver stand from one of the shelves and set it on a long table in the center of the chamber. Three silver dragons stood on hind feet with their tails forming the base of the stand. Their outstretched forefeet supported a wide silver band and their growling snouts rose just above the circle of silver. The whole of it could not have been more than twelve inches high. "Looks a bit Celtic, does it not?" Berinwick queried of the stunned parson, once again turning his back to Dempsey as he searched another row of shelves. "It's not. It was crafted in Italy for Edward the Third."

"I never saw such a thing in all my life," Dempsey breathed, referring not merely to the stand the duke had set before him, but to the shelves and shelves of treasures arranged around the room. "I never dreamed to see—"

"Yes, well, my father collected things," Berinwick muttered. "Artifacts, he called them. Sprinkled everywhere throughout Blackcastle. These are just the leftovers."

"The leftovers?"

"Yes. The ones for which he hadn't any space. Look at the stand I set before you, Dempsey. If you want to know about the lion, you want to know about that, not the rest of this rubbish."

Dempsey forced himself to look away from the treasure-filled shelves to the silver stand. "Incredible workmanship," he said after a moment or two. "Who the deuce—"

"Haven't the vaguest idea who made it," Berinwick interrupted. "Ah, here we are! This sits in it," Berinwick announced, carrying a small, golden bowl to the table and placing it carefully within the ring of silver. "And this," he added, taking the lion Dempsey had brought him, "fits over the rim of the bowl in the space between the dragons' heads, like so. That's why it has that bit of an offset between the crown and the lion."

"It belonged to Edward the Third, you say?" Dempsey could not take his eyes from the thing, though Berinwick turned away to search the shelves once more.

"No, I said it was crafted at his request," Berinwick replied. "He gave it as a gift to the Poles of Wyke when William Pole became a baron. At least, that's what my father said. Yes, here are the other two. See, they're exactly alike. Well, as exact as a craftsman could make them without a mold of some sort."

Berinwick set two more silver lions on the lip of the golden bowl so that the three formed a triangle.

"Incredible," Dempsey murmured in a hushed voice, barely touching one of the dragon heads with the tip of a finger. "Not only an incomparable piece of artistry, but it is fourteenth century as well."

"Fond of antiquities, are you, Dempsey? But then, it's barely an antiquity, compared to most of the other items in this room. When you consider the Roman collection and the Celtic, the Poles' bowl is terribly modern."

"If it was a gift to the Poles of Wyke, how do the Thornes of Barren Wycche come to have it?" Dempsey asked, unable to take his eyes from the thing now that he had committed himself to study it. "And why should my delivering what looks to be the last piece of the set cause you to point a rapier at me? You ought to thank me for bringing the confounded lion into your presence."

"I thank you," Berinwick murmured, studying Dempsey as the parson studied the bowl and stand. "It's not the final piece, actually, your lion. If my father was correct, there are still two lions missing, though I can't think where they fit into the piece. Perhaps there's more to the stand itself." Berinwick shrugged his shoulders. "It's a very long story, the one about the Thornes and the Poles and how we come to have this particular little treasure. A war between the two families began in the fifteenth century and the last battle ended with my father triumphant in St. Milburga's when the Reverend Mr. Dight's blood sputtered out onto the church floor."

"A war? The last battle?"

"The last battle to be fought so far, I mean to say. There may be more on the horizon. The silver lion is taken from the shield of the Poles and the griffin's head rising from the crown is taken from their crest. Thus, that little trinket represents them perfectly. I thought for a moment you intended to present me with the business end of a pistol after you presented me with the lion as sufficient introduction."

"I am not a Pole."

"No. And I doubt there's a descendent of the family left alive. But then, that's what my father thought, too, when up popped the Reverend Mr. Dight who was not the Reverend Mr. Dight at all, but an actual Pole, though only on the distaff side. So, you're not a Pole, eh? Who the devil are you, then? Who are the Dempseys and why should my father seek you out, in particular? Frankly, I doubt you're a clergyman at all."

"You what?"

"I doubt you're a clergyman. It's not greed I see in your eyes as you stand in this room. You're not contemplating the monetary value of each piece and calculating the extent of the fortune you'd have if I gave it all to the church. You would be, were you truly a parson."

"Berinwick!" Dempsey exclaimed. "Enough. I do not care to hear you defame my fellow clerics at the moment."

"I speak from my own experience, Dempsey. And you *may not* address me as Berinwick."

"I'll address you however I please when you vilify the spiritual leaders of the Church of England."

"I've no need to vilify them. They vilify themselves. Greedy toads, each and every one of them I've ever met, and I've made the acquaintance of a goodly number of them, too. It's only you who proves different. Why?"

"Possibly because I am a Dempsey and the Dempseys are a proud lot, eh? Possibly because my father is a parson and two of my brothers as well and we are all proud of ourselves and what we do. We do a great deal among us, let me tell you. I have a great many things to attend to before the sun sets, your grace," the Reverend Mr. Dempsey added, turning away from his study of the bowl and its stand and stepping toward the door. "I have a church to repair. And I should like to speak a bit more with your mother before I take my leave. It goes against my nature to depart without offering her some consolation in her grief over Charlotte and your father. Which reminds me—I have something to ask you."

"What?"

"Do you love your mother?"

"Certainly, I love my mother. Of all the—"

"Impertinent questions?" Dempsey laughed. "I know it. And I know you love her, too. I saw it quite clearly last evening. I merely wished to hear it from your own lips. If you still intend to share a drink with Langton, Hasty, and me this evening at the Fallen Dog, I will be pleased to answer any and all of *your* impertinent questions then, I assure you."

"I'll be there, Dempsey," Berinwick replied. "And impertinent questions will spurt from between my lips the entire evening if I can manage to think of enough of them. Believe it."

Veronica, her tears dried, her manner calm, tucked her hand through Dempsey's arm as they wandered down Blackcastle's drive toward the road. "Do you not ride anymore, Richard?" she queried.

Dempsey smiled, a dimple appearing shyly in his right cheek. "I would ride if I had a horse."

"You have none?"

"None. I did manage to convince the driver of the mail to allow Theophilus atop the coach with me, Veronica, but I am quite certain he would have balked had I suggested he carry a horse up there as well."

"Cease teasing me, Richard. You know what I meant. I simply assumed that you would have your horse, or your carriage and the carriage horses, brought in small stages from Herefordshire."

"Well, I would have done, but I sold my curricle and team to the bishop's new secretary before I departed, and I have not had a saddle horse in three years now."

"Three years? Richard, you were used to love to ride when you were young."

"I still do, but I have not as yet discovered a horse to replace Troubadour, who is even now munching grass on my brother John's farm in Kent. Likely Troubadour is thanking the Lord that he reached the ripe old age of twenty-two at last and has been retired from my service."

"More likely the poor old thing misses you. What a lovely name for a horse, Troubadour."

"Yes, well, he had it when I bought him, though I cannot imagine why. He could not play an instrument or sing worth a pig's knuckle."

Veronica chuckled. The low, breathless sound of it set Dempsey's heart to rejoicing. Her grief was allayed for a time at least. It was a beginning.

"I should like to apologize, Richard," she said once the chuckle had ceased to be. "I ought not to have filled your ears with all my guilt over William. I have never spoken of it to anyone but his father before. I cannot think why—"

"You were right to confide in me," Dempsey interrupted. "And you are not to apologize for crying on my shoulder next, because, to tell the truth, I was honored that you trusted me and that you were not loath to let me see your tears. I should have liked to remain with you and helped you to dry them completely, Veronica. I would have done precisely that had not your son come stomping into the room so unexpectedly. But then, I am pleased that he did step in and interrupt us."

"You are?"

"Yes, because now I can offer you something besides platitudes, Vernie. I can offer you something to buoy you up in that sea of guilt into which you leaped blindfolded all those years ago. Your son has not the least idea that you had anything to do with the loss of his eye. He remembers nothing about it, nor has anyone seen fit to tell him the story."

"William d-does not realize . . . ?"

"Not at all. He assumes he did something imprudent—that he lost the eye through his own fault and no one else's."

"Oh, Richard! That is even worse! For William to believe—"

"Hush, Veronica. That is not the buoy I intend to toss you in my rescue effort. Well, it is a part of it. Only think for a moment. Because the very sight of William reminds you of all that happened and fills you with guilt, you also believe that each time he looks at you, he remembers that horrible night and he cannot possibly forgive you or come to love you. And yet, he remembers nothing and he does love you. I asked him straight out if he did, and he did not hesitate in his reply. 'Certainly I love my mother,' he said."

"How c-can he? Even if he does not remember that night, he very well remembers a mother who could not bring herself to be near him, who allowed his father to send him away."

"I doubt he thinks you had anything to do with it. If it occurs to him that anyone is to be blamed for anything, he blames his father. A gentleman is in charge in his own home. It is customarily so. It would not occur to William that you were involved in his being kept in the nursery or sent off to school. Certainly your husband did never say to him, 'I will not have you in my house more than necessary, Will, because your mother cannot bear the sight of you.'"

"N-no."

"No. So there is hope for you yet, my dear. A great deal of hope. Your son may not know how to show you that he loves you, Veronica, but he attempts to do it nonetheless. I was not mistaken. I saw the love for you in him last evening when he deigned to put up with me for your sake. You will see it as well, if only you look through eyes undimmed by guilt."

"The only eyes I have *are* dimmed by guilt, Richard. Years and years of guilt. One guilty act piled atop another."

"Perhaps, but now you have tools to begin unpiling that guilt, Veronica. You have the knowledge that William loves you and his own innate curiosity about THE ACCIDENT. That is precisely how he refers to it, Vernie, as if it is written large and uppercase. THE ACCIDENT. One word, the vaguest hint, and he will prove eager to sit down and hear you out, to learn at last what happened."

"You want me to tell him?" The duchess shuddered.

"You need not tell him everything at once. It would be best if you did, Veronica, but bit by bit, piece by piece, will do."

"I cannot!"

"Trust in him, Vernie. He's your son. He would reach out to you if he knew how to do it. He attempts to do it in his own brusque fashion, even now. Tell him what you need from him. Show him how to love and laugh and touch another person heart to heart. Reach out to him, Veronica. It's not too late. It's never too late to right the wrongs we have done until we're in our graves."

The Fallen Dog was an ancient, half-timbered building that adjoined the Three Legged Inn at Barren Wycche, though it refused to be a part of the inn. Both buildings shared a wall in common but no door connected the two. If one resided for any time at the inn and wished to drink or dine, one was forced to step out into the street and around to the Fallen Dog's front door. Dempsey was amazed by it. Seated beside Langton at one of the old wooden tables, a tankard of homebrewed before him, the parson glanced from the half-timbered walls to the paintings on them, to the white-painted balcony above the bar—a balcony which appeared to come from and lead to nowhere—to the uneven, pitted wooden floors beneath his feet on which Theophilus lay, happily slurping from time to time at a bowl of homebrewed all his own. Several other hounds hunkered beneath other tables, the lot of them pointedly ignoring each other's presence.

"Why is there a balcony?" Dempsey queried over the sounds of a cheery game of darts being played in the far corner of the pub.

"For Jane and Ellen," Langton replied offhandedly, staring about him, searching for any man to whom he had not introduced the new rector of St. Milburga's of the Wood.

"Jane and Ellen? Who are Jane and Ellen?"

"Two young women from London," Langton replied.

"Two young women from London? The owners of the Fallen Dog built a balcony without entrance or exit for two young women who did not even live in Barren Wycche?"

"Well, they had to do it," Langton said, his full attention returning to Dempsey. "There is no one you haven't met, eh? I've introduced everyone, have I?"

"Yes, indeed, Langton, though I doubt any of them actually wished to be introduced to the new preacher."

"Incorrect," Langton responded with a charming smile. "I asked you to join me here in advance of the duke precisely because all of them wished to make your acquaintance. The entire village is curious about you. Their wives sent most of the men here this evening precisely to make your acquaintance. You are a curiosity and the talk of the village at the moment. 'Met the new parson at the Fallen Dog,' they'll each of them say when they get home. 'Not a bad fellow for a parson. Not uppity and holier than thou, the way ye'd expect.'"

"How do you know that's what they'll say?"

"Because you actually came inside and sat down and are drinking homebrewed with a smile on your face. Because you brought your hound in with you and he's drinking homebrewed as well. They all like you because of it."

"Good. I want them to like me."

"Indeed you do, because if they don't, you will not see one of their faces in the church once we get it repaired enough to use. Send their wives to the services, they will, but they'll not come themselves unless they've a good opinion of you. Stubborn lot, the men of Barren Wycche. They insisted on walking out and standing in midair," Langton added.

"What?" Dempsey was certain that Langton had lost his mind. Men who insisted on walking out and standing in midair?

"Jane and Ellen," Langton clarified, chuckling at the bewildered look that had risen to the parson's face. "That's why the first of the Logans had to build the balcony. It was most disconcerting, even in those days, to have young ladies walking about with nothing but air beneath their slippers."

"More ghosts?"

"Indeed. We be overrun with ghosts in the environs of Barren Wycche. Jane and Ellen, now, were on their way back to London from their auntie's house and paused in Barren Wycche overnight. There was no inn here then, but there were two rooms above the Fallen Dog one could rent for a night or two."

"Allow me to guess," Dempsey grinned. "That very night the Fallen Dog burned to the ground and the young women died."

"Just so. And when the Fallen Dog was rebuilt, it was not in the exact same spot. There would have been an outside balcony on the old place, right above where the bar is now."

Dempsey shook his head in wonder. Not at the idea of the ghosts, but at the way in which Langton referred to the first Fallen Dog as "the old place."

This particular building is most definitely of medieval origin, Dempsey thought. So just how old was "the old place?"

Dempsey was just about to ask Langton that question when Berinwick and Tom Hasty entered through the front door and friendly greetings arose from every section of the public house.

"I hope ye talked his grace inta leaving his sword at Blackcastle, Tom," called a cheeky voice from the dart corner. "We be hopin' ta keep this preacher alive fer a year or two."

"Aye," called out another. "This parson cannot be all bad, Duke. He be drinking Logan's homebrewed."

"Welcome to you, your grace," added a third. "Be you fixin' to buy us all a pint or two?"

"Or three?" called someone else.

"Let the duke be. Cannot you see he means to be on his best behavior to impress our new parson?"

"Ho! That'll be the day!"

Berinwick, spurs jangling, slipped down into the chair across from Dempsey, his eyebrow cocked in silent amusement. Tom Hasty sat down beside him. Two pints of homebrewed appeared before them in less than a minute. "Take them all a pint or two, Nancy," Berinwick said before the barmaid could depart.

"Indeed I will," Nancy replied with a quick curtsy. "And pleased they'll be, too, yer grace. I have never seen such a thirsty lot as they be tonight."

"Is there something more?" Berinwick asked when the barmaid did not take herself off.

"I was wondering, yer grace, about the dogs."

"Take the dogs water, Nancy. Nothing worse than a host of drunken hounds toddling about at one's feet." Berinwick leaned down and peered under the table. "So," he said, returning to his proper height, "did Langton give you the word to bring Theophilus with you, Dempsey?"

"No, your grace, I did not," Langton replied at once. "Mr. Dempsey thought to bring the hound all on his own."

"Fits right in, our new preacher, don't he?" Hasty observed with a wink at Langton. "Perhaps we'll keep this fellow."

They spoke for a bit, the four of them, about the haymaking, the repairs to the church, the number of people who could be expected to appear when Dempsey read himself into his position.

"There will be hurrahs when that happens," Langton said. "People are looking forward to having their own parson again."

Berinwick looked somewhat doubtful at that, but he did not respond and took a long swallow of his homebrewed instead. Then he fixed his glittering, one-eyed gaze on Dempsey. "We will see if they have their own parson or not, Langton. I have a few impertinent questions to ask our Mr. Dempsey here, the answers to which may send him scampering back to Herefordshire."

"I never scamper anywhere," Dempsey replied. "A most distressing sight that would prove to be for anyone watching. But before you begin your inquisition, your grace, Langton, Hasty, and I have something to tell you and we would greatly appreciate it if you would listen without any preconceived notions until we have finished."

"I heard all of this nonsense about the ghost nine months ago," Berinwick protested mere moments after Langton began. "You were drunk, Langton. It was a cold night. You took a few too many sips from your flask and—"

"I vow I did not."

"You were frightfully shocked at the sight of the accident, then fainted dead away and dreamed the lot of it."

"That's what I thought when first Harvey and I talked the whole of it through," Tom Hasty offered, sipping at his pint. "Nevertheless, Harold Belowes and I have been keeping close watch on the ladies of Blackcastle and you, your grace, as best we can. Just in case, you know. But not another thing happened until yesterday."

"What happened yesterday?"

"You were shot at, your grace."

"Someone shot at me? Have you lost your mind, Tom? No one shot at me. I think I would have noticed if someone had."

"The wound in Triumph's hock, your grace. It weren't caused by a thorn or anything else but a piece of lead from a long gun. I knew it when I saw it, but I was loath to bring it up to you. There was no bit of lead to be found, then, not in the wound. But I have it now," he declared, taking the lead ball from his pocket and placing it on the table before Berinwick. "Dug it out of the gate in the south pasture this very morning. I thought I'd best speak to Langton before I broached the subject with you, your grace. And then in walked Mr. Dempsey, in the midst of our conversation like, and suddenly things began to look a good deal less ghostly and more threatening than ever."

Berinwick ran his fingers through his dark curls, setting them awry. "I heard no gun. I smelled no powder. No, wait. I did hear something. A tree branch splitting, I thought it was. Off in the wood. It might have been a long gun firing. But why wait until this evening, Tom, to broach the subject? Why not speak to me the moment you concluded that—"

"Perhaps because you can be a wee bit intimidating at times?" the Reverend Mr. Dempsey asked, staring across at him. "Harvey thought that you might be inclined to hang him from the church tower should he so much as broach the subject of the ghost again. And Tom thought you might lop his ears off for suggesting that you didn't know a gunshot wound from the damage a thorn could do. So, we all agreed to tell you together."

Berinwick glared at the parson. "I can understand Langton and Hasty not wishing to face me down singly, but why should they include you in this meeting? To hide behind the tail of your coat if I should prove recalcitrant? And while I'm thinking about it, Dempsey, why did you not so much as hint at any of this when we spoke this afternoon at Blackcastle?"

"I was a wee bit intimidated?" Dempsey asked with the cock of an eyebrow.

"You were not."

"I beg to differ with you, Berinwick, but I was. When you threatened me with that rapier, I completely understood why Langton and Hasty might wish us all to confront you together in a public place where there were no weapons readily to hand."

"You threatened the Reverend Mr. Dempsey with a rapier, your grace?" Tom Hasty asked, wide-eyed.

Harvey Langton gulped.

"Do not look at me so," Berinwick protested. "Either of you. I did not run him through, did I? And do not call me Berinwick, Dempsey. Forget yourself one more time and I'll nail your tongue to the wall of the rectory parlor. Try preaching then. Why did things seem even more threatening when Dempsey joined your discussion, Tom? You never did say."

"Because he saw the ghost of Owain Glyndwr himself," Hasty replied quietly.

"The evening of my arrival," Dempsey continued. "While Theo and I were making our way back to the rectory from Blackcastle."

"What do you carry in *your* flask, Dempsey?" Berinwick asked impertinently. "And how many nips of it did you take on your little stroll toward home?"

"Most amusing, but not at all to the point," Dempsey replied. "The ghost came riding out of the wood practically in front of us, wailing like a lost soul. I thought at once it must be Glyndwr, because of what it was wearing and where we were."

"What does that mean? What it was wearing and where you were?"

"Well, it was wearing armor. Medieval armor. Rather

dilapidated, it appeared to be, but recognizable. And we are here in the Marches where legends of Glyndwr abound and where your father claimed—but never mind that. What you need to know, your grace, is that I saw the same ghost on the night of my arrival that Mr. Langton saw the night of your father's death. We described him and his horse to each other from stem to stern. He was exactly the same ghost, except I happened to be close enough to discover flour puffing to ground in my ghost's wake."

"Has everyone in Barren Wycche seen this ghost but me?" Berinwick asked, bewildered. "Even the Widow Thistledown claims to have seen him. You would think, if he did murder my father and now seeks my blood, that he would appear before *me*. Flour, Dempsey?"

"Indeed. Langton and I both agree that he looked like a spirit born of mist and hoar frost. It was the flour made it so. I was able to follow his trail past the church and through the cemetery, but lost it once he crossed the lane."

"Why ride past the church?" Berinwick queried.

"To frighten Mr. Langton, whom he threatened the night of your father's death and who just happened to be at the rectory, having delivered my trunk and some dinner for Theo and me. And perhaps to frighten me as well, thinking that the very sight would set Mr. Langton to quivering in his boots and telling me the whole of it. Of course, I was not there, so it did him no good on that account."

"Possibly not. But now that you have heard all that I have heard, are you frightened now, Dempsey?"

"No. But I am quite intrigued."

"Just so. And you, Tom?"

"Me, I'm considerably angry, your grace."

"Langton?"

"I be pleased," Langton said, inexplicably.

"Pleased?" Tom Hasty queried.

"Pleased that the lot of you believe me at last. Thank goodness the blasted spirit appeared before the parson, or you would all be doubting me yet."

"You do understand that it was not actually a spirit that you saw ride out before m'father's coach on a spirit horse, do you not, Langton?" Berinwick queried. "You have grasped the idea that your ghost was simply a man made to look like a haunt?"

"So you all believe, and I am satisfied with it," Langton replied. "Man or ghost, it were him what caused your father's death, your grace, and we must all be on the watch for him from this moment forward."

Hannah, who had spent the day with her dearest friend, Miss Anne Tofar, and had remained to join the Tofar family for dinner, was riding happily home, her groom behind her, through the dwindling twilight. "Davey Lancaster," she called over her shoulder, "do come and ride beside me. It is silly for you to remain in the rear all the way back to Blackcastle. There is no one to notice whether you do or you do not."

"Yes, my lady," Lancaster replied, urging his horse forward until it came even with hers.

"Did you see Eloquent's foal? Did you get a very good look at the little darling?"

"I did, my lady."

"And what think you? Is she sound?"

"Sound and strong, my lady."

"Good, because I am going to purchase the sweet thing as soon as she is weaned. Well, perhaps not quite that soon, because I shall not have enough pin money saved up by then. But she will be mine before Christmas."

"I thought ye was fond of Penn and Marigold, my lady?"

"I am. They are two of the best horses in all of the county. Are you not, Marigold, my dearest?" she added, giving her filly a reassuring pat. "I do not intend the foal for myself, Davey. She is to be a present for his grace."

"For his grace, my lady?"

"Just so. Do not you think it an excellent idea? She is black as coal, just like his Triumph, so I know William will like her.

There is not a blaze or a stocking on her. She will be perfect for him."

"His grace be fond of black," the groom nodded, and then reached out and took hold of Marigold's cheek strap, bringing the filly to a halt.

"Davey Lancaster, what on earth—"

"Hush," the groom whispered.

"Why? What do you hear?"

"Hush, my lady, a moment more."

Hannah ceased to speak and listened to the sounds around her. Settling birds rustled in the trees. In the brush along the road the night creatures scampered. A goodly distance off, in the direction of Little Mynd Moor, a nightingale sang. "There is nothing at all out of place, Lancaster," she said.

"There be something," the groom replied. "I don't be hearing it now, but I did."

Lancaster released his hold on Marigold and Hannah urged the dainty filly forward. "What did it sound like, Lancaster, the thing you heard?"

"Sounded like a pack of Mad Jack's foxes whispering through the woods."

"Mad Jack's foxes? Whispering?"

"Aye, my lady. All soft and quietlike, shushing through the deadfalls where Grydwynn Wood meets the lane at the turning ahead, but they are silent now. Gone, if they were ever there. If it were foxes."

As they reached the turning in the lane, Hannah could not resist slowing Marigold to a walk and peering into the trees to see if perhaps there really were foxes and one or two of them remained. She saw nothing at all exceptional. The twilight was deepening into night and shadows danced along the wood's edge, bringing the underbrush to life and filling it with movement that was not movement at all but merely a trick of the fading light.

"I expect if there were foxes, we frightened them away," Hannah sighed as she looked about her. "Perhaps it was an owl or a falcon or . . ." A small movement on one of the tree branches as she peered upward caught her attention on the instant. "Davey Lancaster, what is that? Just there, on the very tip of that evergreen branch."

"Where, my lady?"

"Just there." Hannah pointed, then urged Marigold from the hard-packed earth of the lane onto the soft strip of grass that was all that separated the road from the wood. Lady Hannah halted beneath the object that had caught her eye and reached up to pluck it off the bough from which it dangled.

Lancaster, his horse just stepping down from the lane to follow her, called out, "M'lady!" and urged his own horse quickly between Hannah and the wood. "M'lady, ride for home as fast as ye can!" he commanded, giving Marigold a resounding whack on one flank. "Do not stop! Not for anyone!"

Marigold lunged forward. Hannah, unable to comprehend what could possibly be wrong, nonetheless stuffed the object she had seized into the pocket of her riding dress and did as she had been taught since first she began to ride. She obeyed her groom's command, turned Marigold back up into the lane, and urged the filly to a full run. She glanced back to see where Lancaster was and saw nothing, no one, behind her.

He has gone into the wood then, she thought, as she and Marigold flew together along the earthen road. Why would he go into the wood? What did he see?

Hannah had grown to be a young woman of stout heart and tremendous curiosity and would like to have reined the filly in and turned back to discover what had happened to Lancaster then and there. But she had also grown to be a young woman of considerable common sense, so she did not. She continued to ride full-out. She turned off the lane at the bottom of Sycharr Hill, set Marigold at a narrow hedgerow, and took the jump with well-trained ease into Blackcastle's east meadow. What she was running from, she had no idea, but the straightest path across the east meadow to the third paddock and then up to the stables, she knew very well, and so did Marigold. No one or nothing would be able to catch them now.

She did not slow the filly until she reached the paddock, when she tugged on the reins and brought Marigold to a canter, then a trot, and at last, as they reached the stables, a walk. The youngest of the grooms stepped out to meet her, took the filly's reins, and led the horse to the mounting block.

"Johnny," Hannah asked as she dismounted, "is Tom Hasty anywhere about?"

"No, my lady. He has gone into Barren Wycche with his grace."

"Trewellyn, then, or Overfield?"

"Mr. Trewellyn be tending to Triumph, but Mr. Overfield be merely cleaning some tack."

"See to Marigold. She has run a goodly distance, John. Walk her before you put her up."

"Aye, my lady."

Hannah gave Marigold a quick pat on the nose and then hurried into the stable. She turned the corner into the first of the tack rooms, but it proved to be empty. She hurried down between two rows of open stalls, beneath a low arch, and peered into the second of the tack rooms. "Overfield," she said as she spied him working on one of the driving harnesses.

"Yes, my lady," he responded, ceasing his work at once and turning to face her.

"Something has happened to Davey Lancaster. I cannot think what. We were coming home along Widowen Lane and we paused to look at something in the trees and he sent me most abruptly home without him. Whacked Marigold on the flank, he did, and said I was not to stop for anyone or anything until I reached Blackcastle. Then he rode into the wood. At least, I think he rode into the wood, because when I glanced back, expecting to see him behind me, he was gone."

"I will go at once, my lady," Overfield responded. "Where in Widowen Lane?"

"At the turning where the wood comes almost to the road."

"I know the place."

"He may be perfectly all right, Overfield, but I should—I

should feel a good deal better knowing that someone has gone to look for him."

"Aye," the groom nodded. "And so I shall, my lady. This instant. And I'll warn Trewellyn and Johnny to keep their eyes and ears open until I return."

Hannah nodded, turned on her heel, and strolled from the stables. She entered Blackcastle through the east door, peered into the farm manager's office, hoping to discover Mr. McClane there and send him off in search of Lancaster as well. But finding the office empty, she hurried past and climbed one of the oldest of the stairways to the first floor. There was light coming from the smallest of the family parlors, so she made her way there, her boot heels hushed by the thick carpeting.

Veronica looked up as Hannah entered. "There you are," she smiled. "Did you have a wonderful day with Anne? Hannah, what on earth? You have lost your hat. Your hair looks like a family of dormice have been nesting in it and you are covered with dust from head to toe."

"Something happened, Mama."

"What? You did not take a fall? You are not injured?" The duchess set aside the volume she had been reading, rose from her chair, and crossed to her daughter at once. She took Hannah's arm and led her to the long, low couch near the windows. "Sit here, dearest. Take a deep breath or two. I will ring for Gaines and send him to fetch you something to drink. Tea?"

"Yes, Mama, I should like some tea. I have more dust in my throat, I think, than is on my person. I rode home as if demons were chasing me. Davey Lancaster has disappeared, Mama."

"Disappeared?" Veronica crossed to a long, wide, velvet ribbon in the far corner of the room and tugged at it insistently for a good minute. "That will raise someone belowstairs," she murmured. Then she returned to Hannah and sat down beside her. "How on earth could Lancaster disappear between here and the Tofars'? Why did you ride home as if demons were chasing you?"

Hannah related all that she knew of what had happened, which was not a great deal, she discovered, as she came to the end of it. "I cannot think what Davey saw, or heard, or imagined, but I did not dare disobey him."

"No. You did precisely as you ought. And you sent Overfield out in search of him. I am thankful you thought to do that at once. Your brother is in Barren Wycche or—"

"Yes, I know. Johnny said Will had gone to the village or I would have told him first thing. I thought to tell Mr. McClane and send him off as well, but he was not in his office." Hannah removed the object she had seized from the tree branch from her pocket and stared down at it. "This is it—what I saw dangling from the evergreen. I have not yet had an opportunity to—Mama, only look!" Hannah could not quite believe her eyes. Resting in her palm was a circular silver pendant on a braided leather cord.

The Duchess of Berinwick took the prize from her daughter's hand and held it close beneath the light of the candelabra nearest the couch. "You found it dangling from a tree on the edge of Grydwynn Wood?" she asked in a hushed voice.

"Yes, Mama, as if someone wished for it to be found."

"Someone did wish for it to be found," Veronica murmured, studying the pendant in her hand with worried eyes. "I wished for it to be found years and years ago."

Seven

"You are certain he is well, Tom?" the duchess asked for the third time as she and the groom rode side by side toward St. Milburga's of the Wood the following day. "Hannah is quite fond of Lancaster, you know, and if he should require a surgeon . . . Well, we have no surgeon near, but we can send to Ludlow for one if it should be necessary."

"Davey's fine, your grace. He was a bit dizzy-like when Overfield found him, and he has bruises from the fall and the fight, but he's up and about this morning. Drove one of the wagons down to the haymaking as though nothing at all happened."

"I cannot believe that Davey Lancaster was actually attacked by a man right there in Widowen Lane."

"Actually, he had followed the man into the wood before he was attacked, my lady. He thought at first it was a highwayman, Davey did. Him sitting his horse so very still as though he was waiting for a coach and four to pass him by."

"It was evening," the duchess replied. "The light was terrible. A highwayman might think to wait in such a place at such a time, but no sensible one would choose Widowen Lane. A highwayman might wait a year or two before any carriage of significance drove in Widowen Lane."

"Just so," Tom Hasty agreed. "The same thought occurred to Davey. But he said the man and horse were so still that it sent shivers up and down his spine, so he yelled at Lady Hannah to ride home and turned back to confront the fellow. And in just that blink of an eye it took for Davey to turn back, the man and horse were gone. Disappeared into Grydwynn Wood, the scoundrel did. Davey swears he didn't hear anything at all, neither the rustling of leaves nor the galloping of hooves."

"But Davey Lancaster rode into the wood, regardless."

"Yes, your grace. Determined to find out who the fellow was and what he meant by peering out so sly-like at Lady Hannah. There ain't an easy passage anywhere through the wood when the light is fading, but whoever the scoundrel was, he had not a speck of trouble. It's a sight too bad Davey was not more careful," Hasty added quietly, almost to himself. "Might have caught the man, else. Fool thing for Lancaster to do, hit his head on a branch and take a tumble."

"I doubt he did it purposely, Thomas."

"No, your grace. I didn't intend to say he had. But then the fellow came back and beat poor Davey senseless. But he's recovered nicely, Davey has. Put a bit of Triumph's ointment on the lump on Davey's head, Overfield did, and bound it up all nice and tight. Put the rest of the ointment on Davey's bruises. He is fine now, Lancaster is."

"I cannot thank Overfield enough for commencing to search at once and sending word to us immediately he brought Lancaster home. Hannah would have fretted the entire night away but for Overfield's swift action."

"Aye, your grace. And likely you would have convinced his grace and me to set out in search of Davey the very moment we returned from the Fallen Dog, too, had Overfield not found the lad already and brought him home."

Veronica nodded. "Likely so, Thomas. Do you think the Reverend Mr. Dempsey will like his present?" she queried, changing the subject.

"I reckon he'll be overwhelmed, your grace, and rightly so. I was thunderstruck to think his grace approved of the idea."

Langton saw them approaching and called down to Dempsey in the church below. "Her grace be riding this way, Mr. Dempsey."

"Her grace?" Dempsey called back, setting another of the overturned pews upright. "She is not alone, Langton?"

"No, sir. Tom Hasty be with her."

"Thank goodness," Dempsey murmured under his breath as he shrugged into his coat and strolled purposefully toward the rear of the church. "We shall have to do something about this floor, Harvey," he called up to Langton. "It has as many pits and cracks as the old coaching road to Hereford."

Pushing aside one of the double doors that hung only by a rusted hinge, Dempsey stepped out into the afternoon sunshine. They were coming up the road at a trot, Veronica and the groom. Dempsey thought Veronica looked the very image of Arduina, the Welsh goddess of the hunt, as she sat her mount proudly, tall and straight, her well-rounded figure adding to her stature. Her black riding dress cascaded over her white horse's side like a faery concept of night consuming day. Her wide-brimmed, black hat with its single white rose shaded her face and revealed merely a hint of the dusky curls which lay beneath. Dempsey inhaled deeply at the sight of her.

"Mr. Dempsey," she said as she drew her horse to a halt before him. "I have brought you a present."

"A present? What?"

"Norville."

Dempsey, his gaze and his mind both focused entirely on Veronica, did not so much as notice the riderless chestnut gelding that danced at the end of the extra set of reins Tom Hasty held, though he did notice the dimple in Veronica's pale cheek that peeked out at him as she began to smile. "Norville?" he asked. "What's a Norville?"

"Open your eyes do, Mr. Dempsey. Norville is certainly large enough that even a nearsighted parson cannot overlook him."

I'm not nearsighted, Dempsey thought, as Tom Hasty led the horse directly up before him so he could not miss it. I'm besotted. But he did not say as much. He dared not. Instead, he stepped forward and took hold of the chestnut's reins. "For me?" he asked. "What a marvelous animal, your grace. But certainly I cannot accept him."

"You can and you will, Mr. Dempsey. My son and I have decided that Norville is to be yours from this day forward. Some of the men will come to prepare your little stable for him before the end of the day. You cannot be a proper parson without a horse, you know. How will you ride out to tend to your flock? They do not all live within walking distance of the church."

"There is a dog cart standing in my stable."

"Yes, but no horse to pull it, Mr. Dempsey. Mr. Langton cannot be expected to give you the loan of his Dolly forever. Norville can be hitched to the cart if you wish. He is accustomed to a hitch as well as to a saddle."

"I do not believe it. Such an animal as this accustomed to pull a dog cart?"

"Well, he does not like to do it, but he will if he must. It is a matter of pride with him to be ridden rather than to pull. The tack he wears is to be yours as well. Come, mount up, Mr. Dempsey, and put Norville through his paces."

The Reverend Mr. Dempsey grinned. He took the reins and stepped up into the saddle. "Will you ride with me, your grace?" he queried hopefully.

"Most certainly, Mr. Dempsey. Thomas, you will assist Mr. Langton until we return, will you not?"

"Yes, your grace," the groom replied. "Pleased to do it."

Side by side, the duchess and the parson rode off together in silence, their horses dancing through shadow and sunlight along a quiet road that would carry them far from the rectory before it would turn and carry them back again. The world was filled with birdsong and butterflies and Dempsey's heart was as content as ever it had been. "You ought not to have done this," he said at last. "I have money, Veronica. I can actually afford to purchase my own horse."

"Yes, but it would not be as fine a horse as Norville, I

think. And you would not have got around to the doing of it for a month of Sundays, would you?"

"Well, possibly not, but—"

"But nothing, Richard. Norville now belongs to you. I wish you to have him and so does William."

"His grace wishes me to have Norville?"

"Indeed. He was the first to mention Norville's name when I brought it to his attention that you had no mount of your own."

"Why?"

"Why?"

"Yes, Vernie. Why did he mention Norville? Is there something about this particular horse that proves a thorn in his grace's side?"

"No. Of course not," Veronica declared, but her lips twitched upward, regardless of the seriousness of her tone.

"I have hit on it," Dempsey chuckled. "There is a particular reason his grace suggested this animal. Tell me."

"It is nothing, Richard. William merely mentioned that a man who had a dog named Theophilus deserved to have a horse named Norville. Which reminds me, where is dear old Theo?"

"In the kitchen with dear old Mrs. Langton. Mrs. Langton is baking gingerbread cookies and—"

"Theophilus is fond of gingerbread cookies."

"Just so. Now, there's a promising field for putting Norville through his paces. I don't expect there will be any haymaking or harvesting there this year."

"None. That particular land is called Hatter's field and ought to have been planted in turnips and mangel-wurzels to restore the soil, but William was preoccupied with the aftermath of Julian's death when the time came, and Mr. McClane, our farm manager, forgot to have it done. One of your parishioners, Richard, lives across the way, beyond that old barn in the distance. You cannot actually see the cottage from here, but do you follow the left fork in the road ahead it will take you to Mrs. Thistledown's. She has been ill and will be glad of a visit from the new parson, I think."

"Then I shall pay her a call first thing tomorrow."

"No, I think we ought to pay her a call once you have put Norville through his paces to your heart's content. I shall be present to introduce you then, and Mrs. Thistledown will like you all the better for my doing so."

Together they turned into Hatter's field and Dempsey put Norville to a trot, a canter, a gallop, a run. Veronica stayed beside him the entire way, changing her mount's pace to match Norville's. "You see," she said as Dempsey brought the horse to a standstill, "there is nothing at all wrong with Norville. He is one of the sweetest goers in all of the county."

"Indeed he is. I cannot possibly accept such an animal. He is much too good for a mere clergyman."

"Perhaps he is," Veronica responded. "He is not, however, anywhere near good enough for my Richard. You did not tell me you intended to meet William at the Fallen Dog last evening," she added as Dempsey dismounted and helped her from her sidesaddle to the ground, forcing himself not to allow his hands to linger at her waist longer than necessary. They began to stroll back in the direction from which they had come, grasses, weeds, and wildflowers bobbing around them, horses trailing behind. "Or did the two of you meet by accident?"

"No, it was a planned meeting. We had some things to discuss, my benefactor and I. Have you spoken with your son as yet, Vernie, about—"

"No," she interrupted, waving her hand in the air as if to shoo the question away. "I *will* speak with him, Richard, when I have gathered every shred of my courage about me. But not now. Not as soon as this. I fear the truth will turn William away from me forever."

"Truth often does make people turn away, at first. But it often compels them to turn back again once they have considered completely what they have been told, Veronica. It is human nature to wish to know all of the truth, to have every question answered, to seek those answers from the person who can provide them, no matter how despised that person may be."

"He will despise me. Even you admit it."

"That is not what I said. I was speaking in generalities, Vernie. I merely intended to say that even if he did despise you for a time, he would not turn away from you forever. I don't believe he could."

"He could," Veronica murmured. "And he would have every right to do so. I know that whether or not William turns away from me ought not matter. I know it is the truth that matters. You are correct about that, Richard. William must know the truth and I must face whatever that truth brings down upon my head. But I do not wish to think about it now, and I do not wish to speak of it any further. Let us change the subject. There is something I brought to show you." With that, Veronica ceased to walk, reached into the pocket of her riding dress, and tugged the pendant Hannah had discovered the evening before out into the sunlight. "I lost this a great many years ago and last evening, at twilight, Hannah discovered it hanging on the branch of an evergreen and brought it home to me."

"There is a story involved in this, yes?" Dempsey asked, taking the silver pendant as she offered it to him and studying it carefully.

"Indeed, and I will tell it to you in a moment. Do you know anything of antiquities, Richard?"

"A bit."

"Can you tell me the least thing about that pendant?"

"It appears to be Celtic and quite old."

"How old?"

"Well, I couldn't say exactly, Vernie. Appearances can be most deceiving. It may just be a copy of something old."

"But if it is what it seems to be?"

"No older than the sixth century, because this open weave knotwork came to the Celts then, with the Saxon monks."

"You do know something about antiquities. Why did you never tell me?"

"Because the subject never arose between us before," Dempsey smiled. "I know, too, that interweaving animals into the knots, as has been done with this boar, likely came from the Vikings."

"This pendant has been in the Thorne family since the tenth century, Julian told me."

"If it is not a copy, it's at least that old then," Dempsey chuckled. "Is the boar intended to symbolize the Thornes? I should think it fits them well enough. If I remember correctly, the boar is a Celtic sign for the warrior—and for fertility, wealth, and courage. The Celts, I think, never did believe in one symbol for one thing."

"Julian gave me this pendant on our wedding night," Veronica said. "He said that Thorne mothers have given it to their firstborn sons to pass on to their brides since first it came to be. I am to pass it on to William to bestow on his bride. I was to do so, that is, until it disappeared. Now that I have it back, I will pass it on to William, even though I doubt he will ever have a bride on whom to bestow it."

"Why do you doubt that, Veronica?"

"Because the young ladies of London are frightened of William. Even the London gentlemen give him wide berth."

"Then he will find a bride outside of London. You think too often and too deeply of his difficulties, Veronica. Think of his possibilities instead."

Dempsey placed the silver pendant on its braided leather cord around her neck. He took her hand in his, and they continued to stroll the field as Veronica told him what had happened to Hannah and Lancaster the previous evening. The heat of her hand came through her riding glove and warmed Dempsey's. He noted it with a private smile and realized at once that the simple act of walking beside her warmed his heart in much the same manner.

"But why would someone hang it on a tree in Widowen Lane?" Veronica wondered aloud as she finished her story.

"Did anyone know that Lady Hannah would ride home along that lane last evening, Vernie?"

"Anyone who knew she had gone to visit Anne would know it. The girls always ride back and forth along Widowen Lane. What? What are you thinking, Richard?"

"That whoever hung the pendant in the tree may have had

no idea of its significance to you. That he hung it there to draw Hannah off the road and away from the groom who accompanied her."

"But why would anyone—Richard? You are not saying that you think someone intended to abduct my daughter?"

"No, I'm not saying that. I'm merely guessing at likelihoods, Veronica. Perhaps it is merely as simple as the fact that someone in the neighborhood found the pendant, realized it was yours, and thought that leaving it for Hannah to find would be the most expedient way of returning it to you while remaining anonymous. They may have feared you would think someone in their family had stolen it all those years ago."

"Yes, that could be. That sounds much more likely, because there would not be the least reason for anyone to abduct Hannah. And whoever it was, he waited there to be certain that Hannah did find it and he punched Davey Lancaster because he did not wish to be recognized by him."

Dempsey nodded. I ought to tell her that her husband was murdered, that her son is certainly in danger, and that she and Hannah may be in danger as well, he thought as he walked beside her. But it's not my place to do it. It's Berinwick's responsibility and he'll not thank me for stepping in and taking it over. He will tell her soon. Certainly, he must. And he has already seen to it that neither his mother nor his sister goes anywhere alone.

"What did Julian write to bring you here, Richard?" Veronica asked, breaking the silence between them. "Did he lie to you, about the living? The living of St. Milburga's was exceptional once and it might well be again, but at present it is more bother than blessing."

"No, it's not an exceptional living at the moment," Dempsey replied, and then he brought her to a halt. He put his hands on her shoulders and turned her to face him. She was nearly as tall as he and yet he could not see her eyes beneath the wide brim of her bonnet until she tilted her head back to stare questioningly at him. "What?" she asked. "Richard? What is it that you wish to tell me? *Did* Jules lie to you to get you to come here?"

Her lips were deliciously red and Dempsey's heart stuttered a bit as he watched her wet them nervously with the tip of her tongue in anticipation of his answer. The perfect alabaster of her brow had wrinkled a bit over the years, but her cheeks were still as sweet and plump as ever they had been and the brown of her eyes still glowed with the golden specks he remembered. He would allow no one to harm this woman. Never. Not her. Not her son. Not her daughter. She had filled his life with love and joy once; he would do everything he could to bring joy and love and peace into hers now and forever.

"You must be the most beautiful woman ever created by God," Dempsey whispered hoarsely, one long finger going to stroke the velvet of her throat, to tremble along that incredibly delicate path to the enticing indentation beneath her chin. "And every year of your life, Vernie, God has added to your beauty inside and out until now, at the very sight of you, my heart cries aloud in wonder."

"You are mad," Veronica replied softly, trapped in the intensity of his gaze, unable to look away from the piercing blue of his eyes.

"Am I?"

"Yes."

Her gloved hand went to Dempsey's cheek and lingered there. His hair was no longer the blond of his youth, but dark now, like honey, sparkling with gold and silver in the sunlight as it whispered down across his brow. His wide, breathlessly beautiful eyes, fringed by thick, dark lashes, blinked down at her in silent inquiry. His lips parted the slightest bit, revealing the ivory whiteness of his teeth. He had grown into a strong man, a man rich in virtue, an honorable man, she was certain. How could he have grown to be anything less than strong, honorable, virtuous? Veronica rose on tiptoe and pressed her lips gently against his.

"I am mad as well," she whispered when their lips parted.

They studied each other in silence for a long time. Then, without a word, the Reverend Mr. Dempsey took her to her horse and helped her up into the saddle. He mounted Norville and they rode together, slowly, silently, across the remainder of the length of Hatter's field.

"Your husband did not lie to me, Vernie. He wrote to me, requesting my aid," Dempsey said as they turned onto the hard-packed road. "We did never meet, but he did read a number of my papers and—"

"Your papers, Richard?"

"Yes. On the antiquities, culture, art, history, and lineages of the people of the Marches. It's a—hobby—of mine. I have presented many papers through the years and—"

"Presented them where?"

"Oh. I left that out, did I? I am a Fellow of the Royal Society of London, Veronica. But there I am not known as the eccentric Reverend Mr. Dempsey who fiddles about in this place and that at the request of the Bishop of Hereford. At the Royal Society, I am R. R. Dempsey, Doctor of Science and Divinity. But I do not like to be called Dr. Dempsey, and so I do not mention that in general."

Veronica's eyes opened wide. "You are a Fellow of the Royal Society of London? Jules was a Fellow."

"Just so. And I should like to have met him, Veronica. Truly. But I never did. At any rate, he knew me by reputation and he wrote to me saying that there were records indicating that the first Duke of Berinwick had sent one of his younger sons to the Parliament summoned at Machynlleth by Owain Glyndwr and that while the son was there, he witnessed Glyndwr presented with a particular—"

"You came to help Jules find the cup," Veronica interrupted. Her previous estimation of his character trembled in her mind, threatening to tumble downward. It could not be true. He had not come here merely to discover Glyndwr's cup and make a name for himself in the annals of the Royal Society.

"You know about the cup?" Dempsey asked in surprise.

"Yes, I know about the cup."

"Then you can under—"

Veronica sliced his word in half as if she wielded a broadsword and the place between "under" and "stand" was Dempsey's midsection.

"I believed you came here to assume the living of St. Milburga's of the Wood, Richard," she declared, her brown eyes abruptly flashing with golden light. "Are you going to tell me now that Julian's offer of the living was nothing but a hoax devised between you to gain you acceptance here? Are you going to tell me that you have no intention of ministering to the people of Blackcastle and Barren Wycche? That your true and only intention was to help Julian pull that poor church apart piece by piece? And now that he is gone, you intend to carry on, to destroy what is left of St. Milburga's in search of some paltry legend and then depart from us?" Veronica brought her horse and his to a halt and glared at him so fiercely that the Reverend Mr. Dempsey gulped. "Well? *Is* that what you are going to tell me, Richard?"

"Not now," Dempsey replied.

"And what, precisely, does that mean?"

"It means that if I were going to say any of those things, I am certainly too terrified to mutter a word of them at this moment, Vernie. By Jupiter, but you can be intimidating when you wish. I barely recognize you with such a fierce scowl and lightning bolts shooting from your eyes."

"No. Likely you believe me to be some weak, watering-pot of a woman who will burst into tears at the least thing. Well, I was once, but I am not any longer. I cannot help that I cried when I confided in you about what happened to William. The grief in my heart over my son is so deep that I must cry sometimes."

Dempsey nodded. He could not think what else to do.

"If Mama had not treated me like some delicate little flower for most of my life with her, if Julian had not continued to treat me so, I might have had the courage to accept my great sin against my son at once. I might have taken that innocent child into my arms and begged his forgiveness on the spot, rather than commit further outrages against him.

I am not yet courageous enough to face William, but I am brave enough now to stand up for my people. I tell you now, Richard Dempsey, if you have come here under false colors, bringing my people the hope of a proper church and a parson of their own, holding out to them the promise of a good man's help and solace in time of need, when all you really intend to do is remain long enough to find that wretched cup or prove that it does not exist in this place at this time, then you had best point Norville's nose toward Hereford this moment. You had best set your heels to his sides, gallop off, and not look back."

Richard Randolph Dempsey could not take his gaze from the tilt of Veronica's chin, the passion that smoldered in her eyes, the smoke and fire he envisioned shooting from her ears. It was the imaginary earfire that did him in. He burst into laughter and had to struggle mightily to force his guffaws and chuckles to subside.

"I fail to see that I have said the least thing amusing, Mr. Dempsey," Veronica declared, her eyes narrowing.

"No, no, you have not. I merely—I imagined—no, never mind what I imagined. Veronica, I give you my word that I have every intention of becoming a responsible rector. I will remain, cup or no, for as long as you and my congregation will have me."

"Then why did you say . . . ?"

"I mentioned Glyndwr's cup because your husband would never have offered me the living if he had not wished my help to discover and authenticate the thing. He wanted me to accept the position so badly, Veronica, that along with the living itself, he offered me full access to his library and the opportunity to study his collection from stem to stern. His letter seemed like a gift from God."

"Perhaps it was."

In more ways than one, Dempsey thought, but he did not say the words aloud. Instead, he said, "I thought I would be forced to work for Hereford for the rest of my days, Vernie. I thought I would never become a rector like my father. The only living I ever had a prayer of getting was in the dreariest place with a patron who would never condone my wasting time on the study of antiquities. And then, finally, along came your husband and St. Milburga's of the Wood."

"Oh. Well then, I do beg your pardon, Richard, for mistaking your intentions."

"You need not beg my pardon," Dempsey said, urging his horse forward once again, thankful to see that she did the same and rode beside him, her countenance returned to a semblance of calm. "I wonder, Veronica," he said as they approached a fork in the road, one lane of which, Veronica explained, would take them past the Widow Thistledown's cottage, and the other back toward the church. "I wonder, Vernie, does your son know about Glyndwr's cup? I only ask because your husband wrote as though he had entrusted the knowledge to no one, and yet you know."

"Julian would not have spoken to William about it," Veronica replied, brushing a tendril of dusky hair from her cheek with the back of her hand. "Will has no interest in antiquities. He is a farmer, our William. And he will be a politician—a fierce politician, I think—when he decides to make use of his seat in Parliament. I would not bother to speak of the cup to him unless you require access to some of Julian's records and must explain why. Do you require access to Julian's records, Richard? I am quite certain they are complete to the final period and easy to follow. Jules was always very methodical in everything."

"No, I do not need to see any of them as yet."

"Now you're frowning. Why? Is there something about my mentioning Jules's records that—"

"No, no, nothing," Dempsey interrupted her. His mind had flown suddenly back to his conversation with Berinwick and the others at the Fallen Dog. It had not occurred to him then, but—had Julian Thorne's murderer wished for access to the old duke's records and collection and been denied? Had Veronica's husband been murdered by a friend, a colleague, someone he had known well? Someone who knew Veronica and William and Hannah well and was even now attempting to cajole the young Berinwick into . . .

"There is something that you ought to know, Vernie," Dempsey blurted out, his mind reeling with the frightful prospect that someone Veronica knew and trusted might well be her husband's murderer and prepared to murder her son, her daughter, even herself if he did not get his way.

"What?"

"N-nothing. I—it is not my place to tell you, Veronica. It is your son's place to tell you."

"Richard!"

"No, as much as I wish to tell you, I cannot. I must allow Berinwick to tell you and in the manner he thinks fitting. Still, I hope you will do me a great favor from this moment forward, Vernie. I hope you and Hannah will not make a fuss over being accompanied by a footman or a groom whenever you ride out or go driving or take a stroll."

"Oh, for goodness' sake!" the duchess responded as they steered their mounts onto the fork in the road that led toward Mrs. Thistledown's cottage. "Have you been listening to Tom Hasty, Richard? Has he filled your ears with all his dire predictions of wandering bands of wretched men gone mad with lust? Honestly, if it is not William ordering someone to attend me the moment I step outside into the sunlight, it is Tom Hasty saddling his horse when the only one he has been told to saddle is mine, or Harold Belowes leaping to the back of my coach and then trailing along behind me through all the shops in Barren Wycche and East Hill Downs. And now I shall have you to contend with as well? I vow, if it were not for the refreshing callousness of Patrick McClane, who cares not if I fall from a horse, tumble into a rabbit hole, or am carried off by a band of lunatics intent on mayhem, I would think every male associated with Blackcastle to be three cards short of a deck."

"I promise, we are none of us three cards short of—"

Dempsey's words were interrupted by an ominous hissing of air past his ear, a quick sting, a sharp crack, and the thud of a lead ball embedding itself in a tree. Norville reared wildly, then lunged forward in panic. "What the devil!" the parson exclaimed as Norville's hooves pounded against the hard-packed earth and trees rushed past Dempsey at a most amazing rate. Something wet dribbled along his jaw and down his neck, but he had no time to investigate it for, quite suddenly, he found himself immensely occupied in an effort to keep Norville from running away with him.

It was late in the afternoon when Berinwick drew his horse to a halt near the kitchen door of the Widow Thistledown's cottage. Patrick McClane had gone off on an errand to Ludlow early that morning and Berinwick had seized the opportunity to spend most of his day in the north meadow spelling the men, women, and children who labored there. He had looked to the horses and wagons for a time and then scythed, spelling the men who required it. He had joined in the gathering, as well, and piled the hay into ricks. It had been long, hot, arduous work, and he had enjoyed it immensely.

His coat, waistcoat, and neckcloth long since abandoned somewhere in the meadow, Berinwick was covered in dust. His face was streaked with it. His shirt clung to him, soaked with perspiration. His curls were in wild disarray. But it did not once occur to him how he must look. He had taken the long way around from the meadow with only one thing on his mind. He wished to speak to the Widow Thistledown, to hear from Mrs. Thistledown's own lips about the ghost she thought she had seen near the Hatter's field barn.

He was just dismounting when he heard the shouts. He turned in time to see two small bodies rushing from the henhouse at top speed, arms pinwheeling, legs pumping. "Duke!" Charlie cried. "Duke!" Millie echoed. And in a moment they were skidding to a halt before him. Charlie put one arm before his stomach, the other behind his back and bowed. Millie took the seams of her skirt in hand and bobbed a curtsy.

"Did you come to visit Mrs. Quillbristle?" Charlie asked.

"No, I did not."

"Good. Because she is sleeping under the woodpile an' prefers not to be waked until evening. She bristles all up if you wake her afore the sun goes down."

"Did you come to visit Charlie and me?" Millie queried.

"Actually, I came to speak with your mother. Is she about?"

"I'll fetch her," Charlie offered and before Berinwick could protest that he was perfectly capable of knocking on the kitchen door himself, the boy had disappeared inside the cottage.

"Ma is feeling a good deal better," Millie offered, staring up at him with a most serious expression, "if you care to know."

"Certainly I care to know. And I am pleased to hear it," Berinwick responded, leading his horse to a post at the corner of the cottage and hitching the animal to it.

"Meg has learned to pluck a chicken and to milk the cow," Millie announced when the beast was safely tied.

"Has she?"

"Yes. But yesterday Ma tried to teach her how to clean out a pheasant's innards and Meg spewed her entire breakfast all over the kitchen floor."

"If I may be so bold as to inquire," Berinwick said with considerable reserve, "why are you telling me all these things?"

"I am entertaining you until Ma arrives, your grace."

"Oh." Berinwick was not certain he desired much more entertainment, so the sound of Mrs. Thistledown's voice came as a great relief.

"Your grace?"

He turned toward the woman at once and was surprised to see that her cheeks were pink and her eyes as clear and blue as Millie's and Charlie's.

"You are looking a great deal better, Mrs. Thistledown," he said, stepping toward her.

"And you look worn to the bone, do I be permitted to say it, your grace. Will you come in and sit awhile and have a glass of milk? The milk be cooler than a cuppa tea is why I say that."

Her cheeks grew pinker with each word, Berinwick noted, and he wondered why that should be.

"He can't come in, Ma," Charlie offered from beside his mother. "He ain't dressed proper."

"His grace may come into our cottage at any time, Charlie, be he proper dressed or not," Mrs. Thistledown instructed.

"But he's practically naked," Charlie protested.

Mrs. Thistledown's cheeks grew pinker still and the lobes of her ears, which were all Berinwick could see of her ears beneath her cap, turned bright red.

Berinwick's dark eye glared down at Charlie. The eyebrow above it tilted upward.

"Well, you *are* practically naked," Charlie declared, unintimidated.

"You don't have your coat or your waistcoat or even your neckcloth on," Millie added. "I noticed at once, but I didn't think it would be polite to point it out to you. It's not, is it? Polite to point it out, I mean."

"No," Berinwick replied.

"Why ain't it polite?" Charlie asked, peering around Berinwick at his sister. "I should think he'd want to know."

"Because a duke does not care to have it pointed out to him that he's done something utterly stupid," Berinwick answered before Millie could. "Especially something as stupid as riding off to pay a call in his shirtsleeves. Better men than you, Charles Thistledown, have been skewered on the end of my sword for less."

Charlie giggled.

"No, sir, it is not a giggling matter. If your mother were not the good woman that she is, I might well be tempted to call you out. I do apologize, Mrs. Thistledown, if I have embarrassed you," he added, turning his attention to the coachman's widow. "I was not thinking beyond having a word with you and so did not give my attire a single thought. I thank you for your offer, but I shan't come in. Are you up to a stroll as far as your pretty little flower garden?"

"Indeed, your grace. Charlie, Millie, be off with you and

finish with cleaning the henhouse. His grace don't be wantin' to speak to the two of you."

"Just so," Berinwick nodded, offering the elderly woman his arm. "Off with the both of you. I really do apologize, Mrs. Thistledown," he added when the children were gone from sight. "I was helping out a bit with the haymaking and—"

"Dearest heavens, you need not be apologizing to me, your grace. I have seen Mr. Thistledown in his shirtsleeves countless times. I cannot think why I colored up as I did. Perhaps the sun is too hot."

"Yes. That's likely it, eh?" He led her slowly along beside the kitchen garden, across a wide expanse of green where four sheep grazed, and into a garden of hawthorn bushes and a veritable riot of wild roses. There was shade to be had here, and a small bench beneath the branches of an oak which looked out toward the lane and across the lane into Hatter's field. He settled her on the stone bench and stood facing her, his hands clasped behind his back, his shoulders resting against the trunk of an elm. "I trust you will not think me addlepated, Mrs. Thistledown," he began, "but I have come to ask you about a ghost."

"A ghost, your grace?"

"Indeed. Millie and Charlie mentioned to me when we went to fetch the hedgehog that you had seen a ghost. Near the Hatter's field barn."

"I did," Mrs. Thistledown nodded. "I saw it from this very spot. It is a goodly long distance from here to the middle of Hatter's field, but I've the eyes of a hawk Mr. Thistledown always said."

"The eyes of a hawk. Amazing, Mrs. Thistledown," Berinwick replied.

"I do so like to come out here of an evening, be it cold or not, and smell whatever flowers are in bloom, and feel the breeze nudging at me here and there, and listen to the nightbirds sing. I cannot thank you enough, your grace, for providing me and the children with such a pleasant place as this. There are others, I'm sure, who would never have done such a kindness for the widow and babes of a poor old coachman."

"You are quite welcome, Mrs. Thistledown. I was pleased to do it," Berinwick responded, shifting his weight from one foot to the other, cocking a hip. "I wonder, Mrs. Thistledown, can you recall when it was that you saw this ghost?"

Mrs. Thistledown smoothed the creases from the skirt of her round gown as she thought the matter over. She had abandoned her apron the moment Charlie had told her that the duke had come to speak with her. She had exchanged her old dusting cap for a jaunty lace one. It was a matter of pride in Mrs. Thistledown's world. One did not appear unprepared for such an honor as a visit from one's duke, whether one was expecting him or not. And when one's duke asked a question of one, why, one did not just blurt out the first answer that came to mind. One strove to remember precisely.

"Can you recall when it was that you saw the ghost, Mrs. Thistledown?"

"It were always after sunset, your grace. I do remember that the shadows were always pooling whenever it appeared, like they do when the twilight comes upon us. Let me think. Four times during Lent, I saw it, and again on Easter Monday."

"On Easter Monday?"

"And three Saturdays in a row following that. But then I come down with the illness, your grace. I have not come out here to look for it since."

"And what did it look like, Mrs. Thistledown?"

"Wispy, it looked, like bits and pieces blowed together by the wind."

"I meant, were you able to tell if it was a man or a woman, Mrs. Thistledown?"

"Oh! It were a man, your grace. It did sit its horse astride. It were Owain Glyndwr, I reckon. Who else would it be but that old haunt? Everyone knows that when he has had enough of his castles in Wales, he comes here to Blackcastle and Barren Wycche to await his time to rise again. My goodness!" Mrs. Thistledown exclaimed abruptly, rising from the bench, her gaze fixed somewhere behind Berinwick.

The duke stepped away from the tree and turned to look. "What the deuce?" he said.

"It doesn't be a ghost," Mrs. Thistledown murmured, as a horse and rider came pounding up the lane. "Unless it be a ghost I have never seen afore."

"No, no, it's not a ghost, Mrs. Thistledown," Berinwick announced, recognizing the wildly running Norville and the man attempting to slow him. "That's our new parson. Gads!" he exclaimed as another rider came into view. "That's my mother attempting to chase him down."

Berinwick set off at a run. If he could reach the lane before Dempsey and the horse passed the cottage, he might be able to grab Norville's chin strap and bring the beast to a halt. His long legs carried him through the remainder of the garden and down a small slope to within eight yards of the lane when the Duchess of Berinwick's mare at last overtook the parson's steed.

Berinwick stumbled to a halt, his heart racing in his breast.

"She cannot possibly," he muttered. "Not riding sidesaddle."

But the duchess did reach out and she did seize Norville's chin strap. The parson continued to pull steadily back on the reins. They were both speaking to the animal. Berinwick could not understand the words, but he could hear the steady drone of their voices as they raced past him. His mother began to slow her mare, in turn slowing Norville, until side by side and step by step, the two animals reached a canter, a trot, a walk. Whereupon, the duchess loosed her hold on Norville and she and the parson turned both animals back in the direction of the cottage. Berinwick, his breathing rapid, his heart beating madly, finished his mad dash to the lane at a fast walk and stood in the middle of it, fists firmly planted on his hips, awaiting the two of them.

"Mother, are you all right?" he asked as she drew the white mare to a standstill before him. "What a fool thing to do! You could have fallen and been dragged to death. Or worse yet, trampled by both animals!"

"Yes, yes, I know all of that, William," the duchess replied.

"But who else was there to help stop that demon of a horse? You know how headstrong Norville can be when he's panicked. I ought to have warned Richard, but who on earth thought anything could happen on such a day as this with a parson on his back, to panic the beast? Help me down, if you please, William. I wish to descend at once."

Berinwick helped her from the saddle and set her feet firmly upon the road before he took his hands from her waist and turned to face Dempsey. "Gads! What the devil happened?" he exclaimed as he got a clear look at the man.

"Richard, you're bleeding!" Veronica cried, moving quickly toward him. "Your neckcloth is soaked with blood!"

"Is it?" asked Dempsey. He began to dismount, then paused in midair as if he could not decide whether to touch the ground or fly up into the clouds instead. "I'm a bit dizzy as well. I expect I've been shot, Veronica."

Berinwick hurried forward on the instant, put an arm out to steady the parson and assisted him, gently, the rest of the way to the ground.

Eight

"They were *what?*" Veronica asked, pausing in her attentions to Mr. Dempsey's ear to stare in disbelief at her son.

"Murdered," Berinwick replied quietly so the Widow Thistledown, busily preparing tea in her kitchen and attempting to keep the children out from underfoot at one and the same time, would not overhear. "I intended to tell you more gently, Mother, you and Hannah both, this evening. But now, with Dempsey having been shot—it's true, I'm afraid. Father, Mr. Thistledown, the footmen, all of them were murdered."

"But why? Why?" Veronica whispered hoarsely, lowering herself slowly down beside Dempsey on Mrs. Thistledown's little couch. "What did Jules ever do to make someone wish to kill him? And why did you not tell me?" she added, between grief and anger. "How dare you keep such a secret from me for so long, William?"

"The boy did not realize what had happened until last evening, Veronica," Dempsey offered before Berinwick could reply. "He believed it to be an accident just as everyone did. If I had not seen Harvey Langton's ghost for myself—"

"Harvey Langton's ghost?"

"Langton saw a ghost, Mother," Berinwick said, pulling a ladderback chair up before the duchess and Mr. Dempsey, swinging one leg over it and sitting, his arms crossed along the chair back. "Langton claimed a ghost intentionally caused Father's drag to overturn when first I spoke to him. Well, naturally, I did not believe it. How could I? A ghost? The ghost of Owain Glyndwr, no less? I will tell you the whole of it when we are back at Blackcastle, but Dempsey is bleeding again. I think you ought to finish tending that ear. And I am not a boy, Mr. Dempsey. Never refer to me as such again. As to what Father had ever done to deserve such a fate," he added, as his mother stood and directed her attention to the rector's wound, "he did kill Mr. Dight and he killed Mr. Dight's cohorts as well."

"A Pole!" Veronica gasped.

"Ouch!" Dempsey exclaimed.

"Oh! Oh! I am so sorry, Richard! I did not intend to tug on your poor ear so. William, do you honestly believe another Pole has come to avenge the last Pole's death? I cannot believe it. Is there never to be an end to these Poles? Is there never to be an end to this nonsense?"

"It is not nonsense, Mother. A significant number of gentlemen died when it all began. A dukedom was forfeit. Kings, countries, and thrones were involved in it."

"Yes, but that was during the Hundred Years War, William. Centuries ago. How can the war itself have lasted merely a hundred years and yet the Thornes' feud with the Poles continue into the present day? The last of their line died in 1525. Thus say the family journals. Thus say the Histories of England. Thus said your father when first he told me the tale. How then come the Thornes to be fending off attacks by Poles in every generation since? I could not credit it at all until the Reverend Mr. Dight appeared here to kill your papa. A Pole of Wyke, he was, two hundred and fifty years after the last of his line fell in battle. How can that be? I do not think such a thing *can* be. And when your papa discovered Mr. Dight's ancestry and his treacherous intentions and killed him first, that must have been the end of it. He must have been the last of his lot. There cannot be any more Poles!"

"Hush, Mama. Mrs. Thistledown will hear you."

"I do not care if the entire world hears me. It is all some great hoax. I do not believe in the Poles of Wyke, I tell you! I believe in them less than I believe in the Stiperstone Strangler or the ghost of Owain Glyndwr or the spirits of Jane and Ellen at the Fallen Dog!"

"Shhhh, Veronica," Dempsey murmured, drawing her down beside him on the couch and giving her hand a comforting pat. "Here comes Mrs. Thistledown with our tea. We will discuss the whole of this later, Vernie, I promise," he added in a whisper, pretending to look over his shoulder for a moment so Berinwick would not hear his added words. "I will meet you tonight at ten o'clock at your gatehouse."

Tom Hasty spread word of the ill-achieved attack on her grace and the Reverend Mr. Dempsey to every ear available when he arrived at Blackcastle. The groom had been stunned when the duke and the duchess had accompanied Mr. Dempsey—with one of his ears awkwardly bandaged—back to the rectory. Hasty's insides had ruffled up like the feathers on a cock's outsides when her grace had explained to him about the shooting. Hasty's pride had been injured by it. He ought to have been up beside her grace, or at least he ought to have been riding behind her grace and the parson. He certainly ought not to have been diddling around the church, helping Langton with this and that.

"My presence might well have discouraged the attack completely," he confided in his mates that evening in the stables. "And if it did not, at the very least I'd have ridden the dastard to ground and battered him soundly about the head, believe me."

"Much good that would have done our new rector, Tom," mumbled Overfield, his head bowed low as he stitched at a piece of harness, "beating the dastard soundly *after* he shot the poor parson."

"But at least then we'd know who the villain was, wouldn't we?" young Johnny asked over his shoulder as he finished currying the last of the cart horses. "I wonder were it the same man you met in the wood, Mr. Lancaster?"

"I wonder," Davey Lancaster replied, offering a freshly made cup of salve to Hasty for Triumph's hock.

"We won't ever know now," Hasty sighed. "I was not with 'em and the blighter has got clear away because of it. What was I thinking, to believe she'd be safe in a parson's company—even a parson as fit and fine as the Reverend Mr. Dempsey?"

"She'd be safe? Her grace?" queried Overfield. "You think the dastard were aiming at her grace?"

"Well, I can't say one way or the other now, can I, as I wasn't there to begin with. But I ask you, Jem Overfield, and you, too, Davey Lancaster, and you, Johnny—who would go shooting at a clergyman who has just barely arrived in the county?"

"The duke?" offered Johnny. "Well, we don't none of us know but that the preacher might already have stuck a thorn or two in our duke's side."

"No, that preacher ain't stuck any thorns in our duke's side," Overfield murmured. "Why, he ain't preached one sermon yet. Besides, our duke would not go shooting at a man from hiding. Walk straight up before the dastard, he would, and invite him to taste the tip of his sword."

Word of Mr. Dempsey's injury, accompanied by Tom Hasty's speculation that her grace rather than the parson had been the object of the attack, traveled from the stables to the Blackcastle kitchens, from the kitchens to all the underservants, from the underservants to the upper servants until the entire staff was abuzz with it.

In much the same manner, the tale of how the new parson had abruptly acquired a most distinctive notch in his ear rode into Barren Wycche in Mr. Langton's dog cart along with Mr. Langton himself, his wife, and his eldest daughter.

"I were that shocked, I were," Mrs. Langton mumbled time and time again. "Were you not shocked, Mr. Langton? I were that shocked! And all that blood on his neckcloth. Who would have thought a parson's ear to have all that blood in it?"

"Thank goodness it were not her grace's blood," breathed

Beth, aquiver with the news and anxious beyond anything to share it with her sisters, her friends, and her betrothed. "Tom Hasty says as how he thinks the shot were intended for our duchess and not the Reverend Mr. Dempsey at all."

"Never!" declared Mrs. Langton. "What a thing to say. As if that sweet lady had ever wronged anyone in her entire life."

"But Ma, who did the Reverend Mr. Dempsey offend? He's not had a bit of time to raise anyone's ire hereabout. Not yet. Has he, Pa?"

"Only the duke's," Langton replied, counting in his mind the number of free drinks this tale would cause to be set before him tonight at the Fallen Dog. The sheer enormity of his expectations on that front prompted him to wish he had a hound of his own to lie under his table at the pub and share in his good fortune. "Not that I think for a moment that our duke actually shot the man, Bethany," he added. "No, it were not him. He'd not have made such a muck of it, our duke. He'd not have done it from hiding, either. Walked right up to the parson and parted his hair with the business end of a pistol, he would have done."

"Then who do you think did it, Pa? And who do you think was meant to be hit? Were the shot intended for her grace?"

"Aye, I believe so, though I cannot say for certain, m'dear. A dreadful thing, when a duchess cannot ride the roads surrounding her son's lands without being put upon so. And as to who did the dire deed, I cannot imagine. It were not the ghost, is all I know. It were not the ghost of Owain Glyndwr. He would not know the first thing about making use of a long gun."

By seven o'clock that evening all five daughters of the Langton household were twittering away about the new parson's ear and the danger that had come so very close to the duchess. Young Mr. Pervis, Beth's betrothed, who had joined the family for dinner, carried the news home to the Pervis household. Tomorrow, he and his father and brothers would certainly spread word of it among the haymakers with as much relish as the younger Langton daughters would tell the tale to every one of their friends in Barren Wycche. Thus, together with those persons in whom their mother and father confided, word of the attack was bound to spread through the village, the farms, the county, like windblown fire through dried grass. Within a day or two everyone, Squire Tofar and his family included, would know of it.

The Blackcastle gatehouse was old, stone, and circular, like the top of a castle tower lopped off by a giant's broadsword and set down by the giant's hand at the entrance to Blackcastle's drive. At ten o'clock that evening the Reverend Mr. Dempsey stepped down from Norville's back, set his lantern on the ground, tied the horse to the nearest tree, knelt to twiddle Theophilus's ears and recover his lantern, then strolled up to the gatehouse. A light winked out at him through a narrow window beside the door. He peered in and saw a lantern glimmering on a small table. He knocked and the door swung inward.

"You did come," Veronica said, drawing him inside and then smiling as Theophilus padded confidently in behind him. "And you brought Theo."

"Yes, well, all of the Langtons have gone for the day and I did not dare to leave him at the rectory alone, Veronica. What with all these ghosts running about, the rectory is not a safe place for a dog alone, especially when no one is in the kitchen baking sweetmeats to occupy his mind."

Veronica stooped down to pet the hound, her dress pooling around her. "How are you, my dear sir? Fit and fine? Your master brought you as a chaperone, I think, and not because he feared to leave you at the rectory at all."

"Arrrrrruph!" Theophilus agreed, his right paw firmly ensconced in Veronica's hand and his long tongue lolling happily. "There is a log fire laid, Richard, if you care to light it, and there are more candles set about. I have not got to them all as yet."

I am babbling like a schoolgirl at her first grown-up party,

Veronica thought, amazed. She released the hound's paw, stood up and attempted to call herself to order. With shaking hands, she removed her hat and set it on a circular table in the center of the room. What is wrong with me? she wondered. My heart is fluttering like a moth at midnight, and I am growing so very warm suddenly. Perhaps I am coming down with a fever. No, of course I am not. It is merely that—that I am alone in the gatehouse with a gentleman who is not my husband.

But it is Richard, she told herself. It is not as though he is some rake with whom I am keeping an illicit tryst. It is merely Richard Dempsey from Arrandell. Richard, whom I once loved like a little brother—whom I still love like a little brother. Richard Randolph Dempsey, whom I would trust with my very life.

Really, Veronica, she scolded herself as she turned to discover Dempsey with his back to her, busily lighting candles. Have you lost your mind? Your husband has been murdered, your son fired upon and you likely fired upon as well, and yet here you stand, taking note of the breadth of Richard's shoulders and growing all shivery inside simply from recalling how it felt to kiss his lips, to touch his cheek, to feel his arms around you.

They'd felt so very strong and comforting in the morning room, his arms, she thought, as the parson moved on to the next candelabra. Whenever I find myself crying again, I shall find myself wishing for Richard to hold me while I do. Most likely he does not even suspect the extent of the comfort he provided me. No, nor the courage his words enkindled in my heart that day.

"I thought Berinwick assured me that Blackcastle had no gatekeeper," Dempsey said.

"No, we do not. Oh, you mean the table and the hearth and the candles?"

"And that sofa and those chairs and this very pretty carpet and that painting on the wall there," Dempsey replied as he lighted candle after candle.

"It is a cozy little place," Veronica replied. "I have always liked it. I cannot think why I have not come here in all the months since Julian's death. It is filled with memories of him, you know. Happy memories."

"Of your husband?"

"Indeed. Jules loved to come out here and . . ."

"And what?"

"P-play dragon at the gate, not that it is any of your concern, Richard Dempsey," the duchess replied, her eyes shining in the flames of myriad candles as her cheeks grew redder and redder with thoughts of herself and Julian and then, most shamefully, thoughts of Richard in Julian's place.

"Dragon at the gate? How do you play that? With cards?"

"No, n-not with cards. Do sit down, Richard. How are you feeling? Does your ear hurt terribly?"

"It merely stings now and then when the wind is in the wrong direction," Dempsey replied, sitting down on the sofa before the hearth on which a fire now sizzled and leaped. "Do not attempt to play the gracious hostess, Veronica. There is no need to take my ear into consideration or to inquire if I will have tea. I wished to meet you here so that we could speak privately, so that I can do something to help settle your mind."

"I know, Richard. I must have seemed most hysterical at the Widow Thistledown's. I cannot think what possessed me."

"You had every reason to be upset, my dear. You had just been told that your husband was murdered." Dempsey patted the space beside him on the sofa. "Come and sit here beside me and we will discuss ghosts and Poles and spirits rising from the mist. Anything and everything. Whatever will set your mind at ease, Vernie. It was a great shock to you, the news of your husband's murder. It was like losing him all over again, I should think."

"No, it was not as dreadful as that," Veronica replied. She walked around the end of the sofa and sat stiffly down beside him on the very edge of the cushion, her back straight as a fence post, her hands clasped together in her lap, her gaze fastened on the fire. "But I was stunned by it, Richard. To think of someone causing the coach to overturn purposely. What sort of a person must one be to do such a thing as that? And to kill Jules by killing them all! I cannot conceive of such evil. As though the lives of Mr. Thistledown and the footmen were meaningless. As though no one would care one way or the other that those innocents should die. As though they, who had done nothing to offend, deserved death for no other reason than that they worked for the Duke of Berinwick."

"It was a heinous act," Dempsey agreed, and then fell silent. The sheer rigidity of her posture beside him dashed the words he might have said from his tongue. He reached out to touch her. His hand moved lightly, up and down, caressing her back, attempting to ease muscles he imagined taut with fear. The very action sent Dempsey's heart tumbling into something approaching despair. How he should like to touch her in a much different manner—caress her for a much different reason.

If I had been born sooner, richer, and with a title, he thought, I might have courted and married this glorious woman myself. She might even now be *my* wife and be living with me a considerably different life than she is now. *I* would be living a considerably different life as well—a life devoid of loneliness, a life overflowing with love, joy, laughter.

"A heinous act," he repeated quietly, "and one I cannot explain. But that is over and done with, Veronica. We cannot prevent what has already occurred. We can, however, prevent this villain from perpetrating more evil, from dispensing more pain. You must not be afraid, not of him, for I will find this fellow and put an end to his evil. I promise you that."

Veronica sighed, the steady stroke of Dempsey's hand along her back and the earnest-yet-serene tone of his voice bringing her a most remarkable sense of peace. She could feel her body give up its unnatural tautness bit by bit. "I am not afraid, Richard," she whispered as she took her feet from the rose-red carpet and tucked them up under her on the sofa.

"Not with you beside me." She leaned gently against him, rested her head thankfully on his shoulder. "But I am so very weary. Old and weary. I wish I had never grown up at all. I was happy in Arrandell with your mama and your papa and you, Richard, and your brothers. There was no evil there, in Arrandell."

"I believe there was, Vernie," Dempsey replied, his arm going comfortably around her as they both gazed reflectively into the flames dancing before them on the hearth. "We were merely too innocent, then, to recognize it for what it was. We were too young, you and I, to be involved with it. But I know what you mean. I do. And if I could carry you back to Arrandell and our youth, I would do it this instant. You do not believe that this person who caused your husband's death and fired on us this afternoon is actually descended from these apparently legendary Poles of Wyke, eh?"

"No. Yes. No. I don't know. I cannot imagine it. Where do they come from? Do they propagate like rabbits? Julian claimed Mr. Dight was a Pole, the man's name notwithstanding. He claimed he had proof of it and of Mr. Dight's intentions. And he did not just jump up and run the man through at the pulpit," she added, the fingers of her right hand going to play thoughtlessly with the buttons of Dempsey's coat. "That's what William told you, is it not? That his papa simply walked up to the pulpit and ran the man through?"

"Um-hmmm."

"Well, Jules did not. Julian stood up in the church and accused Mr. Dight of planning to murder us all in our beds, steal Blackcastle's treasures, and burn our home to the ground. 'No matter what you call yourself, you are a Pole,' he said. Whereupon Mr. Dight replied, 'I share in their blood through my great-great-great grandmother and I am proud of it,' and then he took a pistol from out his pulpit."

"Great heavens."

"Indeed. But before Mr. Dight could so much as cock and fire the thing, Jules pushed William and me to the floor, leaped from our pew into the nave with his rapier in hand,

and ran the man through. It was then that three itinerant laborers, whom Mr. Dight had begged that Jules hire for the harvesting, charged up the aisle. They had knives, each of them. Our own people attempted to stop their advance, but it is such a short way from the narthex to the nave, and none of our people had any weapons at all. Several of our men were wounded before Julian closed with the trio and ran them through, one after the other. Shhh-wish. Shhh-wish. Shhh-wish."

Her soft imitation of the sound of the rapier's bite sent chills up Dempsey's spine as it whispered through the room. His arm tightened around her.

"How can it be, Richard?" Veronica asked quietly. "How can revenge go on and on and on? How can it come to us from men whose names are Dight and Clay and Everrette, whose blood has been thinned through time until what is left of the Pole blood in them can be naught but a drop or two? Why would mothers urge their sons to avenge the wrongs of ancestors they never knew and would not recognize should those very ancestors rise from their graves before them?"

"Perhaps it is not old wrongs they avenge, Veronica," Dempsey murmured. "Perhaps it has little or nothing to do with their ancestors at all. Have you ever thought that revenge is simply an excuse—and what truly drives fellows like that is envy and greed?"

"Envy? Greed?"

"Blackcastle overflows with treasures. It might well be tales of treasure passed down from one generation to the next that draw these evil men here and they only call it revenge to make is seem more honorable."

"I had not thought of that," Veronica replied. "I see nothing honorable in revenge, but I expect men sometimes do. And there have always been treasures about. The Thornes were a rich and powerful family from the earliest days."

"Which reminds me," Dempsey replied, attempting to gaze down at her without moving more than his eyes because his whole being was awed to have her rest against him and his greatest wish was not to disturb her by any movement at all.

"Reminds you of what, Richard?"

"Of the pendant that you showed me. When did you lose it? You never did say."

"Oh, my goodness!" Veronica's head left his shoulder. Her shoes found the floor. She sat up very straight and the abruptness of her movement startled a woof out of Theophilus. "It went missing the very Sunday that Julian skewered Mr. Dight and his cohorts. I had given it to William to play with in the church, to keep him occupied, you know. And the next time I thought to look for it, it was nowhere to be found and William could not remember where he'd put it."

"Did you search the church building for it?"

"We searched everywhere—in the church, in Blackcastle, along the road—but it was not to be found."

"Well, now that I hear what actually happened at the time, Veronica, I wonder. Do you think that amidst all the excitement, William actually did drop your pendant in the church and someone associated with Dight took it? Is it possible that there were more than three men joined with Dight in his scheme? Might that fourth man have stolen the pendant and taken it home with him and now returned?"

"I—I don't know. Wait. There was a man called Tweed—an old, scholarly gentleman whom Jules hired to help catalogue his collection—but he came to us months before Mr. Dight appeared, and even if he has returned, he could not possibly be doing these things, because he would be perfectly ancient by now."

"And yet this Mr. Tweed comes to mind. Why, Vernie?"

"B-because he took his leave of us the day following the incident in the church. I did not think anything of it at the time. He was such a quiet man, you know, and appalled by what had happened. I expected that he would be unwilling to go on working for Julian, but I did not think he would leave us the very next day. Jules called him a poltroon and bid him good riddance."

"And you have never seen this Tweed person again? Think, Veronica. Is there anyone new to the neighborhood who might actually be Tweed returned?"

"No," she replied with a shake of her head. "No one at all who might be Mr. Tweed. He merely came to mind, as I said, because of his leaving the very next day."

"Is there anyone who resembles him? Someone who might be a younger brother, perhaps? Or a son? Someone newly arrived? Well, not newly arrived because it is nine months since your husband's death. Still, did anyone come to work at Blackcastle at about that time?"

"I—I cannot think of anyone. Patrick McClane came to us after David Hancock disappeared, but that was a good four months before Julian's death. And we were lucky to get him, this Patrick McClane. He had just left the Earl of Roderickton's employ with glowing letters of reference and was on his way to seek a position with the Marquess of Erndine. But he paused for a night at the inn and Jules met him in the Fallen Dog. The man so liked our little part of the country that Jules convinced him to come to Blackcastle and manage our farm instead of Erndine's."

"Someone disappeared?" Dempsey asked.

"Our old farm manager, yes. One day he was in his office and the next day he was nowhere to be found. Richard! Could it be that David Hancock did not disappear at all? That he is hiding somewhere and responsible for all of this?"

"He would know of all the treasures at Blackcastle. And know his way about the lanes and the woods as well," Dempsey mused. "And if he was in some way related to this Tweed person, and if this Tweed person actually was one of Dight's associates and did steal your pendant . . ."

The Duchess of Berinwick threw her arms around the parson's neck and kissed him mightily on the lips. "Richard, you are the most wonderful, intelligent, insightful man in all the world!" she exclaimed, once their lips parted and she sat back from him a bit. "I should never have thought anything more about the pendant if you had not come here tonight. No, and

I should still be thinking in terms of vengeance taken on us from the grave. But it is not some vengeful Pole who killed Julian and shot at William and at us. Not some dastardly Pole come to put an end to the Thornes of Barren Wycche. It is some unknown cohort of Mr. Dight's—possibly even our missing David Hancock—hoping to steal Julian's collection and anything else he can cart away. Oh, Richard, I am so relieved. You have not only given me a new perspective on all that has happened, but you may possibly have ferreted out the very man behind it all."

"Possibly, but there were a lot of ifs in there, Vernie. It is merely a theory. One of many possibilities."

"Yes, well, it is a distinct possibility. And I can understand greed and envy, Richard. It was the seemingly endless appearance of single-minded Poles in search of vengeance that had me thoroughly distraught. You are truly the most marvelous man."

"Why are you looking at me in that particular fashion, Vernie? Are you going to kiss me again?" Dempsey asked as she stared boldly into his eyes.

"Yes, Richard, I believe I am. You won't mind, will you?"

"Not at all," he replied, his eyes filled with mirth. "You may kiss me to your heart's content." Whereupon he rose from the sofa, opened his arms to her, and enclosed her within them.

Dempsey could not think what possessed him. Truth be told, he was not thinking much at all. It was the sweetest, soundest, most impractical kiss that had ever come his way and he did not care if he turned blue from lack of breath, or fainted from palpitations of the heart, or if his ear fell off from the way Veronica's arm was pressing against it. He did not want the kiss to end. That was why, when Theophilus pawed at his leg, Dempsey nudged the old hound away.

Theo sat back on his haunches and peered up at his master, mystified. He had not been nudged aside in a con-

siderable number of years. Observing, in his nearsighted
world, that his master and the lovely lady—whom his master had acquired shortly before he had acquired the new
horse—observing that they appeared to be in some distress,
Theophilus pawed questioningly at his master's leg again.
This time he was ignored completely. To the old hound *that*
was confirmation that something was wrong. Never, in all
of their life together, had Theo's master ever completely
ignored him.

Theophilus sat back and peered upward again with great
consideration. While his nose told him clearly that two separate people stood before him, his eyes said that the two had
somehow become one. It occurred to the hound that perhaps
the lady was stuck to his master in the same manner that a
fierce sheet of wallpaper had once stuck to him in his puppy-
hood. Recalling the ruthlessness of that wallpaper and the
mighty struggle that had ensued, Theophilus growled deep in
his throat. Then he stood and rushed at the two of them, leaping up between them and scrabbling madly in an effort to pry
them apart before they stuck too tightly and would require a
trip to the pump, a dousing with great globs of water, and a
thorough rubbing with a bar of soap.

"What the deuce!" Dempsey exclaimed as the kiss was
necessarily ended by the hound's onslaught.

"Oh! Richard! Help!" Veronica laughed breathlessly, attempting to keep from stumbling backward out of his arms.

"Arr-roooohhhh!" bayed Theophilus. His feet touched the
floor and he launched himself again. "Arr-rooooohhhhh!"

"Theo, no! Cease and desist this instant!" Dempsey commanded around a great guffaw of laughter. But the dog forced
his body between them again and then again, baying and
scrabbling, scrabbling and baying.

"What the deuce do you think you're d-doing, sir?"
Dempsey asked, but it was much too late for such a question
as that. Veronica began to tilt away from Dempsey. Dempsey
struggled to keep her upright and they both lost their balance.
Down they and Theo all fell onto the rose-red carpet between

the sofa and the hearth—Dempsey, Veronica, and Theophilus, all in a pile filled with laughter, four kicking, scrabbling dog feet, and one long, wildly licking tongue.

Truly, it was an amazing sight and Berinwick was especially amazed by it as he threw open the gatehouse door and froze on the threshold. "Wh-what the devil is going on here?" he said when he finally caught the breath he had lost from his mad dash along the drive. "Mother?"

"Oh! Oh, William! It is n-nothing, really," the duchess assured him, her eyes bright with laughter as she attempted to rise from the floor.

Berinwick stalked across the room to her at once and helped her to her feet. "No sooner did I walk out to check on Triumph than I heard the Hound of Hades baying down here," he muttered, wrapping his arm possessively around his mother. "All I could think of was that murder and mayhem were being perpetrated upon someone in the gatehouse."

"N-no. No murder. No mayhem, William," the duchess responded. "Well, perhaps a bit of mayhem," she amended, stifling a giggle. "Richard? Are you all right?"

"Yes," the parson replied, struggling to find a deep breath, a serious expression, and his feet all at one and the same time.

Frowning, keeping one arm firmly around his mother, Berinwick offered Dempsey his free hand and tugged the parson to his feet. "What the deuce are you doing here at this time of night—in this gatehouse—alone with my mother?" he demanded.

"We were not alone," the duchess replied before Dempsey could do so. "You forgot the Hound of Hades, William."

"Yes, well, hound or not, you were rolling on the floor together!"

"All three of us," Dempsey nodded and choked on a chuckle. "I cannot think what possessed him, Veronica. Truly, I cannot. Sometimes Theophilus is the most perplexing animal."

"Not near as perplexing as his master," Berinwick muttered. "I have called men out for less than this—rolling about on the floor with my mother and that—that—dog. You're a parson, for gawd's sake. You ought to know better."

"It was an accident, William, truly," the duchess protested, intimidated by the glare in her son's eye. "We merely wished to speak about something without disturbing anyone at the house. Nothing more."

"Yes, well, I hope you have finished your conversation for the night because I am walking you back up the drive myself," Berinwick declared, escorting her toward the doorway, his arm still firmly around her. He seized her hat from the table and handed it to her as they passed by. "Which of these lanterns is yours, Mother? This one? Fine. Extinguish the candles, Dempsey," Berinwick said over his shoulder. "Bank that fire, refrain from moving any of the furniture, take your lantern and your hound, and go home. Your ear is bleeding again, by the way.

"What the devil did you do to start his ear bleeding again, Mother?" Berinwick queried, his attention once again focused on the lady beside him as he escorted her through the door and into the drive. "Never mind. Never mind. I've a notion to set more of his blood flowing, but I won't. Not tonight."

Dempsey moved to the door and watched them as they strolled up the drive toward Blackcastle. His laughter had settled into a wide smile, and the smile was likely to linger all the way home—not merely because of the kiss and the tumble, but because every step of the way up the drive, for as long as they were within Dempsey's sight, Berinwick kept his arm possessively around his mother and not once did Veronica turn to stone, cringe, or appear distressed by her son's touch.

Hannah turned down the last of her lamps, padded across her bedchamber floor to curl up cozily on the pillow-strewn windowseat, and stared out into the night. She had not heard Theophilus bay. She could not see her mother and brother strolling companionably up the front drive. She hadn't the least notion that, at that very moment, a smiling Mr. Dempsey was turning back into the gatehouse to bank the fire and snuff the candles, with Theo padding happily along behind him. She neither saw nor heard nor considered the likelihood of any of these things because Hannah's bedchamber window was the entrance to a land of dreams, and once she chose to gaze through it, the real world had a distinct tendency to disappear completely from her mind.

At the very rear of the west wing of Blackcastle, Hannah's bedchamber window overlooked a wide expanse of lawn bounded on the west by a crumbling rock wall which stood in some places as much as three feet high and in others merely the height of two rocks, one piled atop the other. To the north of the green, Grydwynn Wood sent out its creepers and set its saplings, pondering invasion, considering how far it might grow before anyone noticed it and beat it back again. On the south an underground spring bubbled to the surface just beyond the walls of Blackcastle itself and meandered along for the length of the green, then descended again into the earth, not to reappear for three miles and more. A tiny flock of sheep roamed the green in spring and summer to keep the grass well manicured, but their number varied day by day because one or two or sometimes as many as five of them would be seduced into the maze that stood in the very center of the lawn, equidistant between Blackcastle and the crumbling wall. Fashioned long ago from holly, hawthorn, and wild rose bushes—at the instigation of her great-great-great grandmother, her father had said—the flowering walls of the maze rose eight feet into the air and apparently held a mystical lure for young girls and sheep alike, for Hannah had required rescuing from its clutches by this shepherd or that as many times as the sheep had.

In the light of a moon grown fat and round, the entire scene shimmered before Hannah's eyes like a faery tale world that could be revealed only to a princess who was pure of heart and whose imagination proved strong and innocent enough to people it with the wizards and knights, the witches and dragons who dwelt there. Hannah was peering down now upon a knight in glimmering armor who stood magnificently outlined before the entrance to the maze. His warrior steed—all flowing mane, streaming tail, and rippling muscle—stood proudly behind him. At first, she thought the knight to be Sir Galahad or Sir Lancelot, but then she knew it must be King Arthur himself.

So lost was Hannah in her imaginary world that it did not seem at all odd to spy King Arthur about to meet his Guinevere in the middle of a magical maze. Not odd at all. Especially not to a young lady who had grown up peopling this particular place with all manner of persons she had met in stories and poems. Especially not to a young lady whose eyelids were heavy with sleep and whose mind had taken the first tentative step into dreams.

And then King Arthur's head fell off.

Hannah's eyes opened wide on the instant. Hannah's mind eschewed dreams at once and came directly to attention.

"What on earth?" she murmured, rubbing at her eyes with both fists and staring back out the window. King Arthur was just then scooping his head from the lawn—except that it was not his head at all, because he already had a head. And the horse looked a good deal less like a knight's steed and a great deal more like Hannah's old Penn dipped in cream. And whoever King Arthur truly was, he was not going into the maze. No, he was not. Apparently, he had just exited it.

"I must tell Will about this," Hannah said, rising from the windowseat and beginning to search the chamber for her slippers. "He'll want to know of it at once."

Berinwick gazed at his sister, bewildered. "Tell me again, Hannah," he said. "I hear you speaking, but I cannot seem to comprehend what you say. You came all the way from your bedchamber to mine to tell me that . . . ?"

"There was a gentleman in the maze."

"But he is not in the maze now."

"No, Will, not now. I doubt he is anywhere near the maze now. By the time I found my slippers and relit one of the oil lamps and hurried down to Papa's study—where I did expect you to be at this hour, you know, because you are forever going through Papa's things until the wee hours of the morning. By the time I did all of that and then turned about and rushed all the way across the central wing and up the stairs to find you—"

"Yes, but what about the man?" Berinwick retrieved the coat he had just doffed from his valet's hand and waved that gentleman out of the chamber. "Go read a book or have a cup of tea, Nordstrom," he commanded. "It appears I am about to go for another stroll. I'll ring when I come back. The man was in the maze and he dropped his head, you said, Hannah?"

"I said that I *thought* his head fell off."

"Yes, that was it. Did it?"

"Did it what?"

"Did his head fall off?"

Hannah breathed an exasperated sigh, placed her fists firmly on her hips, and glowered up at him. "Will, do cease acting like a ninny. It was not his head that fell off, but some old hat, I should think. And if you had been where you ought to have been, we might have gone directly out to the maze and caught the fellow and we would even now know who he is and what he was doing there. Who knows but that he was not the very man who murdered Papa and attacked Mama and the Reverend Mr. Dempsey this very afternoon."

"Who knows but that the man you saw was not the Reverend Mr. Dempsey himself," Berinwick replied, shrugging his coat back on.

"Mr. Dempsey? Why would the Reverend Mr. Dempsey be—"

"I don't know. But that gentleman has a knack for being places he ought not to be and doing things he ought not to do," Berinwick muttered as he set a footstool beside his armoire, stepped up on it, and took from the top of that grand cabinet a tooled leather box. "I discovered him just a short time ago, Hannah, in the gatehouse with Mother."

"The Reverend Mr. Dempsey?"

"Yes."

"In *our* gatehouse?"

"Just so."

"Alone with Mama?"

"Well, not precisely. The Hound of Hades was with them." Berinwick opened the box and took one of a pair of silver dueling pistols from it. He loaded it, primed it, then set it back and took out the other. "I shall go out to the maze and see what I can see," he murmured, loading and priming the second pistol as well. "I doubt I'll discover anything. But the moon is nearly full and, if I take a lantern with me as well, perhaps I stand a chance of discovering footprints in the dew or some such thing."

"I'm coming with you."

Berinwick gazed down at his younger sister and almost grinned. "Not in your nightdress and robe, you're not, m'dear, and there's no time for you to run back to your chamber and don something more suitable."

"But, Will—"

"Hush, Hannah. I shan't deny you a share in the fun. Take this pistol. You will accompany me as far as the west door and wait there. If I am luckier than I expect to be, I may yet flush out this rabbit and perhaps be able to send him scampering in your direction."

"And I am to shoot him if you do?"

"No, no, you are only to shoot near him, Hannah. For all we know it might actually be the Reverend Mr. Dempsey and Mother will never forgive us if we are the cause of his being shot a second time in one day."

How the tale of the headless intruder in the maze came to be known by all and sundry, Berinwick could not think. He had failed to flush the fellow out, no shots had been fired, he and Hannah had gone quietly off to their beds, and no one had been privy to a bit of it. Nordstrom's presence at the beginning and the end of the episode had completely escaped Berinwick's mind. The valet had helped him into his bedclothes when he'd returned from the maze and had carried his dew-covered boots down to be polished, just as he ought to have done, and the duke had given him no further thought. Certainly it had not occurred to him that Nordstrom would tell as much of the tale as he knew at breakfast in the upper servants' dining room the following morning. But Nordstrom had done just that, and the story had flown about Blackcastle as swiftly as had the tale of the attack on her grace and the Reverend Mr. Dempsey. And, in the manner of that first tale, this story, too, blossomed and bloomed and burst forth to send its seeds riding on the wind into Barren Wycche and beyond.

It was not surprising, then, that on the Sunday following, when the Reverend Mr. Dempsey stepped up to the pulpit beneath the semi-patched roof of St. Milburga's of the Wood to read himself into his living, every man, woman, and child of Blackcastle and Barren Wycche, and some from the surrounding counties—from the Duke of Berinwick to Ellie, the scullery maid, from Squire Tofar to little Charlie Thistledown, from George Miller, the miller, to Prudence Angser, the woodcutter's daughter, to the five wandering Welshmen Berinwick had hired to work in the fields and Tom Hasty, Davey Lancaster, Trewellyn, Overfield, and Arnold Nordstrom—pressed into the nave, overflowed into the narthex, spilled out through the newly repaired doors, and gathered in the churchyard to keep their eyes and ears open and their hands at the ready as he did so.

It mattered not that some of them were Catholic and some Quaker and so not members of the Church of England or St. Milburga's congregation at all. It mattered not that the church was still in disrepair. It mattered not that the new rector had a bandage over one ear or that an old hound lay beside the pulpit, yawning from time to time, as Dempsey read the

Thirty-nine Articles of his installation. What mattered was that some dastard had had the audacity to shoot a long gun at this new rector in the presence of the Duchess of Berinwick, and likely had been aiming at the duchess herself. What mattered was that some unknown, headless person had been seen prowling about the grounds of Blackcastle—at the maze, for goodness' sake, where no one but the shepherds ever went—and had likely had murder and mayhem on his mind. What mattered—what truly mattered—was that the Thornes of Barren Wycche appeared to be under attack by a person or persons unknown. And such a thing was not to be taken lightly. No, not by anyone. So they had all come to church and they had all come to church prepared.

Because the Duke of Berinwick sat in what remained of the Thorne family pew with his mother and his sister, the Reverend Mr. Dempsey could not help but notice the rapier that Berinwick wore. He wore it in a scabbard at his side like a soldier. But what the Reverend Mr. Dempsey could not see was Squire Tofar's miniature pistol, the knife in Angser the woodcutter's boot, the ready fists in the Welshmen's pockets, the gleaming and newly sharpened scissors and penknives residing in the ladies' reticules. Truth be told, every adult in attendance had come to this first of Mr. Dempsey's Sunday services bearing some sort of weapon with which to protect and defend the Thornes—to protect them to the death if need be, and to protect the new rector, as well, because rumors had also reached their ears that the Duchess of Berinwick was, perhaps, fond of this Reverend Mr. Dempsey and who could guess what might happen between the two of them if the congregation and the visitors could manage to keep this rector alive for a goodly long time.

It was somewhat bewildering to Mr. Dempsey, then, that when he spoke of the Church of St. Milburga's in his sermon as a sanctuary, as a refuge from violence, as a place where forgiveness could be obtained and reparations made, the entire gathering began to shift and murmur uneasily. And it proved even more bewildering to him that, at the end of the service, when he stepped out into the churchyard to greet all who had attended, a great many people tripped over their tongues when they spoke to him or refused to meet his eyes.

"What the deuce did I say, Veronica?" he asked when he and the duchess stood alone before the church entrance. "I worked a goodly number of hours on that sermon. What did I say to make the lot of them so fidgety?"

Nine

"What a lovely place," Dempsey observed as Veronica, her arm tucked neatly through his, led him across the green toward Blackcastle's maze the following Thursday afternoon. Theophilus loped on before them, merrily pretending to chase the sheep who baaaed submissively as he approached and trotted a few feet off when he reached them, thus increasing the hound's happiness while not overexerting themselves in the least.

"Theo certainly appears to enjoy it here," Veronica smiled.

"You need not worry, Vernie. I promise you he'll not harm your sheep or fill them with fear by chasing them everywhere."

"No, and you must not worry, either, Richard, for I promise our sheep will not harm Theo. I believe they will remain content simply to laugh at him as they are doing now. I have not been inside the maze for years, you know."

"But you do remember its secrets?"

"Its secrets?"

"How to reach the center and get back out again? What stands at its center?"

"Well, I believe I remember the way in, but William has a map, just in case I have forgotten a turn here or there. And as to what stands at the center, you will have to wait and discover that for yourself."

"Mama, do hurry," Hannah called from the entrance to the living puzzle. "Will says it is taking you and Mr. Dempsey longer to cross the green than it took him to locate Papa's map—and it took Will a full week to do that."

"And that will tell you how impatient my son is to be inside the thing, Richard. I refuse to run, Hannah. You may tell your brother so. And no, the two of you may not set off by yourselves. We have agreed that we shall all go in together."

"But will we all come out together?" Berinwick asked, as he stepped out from the entrance of the maze, stood behind Hannah, and placed his hands on her shoulders. "Will any of us ever emerge again?"

Hannah giggled.

"I don't expect we shall meet any ghosts at two o'clock in the afternoon, eh, your grace?" Dempsey queried as he and the duchess came to a halt before the two young people. "Theophilus! Come here at once, sir. Enough nonsense with the sheep!"

"It ought to be perfectly safe at this hour," Berinwick observed as the hound trotted to his master's side. "You had best put the lead on Theo, though. We don't want him wandering off without us. And I'll tie a rope around Hannah so we won't lose her, either."

"Oh, Will." Hannah rolled her eyes in exasperation as Dempsey bent to tie the lead around Theophilus's neck.

"But if you should wander off inside the maze, Hannah, you are likely to become lost."

"Will, stop," Hannah hissed.

"I don't wish to lose you, dearest little sister. We both know how easily one can become turned around in there. You know it especially well, I think."

"Will, cease and desist," Hannah pleaded.

"Hannah knows it especially well?" the duchess asked. "Hannah, you have been inside the maze? After your papa and I explicitly forbade you to do so?"

"I know I was forbidden to enter it ever, Mama, but I could not believe that you and Papa actually meant that I should not set one foot inside of it. Why, to grow up with such a remarkable thing calling to me day in and day out, to stare down at it night after night from my own bedchamber, surely you and Papa knew I must go inside if only for a little way."

"Surely, you and Father knew that, Mother," Berinwick agreed. "Even I knew that. I will not mention, of course, Hannah, just how many times one or the other of the shepherds had to go to your rescue, eh?"

"Hannah!" the duchess exclaimed. "And not one of the shepherds ever said a word to me."

"Well, but they understood, Mother," Berinwick explained. "It is just as Hannah said. It's here and therefore must be investigated. They never told you how many times they had to come to my rescue, either. I attempted to get through to its center at every opportunity, even though my opportunities were fewer than Hannah's."

"Too late to scold either one of them," Dempsey offered, reading the duchess's cocked eyebrow and pursed lips correctly. "Especially since we are all going in right this moment and not coming out again until we reach the center."

"Or at least until we discover what Hannah's headless King Arthur was doing in there," Berinwick offered. "He may never have reached the center himself. We may discover his reason for entering merely a few turns beyond the entrance."

Map in hand, Berinwick took the lead, followed by Hannah, then his mother, then Dempsy and Theophilus. The hedges were well trimmed early on, but as the little group progressed, twisting and turning their way through the maze, the hawthorn, holly, and wild roses grew thicker and closer together. Here and there, thorns and branches reached out to snatch at the ladies' skirts and the gentlemen's pantaloons. In places, the inside of the maze became dim and shadowy as the hedges grew together overhead.

"I daresay your gardeners have been a bit lax about keeping the place up, Berinwick," Dempsey called from the rear.

"Lax? *My* gardeners? I think not. It's Crawford and Davis have the care of the maze and they are particularly—particularly—come to think of it, I have not seen Crawford or Davis for weeks now," Berinwick replied, coming to a halt. "I wonder what could have happened to them?" He halted, then rubbed thoughtfully at his chin. Then he gulped a great gulp and turned to stare down at his sister. "Confounded maze must have swallowed them up, Hannah. Set that hound of yours to sniffing around for their bodies, will you, Dempsey?" he called back. "Good men, they were. Deserve a decent burial."

"William, cease and desist attempting to frighten your sister," his mother commanded. "You know perfectly well that Crawford and Davis are out helping to bring in the hay, just like everyone else we can spare."

"Are they? Have you seen them, Mother? I have not," Berinwick replied in hushed tones.

Hannah squeaked, then hurriedly covered her mouth with both hands and giggled behind them.

"By the way, dear sister, did that parson back there just address me as Berinwick?"

Hannah, hands still covering her mouth, nodded.

"So I thought. I amend my previous observation, then. Mr. Dempsey, there will likely be no gardeners' bodies for the hound to discover on our way in, but I do intend to leave a rather large, old body behind me upon our return."

"I'm shivering in my boots, *your grace,*" Dempsey replied.

"Do not refer to Mr. Dempsey as *old,* William," the duchess scolded. "It is rude."

"But he *is* old, Madam, and growing older day by day. There are times when the truth must be faced."

"Will, hush," whispered Hannah, noting an odd, sad light spring suddenly to her mother's eyes. "Mr. Dempsey is younger than Mama is."

"Oh. Right. I forgot. But then, I never would have guessed that to be the case if I had not been told it. Mr. Dempsey has ripened at a greater rate than mother has. But he will be done with ripening soon does he address me as Berinwick one more time, I promise you that."

The Reverend Mr. Dempsey laughed and Hannah giggled, but the duchess simply made a shooing motion with her hands, starting them walking again.

* * *

There are times when the truth must be faced. Her son's words accompanied Veronica as she made her way through the maze. No matter how difficult it seems, she told herself. No matter how much I wish to avoid it, there *is* one particular truth that must be faced. I must face it and William must face it. It can be no more onerous—my admitting the truth and William hearing it—than the harshness of the years we have spent at such a distance from each other. It can cause no deeper, more painful scars than the scars we have each borne for so very long. I will not allow that dastardly night to pervert my perception of my son any longer. Richard does not see a bitter, heartless young man when he looks at William, nor does Hannah. It is the guilt in my heart that makes Will seem that way to me. The guilt and the fear and the wall I have built up between us, brick by brick.

"Now is not quite the time, m'dear," Dempsey whispered from just behind her. His unexpected nearness, the tickle of his breath in her ear, sent a sudden shiver up Veronica's spine.

"What, Richard?" she asked.

"I said, now is not the time to tell him, Veronica. I am walking behind you, you know. I can see your shoulders squaring and your chin lifting. I can feel your courage rising higher and higher, too. And I can hear William's words in my own mind as clearly and insistently as you must be hearing them in yours. 'There are times when the truth must be faced.' Over and over, I hear them. But now is not the time, my dear. Hannah is present, and I am present as well."

Veronica ceased to walk and turned to him, putting her hands in his. "But I do not wish it to be a secret any longer, Richard. I must not. You said that, and I agree with you. I want William to know all. You already know of it. William *must* know of it. And I wish Hannah to hear and understand what happened as well. I want Hannah to realize what dreadful things can occur when young women are encouraged to think only of themselves—of their own comfort and pleasure and feelings—and thus lose sight of what is truly important in their lives."

"Which is all well and good, Vernie. I applaud you for it. But first you must speak to William alone. He is the one you've harmed and his feelings and wishes are the ones you ought to consider and respect. You don't know how he will react to your words or what he will choose to do about them. Perhaps he won't wish anyone else to know. I should think he would not. Not at first. Perhaps he will not want Hannah to know what happened ever. Certainly he will not wish to learn of such an extraordinary event while I am present. We are friends, you and I, from long ago, but to your son I am, as yet, a stranger."

"How can I be so stupid?" Veronica replied. "How can I still be so centered on myself that it did never occur to me how different William's wishes on the matter might be from my own?" She sighed. A sad, weary, impatient sigh. Releasing his hands, she put her arms around the Reverend Mr. Dempsey's waist and nestled against his broad chest, taking solace from the mere act of touching him. "I was never used to be such a featherhead, Richard. I am positive I was not."

How could Dempsey resist wrapping his arms around her, drawing her even closer? He could not. With Theophilus's lead still in his hand, cautiously gazing over the duchess's head to discover if Berinwick and Hannah were anywhere within sight, he hugged her to him. Deep in his heart, the Reverend Mr. Dempsey desired nothing more than to hold the Duchess of Berinwick in just this way, with perfect love, understanding, and tenderness forever.

Not that I am in the least bit worthy of such an honor, he thought, touching his cheek to the soft, dusky, sweet-smelling hair he loved. Not that she will ever think of me as anything but an old friend—but that is enough. It is all that is available to me, so it must be enough. But in the deepest, most secret chamber of my heart, I will allow myself to love her with all my heart and all my soul. Now that I have found her again, I will never let her go.

"Veronica," he murmured, "do not worry so, and don't be sad. All will be well in the end. You'll see. You will tell your son the truth. He will understand and forgive you and he will come to love you even more than he does now. And we will discover together who it was that fired upon us and why, too, and put a stop to that. You will find peace of mind, my dear, *and* peace from ghosts, goblins, and Poles as well. I will see that you do. You have my word on it."

Veronica nodded against his chest, then stepped back, breaking the circle of his arms. "We must catch up with the children, Richard," she said, "before they come back in search of us. They will wonder what we were doing to lose sight of them in a matter of moments."

Dempsey nodded, took her hand into his own, and set off, confident that Theophilus, nose to the ground, would lead them directly to Berinwick and Hannah, which, thankfully, the hound did, and before either of the young people had noticed their absence, too.

"One more turn," Berinwick called, without looking back, "and we ought to reach the center. Yes, here we are. Well, I'll be deviled."

"Why is he being deviled?" Dempsey asked.

"Because he sees what is at the center of the maze, of course," Veronica replied.

"Oh, goodness!" Hannah exclaimed breathlessly.

The Reverend Mr. Dempsey was so curious to see what the younger people saw that he sprinted around the final turn, tugging the duchess with him. Veronica had to run to keep up. In her heart, she paused to smile at his boyish excitement, though her feet dared not pause at all.

"It's a belvedere," the duchess explained as Dempsey and her children stood and stared at the open-sided, rectangular wooden building, fronted by three shallow steps, its roof supported by richly carved columns, all of it painted a brilliant white and as thick and lush as marble.

"Belvederes are meant to be situated on hills," Berinwick muttered. "What the deuce is one doing at the center of a maze?"

"Yes, and why should it draw Hannah's headless King

Arthur?" Dempsey added. "I saw nothing to suggest his presence anywhere along the way, or no reason for him to enter, unless he is inordinately fond of foliage."

"Are you certain you saw someone exiting the maze, Hannah?" Berinwick asked. "You were not dreaming the whole of it?"

"There was a man," Hannah whispered, enthralled with the belvedere as it glistened in the sunlight. "I saw a man, and a horse who looked a good deal like Penn dipped in cream."

"Dipped in cream? Might the horse have been dusted with flour?" Dempsey asked, as Theophilus tugged mightily at his lead.

"Flour? Truly dusted with flour, do you mean? I merely thought to describe the horse in terms of Penn's size and the color of cream. But flour would do, I expect."

"Just so. What is it, Theo?" Dempsey asked as the hound bayed loudly and lurched against the lead once more. "All right, then, lead on."

Theophilus, nose to the ground, tugged the parson toward the back of the building while the duchess, Berinwick, and Hannah climbed the three shallow steps and entered the structure.

"There's nothing in here but space," Berinwick announced, gazing about.

"But there is something back here," Dempsey called. "Good dog, Theophilus. You have solved one mystery."

"What is it, Richard? What have you discovered?" the duchess asked, hurrying to the rear of the building and gazing down at Dempsey. He reached up to her and swung her to the ground as though she weighed but an ounce.

"Something most remarkable, m'dear. Only look."

"Oh, my! William, come here at once," the duchess called. "You and Hannah will wish to see this."

Patrick McClane sat on the back of one of the Duke of Berinwick's horses and stared out over the meadow, pondering. He had returned from Ludlow with a number of things the new parson had requested of the duke to repair the old church and now had resumed his regular duties, only to discover that a goodly number of his laborers were armed. It was disconcerting, to say the least. The men wielding the scythes, of course, had no need of other weapons—the scythes themselves were deadly. But the wagoners were keeping fowling pieces and pistols beside them on the wagons. One of them even had a bow and arrows, and another stood near his horses' heads with a thunderous big whip. A number of the women had knives or scissors ready to hand and the children were armed with slings and stones. It was the most outrageous thing he had ever seen.

Not merely outrageous, he thought, frowning. It's downright dangerous.

And it was, for each time the haymakers thought they heard an odd sound—a rustling of leaves or the cracking of a twig in the woods close by—they paused in their tasks and took up whatever weapon they had with them. McClane, himself, had discovered a fowling piece, two slings, and an arrow aimed in his direction when he had entered the meadow that morning from a path through the wood.

Devil of a thing, he thought. And it slows down the work abominably. I must speak to his grace about this. We shall never finish making the hay with people pausing and reaching for their weapons at the least little thing. Five pauses this time and three that and seven another. It's perfectly senseless. What the devil do they expect to happen? Do they actually expect some madman to come charging at them out of Grydwynn Wood, swinging a broadsword as he approaches, and cutting them down one by one until they are all lying dead in the field? It's the Thornes who are the object of the attacks, not a scurrilous group of haymakers.

McClane had asked them, of course, the moment he had taken note of it, why they thought they required weapons. Angser, the woodcutter, had told him bluntly that the Duchess of Berinwick had been fired upon and that the duke had been fired upon as well, according to Thomas Hasty.

"And we ain't none of us agoin' to put up with it," the woodcutter had said. "Not a bit of it. Does anyone come asnoopin' about here with a long gun to hand, hopin' to find the duke alone and us all busy and not payin' the least attention—be he a stranger or be he someone we knows—we intends to take him prisoner and carry him to Blackcastle, we do. Does it take one of us or all of us, we'll do it, too. Ye can't trust no one when it comes to protectin' the Thornes of Barren Wycche. We remembers the Reverend Mr. Dight, we does, even though you do not. The Thornes' enemies be so skullduggerous they will go so far as pretendin' to be parsons."

"You don't think it likely that the Reverend Mr. Dempsey—" McClane had begun, only to be rudely interrupted.

"No. Whoever it be, it bean't the new rector. He were shot, he were. Not likely as he shot himself."

McClane mumbled under his breath as he recalled that conversation. The new rector was the only actual stranger around and apparently he was now beyond suspicion.

No, wait, he thought. There are the Welshmen—the Welshmen Berinwick hired when I told him not to do so. Certainly, they ought to be considered strangers. How can they not be considered strangers? I expect these simpletons think of the Welshmen as familiar because they happen to be working together in the same meadow, but the fact is, they've not been here all that long and we know nothing about them but what they wish us to know. "I had best drop a word in an ear here and an ear there," he muttered. "Suggest to a few of our loyal laborers that the Welshmen may not be precisely whom and what they claim to be."

McClane smiled to himself and nodded. Yes, that would be just the thing to do. Everyone knew by now that he had not trusted those men enough to hire them in the first place. Simply because the duke had chosen to trust in them, did not make them worthy of that trust.

* * *

"By Jupiter," Berinwick murmured, staring down from the belvedere at the dusty armor—apparently hastily discarded—tucked against the rear of the building.

Dempsey reached down and lifted a helmet from the ground. Forged from steel and brass, it had once covered some warrior's entire head, including his face. An animal skin with deep reddish-brown fur spotted white with flour dust was attached to the top of the helmet and above the skin rose the figure of a griffin rampant. "This will be the head that your King Arthur lost, Lady Hannah," Dempsey said, showing it to the girl as she came to stand beside her brother. "It does rather look like a head. From a distance this bit of fur might be mistaken for a man's hair. And the griffin atop it, you might think that was his hat."

"So, that's what the fellow was doing in the maze, donning his disguise," Berinwick mused.

"Just so. Or taking it off. It must take him a while to get it all on and off, and he wouldn't want anyone to walk in on him while he was in the midst of it."

"I'd think he'd need someone to fasten all that for him," Berinwick observed quietly. "Are you sure you didn't see two men, Hannah?"

"Only one, Will."

"Well, I don't think all of it was fastened," Dempsey offered. "The way it clanked when he rode past Theo and me that night in the wood, pretending to be the ghost of Owain Glyndwr, it sounded fairly much as though his armor *was* falling apart. And it looked it, too. Looked like bits and pieces of armor, I mean. Floating about."

"What else is down there, Dempsey?"

"Let me see. Chain mail. A breast plate. A pair of greaves."

"A pair of what?" the duchess asked, on her knees just as Dempsey was, beside the pile of armor.

"Greaves, Vernie. These things here. They're worn over a knight's shins and calves. And these are salvatons."

"Shoes," Berinwick clarified, jumping from the belvedere to the ground and lifting his sister down after him. "And a pair of quisses to protect his knees and thighs, and those are paldrons which fit over the arms and shoulders."

"And *that* thing?" Hannah queried as Dempsey lifted a medallion-shaped piece of metal into the sunlight.

"One of a pair of bezagews," Dempsey replied. "They are made to slip around under a knight's arm when he lifts his weapon. You will know what these are, Lady Hannah," he added. "These I'm certain you can name for us without the least hesitation."

"Oh, gauntlets!"

"Just so," Berinwick nodded. "It looks as though someone has taken an entire set of armor from the Great Hall and stored it out here. It's odd that Gaines did never notice that any of the armor was missing."

"This armor was never on display in the Great Hall," the duchess said, taking the helmet into her hands. "I would have remembered this helmet. It is most unlike all the others."

"I have actually seen a helmet quite the twin to that before," Dempsey murmured, taking it from her and studying it himself. "Yes, indeed I have."

"Where?" asked the others simultaneously.

"In a drawing in the Bishop of Hereford's private collection, and on our own Owain Glyndwr's ghost. It was too dark to recognize the piece atop it as a griffin rampant when I saw the ghost, but I don't doubt this was the helmet or its twin. Not at all, I don't."

"Arrrrosh!!!"

"God bless you, Theophilus. Indeed, this flour has dried and is dusty again."

"He must be a regular giant of a man to be able to ride with so much metal on him," Hannah observed.

"No, not a giant. But strong," Dempsey observed. "See here, the size of the breastplate and the greaves and the quisses? They are made to fit a man about the size of your brother. Of course, in medieval times the man who wore these must have seemed a giant to his foes. If this helmet is not a copy, Veronica, it once actually belonged to Owain Glyndwr. In the only drawing I have ever seen of the man, he is wearing it."

"Well, it cannot be the original," Berinwick observed. "Where would it come from? If anyone of Father's ilk had discovered such a thing as Owain Glyndwr's battle helmet, word would have spread like wildfire through the Royal Society. And if any Welshman had discovered it, all of Wales would know in a day's time and be expecting Glyndwr's resurrection at any moment to lead them to independence at last."

"You are very quiet, Veronica," Dempsey observed, drawing one of the gauntlets on his own hand as Berinwick knelt down and drew on the other.

"Am I? I am thinking, merely. This armor must belong to the man who murdered Julian and Mr. Thistledown and the footmen and he is likely the same man who fired upon us, Richard, and on William. How large a man was Mr. Hancock, Hannah? Do you recall?"

"Mr. Hancock?" Hannah stared at her mother, bewildered. "I expect he was Will's size, Mama. But Mr. Hancock has been gone from Blackcastle for more than a year. You cannot possibly think that Mr. Hancock is still here, sneaking about, pretending to be a ghost?"

"It is a possibility, Hannah, though it's yet to be proved. Mr. Dempsey and I discussed it and—"

"And Mother told me, and I thought it possible as well," Berinwick offered.

"Well, it is not possible," Hannah declared. "Mr. Hancock would never murder Papa. He and Papa were friends, and he and I were friends as well. Something dire happened to Mr. Hancock or he would never have left us. He wouldn't shoot at you, Will, or at Mama. Do not you remember what a fine gentleman Mr. Hancock always was?"

"Not really, but then I was away a good deal of the time," Berinwick replied, studying his sister's frown with some consideration. "You don't believe the disappearing Mr. Hancock is our villain, eh?"

"Never."

"Well, perhaps he's not. Perhaps we shall be proved wrong."

"I daresay we will be proved right or wrong shortly if we do things correctly from this point forward," Dempsey offered. "The first thing we must do is put everything back exactly as we found it. And then you, your grace, must set some of your people to watch over the maze day and night. When the villain returns to don his garb, we want to be prepared to seize him with his armor on so he cannot protest his innocence."

"Trust you to go directly to the heart of the matter, Richard," Veronica observed quietly. "And I should like to go there with you, if I may. It is someone who knows us and Blackcastle well, Hannah, William. There are no strangers who would know the way to the center of this maze. And if it is not our long-absent Mr. Hancock, then it will be someone else in whom we have placed our trust. You must both think about that and be prepared for it."

"Crawford and Davis must know the way in and out of the maze blindfolded," Hannah whispered. "You don't think—"

"No!" Berinwick protested heartily. "Neither of them would think to threaten anyone at Blackcastle, especially not Father or Mother!"

"Someone has thought to threaten the lot of you, however," Dempsey murmured. "And if Lady Hannah is correct and it is not this Mr. Hancock, then it is someone else who has had access to the maze and learned to find his way in and out of it in the dark. One of your shepherds, perhaps?"

"No."

"You're positive? They certainly may go in and out of the maze without raising an eyebrow all day long."

"And they check on the sheep twice after sunset, William," the duchess pointed out. "Once at nine and once again at eleven. At either time, one of them could easily slip into the maze, don this armor, and—"

"We cannot trust the shepherds then, to watch over the

maze," Berinwick mumbled, scowling. "And perhaps, despite my trust in them, it would be unwise to set Crawford and Davis on watch. What about my butler, my valet, my footmen, Dempsey? Am I not to trust them, either?"

"I would not."

"Tom Hasty!" the duchess exclaimed. "If I trust anyone implicitly, it is Thomas Hasty."

"And Harvey Langton," Berinwick added, brightening a bit. "Though if I ask Langton to watch the maze at night, he'll not be worth a pig's eye in the morning when you need him, Dempsey."

"No, we needn't take Mr. Langton from Mr. Dempsey's service," Hannah declared. "Davey Lancaster, Overfield, Trewellyn, and young John can all be counted upon in any situation, can they not? They are as loyal as loyal can be. Why, they did all of them carry pistols to Mr. Dempsey's reading-in."

"They did what?" Dempsey asked.

"Everyone carried weapons to your reading-in, Richard," the duchess replied, a sudden smile lighting her face. "Even I had a lovely Italian stiletto in my reticule."

"And I had a pair of scissors, newly sharpened," Hannah giggled.

"And I had my rapier. But then, you saw my rapier," Berinwick added. "I was the only one did not care whether you saw a weapon on my hip or not."

"*That's* why people kept stuttering and staring at their shoes and shuffling about when I spoke to them after the service?" Dempsey stared from one to the other of them. "Do you mean to say that I stood before them, rattling on about the sanctity of the church, and sanctuary, and peace, and forgiveness, and all the time my entire congregation was armed to the teeth with weapons of death and destruction?"

"Ahhh. Yes," Berinwick admitted.

Dempsey set the gauntlet with which he played aside. He rocked back on his heels and began to laugh. He laughed so hard that tears mounted to his eyes and ran down his cheeks.

"Will, do something," Hannah urged. "Mr. Dempsey is hysterical."

"N-no. N-no," gasped Dempsey. "It's s-simply the funniest thing I have ever d-done. Oh, how I wish I had known precisely what I was d-doing to the lot of you!"

It was the evening of the following day when the Duchess of Berinwick stepped into St. Milburga's of the Wood to discover the Reverend Mr. Dempsey on his knees, digging about in a hole in one of the church walls, a lighted lantern on the floor beside him.

"You are looking for the cup," she declared from just inside the church doors.

"Veronica! What are you doing here?"

"I came to share something I discovered about the maze with you. I ought not have come so late, but I pondered and pondered over it and at the last, I thought that you have more right to know than even I do myself. Cannot you deny yourself the cup, Richard? Is it such an important thing that you must work all day long to restore the church and then at night tear the poor building apart again searching for the dratted thing?"

"I am not tearing the building apart again, m'dear," Dempsey protested, rising, brushing off his knees with his hands and then rubbing his hands clean on his breeches. "What I'm doing is digging into every niche and crack I can in the evening when the Langtons are gone, and then those are the cracks that we seal up the following day. At first I believed the cup would have been more safely laid to rest in the rectory, that perhaps a new rectory had been built with the intention of adding to its design a particular hiding place for Glyndwr's cup, but I have since changed my mind. You did not come alone, Veronica?"

"No. Tom Hasty is with me. He is standing guard outside, even as we speak." She smiled a bit then, and as Dempsey approached her, she reached out to take his hand. "Come outside with me. I have something to give you, Richard. Tom is holding it for me."

The Reverend Mr. Dempsey took her hand in his and gave it a slight squeeze. Veronica would think it was intended to show his support for her, that subtle squeeze. He was certain of that. But it was not intended to show his support for her at all. It was intended—selfishly on his part, he supposed—to provide him with the thrill of a secret intimacy. It allowed him to release the tiniest bit of the passion that continued to grow in him with their every meeting, their every shared experience. It set his pulses racing for a moment, that seemingly innocuous squeeze.

"What is it?" he queried as they exited the church to discover Tom Hasty astride his horse, waiting most patiently. The groom held his horse's reins and the reins of Veronica's white mare in his right hand. A heavy-looking volume rested in the crook of his left arm.

"Good evening, Thomas," Dempsey greeted.

"Mr. Dempsey," Hasty nodded in return.

"I will take the volume now, Tom," the duchess said, and freeing her hand from the parson's, she stepped up beside the groom and he handed the book down to her. Then she stepped away again and strolled off in the direction of the rectory, forcing Dempsey to follow her without a word. The rector nodded to Hasty and hurried off behind her on the instant.

"What is it, Veronica, that you cannot tell me of it before such a loyal groom as Tom?"

"It's a journal of sorts," she replied when she judged them to be far enough away from Hasty that they would not be overheard. "A diary, I suppose one would call it, because apparently, among the Thornes of Barren Wycche, only men were important enough to have actual journals. At any rate, it was written by one of Julian's grandmothers. I cannot remember how many greats to put before that title of grandmother, but a number of them. Jules gave it to me years ago. He gave me all the writings of the ladies in his family. I do not think he ever read any of them."

Dempsey cocked an eyebrow in the lingering twilight. "He did not read any of them? Not even one?"

"I found it foolish of him as well," Veronica replied. "Jules was always so serious about his research and yet, he apparently thought there could be nothing worthy of notice in anything written by a woman. You do not have the same prejudice, do you, Richard?"

"No."

"No. Just what I thought, after giving it due consideration. Despite all the years gone by, in your heart you are still the boy I once knew—the boy who thought me worthy of sharing in the Lord's Chamber, who thought me capable of learning to behead a chicken, who trusted me to explain to him the lessons he could not quite grasp. You did never expect less of me because I happened to be a female."

"You never gave me reason to expect less of you simply because you were a girl, Veronica."

"No, I did not, because I did not expect less of myself then. I was not pampered and petted and indulged into stupidity until my mother and my stepfather returned and took me off to London. Thank goodness you and your family did not think of me as some delicate flower to be nurtured and protected and never allowed to think for herself or I would not have the least grain of independence and courage in me now, when I most require it."

"I have never thought of you as some delicate flower."

"No." She smiled at him. "Even now you expect me to stand up and do what is right for everyone, no matter what the consequences, which is why I came to give you this." She passed him the volume. "Cease looking for Glyndwr's cup tonight and read the pages I have marked with red ribbons, Richard. You will not be sorry that you did." She turned away from him then and began to stroll back toward Tom Hasty.

"Can you not stay awhile, Veronica?" he asked, catching her up. "I can make some tea and we can peruse the volume together."

"No, I cannot, Richard," she replied, turning to face him

once more. "I should dearly like to do so, but I wish to look in on Mrs. Thistledown for a bit and I promised William to be home before dark. He is frightened for me, you know. I should never have believed it of him, and no one would ever guess by the words he chooses that he is afraid on my behalf, but I am learning to see him through clearer eyes, and he is worried about my safety. He made Tom carry a horse pistol in his pocket tonight." She raised a hand gloved in soft leather and touched Dempsey's cheek. "How I wish that you could find . . ." she began, and stopped in the midst of it. "No. Never mind. You need not accompany me back to the horses, Richard. Tom will assist me to mount." Then she caught her lower lip between her teeth, turned again, and made her way to the mare. Hasty assisted her to the saddle and the two of them rode off in the direction of Mrs. Thistledown's cottage, leaving the Reverend Mr. Dempsey, his arms around the enormous volume, staring after them in silence.

"How you wish I could find what, Vernie?" he whispered when the sound of their horses' hooves had faded. "Not Glyndwr's cup, I'll wager. The man who murdered your husband? I *will* find him. I promise you that. Or is it something else? Only tell me and I will do whatever it takes to find whatever it is and lay it at your feet."

Richard Randolph Dempsey discovered that his hands were trembling, that he had grown cold, and that there seemed to be an empty, hollow ache in the region of his heart.

Blackcastle fairly roared with the pounding of boots, the rustle of clothing, and male and female voices shouting one to the other. In the stables, the grooms scrambled madly to saddle horses and to hitch teams to the curricle, the dogcart, and three of the farm wagons.

"I am going with you, Will," Hannah called, racing after her brother as he dashed out into the corridor toward the nearest staircase. "I can pass a bucket as well as the next person."

"Yes," Berinwick called back over his shoulder. "We'll be

glad to have you. But fetch your riding gloves first. They will give you some protection for your hands. I'll see Marigold is saddled for you. Gaines, you cannot go," he added as the butler sailed past him down the staircase.

"Cannot go? I cannot go? But, your grace," Gaines pleaded, skidding to a halt at the main floor landing, "I cannot possibly remain behind."

"Someone must wait for my mother to return and tell her what has happened and then send Tom Hasty on to help us, Gaines."

"No, no, take Gaines with you," Patrick McClane shouted, hobbling toward them along the corridor. "I'll wait. I'll tell her. I'll send Hasty on."

"What the devil happened to you?" Berinwick asked as he nodded his consent to Gaines and the butler raced off in the direction of the summer room, where he might exit through the French doors and be at the stables in less than two minutes if he ran fast enough.

"Slipped," McClane replied, gritting his teeth in obvious pain. "Caught my bootheel on something and went down hard, your grace. I think I have broken my ankle. Never mind," he added. "Go. I shan't die from it. Time enough to do something about it when the Tofars are safe and the fire is out. The flames are mounting higher. You can see them from the stableyard now. Go! Go!" he urged.

"I am right behind you again, Will," Hannah called, pounding down the last bit of the staircase. Berinwick turned, grabbed her gloved hand, and together they dashed toward the summer room and out into the yard. All around them, men, women, and children ran toward the stables as the Tofars' fire bell tolled relentlessly through the deepening twilight.

Dempsey did not turn at once to the pages Veronica had marked with bits of ribbon, but began the diary at the very beginning, attempting to lose himself in another world—in the world of a woman named Dilys Thorne, who had become, through no desire of her own but through the machinations of her husband and by order of King Henry IV, the first Duchess of Berinwick. He read page after page written in a fine—a lovely, in fact—hand, a very feminine hand. In his mind her voice seemed to rise from the pages. She spoke the written words aloud, just to him. He heard. He listened. And he understood. She was a chronicler of history, Dilys Thorne. But more than that, she was a watcher and a recorder of the hearts, the minds, and the souls of all of the Thornes of Barren Wycche who lived and fought and died, who loved and laughed and cried through the final years of the fourteenth century and into the early years of the fifteenth. By her hand, all those who had lived then, in a great pile of stones called Blackcastle, lived again, for him, this very evening.

The pages that Veronica had marked lay very near the end of the volume. By the time Dempsey reached them, his eyes had grown weary, his candles had burned to stubs, and Theophilus had fallen into a deep sleep beneath the kitchen table on which the diary rested. But by then, Dempsey had entered so fully and so completely into Dilys Thorne's world that he could not bear to depart from it. He longed to know more, to understand more, to feel more of what it had been like to be one of those Thornes of Barren Wycche, to live in that time, in that place.

It was not surprising, then, that rather than leave the remainder of the volume until the following morning, Dempsey pushed back from the table, stood and stretched, and then made his way to the kitchen cupboards where he found fresh candles, set them in the candelabra, and took up his reading once more.

Here, the bright red ribbon seemed to whisper to him as he turned the page and met it head-on. *Here is the most important part. Here is the part that brought Veronica to you this evening. Treasure each and every word.*

Dempsey nodded to himself. His long, lean fingers stroked the ribbon gently as he lifted his gaze from the volume and stared off into an inner region somewhere near his heart where the image of Veronica this evening, the shadows of St. Milburga's gathered around her, her chin held high, her stance proud, lingered still.

"I have never felt the loneliness of my life so completely as I do of late," he whispered. "I have never longed for a woman so fully, so deeply, as I do now—as I have done from the moment I saw her face again."

Dempsey sighed and returned his attention to the volume. He read to the middle of the first of the marked pages, then muttered a quiet curse and returned to the top of the page to read the passage again. "What the devil?" he hissed under his breath, and then he continued on. Beneath the kitchen table, his feet shuffled uneasily, causing Theophilus to stir. The Reverend Mr. Dempsey took in a great breath of air and expelled it in a low whistle.

In faith, I cannot but think that he dies of a broken heart. Dilys Thorne had written. *Betrayed, deserted, forgotten in his defeat, his strength at last deserts him. He is too ill to return to Wales again. Thus, he must remain here among the Thornes. We are the only ones who offer him sanctuary in the Marches where once many would have offered him that and more. No matter now how I perceived him when first he rose to plague Robyn's loyalties and to send my family into turmoil, this Owain Glyndwr has made a home for himself in my heart. He is a proud man, but kind. He is a man who continues to dream of freedom, of unity, of equality for Wales. And though he dies in England, his dreams for his homeland do not depart from him.*

Dempsey's heart pumped exceedingly fast. Can this be true? he wondered. But it must be true. Why would she write lies to herself and her descendants? Owain Glyndwr, in his final days, had taken shelter at Blackcastle! Had he remained? It sounded very much as though he had remained until his death.

No one has been able to discover the date of Glyndwr's death or the place he was interred to this very day, Dempsey thought. What a triumph it would be for me to present a paper before the Royal Society that actually does name them. How could Julian Thorne make reference to Glyndwr's death in his letter, assure me that Glyndwr gave the cup bestowed on him at Machynlleth into Thorne hands, and yet mention nothing of Glyndwr having actually died at Blackcastle? Why should he not write me a word about that?

"Perhaps he didn't know," Dempsey murmured to himself. "Veronica said her husband thought the writings of women to be worthless to him in his historical investigations. He considered women's writings to be nothing more than emotional scribbling, I expect. And perhaps none of Berinwick's male ancestors did ever think Glyndwr's death worthy of note in one of *their* journals."

They certainly thought possession of the cup and a written record of *that* important, Dempsey mused. Well, but what man born and bred anywhere in England or Wales would not think the cup important? Especially men wrapped in the legends and mysteries of King Arthur. But once they had the cup, would they have taken the time to record and analyze the last days of Owain Glyndwr's life? Glyndwr was not King Arthur, after all. To the Thorne men of that time, he was likely nothing more than a troublesome old rebel who came near to getting them all hanged at one point in history. How would they know he would become a legend himself? But the women knew—apparently the most important of the Thorne women knew.

Dempsey read on, his heart rising into his throat as he progressed from one ribbon-marked page to another. "It cannot be," he whispered. And moments later, "The belvedere?" And then again, "She planted the maze to grow up around him and protect his spirit for all eternity?"

It was all too much for the parson. He closed the volume and stared at the kitchen walls. He stood and paced and sat down again. Can it be true? he wondered. But why *wouldn't* it be true?

"I must speak with Veronica first thing in the morning," he said then, his voice trembling with anticipation. "Langton will have to patch that rear wall of the church without me. This cannot wait. As it is, I ought to saddle Norville and ride to Blackcastle tonight. No, no, I certainly cannot do that. Veronica will not thank me for setting her household on its ear this late in the evening. It is full dark already. How can the night have descended so swiftly? But I ought to go, regardless, and beg her to discuss this entire volume with me before we sleep."

And while I am begging her for that, he thought, calming himself, forcing his heart to beat more steadily—while I am begging Vernie for that—why should I not beg her for something else as well, something a great deal more important? Why should I not open my mouth and beg her to consider, merely consider, marrying me one day? She need not do it, after all, simply because I ask.

But then he called himself a fool for even thinking of such an audacious thing as the proposed alliance of a duchess with a mere parson. Calling Theophilus from his nap, Dempsey opened the door and stepped out into the night.

Ten

The Reverend Mr. Dempsey took a deep breath of the fresh night air and heard the slow clip-clop of a horse's hooves and a hissing that sounded very much like "Missserrr Demmmsssseyyyy" coming from the direction of the church. Dempsey turned on his heel, sprang back inside through the kitchen door, and fumbled about in search of a lantern. Trembling, Theophilus scurried in after him, sat down on his haunches in the middle of the kitchen floor, and bayed three times while Dempsey found and attempted to light the blessed thing.

"Getting on your nerves, eh, m'boy?" Dempsey muttered when the lantern light flared at last into being. "I must admit this nonsense is getting on mine, too, Theo. Too many ghosts around here for such delicate sensibilities as ours." He went first to the dog, knelt and scratched the hound's ears, and spoke kindly to him, calming the poor creature. Then he stood, took the lantern in hand, and stepped outside once again.

The slow clip-clop of the hooves was closer now and the hissing sounded again. "Missserrrr Demmmmssseyyy."

"Yes, I am right here," Dempsey replied to the hiss, holding the lantern at shoulder height. "Can you see me well enough with this light before me? Come for me, then."

It was a foolish thing to say, that, for the only weapons the parson had were his own fists. But Dempsey would not have refrained from saying it even if he had stopped to think before opening his mouth.

"You need not believe you will frighten me by hissing at me from the darkness," he called more loudly. "For one thing, I am not afraid of ghosts, nor have I ever been. And for another, you are not a ghost. You are nothing but some pitifully inept villain pretending to be a ghost. I have seen your armor empty, sir. Step into the circle of my light now and let me see it filled."

Clip-clop. Clip-clop. Clip-clop, replied the horse's hooves, moving slowly, unswervingly in his direction.

"Missserrrr Demmmsssseyyyy," came the hissing, once, twice, three times more.

Dempsey took a step in the direction of the spine-chilling voice. He took another. The horse's hooves ceased to make any sound at all, but the horse snorted through its nostrils.

Dempsey took a third step forward.

"Demmmmsssssseyyyy," the voice hissed again, so softly this time that it was barely audible.

The parson took a fourth step and the light of his lantern glinted off a piece of tack. He raised the lantern higher and found his gaze fixed on a bay's withers wet with blood, and then on the entire horse, and then on the rider slumped forward in the saddle. Behind Dempsey, in the kitchen, Theophilus bayed and bayed as if his heart would break.

Far from the rectory of St. Milburga's of the Wood, the Duchess of Berinwick turned on her side and groaned. "How I wish you could find it in your heart to love me, Richard," she whispered.

She did not hear herself speak, had not the least notion that she had said the words aloud, and yet, the earnestness of those words and the longing of her heart that they conveyed, instilled a wistfulness, a melancholy into the night. They lingered and filled the darkness in which she lay, wrapping themselves around her like a sad, lonely shroud.

In her mind, Veronica cupped Richard's cheek in her palm and peered into the brilliance of his eyes to discover them filled with sympathy, with compassion, and with a hint, a glimmer, of something else. What could that glimmer be? Might it be love? Desire? No, it could not be, not after all these years of separation. They had grown to adulthood in such different worlds, Richard and she. Surely, they could not now recover what once had been and see it bloom and grow. Veronica's heart pivoted painfully in her breast and she dropped her hand to her side, bowed her head. What a fool I am, she thought. Merely because I wish a thing to be true, I think to see it. But it cannot be. Once he loved me, but it was so long ago and we were both so young. It was a different sort of love entirely. Richard's arm went around her shoulders just then, and though she could find solace in that supportive gesture, it was not merely his sympathy, his compassion, his friendship for which she yearned.

Her eyes ached, her neck felt stiff and sore, the back of her head burned fiercely as if her hair had been set afire. Veronica rubbed her forearm across her eyes and groaned. And then she opened them, squinting painfully into the darkness. "Richard," she murmured, and this time she heard her own voice clearly. The very desperation in it caused her to sit up at once and that sudden movement sent pain shuddering through her.

"Gracious heavens," she mumbled once the pain subsided into a dull ache at the back of her head. "Why do I feel so ill, and why is it so very dark in here? I cannot see my fingers before my face. Has my lamp gone out completely? Why would Martha allow my lamp to grow so low on oil that it refuses to burn the length of a night even with the wick lowered? And what in heaven's name has happened to my mattress? It is as hard as a rock."

Veronica realized then that she was inordinately cold as well, and she reached for the counterpane to pull it up close around her but it was nowhere to be found. Am I still asleep? she wondered. I must be still asleep and this a most aggravating dream. And then her head began to ache more severely. She lay back down, curled into a fetal position to fend off the chill and closed her eyes. Within moments, the Duchess of Berinwick lost all thought of the cold, the darkness, and the pain.

Just a few yards from the rectory door, Dempsey set the lantern on the ground and reached carefully up. "Steady, m'boy," he murmured. "Hold still, now. I merely mean to take Tom from your back."

The bay nickered and burred. He shifted his weight slightly but then held steady as the parson, with slow, decisive movements, unclasped the near death grip Tom Hasty had around the horse's neck, freed the groom's boots from the stirrups, and tugged the man to the side until the groom's own weight caused him to slump over Dempsey's strategically placed shoulder. Then, shifting the man's weight until he could stoop without danger to his burden, the parson picked up the lantern and made his way back to the kitchen door. He fumbled a bit in his attempt to work the latch without dropping the lantern, but he managed to do it at the last and stepped into the kitchen.

"Missserrr Demmmsssseyyyy," Tom Hasty whispered again, forcing the words from his throat on a tortured breath as he dangled awkwardly over Dempsey's shoulder.

"It's all right, Tom," Dempsey replied, depositing the lantern on the kitchen table and making his way carefully toward the staircase. "You've found me. I am right here. Don't talk any more, lad, until I have got you safely down on my bed."

With Theophilus toddling along behind him, licking at Hasty's dangling hands, Dempsey carried the groom up the staircase and into his bedchamber, where he placed the man carefully atop the counterpane. The parson's heart was in his throat. It had been there from the moment he had recognized the burden the bay carried and it was not likely to return to its proper place now—not until he knew what had happened and whether or not, somewhere out in the night, Veronica was lying injured or dead.

Oh, God, he prayed silently as he lit the rest of the candles in the candelabra on his bedside table and then hurried to his chest of drawers to seize his penknife from atop it so he could cut away Hasty's coat and shirt and discover precisely where all the blood was coming from. Oh, dearest God, please keep Vernie safe. Wherever she is, whatever has happened, keep her safe until I can reach her.

Hasty's bloodied clothing at last cut away, Dempsey filled the basin on his washstand with water and set it on the bedside table. Gathering every towel he could find, he began to soak up the blood. It was coming from a small, roundish wound just above the groom's left breast and a much larger wound almost opposite it in the groom's back. The parson set himself to stanch the flow of blood. A pistol ball, he thought, as he worked. By gawd, whoever fired the thing barely missed Tom's heart, and he was close to him. Very close. There are powder burns on Tom's chest. At least the ball has gone clear through, though. Ought to consider that a good thing, I expect, especially since there is not a surgeon to be had, not even in the village.

Dempsey's thoughts lurched, then, to Veronica. Was she, too, lying somewhere as badly wounded as Tom? Was she lying there alone? Without anyone to fight for her life?

I will never know, he told himself as he worked over Hasty. Not in time to save her. Not if I do not fight for Tom Hasty's life this very moment.

Binding the groom's wounds as tightly as possible, Dempsey hurried to his trunk, dug hopefully through it, and found, thankfully, that he had in his small collection of bottles and packets, a goodly portion of powdered sweet basil leaves, and both the striped and the spotted elder that his brother Geoffery had brought back with him from his travels in America. He had a goodly portion of ground hazelnut as well. He made a paste of each and dipped the thin, porous strips of lint into them. His hands trembled as he did so. He had never before tried the elder and the hazelnut. Geoffery said he had seen their use stop hemorrhaging, but Dempsey had not, nor did he know precisely how much he ought to use. Nevertheless, he returned to Hasty, unbound the groom's wounds, and packed the medicated lint into them, then bound them up again. The sweet basil would help to keep any infection slight. But what good would that do, if the two different elder powders and the ground hazelnut did not stanch the flow of blood?

Hasty was as pale as a waning moon as Dempsey removed the groom's boots and stockings and covered the man with the counterpane from the other bedchamber. Hasty's breathing was swift and shallow, his heart beat rapidly, and yet the man fought to open his eyes, fought to speak.

"Her g-grace," he said. "T-taken near the f-fork."

Dempsey's heart fell from where it had lodged in his throat, down into his stomach. *Taken,* he thought. *Someone has taken Veronica.* Near the fork. Near what fork?

"Where?" he asked Hasty. "Where, Tom? What fork?"

Hasty moaned and moved his head weakly on the pillow. "H-Hatter's f-field."

The fork that leads to Mrs. Thistledown's cottage. Of course, Dempsey thought. Vernie intended to stop in and visit with the Widow Thistledown. But if she and Tom were attacked at the fork in the road, then they never reached the cottage. The rector shook his head as if it were filled with cobwebs and he could clear them away with the motion.

If Berinwick expected them home before dark, he thought, then Berinwick most certainly went in search of them when they did not arrive. He will have long since discovered that they did never reach Mrs. Thistledown's. So where is the lad? Why is he not here pounding on my door, demanding to know what I have done with his mother? Has something happened to Berinwick as well?

Dempsey took one long look at Hasty, who had at last given up his fight to keep his wits about him and tumbled into complete senselessness. There was nothing more he knew to do for the man, and Veronica might well be . . .

He dashed from the chamber, ran down the staircase and out through the kitchen door, seizing his lantern on the way. Tom Hasty's horse burred as the Reverend Mr. Dempsey approached it, took the reins in hand, and, ignoring the blood and his own lack of riding boots, mounted the beast. With a quick word to the animal, he turned the horse toward the road in the direction of the fork and urged it into a gallop. Theophilus, having scrambled through the door on Dempsey's heels, blinked bewilderedly after them. Then the hound put his nose to the ground and trotted off in their wake.

Unaware that anything at all had happened to his mother or Tom, the Duke of Berinwick focused his total concentration on the task he had set himself. If there truly is a Hades, it cannot be much worse than this, he thought as he stumbled to his left, barely avoiding a great chunk of the Tofars' vestibule ceiling that came crashing down at him. He waited a moment to see if any more would follow and when it did not, he began to move forward again. He had thought himself accustomed to the loss of one eye after all these years. He had thought himself well-adjusted to it. He had learned to ride, to fence, to climb, to run just like any other boy. But the loss of his eye was hampering him now amidst the thickening smoke and the sudden flames that seemed to burst out at him from everywhere. He had no warning of what was happening on his right. He could catch no glimpse of flames, no glimpse of movement out of the corner of his eye because, of course, the eye was gone. For a brief instant, Berinwick thought that he would do best to turn back. If Anne Tofar was in this house—and where else could she be, since she was not to be found among the crowd striving to fight the fire—if she was in this house, then she had likely been smothered to death by the smoke.

Smothered or burned to death, Berinwick thought, the wet rag he held over his nose and mouth doing little to keep the smoke from seeping down into his throat. If Tofar had realized sooner that Anne was not—no. Unfair, he thought. Not the man's fault. And he would be in here now instead of me if I had not convinced him that I am more capable because I am far younger than he.

When the fire had begun in Squire Tofar's main stable—*set,* one of the grooms had declared, set by someone in a pile of hay at the very back of the place. He had seen someone running from the scene. When the fire had flared into being, the squire and every other able-bodied man had run to lead the horses out of the building. All of his servants—men, women, and children—had spilled out of the house and scrambled down to the stable to douse the flames lest they spread to the other outbuildings. But they had not managed to put out the flames before an ill-timed wind had carried a multitude of sparks up into the air to travel across the stable yard all the way to the roof of the house itself, which welcomed them, feeding them as they grew into flames. By that time, though, everyone ought to have been out of the house. Anne ought to have been out of the house. But Hannah had been unable to find her best friend anywhere among the crowd and the girl's mother had been hysterical and incoherent.

"I am going to box the chit's ears until they fall off if she grew as hysterical as her mother and is hiding away, perfectly safe, outside somewhere, while I am roasting to death in here," Berinwick muttered and then he coughed raggedly. He took the wet rag from his mouth and attempted to shout over the fire's roar. "Anne! Annie!"

He listened, expecting no answer. Even if she were in the house, even if she were not unconscious or dead from the fire or the smoke, it was unlikely the girl would hear him or he hear her with the roar of the flames increasing in intensity and things—like that bit of ceiling—beginning to crash down around them. Berinwick was perfectly amazed, then, when a rhythmic pounding reached his ears. *Bam! Bam! BamBamBam!* it went. And again in the same rhythm. And a third time.

It is coming from somewhere here on the ground floor, Berinwick thought. It must be Anne pounding. It's certainly not an accidental noise caused by the burning. Thank gawd she's alive and thank heaven she's not up those stairs. "Again! Pound again, Annie!" he shouted.

Bam! Bam! BamBamBam! came the response from down the main corridor before him. Somewhere near the rear of the house, she was. Berinwick moved forward, stepping carefully over pieces of burning ceiling.

Veronica woke again. This time her mind was clearer than before and the darkness was not complete. Her eyes still hurt and there was yet a stinging at the back of her head. She seemed to ache everywhere as she lowered her feet to the floor and sat up on the edge of what she could now see was a small cot. But the floor was not a floor at all, she noted with dismay. It appeared to her to be more of a lane, a most uneven lane formed of hard clay and stone.

"Now that's perfectly ridiculous," she murmured. "I have certainly not been sleeping on a cot in the middle of some lane." She gazed about her to discover that the bit of light she now had came from a silver candelabra that held three un-equally burning candles. It had been carefully wedged between two odd formations of rock. Someone had come into this strange chamber while she slept and placed the cande-labra there. Who? Where in heaven's name was she? Why had the person who had furnished her the candles not remained? Veronica shivered. Her jaw tightened and her teeth chattered the merest bit. Wherever she was, it was a cold, damp, horri-ble place and she could see nothing beyond the light of the candles. And someone had come into this place and departed again without her being the least aware of it. "Why did I not wake when the person came?" she whispered, and her whis-per echoed around her. "Who was it? Where am I? How did I get here?"

She tried to stand, groaned, and sat back down at once. I am frightfully lightheaded, she thought. And there is not a bone in this poor old body that does not ache. Why?

And then she remembered. *We were attacked! Thomas Hasty and I were attacked on the way to the Widow Thistle-down's cottage!*

"Oh," she whispered. Veronica balled her hands into fists and pressed her knuckles against her lips as the memory of everything that had happened rushed back to her with full force.

She could hear the wretch calling out to her and to Tom just as clearly, with just as much urgency in his tone as he had called then—in the deepening twilight—at the fork that led to Mrs. Thistledown's. "Your grace, Hasty, you must come at once. There has been an accident! The duke has been gravely injured!" And then that monster of evil had ridden straight toward them—brought his horse to a halt almost muzzle to muzzle with Tom's, raised his hand and shot Thomas Hasty in the heart before the poor groom had even suspected that something was odd and thought to reach for his own pistol.

"Oh, Thomas," Veronica sighed. Tears rose to her eyes. She had known Tom Hasty since first he had begun to toddle about on fat little baby legs. He had been born merely three years before her own William. And though his mama and papa had died, taken by the same fever that had taken little Charlotte, he had thrived and grown to manhood at Blackcastle, as sweet and charming a scamp as ever she had known. "Oh, Thomas, how could that beast have murdered you? And without so much as the slightest warning! What did you ever do to him? Nothing! Nothing!"

Veronica saw herself in shock, reaching out to the groom as he slumped in his saddle, then slid toward the ground. She felt Tom's blood on her hand. Smelled the gunpowder that lingered in the air. Heard the scream as it began to escape her lips. And she heard, too, how it cut off as swiftly, so swiftly, as the fiend reached out and pulled her from the saddle with such strength that she had actually felt herself flying through the air.

I hit the ground with a tremendous whack, she thought. It knocked all my breath right out of me. And then he was standing over me and he reached down and lifted me from the berm and began to beat me with his fists.

"Oh," she said on a strangled gasp, remembering her terror, her pain, her struggle to escape him. "Oh, dearest God, I thought he meant to kill me then and there."

But he did not, she reminded herself, for here I am, sore and shivering and frightened to death, but alive. I must be thankful for that. I'm alive. And because I am, I have hope of escaping this place, whatever this place is.

That bothered her immensely. She could not think where she was. Cautiously she stood again and waited this time for the dizziness to depart from her. Ignoring her pain, she stepped toward the candelabra. Stones. It *was* wedged between two enormous stones, but not tightly. She took it up into her hand and held it high, gazing around her. She took three steps to her right, stumbled, lowered the candles to gaze at the rocky floor beneath her, took another three steps and raised the candles high again. Step by careful step, she made her way around the perimeter of the chamber, her heart sinking with each remarkable thing she saw. Her mind attempted to form the glimpses allowed her by the candlelight into one large image, but it could not quite do so. At one point, she discovered an arched opening and moved toward it, only to discover that it led into more blackness. Blackness as deep as death itself.

The ground upon which she walked was uneven, dangerous in the dark. Pitted in some places, stones rose raggedly from it in others. In some spots water pooled, dripping down from above, from a ceiling she could not see because the light of the candles did not reach as high as that.

I am underground, she thought when she returned at last to the cot and sat down upon it. This is a cave of some sort, though much larger than the caves that Jules took me into all those years ago when he thought that King Arthur might be buried in one of them. Surely this is a cave. Surely there is no such place as this that can exist above the ground.

"Oh, God," she whispered then. "Please, please let that beast have lied to us about William. Do not let my Will be gravely injured by some horrid accident or by that fiend, either. No, and do not let Thomas Hasty be dead. By some miracle let Tom be saved. You can perform miracles. Perform one this day. Allow Mrs. Thistledown to find Tom, or someone coming along the lane find him, and let Tom still be breathing and fighting to live when he *is* found. He looked to be dead, but he need not be, not if You should take pity on him. And protect my dearest Hannah from the machinations of that unholy demon. She is such an innocent. Have mercy on her innocence and keep her safe from him. And please send me an angel to rescue me from this dank and blinding prison," she added in a wistful voice. "I vow I will make all right in my life and in William's, and in everyone else's life, too, if only you will send me an angel to guide me from this hellishly dark cavern into the light of day. He need not be a magnificent angel or an important angel. A small, insignificant angel will do, someone to take my hand and lead me out of this darkness into the light."

Dempsey whispered a prayer of thanksgiving. Veronica was not lying crumpled and dead at the fork. There was blood in the lane, staining the hard-packed ground, but he could only think that it was Tom's blood, for the man had lost a good deal more of it than had stained his coat, his shirt, and his horse's hair. It had to be Tom's blood. He could not bear the thought that it might be Vernie's.

"Unbelievable," he murmured. "Could Hasty actually have fallen from his horse when he was shot and managed to climb back on? What courage and determination there is in the man. And to stay aboard all the way back to the rectory to fetch me—how deeply he cares about Veronica. How incredibly loyal he is."

The sky above Dempsey was cloudless; stars winked down, adding light to his search though a full moon would have proved considerably more helpful. But the moon was barely a quarter of itself. Dempsey shrugged. A quarter-moon, stars, and a clear sky were far better than fog and drizzle and no light at all. And the hope that rose in his breast because of the absence of Veronica's lifeless body was better than anything he could think of at the moment. On his knees, the parson squinted at the lane and the berm beside it. There was one place on the berm that seemed not quite like the rest. Some of the grass stood tall, but some of it was only now rising and other bits of it were crushed flat, but he could draw no firm conclusion from that. It might tell of a struggle between Veronica and her attacker, or it might simply be the evidence of a fox having rolled about at the side of the road, enjoying the fine evening. Dempsey stood and held the lantern at shoulder height. He turned in a circle, called out Veronica's name, and waited. There came no reply. He whistled, and waited again, hoping to hear a responding snort or a burr from Veronica's mare. He heard nothing of the sort, only the usual scamperings and twitterings, the calling of the creatures of the night—and a breathless snuffling.

A smile crept slowly to Dempsey's face. "Theophilus, is that you?" he called. "Have you followed me, you old rascal?"

The snuffling ceased, replaced by a joyous bark and the sound of a happy hound rushing at Dempsey out of the darkness.

"Yes, you have found me, Theo," Dempsey said, kneeling, setting his lantern aside, and taking the elderly hound into his arms. "What a good dog, you are, Theophilus. What a fine dog, to have come all this way with nothing but your nose to guide you. Come, my lad. We'll walk on a bit, you and I and Tom Hasty's noble steed. Perhaps Veronica escaped the man. It's possible, you know. Perhaps she rode to the Widow Thistledown's and is safe and sound there even as we speak."

Dempsey took the horse's reins in hand and led it along the lane in the direction of Mrs. Thistledown's cottage, Theo trotting proudly beside him. Please let her be at the Widow Thistledown's, he prayed silently. Or at the very least, Lord, let the Widow Thistledown have seen Vernie riding neck-or-nothing for the safety of Blackcastle. You can reach Blackcastle from here, can you not? Yes, I believe so. Did not Berinwick mention that day I was shot that he had stopped in at the cottage on his way home? Yes, he did. I am certain of it. Perhaps the dastard was preoccupied with shooting Tom Hasty and Vernie had that one moment of his preoccupation, that one opportunity to spur her mare into a run and escape him. She could do it. I have seen Veronica ride. She could outride any man, did she have but a few moments head start on him.

"There is nothing Veronica Longwood cannot do, I think," Dempsey said aloud, "once she slips out from beneath the guilt, sloughs off that shell of dependence that her mother and that dreadful stepfather of hers—and her husband, too—forced her into. Once she gathers all her courage about her, Vernie will be able to conquer the world. I know she can conquer the world if she wishes, Theo. I have seen the remarkable power of her, because I knew her in the best of times, you see, before she was tamed and pampered and taught to be nothing but a bit of decorative braiding on some duke's sleeve.

"No, no, that's unfair," he continued, his long stride carrying him quickly along the lane. "I don't know a thing about Julian Thorne. Not anything but what I have gleaned from all he has written. He might well have complied with Veronica's every whim and encouraged her in her weakness without knowing what it was doing to her, simply because he loved her with all his heart and not because he intended her any harm whatsoever. Certainly she meant more to him than a decorative braid on his sleeve. How could she not? She was his wife. Why do I blame him for something I might well have done myself? Do you know what it is, Theo?" he asked in surprise. "I believe I'm jealous. Yes, well, I know I am. Jealous of a dead man because he married the only woman I have ever loved. What a stupid thing, eh? Well, but now that it's come to my attention that I can seethe with jealousy, I shall cease to indulge in it. Veronica loved him, after all. She loved him very much, from what I can tell. I shall set myself to learn to admire and respect Julian Thorne's memory, that's what. I will make it easy for Vernie to share her memories of him with me whenever we speak. A woman who has lost a beloved husband must be allowed to speak of him when she wishes to do so. I will urge her to speak of Julian Thorne to me whenever she likes."

Dempsey knew that he was babbling. It was the tension, the uneasiness of not knowing if he would find Veronica at the Widow Thistledown's or not that made him do it. And Theo did not seem to mind in the least. Had the hound not appeared, Dempsey would have mounted Hasty's horse and ridden like a madman for the little cottage, but Theophilus was old and could not be expected to keep up with the horse for such a long distance. And besides, if Veronica were not at the cottage, he would be forced to ride to Blackcastle next, and quickly, too. The horse, as well as Theo, could use this bit of walking in case they should be forced to set out again at anything approaching a lively pace.

Mrs. Thistledown, in a flannel nightdress covered by an enormous shawl, her feet bare and her nightcap wildly askew, stood on the threshold of her little cottage, candlestick in hand, and stared at the parson. "Her grace?" she asked. "You are seeking her grace here, Mr. Dempsey? I cannot think why you should come looking for her grace here."

She could not think why he should be looking for her grace anywhere at all at such a late hour as this, but Mrs. Thistledown was much too polite to say such a thing aloud to the man.

"You did not see her ride down the lane earlier this evening, did you, Mrs. Thistledown?" he asked. "It would have been several hours ago, I should think. Still twilight. She would have been riding the white mare and traveling at an outrageous speed. Perhaps she veered off into Hatter's field? Can one reach Blackcastle by cutting across Hatter's field?"

"Should you like to come inside and sit down for a moment, Mr. Dempsey?" Mrs. Thistledown offered. "You and the hound?"

"No. No. Thank you very much. If you have not seen her

grace, then I must go on to Blackcastle. Can one reach Blackcastle by cutting across Hatter's field? You did not say."

"It's possible. But I wouldn't do it if I were you, Mr. Dempsey. It be far too dark of a night and there be things in Hatter's field and in the field beyond . . ." Mrs. Thistledown's voice faded into nothing.

"What sort of things, Mrs. Thistledown?"

"Haunts," she said on a breath of a whisper. "I did see a haunt in Hatter's field only tonight. A fierce thing it looked to be, too. Not Owain Glyndwr or even the Stiperstone Strangler. Not at all. A demon from Hades, I should think this one were, with two heads and arms and legs flopping all around it instead of where arms and legs be intended to be."

Arms and legs flopping all around it. Arms and legs flopping all around it. A vision arose in Dempsey's mind. Might not a man carrying a woman who had fainted or lost her senses look like a demon with two heads and arms and legs flopping all around it?

"Where did it go, Mrs. Thistledown? This demon?"

"Into the barn and it never did come out again, it didn't."

"Perhaps it waited to reemerge until you had departed, Mrs. Thistledown? Did it have a horse with it? A white horse?"

"No. No white horse. No horse at all what I noticed. And I didn't wait to see if it came out again. That be the truth. I were so upset by it that I hurried back to my little cottage as quick as a fox before the hounds."

"Just so." Dempsey nodded. Hope fluttered in his stomach. Veronica had fainted and her attacker had carried her into the Hatter's field barn. Perhaps she was there now! Perhaps he would arrive in time to capture the villain and save Veronica's life, and she would prove so grateful for his assistance that she would listen to his proposal and agree to marry him. And then the hope in his stomach ceased to flutter and dropped like a stone to the bottom of a lake. "Mrs. Thistledown," he asked, tapping the bottom of his lantern against the side of his knee nervously. "You did not, perchance, receive a visit from the duke this evening, did you?"

"From his grace? No, Mr. Dempsey, I did not," replied the widow. "The only visitor I be having all the entire day and night be you."

Just so, the parson thought. No sign of Berinwick. What am I to do if I manage to capture the villain and rescue Vernie, only to discover that Berinwick is in dire straits? Or gravely injured? Or dead? What do I do then? She will not thank me for saving her life before her son's, Veronica will not. I am certain of that.

"I beg your pardon for disturbing you, Mrs. Thistledown," Dempsey said, attempting to be polite when all he wished to do was mount Hasty's horse, charge down the drive, cross the lane, and ride into the field to thc barn. "If you will simply explain to me the most expedient way to reach Blackcastle from Hatter's field, I will leave you to your sleep. And I thank you for your kindness in speaking with me. I most certainly do."

"You be taking the road at the bottom of Hatter's field. You be taking it to the left," Mrs. Thistledown explained slowly. "And you will come upon a small field planted in wheat. It be cut from the midst of Grydwynn Wood, it be. You cross that perticuler field and follow the road what is on the other side of it to the left, Mr. Dempsey, and that will be taking you to Blackcastle. But I would not be doing it, not tonight," Mrs. Thistledown warned. "Good night to you, sir."

"Good night, Mrs. Thistledown." Where in Jupiter *is* Berinwick? Dempsey wondered as the cottage door closed behind him and he hurried to where he had tied Tom Hasty's horse, Theo trotting at his heels. The lad expected his mother to be home before dark and she was not. Why was the lad not here, pounding on the Widow Thistledown's door, hours ago? Why did he not come pounding on my door? Does that mean Vernie did escape the fiend's clutches somehow and did get home to Blackcastle? But if she did, she most certainly would have told Berinwick about Tom Hasty and Berinwick would have come looking for his groom. Even if he thought the poor man dead, he'd not have left Tom's body to lie at the fork in the road through the night. Not Berinwick. Which means he still would have called upon the Widow Thistledown, and then me.

The smoke in the squire's study was not as thick as that in the vestibule, not yet, because it was on the opposite side of the house from where the first of the sparks had set the roof ablaze. But there was evidence that the fire had crossed the upstairs corridor. A beam had fallen through the ceiling and smashed into the side of an enormous French armoire, which now tilted precariously to the right, balancing on two of its four feet only, the entire weight of the piece upheld by the left curlicue on its top right corner, which rested against the corner of the room itself. The sound of pounding that Berinwick had followed was coming from inside the armoire.

"Anne?" he called.

"Is that you, Will?"

"Yes."

"Oh, good! I'm in here. In the armoire. Thank heaven you found us."

Us? What does the child mean by us? No one else was missing as far as Berinwick knew. Only Anne.

"We cannot get out, Will. This huge thing came crashing down out of the ceiling just as I was gathering everyone up and I jumped in here—to avoid getting squashed, you know—and I cannot get out. I have been thumping and thumping against the doors, but it is no use. And it is frightfully hot in here. It gets hotter and hotter by the minute."

"I should think so," Berinwick replied. "The blessed house is burning to the ground, Anne." Berinwick dropped the wet rag from before his nose and mouth, crossed immediately to the armoire and began to pull on the door nearest the floor. It moved not at all. He transferred his energy to the door above it, but though he pulled until his muscles strained to the breaking point, that door would not open either. "What the devil is holding them closed!" he shouted with exasperation.

"They're locked, I think."

"With what? Three brass bars straight across?"

"I don't know with what, Will," Anne Tofar replied, a teariness in her voice that Berinwick noted at once, despite the courage that he knew she intended to convey. "But there is a lock of some kind. Papa always kept it locked when he was not here—at least he did until Liddy jumped inside and had her kittens."

"Do you mean to say you are in there with a cat?"

"And six kittens. I came back inside to fetch them."

Berinwick had already turned away and was searching madly through the squire's desk drawers for a key to the thing. The smoke was increasing and the smell of it, which had long since set his head to aching, was now beginning to nauseate him as well. "Of all the stupid things to do," he growled, throwing the first of the drawers over his shoulder, sending it crashing into the wall behind him. "To come back inside once you were out of the house for a cat and a bunch of kittens!" He tossed the next drawer over his shoulder as well, sending its contents spilling into the fireplace. He pawed madly through the next drawer, his eye watering, the heat increasing around him. Something else was about to come tumbling through the ceiling. That, or the ceiling itself was coming down. He could sense it.

"I couldn't leave them to burn to death, Will. You would not have done so. And do not say that you would, because you would not. You may fool everyone else into thinking that you are gruff and cruel and uncaring, but you cannot fool Hannah and me. We know it is all a role you play. Oh, Will, cannot you f-find the key? It is so hot in here and I—I—"

Berinwick snatched a key from the third drawer, rushed back to the armoire, and stuck it into the lock. He turned it to the right, heard a satisfying click and tugged the bottom of the two doors open. He reached in, scooped Anne Tofar up into his arms and spun toward the study door.

"Wait! Will, wait!" Anne cried. She was very near tears, and her eyes were red with the smoke. "I haven't got them all. I only have Diddle and Marshall Newman."

"Oh, for the love of Jupiter!" Berinwick shouted, but he set the girl's feet on the floor and rushed back to the armoire. They were mewling and crying, the rest of the kittens. One clung to the spine of a ledger. Another curled in a corner on the top shelf. A third clawed at the bottom shelf, hoping to make its way into the drawer beneath. The fourth was caught up in the mother cat's mouth by the scruff of its neck. "Don't move, cat," Berinwick ordered, pinning the mother cat in place by the sheer force of his glare. He reached out, scooped her up, took the kitten from her mouth and stuffed the tiny thing into his coat pocket. Then he tucked the mother cat securely under his arm. He heard Anne moving about, coughing raggedly behind him, but he did not turn away from the armoire to see what she was doing. Instead he snatched the yellow striped kitten from the top shelf and stuffed it in his pocket with the black kitten. "Where the deuce I'm going to put you two," he grumbled at the remaining kittens, "and still get us all out of here, I cannot think."

"In here, Will," Anne said, tugging at his sleeve. She had torn one of the draperies down from the window, folded it, and placed her two kittens atop it. "Give me Liddy and those in your pocket and get the other two. Quickly, or we will all burn to death."

"Now you think of that," Berinwick replied, handing her the cat and kittens and turning back for the last two.

"I thought of it before I came back in, but the fire was not so very great then. At least not back here. I came in through the door from the rose garden."

Berinwick set the remaining kittens onto the drapery, wrapped it around the lot of them and tied it together at the top. Then he placed the squawling bundle in Anne's arms, lifted Anne up into his own, and leaped for the threshold just as a great creaking, a whoosh of fiery air, and a tremendous crash informed him that the study ceiling had fallen to the floor as he had sensed it might. "Where is this door to the rose garden?" he asked. "I cannot recall it."

"Just around the corner there." Anne pointed. Then her eyes grew wide with fright as she peered back over his shoulder at her father's study, suddenly awash in flames.

"Veronica!" Dempsey called one last time, looking around at the empty barn, his lantern held high.

"Arrrr-rooooh!" Theophilus bayed plaintively, hearing the sadness in his master's voice. "Arrrr-rooooh!"

"Never mind, Theo," Dempsey said, reaching down to the hound and tugging him close, stilling him so that he might hear the smallest of sounds should there be any. But this time, like the time before and the time before that, there was no answer to his call. None at all.

"She's not here, then. He has taken her somewhere else, Theophilus, if it was Veronica's attacker whom the Widow Thistledown saw, and if it was Vernie whom he carried."

Dempsey attempted to convince himself that it was not— that Mrs. Thistledown had not seen anyone or anything at all. That she had, in fact, completely imagined the supposed demon. If only that were true it would be the reason he could not find a single sign of Veronica in this place, and he need not feel such a useless old fool because he could not see as well as he ought by lantern light.

"If the Widow Thistledown did truly see the man and he *was* carrying Veronica, Theo, we have lost all trace of them for tonight, I'm afraid. It will not do us a bit of good to attempt to follow them through Hatter's field in the dark when we don't know where he's bound or in what direction he's taken her, or even if he is walking or riding."

Theophilus, stirred to the core by the tone of his master's voice, jumped up and attempted to lick the parson's cheek. Then he pulled free of Dempsey's grasp and snuffled his way through the darkness at the edges of the barn. He covered the entire perimeter of the old outbuilding while Dempsey waited with a sad smile on his face for the elderly hound to return.

I ought to go back to the rectory and see to Tom, he thought. I ought not have left him alone. And yet, he, himself, would have wished me to come in search of Veronica. I am certain of that. "Why the devil did you make me only one person, Lord?" he asked, exasperated. "What do You expect of me? I cannot do everything and be everywhere at once."

I might go back and ask Mrs. Thistledown to go to the rectory and look after Tom, he thought then. But it's the middle of the night and she has children to look after—the eldest of them is merely a child herself. No, I cannot ask her to leave them alone when there is some lunatic running about shooting at people. And I cannot ignore the fact that Berinwick has not come looking for his mother or Tom Hasty, either. The wind smells most queer in that particular quarter.

"Come, Theo," he called quietly. "We'll go on to Blackcastle, old fellow, and see what we can discover there. Perhaps our lovely lady is safe and sound and we are frittering away our time in this old barn for no reason at all. What the deuce is that you've found?" he added as the dog returned to him, something dangling from between his teeth.

Theophilus whined and dropped the prize down before him.

Dempsey knew what it was the moment he touched it, before he held it near the lantern's glow. It was the pendant Veronica had shown him as they were walking here in this very field on the day she had given him Norville. It was the pendant that Julian Thorne had given to her on her wedding night. The pendant she intended to pass on to her son.

"She *was* here," Dempsey hissed. "Theo, where the devil did you find this? Show me, old fellow. Can you?"

The hound merely stared up at him.

"It belongs to the lovely lady, Theophilus," Dempsey said, and laying the pendant on the flat of his hand, he held it out for the hound to sniff. "It belongs to the lovely lady who likes to take your paw and laughs at you when you are being a rascal. Veronica, Theo. Can you find her? Can you find her for me?"

Theophilus sniffed the pendant thoroughly, took it carefully from the parson's hand, and trotted off toward the very back of the barn, tail wagging.

It's too much to hope for, Dempsey thought, picking up the lantern and following in the dog's wake. He thinks it a game, merely. He only wishes to please me, but he has no idea what I want from him. None at all.

And yet the hope of finding Veronica alive, of freeing her from the fiend who had taken her, and escorting her home to safety had risen once again in Richard Dempsey's heart.

Eleven

Soot-covered, bedraggled, exhausted, the intrepid group of firefighters straggled along Widowen Lane toward Blackcastle. Some of them walked, but most rode in a little caravan of saddle horses, carriages, dog carts, and farm wagons. They were silent for the most part, the lot of them, except for the coughing and the sobbing. It was Mrs. Tofar who sobbed the most. And rightly so, for the poor woman had watched her home, her possessions—and, almost, her daughter—licked at and eaten by the flames. And though orange-reddish flames no longer stroked the sky behind them, smoke continued to float upward, obscuring the starlight over Tofar Farm. Each time Mrs. Tofar looked back, she could see the smoke rising and knew clearly that almost everything was lost.

They had left a goodly sprinkling of men behind them at the scene of the fire to keep watch over what did remain of the house and stables, to extinguish any flames that dared to rekindle, to save what could be saved from the rubble. Berinwick had instructed his grooms to join with the squire's men in rounding up Squire Tofar's animals—those that had escaped the blaze. They were to bring them, in whatever manner seemed the most expedient, to the Blackcastle stables where their needs could be tended to one by one. It would prove a daunting task.

It would prove a daunting task, as well, for the staff of Blackcastle to prepare enough beds for the Tofars and the Tofar servants before the morning dawned, to provide enough water for their washing up, and gather enough nightdresses and clean clothes for them. And then there were the inevitable injuries to be tended to—the cut and blistered hands, a burned cheek here and a sprained wrist there, a stubbed toe, a dislocated finger or elbow.

"I cannot thank you enough, Berinwick," Squire Tofar said gruffly, as he brought his horse up beside the duke's.

"Think nothing of it, Tofar. Any neighbor would do as much. I am sorry we could not save more of the house, though."

"The house? Pah! Houses may be rebuilt. It takes merely money and time to do that. I am thanking you, most especially, for saving my Annie, Berinwick."

"Oh. Well, as to that, you're welcome, I'm sure. She's a brave girl, your Anne."

"And foolish, to go back into that conflagration for a stupid cat and a litter of kittens. I ought to box the child's ears soundly."

Berinwick drew his horse off to the side of the lane and halted, which forced Tofar to draw off the road as well if he wished to maintain the conversation. The ragtag little army tramped past them, weary and woebegone.

"I think you ought not do that," the duke said, studying the exhausted, begrimed older man with sympathy. "Box Anne's ears, I mean. What you ought to do, Tofar, is to take Anne in your arms and hug her to you as heartily as you can."

Tofar had done precisely that already. Three times, in fact. And he was inclined to do it again the moment he dismounted and located Anne among the crowd that would soon be milling about outside Blackcastle. But he was amazed to hear Berinwick say it. The young duke was not generally known for such sentimentality.

"I am sorry about Eloquent's foal, too," Berinwick added. "I found Trewellyn handing her up to Hannah in one of the wagons. Eloquent was near to mad with worry, watching him do it."

"Too much smoke for such a tiny thing," Tofar muttered. "Does it survive, it will never be sound in its lungs. I ought to have put it down, but I could not bring myself to do it, and I could not put such an onerous task on any of my men. Not this night, I could not."

"Time enough to put her down tomorrow or the day following if she shows no improvement," Berinwick replied. "Don't worry your head over it now, Tofar. You have lost enough this night. We will fight for the foal, my men and I. If anyone has a chance to save that little one, it will be Tom Hasty."

"Aye," the squire nodded. "Tom's a miracle worker when it comes to horses. But I did not get one glimpse of him tonight, Berinwick. Was he not with you when you came? Has he gone off somewhere?"

"He accompanied my mother to the rectory," the duke said. "They set out well before we heard your fire bell. She found something she thought Mr. Dempsey ought to have, my mother did, and I could not persuade her to wait and deliver it in the morning. She intended to drop in for a moment on Mrs. Thistledown as well. A double reason to go. She was worried, I think, about the state of things at that particular cottage, though they all seemed to be doing well enough the last time I looked in on them.

"Tom and she will not have heard your bell at the rectory or the cottage," he continued, "but I did tell McClane to send Tom to Tofar Farm after us once he had brought Mother safely home. Perhaps my mother requested Tom's aid in preparing Blackcastle to receive your people," Berinwick added with a smile, visions of the groom attempting to make beds popping into his mind. "McClane was the only one we left behind us, you know, and he with an injured ankle. Not much help to be had from a man with an injured ankle when it comes to preparing beds and all. About the fire itself, Tofar."

"Yes?"

"One of your men said the stable was set alight purposely."

"Aye, that would be Michaels. Michaels saw a man dashing away. Said the fellow mounted a horse that was tied a goodly distance from the stable and rode off as though the devil were after him."

"He did not recognize the fellow?"

"No. Did not give chase, either. Ran for water and yelled to warn the others to get the horses out."

Berinwick urged his horse back into the lane at the rear of the caravan and Tofar did the same. "I cannot think why anyone would set your stable alight, Tofar. Has the entire world gone mad? What could the fellow hope to gain by it?"

"I can't guess," murmured Tofar. "Bless me, but I haven't a notion."

Both men were exhausted and not inclined to push their animals beyond a sedate walk, nor were they inclined to invest their remaining energy in further conversation.

When at last the caravan arrived at Blackcastle, that old pile of stones proved a welcome and heartening sight. Blackcastle fairly danced with light. Torches lighted its perimeter; McClane had obviously set every lamp and candle inside the place aglow. "Now that should put a bit of cheer into Mrs. Tofar's heart," Berinwick said. "She must at least feel welcomed by such a sight as that."

"Eh?" asked Tofar.

"Nothing," Berinwick replied. "I was merely thinking aloud."

It seemed to Berinwick, as he gazed at his home, that all the doors of Blackcastle stood open wide, ready and willing to take him and all these poor, bedraggled humans to its heart. He always thought of Blackcastle that way, as a living, breathing thing, ready, waiting, and more than willing to provide him succor when most he required it. It was a stupid way to look at a mere pile of stones and he would never admit to such thoughts in front of anyone. But they were there. They had been there since first his papa had sent him off to school.

And then Berinwick noticed McClane limp quickly through one of the doors and rush as best he could into the milling crowd. Urgently, it seemed, the farm manager peered into wagons and carts. He spoke first with one man on horseback and then another. Finally he stood in the midst of this small sampling of weary humanity and called Berinwick's name.

The duke urged his mount forward. "What is it, McClane?" he queried, dismounting beside the man.

"It's her grace," McClane answered at once. "She has not yet returned, your grace. Neither she nor Tom Hasty. I waited forever, it seemed, but no one came and the twilight disappeared and it was full dark. I lit the torches for them and went inside to light up all of the windows. And then I thought I would go down to the stables to see if you had left one of the horses behind you. I thought to saddle it and ride off in the direction of Mrs. Thistledown's cottage, despite the pain in my ankle, but then—but then—"

"But then what, McClane?"

"Then I heard hooves pounding up the drive and I hurried out the front doors to see who it could be coming at such a pace."

"And?" Berinwick urged when it seemed the man would not continue.

"And it was her grace's mare—her grace's white mare— thundering toward the stables as though the devil himself were on her heels. And her grace was not in the saddle! She was not in the saddle, your grace. Something dire has happened! I cannot help but think that something dire has happened to her grace and Tom Hasty both!"

With a sigh, Dempsey turned away from the corner of the barn where Theophilus sat. There was nothing there but an old, broken plow leaning against an ancient, topless trunk. He had assumed, because Theo had led him directly there, that it was the spot where the hound had found Veronica's pendant. And for an instant, Dempsey's heart had come to a stop. A horrifying vision had assailed him, a vision of Veronica lying cold and still inside the ugly box. He had had to force himself to step forward and gaze down into it. But Vernie had not been there, lifeless or otherwise. He had peered behind the trunk with equal anxiety, fearing the very worst, but there had been nothing behind the trunk but a dirty floor.

"Come, Theo," he called, making his way toward the door. "The lovely lady is not here. There is nothing here. This is a big, empty barn and nothing else. We know now that the fiend did carry her in here. We have her pendant to prove it. But he has carried her out again and we are not like to find any trail to follow tonight—not when my eyes are so bad and you do not quite understand that I wish you to take Vernie's scent from this bit of jewelry and follow it to her. I wish I had not read that diary. I really wish I had not. I would likely see better then. My eyes would not be so weary."

Theophilus merely sat where he was and whined.

"Theo! Come, sir!" Dempsey demanded.

Theophilus put his head back and bayed.

The Reverend Mr. Dempsey could not think what was wrong with the hound. "Please come, Theo," he said, softly. "I am worried beyond belief. We are not like to find our lovely lady tonight, and we must still go on to Blackcastle. Something has happened to Berinwick. We will be forced to snoop about a bit, I think, before we knock on his door. If we discover nothing sinister by spying on the place, we'll raise the dead at that old pile of stones, you and I. I promise we will. You shall bay and I shall pound on the door and we shall both make ourselves thoroughly obnoxious until someone explains to us satisfactorily why the duke did not come looking for his mother."

The hound followed him reluctantly out into the night where the parson once again mounted Tom Hasty's horse and, steering it carefully through the dark, brought the steed safely into the road at the bottom of Hatter's field, a goodly two miles and more from the Widow Thistledown's cottage. There was one more field to cross before he came upon the road that led directly from his church to Blackcastle. By the light of the flickering lantern, almost out of oil now, and with the luck of a gentleman who was never loath to push on, regardless of the odds, when he had some idea of which way to push, Dempsey found the field Mrs. Thistledown had described and crossed it without injury to himself, his horse, or his hound. He kept to the side of the road when they gained it and held the horse to a walk until he reached the entrance to Black-castle, where he entered and dismounted before the gatehouse. He shuttered his lantern and led Tom Hasty's horse cautiously up the drive.

The Reverend Mr. Dempsey could not ease the tension from his shoulders. The nearer he drew to the castle, the more tense he became. Something had happened to Berinwick—he knew not what. He could not afford to let anything untoward happen to himself or there would be no one to say that the Duchess of Berinwick had been abducted and that Tom Hasty lay gravely injured in the rectory's master bedchamber.

As he rounded the bend nearest the castle, Dempsey was amazed to see the house shining like heaven at midnight. There was light throughout—in every room with a window, he thought—and torches blazed along the turnaround and around the side of the place. And just as he reached out to grab the scruff of Theophilus's neck to keep the hound from dashing forward, a horse thundered from the side of the castle into the turnaround, reared wildly, and pawed at the air before the rider on its back settled it and turned it down the drive in Dempsey's direction.

They were as black as the night, horse and rider both, and were it not for the torches flaming behind them, Dempsey doubted he would have been able to see them at all. "There'd be nothing but the thunder of those hooves to set us scurrying out of his path," the parson muttered, holding tightly to Theo and Tom Hasty's horse, pulling them from the drive into the shadow of the trees that lined it. "Who the devil is that? He's more frightening than Owain Glyndwr's ghost could ever be. Theo!" Dempsey shouted abruptly as the hound wiggled from his grasp and shot out into the drive directly into the path of the horse and rider, barking wildly. "Theo, no!" Dempsey yelled. He dropped the horse's reins and lunged out into the drive himself, diving at Theophilus in a mad effort to save the old hound from being trampled to death.

"Son of a sea serpent!" Berinwick exclaimed, hearing the frenzied barking and then Dempsey's shout before he could see either man or dog. He pulled powerfully on the reins, turning Triumph's head and thus forcing the stallion's feet off to the left side of the drive, causing the horse to stumble a bit, but bringing him, in the end, to a swift halt. "Damnation!" the duke exclaimed, leaping angrily from the saddle. "Who is it? What the deuce is going on?" Then his one eye noted the shadow, blacker than those around it, hunched in the middle of the drive. He stalked forward, his shoulders squared, his riding crop beating in indignant exasperation against his leg.

"I'll be deviled! Berinwick, is that you?" Dempsey asked, straightening, but not freeing Theophilus from the circle of his arms. "I hate to tell you what you looked like, coming down the drive like that."

"Dempsey? What the deuce are you doing skulking around my house in the middle of the night? Was it Theo barking? Is he all right? Did Triumph miss him?"

"Missed us both, barely," Dempsey replied, releasing a much quieted Theophilus and gaining his feet.

"Good. I wouldn't want to hurt the hound. What have you done with my mother, Dempsey? She and Tom went to take you some journal or other and she's not been seen since. Her mare came back without her."

"Yes, I know."

"You know?"

"Well, I know about the volume. She brought it to me. She was going on from the rectory to visit with Mrs. Thistledown for a bit after she dropped it off."

"Indeed. She told me as much before she departed."

"But she never reached Mrs. Thistledown's, Berinwick. She and Hasty were attacked along the road. Tom was shot and is lying, gravely injured, at the rectory. Apparently your mother could not escape her attacker and has been abducted."

"My mother has been—?"

"Where the deuce were you, Berinwick?" Dempsey ruth-
lessly interrupted. "Why did you not come pounding on my
door the moment night fell and your mother had not returned
home? If Tom Hasty had not managed to remount and ride
back to the rectory—never mind. Never mind. At least you're
not dead or abducted or held prisoner in your own house as I
feared. I thought I was going to be forced to rescue you before you could help me to rescue Veronica."

Veronica could not remember when she had fallen asleep
this last time, but she must have done for her eyes were
even now just beginning to blink open. All but one of the
candles had sputtered out and the world around her was almost totally black again, though she did not feel as cold as
she had at first.

I am growing accustomed to the temperature, she thought.
It is not as cold as I imagined it to be. It is more damp than
anything else. But I am growing very tired of this darkness.
What the deuce did the man mean by confining me in such a
place as this with so little light to see by? Is he hoping to blind
me? Well, only let him make an appearance in this chamber
and we'll see who blinds whom.

"Is anyone there?" she called loudly. "Hello? Can anyone
hear me?"

Her voice echoed and reechoed for the longest time, but
no answer came. She pondered whether she ought to make
her way along the cave wall to the arch that she had noticed
when all three of the candles had been alight—however
long ago that was—and then go through the arch into the
adjoining chamber. She would not take the entire candelabra with her, of course. Merely the stub that continued to
burn.

I did not see any light in that chamber before, she thought,
but perhaps it was still night and there was no sunlight to seep
in. Perhaps it is daylight now and there will be bits of light filtering through the ceiling or one of the walls. Perhaps there

is even an entranceway in the next chamber, or the chamber beyond that one, if there is a chamber beyond that one.

But then Veronica recalled the two caves she had entered with Julian and she hesitated. Caves did not have flat floors or regular walls. They had, instead, great piles of rocks and rubble, unexpected crevices, paths that ended abruptly at the edges of deadly cliffs, stalactites growing down from the ceiling and stalagmites reaching up from the floor, some of them dense and solid enough to break a man's nose did he not see them in time and run into one. And in some caves, Julian had explained, streams rushed through underground channels at a violent rate and sometimes formed themselves into tremendous waterfalls. If one were not very careful, a single misstep could end one's life in the world beneath the ground.

And all I would be able to see by the light of that one tiny candle stub would be the area immediately before me. I would not so much as see the floor and the ceiling together at one time.

"Well, what are you going to do, Veronica Longwood Thorne?" she asked herself aloud as she sat idly on the cot, ignoring the aches that plagued her from the beating. "Are you just going to sit here and await the fiend's entrance, or can you think of a way to escape in spite of everything? I must think of a way to escape in spite of everything," she replied with a soft smile that caused her lower lip to hurt. She ran her tongue gently along that lip and tasted blood.

Damnation, she thought. When I get my hands on that dastardly poltroon, I will whip his sorry hide from here to Ludlow and laugh every inch of the way.

And then Veronica had an idea. An inspiration, actually. Cautiously, she took the still-lighted candle stub from the candelabra and, cupping it in her hands, she began to move cautiously around the chamber, holding the light low, first, to see what lay immediately before her feet, then raising it to the height of her waist, then higher, above her head. If she remembered correctly, the ceiling stretched high above her, but at one point—at one point—a fall of rocks led up to it, nearly touching it. If this cavern were like other caves, there would be roots growing down through the ground. Perhaps there would be a root thick enough to form the base of a torch.

Berinwick arrived at the rectory shortly after dawn with the youngest of his grooms beside him. They ignored the front door and rode around to the kitchen entrance. "There's nothing to fear, John," Berinwick said reassuringly as they dismounted and tied the horses. "If Tom Hasty made it through the night with the Reverend Mr. Dempsey as the only person in attendance, you certainly won't be able to kill Tom."

"N-no, your grace," young John replied nervously.

"I wouldn't ask it of you, Johnny, except that so many of our men remain at the Tofars'. There is much to be done there. And I cannot send a female to look after Tom. He'd comb my hair with a milking stool if I did that."

"J-just so, your grace."

"Besides, Langton will be along soon. He'll lend you a hand. And his wife and daughter will be with him. They will be pleased to give you advice on how to care for Tom— women always will, you know—give men advice. They are excessively good at it. Dempsey, open up!" Berinwick called, pounding his fist against the door.

"I swear you were born to open graves and awake the corpses," Dempsey declared, unlatching the door and opening it wide. "Have you ever heard of knocking on a door, your grace?"

"I did knock."

"No, you pounded. There is a difference."

"Never mind that. How is Tom? You didn't manage to kill him, did you? I've brought young John here to sit with him until we return. Tom *isn't* dead, is he?" Berinwick asked more quietly when Dempsey did not answer at once.

"No. No. He is a bit better, I think. His breathing is easier and more regular and the bleeding has ceased. You can look in on him if you like. He's at the top of the stairs, first room on the left." The parson followed them to the vestibule and watched as the duke and the youngest of the Blackcastle grooms took the stairs two at a time. Dempsey shook his head in wonder.

"There was a time when I would have had that much energy coursing through me after I'd fought a fire and then remained awake to cope with the aftermath the entire night, Theo," he commented, staring down at the hound beside him. He could tell Theo was longing to hurry up the steps after the two men, but the hound did not. He refused to leave his master's side. "I hate to admit it, Theophilus, old fellow, but I'm forced to climb that staircase this morning merely one step at a time."

Berinwick pulled a chair up for young John beside the bed, then sat down on the very edge of the mattress himself. Tom Hasty's face was as pale as a winding sheet, but he was, as Dempsey had assured the duke, breathing easily and he appeared to be resting comfortably. Still, Berinwick's hand trembled a bit as he placed it on the groom's brow.

"He is not as feverish as he was," Dempsey offered from the threshold. "I vow, I thought surely he'd be dead when I got home last night but I did what I could for him. I could not remain, Berinwick. I had to go out and search for your mother. And I had to go as far as Blackcastle, too, when I found no sign of her, because—"

"You need not feel guilty about your decisions last evening, Dempsey," Berinwick interrupted. "I can only think that I'd have done the same had I been in a like position. And Tom is not dead. Whatever you have done for him, it has gone a great way toward saving his life."

"Yes, well, the powders my brother gave me halted the bleeding quickly and the sweet basil powder ought to drive out the fever sooner or later."

"I sent Davey Lancaster off to Ludlow for a physician," Berinwick murmured. "You said Tom didn't require a surgeon, that the ball had gone straight through?"

"Indeed. How long will it take for the physician to arrive?"

"I doubt he'll arrive before tomorrow, even if Lancaster

convinces him to drive the entire night through. But I told Gaines to send someone to East Hill Downs to the apothecary there. Stupid not to have a physician of our own hereabout. But they don't wish to come. And if they do come for a time, they don't stay. They all wish to reside in London or the larger cities, you know. They are like to feel more important in places like that, tending to the fribbles of the aristocracy. Did Tom say anything more this morning? Did he say who attacked them?"

"No. His mind was wandering and his speech beyond understanding. Perhaps later in the day he will make more sense, but we cannot wait for Tom to make sense, your grace. There is no telling the danger in which your mother lies."

"Just so."

"There is water for him there in that pitcher, John," Dempsey said. "His glass is beside it. Give it to him whenever he asks, eh? But the best thing is to allow him to sleep for as long as possible."

"Dempsey and I must be off, John," Berinwick added, standing. "You'll tell Langton what happened and that we've sent for help—and you'll look after Tom for us, eh?"

"Look after him as though he be my own pa," young John replied. "You may place your trust in me, your grace."

Berinwick nodded and crossed the room, ushering the parson out before him. "Gaines found this note on the hunt table in the Great Hall after we attended to everyone last night," he said, taking a piece of paper from the pocket of his hunting jacket and unfolding it as he and Dempsey descended the stairs together, Theophilus padding along behind them.

"What does it say?" Dempsey led the way along the corridor, into the kitchen, and out through the side door. "I must go down to the stable and saddle Norville," he added. "Will you wait here or join me?"

"I'll join you, but do hurry, Dempsey. I realize you're old and all, but we haven't a great deal of time. There's no telling what that monster has done with my mother."

The parson increased his pace to match Berinwick's. Behind

them, Theophilus attempted to trot and yawn at one and the same time. Dempsey had intended to have Norville saddled before Berinwick arrived, but he'd fallen asleep on the sofa for an hour or two, and changing Tom Hasty's bandages had taken longer than he'd planned. And to tell the truth, he'd not expected the duke to be on his doorstep with the rising of the sun. Obviously Berinwick had taken no time to sleep at all. He'd not so much as changed his clothes. His jacket and breeches and boots were covered in soot and saturated with the smell of smoke. He had washed his face and hands, though, and brushed the debris from the burning buildings out of his hair.

"What does it say, the note," Dempsey asked again as they entered the stable.

"It says that the villain has my mother, of course," Berinwick grumbled.

"I assumed it would say that. What else does it say?" Dempsey gathered Norville's tack and began to saddle the animal.

"That if I wish her returned to me, I must prepare to part with that old bowl and stand I showed you of the Poles—"

"The Poles? Good heavens, you don't mean to tell me the villain is another Pole?"

"I don't know, Dempsey. I don't believe he is. There is no raging about past wrongs in the thing. No talk of revenge. He does not even mention the bowl as belonging to the Poles, though he describes it well enough that I knew at once which bowl he meant. He didn't weigh the paper down with a silver lion holding a crown with a griffin rising, either. Which, I should think, an actual Pole would have done. There are two of them missing yet—lions—according to my father's writings. Whoever wrote this simply set a stone on it, Gaines said, to keep it from fluttering off the table. I expect he requests that particular bowl because it can be easily carried and it's worth a small fortune. The rest of the things he requests are equally as portable and quite as valuable. There's an entire list here. Obviously it is someone familiar with m'father's collection."

"Are you willing to part with everything on that list?"

"Of course, if I must. Though what I truly long to part with is my rapier, Dempsey. I long to leave it buried in this fiend's heart. And I will, too, once I discover who the fellow is."

"I think not, your grace," Dempsey murmured.

"What?"

"I think you will not run the man through."

"And what makes you think that?"

"There are laws in England. Laws that will see that this man is adequately punished. You'll not kill him unless you must do so to protect your life or someone else's. I will not allow it."

"You will not allow it?"

"Precisely so. I will not allow you to murder anyone. To kill in self-defense or in defense of those you love is one thing. To murder a dastard simply because he is a dastard is quite another."

"Blasted parson," Berinwick grumbled.

Dempsey smiled. "Just so," he acknowledged. "I am a parson and though, as your rector and simply as a man, I have a duty to your person, m'boy, I have a greater duty to your soul. You will discover that I take *both* duties seriously."

"Do not call me that," Berinwick ordered petulantly. "I am not a boy. And I would not be *your* boy, even if I were still a youth. We will see whether I skewer this fiend or not, Dempsey. We will see about that."

"What is it now?" Dempsey asked as Berinwick glanced back down at the note and began to nibble at his lower lip.

"Eh?"

"I asked what it is that's written on there that seems to be upsetting you so."

"Nothing. It doesn't matter what's written on here, Dempsey. The fiend is not going to get any of it. We are going to find my mother and rescue her. She will tell us who the villain is, and I will dispatch him with alacrity. It is merely that, if we cannot find her—if we cannot—There is something listed here at the last that I have never heard of before. I cannot think what it can be. I shall have to go through Father's catalogues and hope his Mr. Tweed from all those years ago made a note of it and described it accurately."

"What is it?" Dempsey asked, leading Norville out of the stable and toward the spot where the duke's Triumph was tethered.

"Some kind of chalice, I assume. Father has a plethora of chalices from the old monasteries. It says here that I must provide this poltroon with something called Glyndwr's cup. You don't suppose that refers to *Owain* Glyndwr, do you? Why would Owain Glyndwr have been running about fighting battles with a chalice at his side? Or perhaps he kept it stuffed inside his breastplate? Dempsey? What's wrong?" Berinwick asked, as the rector's steps slowed considerably.

Patrick McClane, who had assured Berinwick that his ankle was not broken and that he would not require a surgeon, limped out to the stables. He was forced to saddle his own horse—a labor he found tedious and aggravating but necessary, since not one of the Blackcastle grooms was anywhere to be seen.

Fire at the Tofars' or no fire at the Tofars', I have the haymaking to see to, McClane thought, and it's likely—with so many of the laborers from Blackcastle absent from the field this morning—that things will go abominably ill. There will still be the laborers from the village, of course, and the tenant farmers, and those confounded Welshmen. But I'll be forced, first thing, to send some of the men back here to hitch up the farm wagons and drive them down. That alone will set us back considerably. I hope Berinwick does not expect me to actually join in the haymaking. Overseeing the task is one thing, doing it is something else again. I ought to have stood up to Berinwick that first day in the meadow when he hired those blasted Welshmen over my head, he thought as he stepped up into the saddle. Ought to have quit my position then and there. "I was born to be a gentleman," he whispered.

"What the deuce business have I to play the role of Berinwick's servant?"

Oh, he doesn't call me a servant, McClane thought. No. But he treats me with no more respect than he treats his valet or his butler. And his father treated me no better. Well, but at least his father did not come out into the fields, sticking his nose into my business every time I turned around.

"But I will not be forced to put up with Berinwick's highhandedness for much longer," he mumbled as he ducked beneath the stable door and rode off.

"What did he say?" asked Anne.

"I don't know. I was not listening," Hannah replied, stroking the black head that rested in her lap. "I wish Tom Hasty were here. Tom would know what to do for this poor little thing."

"I don't know how you can be so worried about Eloquent's foal when you ought to be worried about your mama," Anne offered, patting the foal's withers tenderly and watching Liddy, in her nest in the straw in the corner of the stall, gently washing her kittens one by one. "I should be thoroughly overcome with shock and fear if my mama had been abducted."

"No, you would not," Hannah protested. "You were not even overcome with shock and fear last night when your house was burning down around your ears. I do believe that it was you, was it not, Anne Tofar, who ran back into that conflagration to save Liddy and her kittens?"

"Yes, but I was frightened beyond belief when I thought I would never escape from that armoire and we would all of us be burned to cinders. If Will had not come after me—"

"Yes, but that is just the thing," Hannah interrupted. "Will *did* go after you, and here you are, safe and sound. Yes, and Liddy and her kittens are safe and sound as well. And Will has already set off to rescue Mama, so I am not worried at all. Whatever Will sets out to do, he does, and admirably well, too."

"That's so," Anne nodded. "He is, perhaps, the greatest hero of all time, your brother."

"Do you think so?"

"Yes. And I am madly in love with him, too," Anne giggled. "But do not say a word to anyone. You won't, will you, Hannah?"

"Certainly not. But Will is much too old for you."

"He is merely ten years and two months older than I am. I know that seems like a tremendous gap now, but it will not seem so when I am twenty, and it will seem an even smaller gap when I am thirty."

"You are not thinking to wait until you are thirty to marry Will? Of course you are not. You will find someone you like a good deal better than my brother long before that. Oh, there is Trewellyn. Trewellyn!" Hannah cried, transferring the foal's head carefully onto Anne's lap and quickly gaining her feet. "Trewellyn, are you terribly exhausted?" she called, hurrying from the stall. "Oh, but I know you are." Hannah sighed, then, clasped her hands behind her back and stared down at the toes of her walking shoes. "You spent half the night fighting the fire and the other half attending to Squire Tofar's horses, bringing them here and caring for their burns and their lungs and all."

Trewellyn, a smile playing about his lips, studied the young lady before him with weary but sparkling eyes. "What is it you wish of me, my lady?" he queried, his voice still scratchy from the smoke.

"I—I merely hoped that perhaps you would—" Hannah peered up at him from beneath her slightly lowered lids. "That is to say, I hoped you would come and take a look at Eloquent's foal."

"The foal? I thought Tom Hasty were looking after that one."

"No," Hannah replied, abandoning her waiflike pose at once and fixing her gaze full on the groom. "Did you not hear? Tom Hasty has been shot and my mama abducted."

"What?" Trewellyn roared.

"Tom is not going to die," Hannah added quickly. "Mr. Dempsey took him in at the rectory last evening and ministered to him. The Reverend Mr. Dempsey can work miracles, you know. Mama believes he can. He is near to being a saint, I think. And Will has sent Davey Lancaster off to Ludlow for a physician for Tom, and Gaines has sent Tibbs to East Hill Downs to the apothecary, too. And my mama will be rescued shortly," she added, "because both Will and the Reverend Mr. Dempsey have gone to save her. But there is no one to save Eloquent's foal. Anne and I would, if we had the least idea what to do. Would you be kind enough to tell us what to do, Trewellyn?"

Veronica sat at the top of the rockfall, attempting to chop through a root as thick as her forearm with the sharp point of a small stone gleaned from the fall itself. She had set aside the bit of candle, had set it far enough from her so that her movements would not extinguish its tiny flame. But its light was necessarily lost by doing so and chopping at the root without being able to see it was proving to be dangerous and difficult work. She had missed her mark any number of times and her hands were cut and bruised inside her gloves. Her arms ached from holding them above her head. Pieces of soil caused her to lose precious moments when they filtered down into her eyes.

"Do give it up, you blasted root," she grumbled, her heart thumping fearfully inside of her as she peered at the candle. "I've only minutes before I am completely in the dark again and I do not wish to be left in the dark again without a single hope of finding my way out of here."

As if in response to her words, the root came loose in her hands and she breathed a thankful sigh. But now was not the time to sit back and glory in such a small victory. Instead, she must somehow build a torch on the thing. Hurriedly, she divested herself of her gloves in order to unfasten her riding skirt. Already torn in several places from the poltroon's attack, Veronica proceeded to tear the skirt further, making strips of it and wrapping them—one after the other—quickly around the root. She did the same with strips from the bottom of her shift until the top portion of the root became a great, hulking thing. Then she reached into the little pocket that she always kept fastened around her waist beneath her skirt to take the pendant from it, unbraid the leather, and use those strands to hold the whole together.

"Where is it?" she cried, feeling for the pendant in the dark and not finding it. "Oh, my dearest God, where is it? How am I going to keep all the material together without it? It will all burn up in a flash and fall off before the root itself can catch fire." She felt like crying. Tears rose at the back of her eyes. She wanted simply to toss the makeshift torch away, rest her head on her arms, and sob. But she called herself to order at once. What good would sobbing do her? None. If she surrendered to tears now, not only would she be unable to search for an exit from this place, but if her captor did not return quickly, she'd freeze to death in nothing but her bodice and her shift—a greatly shortened shift, at that.

And then it occurred to her. She would put the pocket over the strips of cloth and tie it to the root with the ties that kept it around her waist. Quickly she undid the pocket, took from it the little bottle of Balm of Mecca that she kept near her to rub into her hands and keep them smooth, and she placed the open pouch over the thumping great mass of strips of material. She knew that the torches that blazed in the turnaround were dipped in pitch to keep them alight for a long period, but she had nothing that resembled pitch. What she did have was the Balm of Mecca. Veronica shrugged her shoulders, poured the oil over the pocket, tossed the bottle aside, and waited impatiently for the oil to soak through the pocket into the strips of cloth beneath.

The little stub of a candle was nearly gone by the time she made her way carefully to it. Holding her breath, praying silent prayers, Veronica lifted the stub carefully to her makeshift torch and applied the flame to the oil-soaked pocket. It did nothing at first, but then it began to sizzle and spit, and then a tiny flame appeared—a flame separate from the candle flame—and that flame, that blessed flame, meandered slowly up and around the oil-soaked pocket.

* * *

Theophilus trotted immediately toward the old barn in Hatter's field, tail waving happily.

"That's where I discovered the pendant I gave you last night," Dempsey said as he tethered Norville. "In that barn. Well, Theo discovered it, actually. I couldn't see much of anything myself."

"There isn't much of anything to see in that particular barn," Berinwick replied. "It's used to store wheat. Hatter's field was once one of the best wheat fields in the county, but there hasn't been any wheat grown here for the past two seasons." Berinwick finished tying Triumph to a sapling, gave the beast's rump a farewell pat, and started off toward the barn with long strides. Dempsey, hands thrust into his breeches' pockets, kept pace beside him.

"You're quiet, Dempsey."

"What? Oh, yes. Pondering."

"Pondering what?"

"Your mother said something to me about this field. She said it was to have been planted in mangel-wurzels and turnips."

"Yes, to restore the soil, but McClane forgot."

"Just so. You were busy with the aftermath of your father's death and your farm manager forgot. Why did he forget, do you think, your grace?"

"Why?" Berinwick shrugged. "It was an upsetting time for everyone at Blackcastle—even McClane, I expect."

"And yet, he is paid not to forget such things, is he not?"

The two of them entered the barn to discover Theophilus sitting beside the ancient, topless trunk, his tail sweeping back and forth across the dusty floor.

"Wait," Berinwick said, extending his arm to keep Dempsey from progressing. "There might be footprints."

"There *are* footprints—everywhere," Dempsey replied. "I noticed as much last evening. Prints of boots, mostly, and some children's shoes—"

"Right," Berinwick nodded. "Mine and Charlie's and Millie's, but we never did go over there where the hound is sitting."

"I did," Dempsey murmured, gazing at the floor between himself and Theo. "Went to have a closer look at the place where Theophilus found your mother's pendant. I wasn't thinking about finding footprints by then. I was only thinking that she might be—that she might be lying in that trunk or behind it. But I did not make the trip twice," he added, staring at the patterns on the floorboards. "No, and I did not wear my shoes one time and boots the next, either. I hadn't time to don my boots before I set out after her."

Theophilus whined impatiently as the men studied the pattern of shoe and boot prints across the barn floor. There were three sets of prints, besides Theo's: one set made by a gentleman's walking shoes, which went directly to the trunk; another set of that same pattern, which returned; and a set of prints made by riding boots that led to the place where Theophilus sat, and did not return at all.

Theophilus stood and turned and began to scratch at the trunk; then he turned back toward the gentlemen, sat down on his haunches, and bayed.

The two hurried toward him. "Move that plow," Dempsey ordered. "I'll move the trunk."

"What the deuce?" Berinwick, having fairly tossed the plow out of the way, grabbed the other side of the trunk to help shove it aside. "What the deuce?" he repeated, staring down into a hole in the floor. "How did that get there?"

"Someone put it there," Dempsey said excitedly. "The same someone who carried your mother in here, I should think." He sank to his knees, shouldered Theo aside, and shouted down into the opening, "Veronica? Vernie, can you hear me?"

". . . ronica? . . . nica? . . . hear me . . . me . . . me," echoed his voice back up at him.

"Don't," Berinwick whispered, kneeling down beside the parson. "What if the villain is down there with her?"

"Then he will know we have discovered his little secret," Dempsey replied, shouting his answer down into the aperture. "And he'll know I am about to come down there and rip his head from his shoulders!"

"You're the one who told me I couldn't run the dastard through," Berinwick said, as Dempsey's voice echoed back at them.

Dempsey fixed the duke with a most intimidating stare. "Only because I'm a parson and responsible for saving your soul," he replied from between tight, dry lips. "Whether or not I choose to save my *own* soul is entirely my own business. How dare he? How dare the man abduct Vernie and stuff her under the ground as though she is nothing but a sack of potatoes to be saved for the winter's dining!"

"If she is down there, why doesn't she answer?" Berinwick muttered. "Why doesn't she make some sound, any sound?"

"I am going down," Dempsey declared, turning about, swinging his legs over the side until he was hanging only by the grip of his hands on the broken flooring. "There's no ladder," he observed for Berinwick's benefit, and then he released his hold.

Berinwick heard a number of rocks clatter, an "Ouch!" and a definite thump. "Dempsey? Are you all right? Can you see her? Is she lying there senseless?"

There was no immediate answer but Berinwick and Theophilus, peering down into the hole side by side, could both hear a groan, then the muffled movement of cloth, and at last the sound of boots against rock. Mr. Dempsey's footsteps sounded tentative at best as he moved about below them.

"I am coming down," Berinwick called.

A low whistle answered him, and then the sound of boots again, and just as the duke sat down and swung his legs over the side, he saw the Reverend Mr. Dempsey's face looking up at him.

"Don't come down just yet," Dempsey said.

"Why not? What's wrong? Oh, m'gawd! She's not dead, is she? Not my mother!"

"No, your grace, not dead. She's not here. That is to say, she's not in this particular chamber."

"Chamber? Particular chamber?"

"It's not a root cellar," Dempsey replied. "Your grace, we are going to require a ladder and some lanterns."

Twelve

Theophilus padded back and forth before the hole in the barn floor. Then he sat. Then he padded back and forth behind the hole in the barn floor. Then he sat. Then he padded all around the hole in the barn floor, sat down, and bayed plaintively.

Twelve feet below him, the Reverend Mr. Dempsey was pacing as well, but he could not sit, not even for a moment. He would have bayed if he thought it would do him the least bit of good, but he failed to see how it would. He shouted instead. He shouted Veronica's name over and over, but the only answer he received was a series of echoes.

Where the devil did the lad go for those lanterns? he wondered. I hope he wasn't attacked along the way! No, that would be stupid. The villain is demanding a ransom. How can he expect the duke to pay it if he kills the duke? Still, he killed Berinwick's father. Wasn't thinking about any ransom when he did that. "Veronica!" he shouted again in the midst of his pacing.

It was light enough where Dempsey paced to see almost all of the rocks and crevices that surrounded him—because of the daylight filtering in through the gaps in the old barn and down through the hole in the floor. But it would be pitch black farther back in the cave. No matter how much he longed to go charging in after Veronica, Dempsey knew perfectly well that he would be forced to a standstill by the complete lack of light.

And then the Reverend Mr. Dempsey, too sure of himself in the little light he had and not paying the least bit of attention where he set his feet, veered from the path he had been pacing onto an even wider path. He stubbed his toe and banged his knee on a stalagmite rising from the previously untrod portion of the floor, did an odd little dance attempting to keep his balance, and at the last, stumbled against the cave wall, yelled "Ouch! Confound it!" as his elbow and his backside smacked against the stone, slipped unceremoniously to the clay floor, and watched angrily as a miniature rock slide began to tumble down around him. "Damnation!" Dempsey roared. He hunched his shoulders and hid his face behind his arms as stones bounced over him and dust attempted to gobble him up. He coughed. He groaned. He tried to hold his elbow, his knee, and his toe at one and the same time. And as the last bits of shale slithered down around him, three candles bounced off his head and into his lap, one after the other after the other.

"Well, I'll be," Dempsey mumbled, wiping his face on his coat sleeve, thus smearing the dust and dirt around without getting rid of any of it. "If ever a man was blessed by God!" The parson shoved two of the candles into the pocket of his riding coat, fished his flints from his other pocket, lighted the single remaining candle and, with stern words to Theophilus to remain in the barn and wait for the return of the grouchy duke in the buckskin breeches, he gained his feet and cautiously limped deeper into the cavern. The farther he moved away from the opening above him, the darker the world around him became. The darker the underground world became, the less help a single candle flame proved to be. Dempsey took the other two candles from his pocket and lit them from the flame of the first. It will not matter much do I burn them all to nothing at the same time, he thought. Berinwick will be here soon with the lanterns.

The more Patrick McClane considered the idea, the better it seemed. Certainly no one would find such a decision odd under the present circumstances and it would suit his own needs especially well. What good would it do, after all, to attempt to finish in the north meadow today when he was unavoidably short on laborers, horses, and wagons because of the fire at the Tofars?

The entire thing is going to work out a great deal better than I ever imagined, he thought with a mounting sense of satisfaction. I shall have the time I need to visit my chamber and see that my guest is quite cozy, and yet, I will still be present to assist the duke in whatever he might require of me as regards his missing mother. It's amazing, really, how one thing leads to another. When Lady Fortune smiles on a man, even the most annoying obstacles can be overcome. With a smile replacing the thoughtful scowl on his handsome face, McClane urged his horse into a gallop. He was certain that Lady Fortune had begun to smile on him last evening and was continuing to smile on him today. If only he could convince her not to turn her face away until all of his plans were brought to fruition.

When McClane reached the path through the wood that led into the north meadow, however, he declined to place all his trust in the fickle lady, Fortune. He'd spent a goodly number of months in charge of the farmers and field hands at Blackcastle and he knew—he absolutely knew—that despite the warnings and the threats he'd bestowed on them, the stupid fellows would still have their weapons ready to hand. McClane did not treasure the thought of facing more fowling pieces pointed in his direction. No, most certainly he did not.

"Peasants," he muttered under his breath as he rode his horse past the tempting shortcut. "As if they would know a man were an enemy of the duke's without the fellow standing directly before them and declaring aloud that he was. They will likely kill each other in the end, pointing arrows and fowling pieces and slings at everything that moves. Thank goodness I shall not have to put up with it for much longer."

He entered the meadow from the road in plain sight of them all—a tall, broad-shouldered gentleman in a black riding coat and buckskin breeches—his back ramrod straight, his hands light on the reins, a rather strained smile on his lips. When he reached the place where they'd gathered, he swung down from the saddle and strolled straight into their midst. "I expect word has not reached you as yet," he said, a frown creasing his brow.

"Word o' what?" asked one of the men.

"Squire Tofar's establishment caught fire and was badly damaged last night," McClane provided. "Terrible thing."

A series of mutterings arose in response to this news.

"Lost a large portion of the house and the main stable, the squire did. However, everyone escaped with their lives," McClane assured them, "servants and family alike. But because of our efforts to put out the blaze, a goodly number of Blackcastle people are only now sinking down into their beds, which quite diminishes our labor force, eh?"

"Considerable," sighed one of the freeholders who had already taken in his own hay, but was depending upon his wages from the Blackcastle haymaking to plow and plant three more acres of wheat next season and to build a new barn as well. "I expect we'll be forced to do double the work for half the price, eh?"

"Not precisely," McClane replied. "Actually, I thought it might prove expedient to abandon the haymaking for today and to send the lot of you over to the Tofars' to see what help you can be in clearing the rubble and setting things to order. You'll be paid your day's wages, of course, for the doing of it."

"Be ye aplannin' ta accompany us, Mr. McClane?" the woodcutter, Angser, asked from somewhere near the rear of the group.

"No. I think not. There has been a spot of trouble at Blackcastle as well as at the squire's. I rather think I shall see what help I can be to the duke."

"What be going forward at Blackcastle?"

"Are the duke and the duchess safe, Mr. McClane? They have not been shot at again?"

The queries came rapidly, one after the other, and McClane answered them as best he could.

"It is really nothing of significance," he said at last. "A small annoyance, merely. But I think his grace will be glad of my assistance and I feel he will wish me beside him.

"So, you will take yourselves off to the Tofars', yes? And I shall ride back to Blackcastle and make myself of use there, and we will all come prepared to finish our work in this meadow first thing tomorrow morning."

"Aye," grumbled one of the Welshmen. *"We* will all come prepared to finish *our* work. Indeed, *we* will."

Heads nodded. Some of the men, women, and children turned away toward saddled farm horses, hitched carts, and wagons. Others began to walk in the direction of Tofar Farm. McClane, brushing at his coat, imagining himself somehow physically soiled from having merely stood in the midst of them, mounted his horse and turned the beast's head toward Blackcastle.

Veronica wedged her torch into a crevice in a rock and sat down beside it. She ran her gloved fingers through her hair, scattering the few remaining hairpins hither and thither. Her dark, silver-streaked tresses fell the rest of the way down her back to her waist. Shorter wisps curled along her cheeks, clinging to patches of dampness left by the water droplets that fell sporadically from above. She was chilled, weary, sore, and now she was hungry.

Of all things, she thought, a smile curving her lips despite the seriousness of her situation. My stomach is gurgling.

For some reason she found the sound and the thought of it extremely funny. She leaned back and laughed loudly—laughed and laughed—until she leaned forward and buried her face in her hands. Tears spilled down her cheeks and she sobbed as though her heart would break. She allowed herself to sob for a minute or two more, but then she took a deep, shuddering breath, inhaled the stink of the burning Balm of Mecca, and ceased to cry. She could not afford to waste what remained of her torch's light sitting here feeling sorry for herself.

If I am not traveling in circles, I shall be free of this place soon, she told herself, swiping at her tears. Unless I am not walking toward the entrance. Unless I am walking deeper into the cave. "Oh, please, God," she whispered, "let me be going in a straight line. Let me be walking toward the entrance. Do not allow me to wander lost and alone beneath this ground until I die. Do not let me die here alone with no one to take my hand and bid me farewell."

She stood once again, took her torch firmly in hand, and walked cautiously onward, one small step after another, a wraith of a woman, outlined in flame, determined to conquer the underworld.

Eloquent's foal was on its feet and nursing. Eloquent herself was overjoyed to have it so. Trewellyn grinned wearily at the two young ladies who were leaning in a most unladylike fashion on the paddock fence and strolled toward them. "The little one will do for now, Lady Hannah, Miss Tofar," he assured them as he reached them. "A brave little thing the foal is, and a fighter, too. Does she stay on her feet and begin walking about some, her lungs will do better than they would with her lying down. Ye need not remain, my lady," he added, his smile especially for Hannah. "You've talked me into caring for the little beast, and that I will, though I do think I'll take a moment now to wash the dirt from my hands and face and put a pot on the boil."

"Oh, Trewellyn, I am so sorry!" Hannah exclaimed. "I did not truly think. You have been up and working the entire night and now I have asked you to care for the foal."

"It's no trouble, my lady," Trewellyn assured her. "I will simply bring a blanket out here and settle down in the paddock with the two of them."

"We could remain," Hannah suggested, "and you could go to your own bed for a time."

"And what would his grace say to that?" Trewellyn queried, knowing the answer as well as Hannah did. "He would say that it is you young ladies who ought to be inside the house sleeping after such a night as you have had, and if I am not man enough to allow you to do so, he'll find himself a groom who is."

"No. Would he really say that?" Anne asked.

"Precisely," Hannah replied with a sigh.

"But we have slept," Anne protested to Hannah as they thanked Trewellyn and wandered off in the direction of the house.

"Because we shared my bed, which was already made up," Hannah pointed out. "Almost everyone else was up and fumbling about very late into the night. Even Cook and Gaines were not to be seen when we came downstairs. Remember?"

"Yes, but Mr. McClane rose early and went out to see to the haymaking."

"Only because he did not go to help fight the fire," Hannah replied. "And aside from lighting the candles and the lamps and the torches, I have no doubt Gaines found Mr. McClane to be useless and sent him off to bed early to get him out of the way."

"Do you think so?"

"I am almost certain of it. Oh, I have got the most brilliant notion!" Hannah exclaimed.

"What?"

"This is the perfect time!"

"The perfect time for what?"

"The perfect time for us to go to the center of the maze. You said last night, just as you were falling asleep, that you wished to see the armor and the belvedere, and this is the most excellent time to do it. There is no one watching over it now. All the grooms, except Trewellyn and Tom Hasty, are still at your house. Will has gone to fetch Mama home, and the shepherds are still asleep. There is no one to say we cannot go in."

"Do you have the map?" Anne asked excitedly.

"No, but I saw exactly where Will put it."

The two young ladies hurried inside and rushed through

the silent corridors to the Duke of Berinwick's study, where Hannah opened a book and removed a piece of vellum from it.

"Is that it? Will doesn't hide things very well, does he?" Anne commented, taking the map from Hannah and gazing down at it in wonder. "It is very old, I think."

"He was not hiding it, Anne. He put it there so he would remember to take it back to the muniments room."

"Oh. It looks to be very easy to follow."

"It is. We had not the least bit of trouble when we all went inside the other day. I rather think I remember the way without the map."

"We will take it with us regardless," Anne declared. "We will feel like utter ninnyhammers if we leave it behind and then get lost and someone must come to rescue us."

It took the excited young ladies less than five minutes to make their way through the labyrinthian corridors of Blackcastle to the door that opened at the very rear of the westernmost wing. Hannah tugged it open and paused on the threshold. In the distance, the sheep baaaed and the maze beckoned.

"Who is that?" Anne asked, peering out over Hannah's shoulder.

"Why, it's Mr. McClane," Hannah replied, watching as the farm manager strolled from the wood on the northern edge of the lawn directly toward the maze. "What on earth is Mr. Mc-Clane doing here? Where has he left his horse? Oh, there it is, tied back in the wood, just under those oaks. But why is he not in the north meadow overseeing the haymaking?"

"He is looking all about him," Anne observed. "Is he looking for the shepherds, do you think?"

"Oh! Oh! He is looking to see if the grooms are back and on watch!" Hannah exclaimed in a hushed voice, pushing Anne back inside and closing the door quickly behind them. "He is the one, Anne! Mr. McClane is the villain who wore the armor and murdered my papa!"

"No, he cannot be," Anne protested. "He is nothing but

your farm manager. How can your farm manager know that the grooms are to be on watch, Hannah? You said it was a great secret and no one else in all of Blackcastle knew of it but the grooms, the family, and Mr. Dempsey."

Hannah gave her friend a thoughtful look, then slowly opened the door again. McClane had disappeared from sight. "I expect he overheard the grooms discussing it. He went into the maze," Hannah declared.

"Or he saw that the shepherds have not yet appeared and went back through the wood to the north meadow. No. No. His horse is still there. Hannah? Where are you going now?"

"I am going to fetch us weapons," Hannah replied, "and then we are going into the maze to see which of us is correct about Mr. McClane. Are you willing, Anne?"

Anne nodded. "But you will see, Hannah, Mr. McClane is seeking the shepherds and nothing more. He cannot possibly be a villain. Farm managers just are not."

"What the deuce is that?" Dempsey, his gloves covered in hardening candle wax, paused and sniffed at the air. "Phew!" he muttered. "Smells like someone burning a bushel of lemons. Veronica?" he shouted. He didn't know why he shouted, precisely. He had ceased to shout for her a while ago when his candles had melted to half-mast, having come to believe that she was either lying senseless somewhere in this dank prison or that her abductor had tied and gagged her and left her unable to answer his calls.

"R-Richard!?!"

Dempsey was stunned when she called out to him in reply. His own name echoed and re-echoed in the air around him, drowning him in the sweet, welcome sound of her voice.

"Vernie? Stay where you are. I am coming for you!"

"Richard!" Veronica called again. "I am here! I am over here! I am lost in this confounded cavern!"

The smile that spread across the parson's face was unequaled by any other he had ever smiled. His ears sorted through the echoes for her original voice. She was straight ahead of him, he thought. He need but keep his toes pointed in the present direction. "Can you hear me if I do not shout, Veronica?" he asked. "Can you understand what I am saying to you at this moment?"

"Yes," she replied, not shouting this time, either, merely speaking loudly, as though he were on one side of the Great Hall at Blackcastle and she on the other.

Dempsey pushed on, attempting not to increase his speed for fear the breeze would extinguish his candle flames. But he did increase his speed. He could not help himself, and the candle flames wavered wildly.

"Richard! Oh, Richard, is that you? That tiny speck of light before me?"

The Reverend Mr. Dempsey came to a halt. A goodly distance ahead of him, flames danced and shadows scuttled along cave walls. And just below the flames, if he squinched up his eyes a bit, he could see her. He squinched up his nose at the exact same time. "Vernie? I can see you now. Do not come any farther. Your light is bigger than mine. I will come to you, eh? What the devil is that smell?" he added in a low whisper to himself.

He extinguished the faltering flames of his own candles as he closed the distance between them. He waved the candle stubs in the air to cool the wicks and then stuffed them into his coat pocket. His nose wrinkled again as the stench that assaulted it became more powerful. But then, he no longer cared about the smell at all, or the pain in his elbow, his knee, his toe, his backside. She was merely six feet from him, then four, then two. He took the odd-looking torch from her hand and wedged it between two rocks. He took off his coat and helped her don it, even if it was a good deal too big, even if its sleeves hid her hands and fingers completely unless she kept her arms raised. He buttoned each button slowly, carefully as she stood smiling at him. Then he took her into his arms and hugged her to him like a great, lumbering bear hugging a favorite honey tree. He rained kisses down on her brow, her eyes, her cheeks, her chin, and finally he touched his lips to hers. But then he called himself to order, ceased to kiss her, and stepped back, allowing a particle of space to separate them.

"I—I beg your pardon, Veronica," he said softly, his eyes gazing down into hers, the shifting torchlight setting the gold of his hair aglow through the dust that covered it. "I was not thinking. I simply—I could not—are you all right? You are not injured at all?"

"I am bruised from top to toe, I believe, Richard. No, do not loosen your hold further. There is nowhere else I wish to be at this particular moment than in your arms. And tightly in your arms, too."

"Truly?"

"Just so," she whispered. Placing a hand tenderly on each of his cheeks, she brought him down to her and caressed his lips with the cool silk of her own. Her hands slipped around his neck. Her fingers tangled in his hair. She grew flushed and breathless and her heart fluttered like a wild thing in her breast. With a sigh, she continued to kiss him until her spirit soared beyond the sad dankness of the cave, up into a world of crystal sunlight through skies the exact color of Richard Dempsey's eyes.

The dull ache of emptiness that had lingered silently inside the Reverend Mr. Dempsey the whole night through was filled to overflowing with love at the mere touch of her lips on his. His heart thundered joyously in his ears as she clung to him. To have her soft, supple body safe in his arms caused his very soul to sing with triumph and rise into the heavens like a shooting star in reverse.

What the deuce is that smell? the fiend wondered, his nose wrinkling at the acrid odor that the burning Balm of Mecca had left to linger behind in the chamber. He held his lantern higher. A perplexed frown creased his handsome brow. His gaze then fell upon the empty cot and the burnt-out candles in the silver candelabra. Where the devil is that blasted woman? I did not leave her with candles enough to actually go anywhere. I intended merely to give her enough light to calm her when she woke. She was in no condition to wander off. I thought I made certain of that. How hard must one pummel the woman, and how many times, to keep her down?

"One of the three candles is missing," he mumbled. "Well, but she cannot have gone very far with the light of one small candle. She is nearby somewhere. Fainted and lying in a puddle on the floor, no doubt. Or she ceased to wander about at whatever place the candle flame died and cried herself to sleep in the darkness."

With an aggravated sigh and a muttered curse, the villain began to search for her. He had not tripped over her on his way into this tiny chamber in which he, himself, had eaten and slept from time to time, so he must assume that the duchess had walked off in the opposite direction—had gone toward the entrance in the Hatter's field barn, the entrance through which he'd carried her last evening. That was not a good thing. There was a deep and dangerous crevice in that direction, just to the side of the path he had cleared and kept clear over the past fifteen months. Yes, indeed, it was an extremely perilous fissure in the rock floor. He knew from experience. He had been careless early in his exploration of this cavern and had nearly fallen into it himself.

"I am not going after her if she fell," he said, annoyed, keeping his eyes wide open for a glimpse of her on all sides of him as he walked. "If she has fallen into that crevice and broken her bones, she may stay there and die, for all I care. I shall be forced to kill her anyway, once I have got what I want from Berinwick."

Except that Berinwick may not bring me what I desire without I give him a glimpse of her. Bah! he thought. If she's dead, I'll merely seize Lady Hannah. She will do just as nicely for trading purposes, I should think. Could I get into that blasted treasure room of his myself, I would require no one to hold to ransom. I could kill them all and walk off with all I could carry. But I cannot discover where he hides that key and I cannot get in without it.

The dastard had advanced merely four or five yards deeper into the cave at a cautious rate when something on the cave floor, just at the foot of the rockfall, glinted oddly in the lantern light. He stooped down beside it and took it into his hand. "What the deuce?" he muttered. He held the bottle beneath his nose and inhaled the scent of lemons. Then he stood, stuffed the bottle into his pocket, and turned in a slow circle, holding his lantern high. He saw her kidskin gloves higher up on the rockfall and climbed up after them. Setting the lantern on one of the rocks above him, he sat down for a moment and studied the gloves under the light. There were slits across the palms and the fingers and blood inside of them, sticky and smelling of iron.

Why the devil should her gloves be slit and her hands bloody? he wondered. What did she do to herself? Climbed up the rockfall, obviously, but that should not have injured her hands to such an extent. Most of these rocks are dull and rounded.

He stood again, took hold of the lantern, and gazed carefully around the rockfall. Tiny shreds of black cloth and white cloth were sprinkled among the stones. The missing candle stub from the candelabra lay abandoned on a tilted ledge. The fiend cursed under his breath and climbed to the very top of the rockfall. Tiny droplets of blood spattered the rocks; above the blood, a short, shredded piece of tree root hung down.

"Blast and damn!" he hissed. "Blast and damn! How did she ever think of that? How could any woman come to think of that? I will break the she-devil's neck with my own hands when I catch up with her!"

"Why does the Reverend Mr. Dempsey be kissing our duchess?" asked a small voice from somewhere behind Dempsey's back.

"And why does our duchess be wearing nothing but her

shift an' Mr. Dempsey's coat?" queried another voice, equally as small and sounding perfectly amazed.

"What the deuce do you think you're doing, Dempsey?" growled a louder, deeper voice. "Unhand my mother this instant, you old reprobate, or I'll have your guts for garters!"

"William?" the duchess murmured, peering around the parson's well-muscled arm and smiling at the sight that met her eyes.

"It is Berinwick, is it not, Vernie?" Dempsey whispered, pressing his cheek against her ear, enjoying the tickle of her hair against his face, determinedly keeping his back to the duke and what he perceived to be a steadily growing crowd.

"Yes, it's William, and little Millie and Charlie Thistledown with him."

"Tell them to go away, Veronica."

"Mr. Dempsey would like you to go away for a bit, children," the duchess said, without removing her cheek from the soft lawn shirtsleeve against which it nestled. "I believe I should like you to do the same—for merely a moment or two."

"Not on your life, Madam," Berinwick replied, stepping closer to them, lantern in hand. "I am not about to let this parson take advantage of you in your—Mother, you're injured," he said on a quick intake of breath as his light betrayed the bruises on her face, her slightly swollen lips, a most grievous scratch along one cheek, and a cut above one eyebrow.

Dempsey sighed. Reluctantly, he surrendered his dream world and stepped away from the duchess. "Yes, she is injured, Berinwick," he said, turning to face the duke and the children. "And she requires all the comfort with which we can provide her."

"I am not *gravely* injured," Veronica protested, going to her son and taking his free hand in her own. "You are both making it sound as if I shall die in the next five minutes. I am perfectly capable of surviving this escapade without either one of you making a fuss over me. Lead us out of this cavern, William—you and Millie and Charlie—and while you do, tell me that you found Tom Hasty and that he is not dead nor likely to die. Richard," she added softly, extending her hand to him, "come with us now. It is time to leave this place."

Berinwick had brought not only Millie and Charlie and three lanterns, but a ladder and Mrs. Thistledown as well. He had hitched Norville to an old dog cart from behind the Thistledowns' henhouse and driven the lot of them, bouncing and jouncing across Hatter's field, to the barn.

"I didn't know, Mother," he said, as he shooed Millie and Charlie up the ladder, "if you would require a woman to attend you or not. We had no idea what the fiend did to you, Dempsey and I. And so, when Mrs. Thistledown suggested that we would do better with the children to carry extra light and with her to attend to you, I said yes."

"I am glad the children wished to help and equally as thankful for Mrs. Thistledown's presence," Veronica assured him, smiling up at the widow, who was just then scooping her children off the ladder and setting their feet firmly on the barn floor. "I should like to take advantage of Mrs. Thistledown's kindness, William, before we return to Blackcastle. I should like to wash up at the very least, and perhaps she will have an old round gown that will fit me so I will not be forced to appear on my own doorstep in nothing but Mr. Dempsey's coat and my shift."

"Just so," Berinwick nodded.

"The man who did this to you abides at Blackcastle, does he not, Veronica?" Dempsey asked.

"Yes."

"Who is he, Mother?" queried Berinwick.

"Patrick McClane," the duchess replied, setting her foot on the first rung of the ladder. "And I do not wish you to go riding off neck-or-nothing after the man, William," she said, advancing to the second rung. "Or you either, Richard Dempsey," she added as she gained the third. "I wish us to sit down in Mrs. Thistledown's little parlor and devise a plan that will allow us to catch that fiend without granting him a single opportunity to injure or kill any more of the people I love.

I am coming, Mrs. Thistledown," she added, looking upward to smile at the woman who waited at the top of the ladder with one hand held out to assist her from the final rung to the safety of the barn floor and the other hand holding tightly to a stout stick.

Around the Widow Thistledown, around the hole in the barn floor, Veronica could see Charlie, Millie, and Theophilus dancing a little jig of joy—with a step and a step and a rarf-rarf-rarf! and a rarf! and a step and a step-step-rarf!

The darlings are dancing for me, she thought. They are celebrating my return from the underworld. In defiance of all that evil has done, can do, might think to do—innocence, loyalty, faith, and trust are not cowed this day, but jubilant in triumph. And this is the day that counts. This day. The day I am living now.

"Oh!" Anne exclaimed, seeing the belvedere for the first time. "How lovely it is. And what a strange place for it to be."

"Shhh," Hannah warned, looking about her suspiciously. "He will hear you."

"Who?"

"Mr. McClane."

"He is not here, Hannah. Certainly we would see him if he were here."

"Not if he is hiding down behind the belvedere," Hannah whispered.

"I did not think of that. I expect we ought to check," Anne whispered back. "You go that way and I'll go this."

"Keep your weapon at the ready," Hannah warned as they stalked forward, separated before the steps of the building, and proceeded cautiously, Hannah walking along one side of the belvedere and Anne along the other.

They came together at the rear of the belvedere, Anne with a smile and Hannah with a frown.

"I told you," Anne announced. "There is not a sign of Mr. McClane anywhere. He is a farm manager. He cannot be a villain. Doubtless, he came looking for one or another of the shepherds to help him with something."

"I think not," Hannah replied at once. "Annie, this is where we discovered the armor. Right here in this precise spot. And we left it here, too. Now the armor has disappeared and Mr. McClane with it."

"But he did not have time to come all the way to the center of the maze, collect the armor, hurry back out again, and disappear, Hannah. It did not take us that long to procure our weapons and come out here to the maze. Either someone else took it, or Mr. McClane is still here within the maze, hiding."

Hannah turned at once in a clockwise circle, her weapon at the ready, peering into the barrier of foliage nearest the belvedere and then scrutinizing the tall, narrow columns of the building itself to see if any speck of McClane's clothing peeped out from behind them. Anne turned in a counter-clockwise circle, her weapon at the ready as well. "Do you see him?" she asked in a hushed voice.

"Not yet," Hannah whispered back.

"Then he is gone," Anne said, letting down her guard.

"We would have passed him in the maze on our way in, Anne. There are not two paths into and out of this maze. There is only the one."

"Then he has gone without making his way back through the maze." Anne allowed the fireplace poker she had taken from the blue salon in the west wing to dangle at her side.

"How could he have gone without going back through the maze?" Hannah asked, allowing the rapier from her father's study to rest on her shoulder. "Unless there is a secret door hidden among the hawthorn bushes."

"Or a door beneath the belvedere!" exclaimed Anne. "Where was the armor, Hannah? Precisely where?"

"Precisely here."

The girls dropped their weapons, got down on their knees, and poked at the wood between the floor of the belvedere and the blocks of stone upon which it sat. They poked and prodded and prodded and poked.

"This part wiggles," declared Hannah excitedly.

"Where?"

"Here. And there is the merest line. Wait, Anne." Hannah scrambled backward, seized the poker, and pried at a barely visible vertical line in the wood. A goodly section of the base at the rear of the belvedere fell out onto the ground.

Thoroughly excited, both girls hurried to look inside and then felt about with their hands.

"I cannot see a thing," Hannah sighed, sitting back on her heels. "Or feel anything but dirt."

"Nor can I," Anne agreed. "We shall need to fetch some candles or a lamp or a lantern if we are to discover anything at all. You wait here, Hannah. You must just sit right up there on the floor of the belvedere with the poker in hand. Right above this very spot." Anne took the loosed piece of wood and set it back into the base as she spoke. "If Mr. McClane believes we are gone and comes sneaking out, you must whack him in the head with the poker at once."

"Just so," Hannah nodded in agreement. "I can do that."

"Good. Then I will go back through the maze and fetch a lamp or something."

"And someone to help us. But not Trewellyn. He is doing quite enough for everyone already and I cannot bear to ask more of him."

"All right then, not Trewellyn. Give me the map, please, and I will go and return as quickly as I can."

Hannah stood and reached into the little pocket, much like her mama's, that she kept beneath her skirt. She could not feel anything inside of it. "Annie? It's not here."

"Are you certain?"

"Yes. It's not here."

"Perhaps you did not put it in your pocket, Hannah. Perhaps you set it down somewhere."

"Where?"

"Inside the belvedere? Over there where you first raised your weapon? Here, when we were feeling for a door?"

The girls searched everywhere. Up and down, back and

forth along all four sides of the building. Then they walked farther out from the belvedere, through all the grass that surrounded it. Then, right beside the bushes that formed the inner square of the maze, avoiding the thorns as best they could to peer under them. The map was nowhere to be found.

McClane moved quickly through the darkness with only one side of his lantern unshuttered. He had traveled back and forth on this same path so many times that he barely needed any light at all. Here was the spot where the trail sloped downward ever so slightly. Five steps ahead was the enormous stalactite that had to be ducked under or it would take a man's head clean off. Eight paces beyond that, on the right, the rift began, slitting through the floor of the chamber like a snake slithering through grass. He halted at the edge of the crevice, opened the second of the lantern doors, and peered cautiously over the edge. There was no telling how reliable a torch the duchess had been able to fashion or how long it had lasted. She might well have made it only as far as this fissure, and not seeing it, stepped off the edge. But the only thing the dastard saw as he dangled the lantern over the jagged opening were David Hancock's bones rotting away in the damp.

"I will get her back before she escapes this place," he hissed down at what remained of Blackcastle's previous farm manager. "See if I don't. I have not been waiting all these years to avenge my father and gain a fortune at last merely to see my hopes dashed by some beetle-brained female. I will have my revenge on Berinwick and his family for killing my father and I will have everything they own of value that I can carry away with me, too. See if I don't, Hancock. See if I don't!"

He reshuttered the second lantern door. No sense announcing his approach to the duchess by giving her an extra gleam of light to see him by. Once he passed the crevice, once it snaked its way farther out into the center of the cave where it was of no danger to anyone who held to the path, there were merely odd turnings, low ceilings, uneven and slippery floors, and falling shale with which to contend. The going became a good deal easier.

But the Duchess of Berinwick, he thought, will not realize there is nothing else of great significance waiting to entrap her. She will still continue slowly, since she knows not what to expect. Oh, I will catch up with the lady, I will. And when I do, I will see to it that she never attempts to escape me again.

McClane was truly amazed when he had traveled two miles and more without a sign of her. Even if the torch she had fashioned had proved amazingly bright and durable, he could not fathom how she had kept going for such a stretch, not knowing if she was bound in the direction of an exit or twisting and turning deeper and deeper into the cave. "No other female could do this," he whispered to himself. "It is because she's a Thorne and has powers beyond those of any human woman."

The pendant! he thought then. The blessed child took the pendant home and gave it to her mother. That's where the witch is getting her power—from that blasted pendant! He cursed himself for having given up the trinket, and cursed himself again for having given it up to a Thorne, in particular. But when the opportunity had arisen to seize Lady Hannah, to hold her to ransom and bring both mother and son to their knees at one and the same time, he had not been able to resist it. The sweet thought of it had lured him into an abominable decision. A spur-of-the-moment thing, really. No plan. No thinking involved. Simply an opportunity that presented itself for the taking. And the child had seen the trinket, too, and ridden off the lane practically into his grasp.

And then she had ridden out of his grasp in an instant. One shout from Davey Lancaster and she had grabbed the pendant and ridden off at full tilt, leaving him to lead the groom on a chase through Grydwynn Wood, until he could come around behind Lancaster and knock the man senseless.

"Imagination. Nonsense. Pure rubbish," the villain mumbled to himself. "I will not be intimidated by a piece of ancient jewelry. Such things have no power nor do they bestow any upon those who wear them. I have been playing at superstitions and ghosts so long that I am losing my mind in the quagmire. When I get my hands on that she-devil of Julian Thorne's, I will rip the pendant from around her neck with my bare hands. Then we'll see who has power and who has none." Just as he said the words, the acrid smell that had cloyed its way up through his nostrils and into his head for the length of his journey beneath the ground seemed stronger, more pungent. He stopped and shuttered his lantern completely. Yes! There was a flicker of light up ahead.

As silent as a spider on a wall, the poltroon scuttled forward. The light that did not belong to him increased and he smiled widely. It was not moving, that light. He could see that it remained, flickering and sputtering—he could hear it sputter now—in one spot.

She has given up, he thought. She cannot imagine how close she is to freedom and so she has set her torch aside and surrendered to the hopelessness of it all! The damnable woman is mine! Victory swelled McClane's chest as he closed in on the vile torch she had fashioned. She would never fashion such a torch again. Never again. And then he was upon her. He was upon . . .

McClane halted and blinked in astonishment. There, wedged between two rocks, the torch the duchess had made from a root and some cloth continued to burn, emitting the foulest odor, but the Duchess of Berinwick was nowhere to be seen. McClane muttered, unshuttered his lantern, turned back onto the path, and hurried forward, not caring now whether she heard him or not, not caring if she looked back over her shoulder and saw him closing the gap between them. He had to catch her up. She was almost at the spot beneath the floor of the Hatter's field barn.

But the floor is too far above her, he reminded himself, attempting to calm his sudden panic. She will be forced to look for my ladder, and she'll never find it, as well-hidden as it is, without that torch.

Whatever possessed her to leave the torch behind? he wondered abruptly. She came this far with it. Why leave it behind? He slowed then, forcing himself to think. Why? Why? Why? He urged himself to gather his wits about him before he did something stupid—something he would dearly regret—like walking right past a woman with a large rock in her hands—a rock that she was waiting to bounce off his head. He reined in his anger, his antipathy, his frustration. He reshuttered all but one door of his lantern again and moved from the center of the path to scuttle along silently, close against the rock wall. He was rewarded for his suspicions and his stealth by the sight of more and brighter light before him and the sound of her voice.

"Patrick McClane," she said. "And I do not wish you to go riding off neck-or-nothing after the man, William. Or you either, Richard Dempsey. I wish us to sit down in Mrs. Thistledown's little parlor and devise a plan that will allow us to catch that fiend without granting him a single opportunity to injure or kill any more of the people I love. I am coming, Mrs. Thistledown."

McClane pressed himself against the wall. Saliva welled behind his lips. He gulped it down. So, he thought. The duke and that wretched parson have rescued her. And the three of them think they will capture me without the least injury to anyone. We'll see about that, we will. Lady Hannah is at Blackcastle even now. At Blackcastle, and purely innocent of everything that has occurred. She will not know to be wary of me until these three return there. No one at Blackcastle will know to be wary of me until then. And they think to waste time formulating some fool plan or other at the Widow Thistledown's cottage before they ride for Blackcastle. Ha! Much good *that* will do them!

For the first time this particular day, Patrick McClane put his hand into the pocket of his riding coat and lovingly stroked the hard steel of the little pistol that fit so nicely there. He smiled—a cold, lifeless smile. Then he turned back along the track he had just taken and made his way toward Blackcastle and the maze.

Thirteen

"We are trapped here forever," Anne sighed, seated dejectedly beside Hannah on the floor of the belvedere, their legs dangling over the edge. "Look in your pocket again, Hannah."

"I have looked in my pocket five times already. I am not looking there again," Hannah replied with a pout. "And I am not looking anywhere else, either. I am quite sick of looking for that map. It has completely disappeared."

"It cannot have completely disappeared," protested Anne. "Things do not, you know. It must be somewhere."

"Yes, but we cannot find it, so it is not the least help to think it is *somewhere*. Where is somewhere? That's what we need to know so we may go and fetch the wretched thing."

"Perhaps we simply ought to begin walking and we will remember the way out as we go along."

"Pooh! I thought I remembered the way *in* this morning. But did I? No. We had to consult the map any number of times. If I could not remember the way in when we came, why would I remember the way out now? No, I am afraid we must wait here until someone hears us calling for help and arrives to save us."

"But we are not calling for help," Anne pointed out.

"I expect we ought to, but I am so utterly disgusted with myself that I do not feel in the least like doing so." Hannah's shoulders slumped ever so slightly as she leaned forward and began to thump the heels of her walking shoes against the rear wall of the belvedere. "I thought we would be heroines, you know, and make everyone proud of us by disclosing to them that Mr. McClane is the villain they seek and by capturing him."

"You intended for us to capture him? Truly?"

"Well, I hoped we might. But, of course, we have not. I expect Mr. McClane has gone far from here by now and Will has already saved Mama and is close on the fiend's heels. All I have done is to get us into a place from which we cannot exit—not without help, at any rate. Oh!" Hannah exclaimed as her heel abruptly kicked against nothing at all. "Oh!" she cried again as she felt a hand seize her ankle and give it a mighty tug. "Annie, it's the villain and he has got hold of my ankle!"

Anne pulled her legs up and scrambled away from the edge of the belvedere at once. She grabbed the weapon that lay nearest to her on the floor behind them. "Unhand Hannah at once, you wretch!" she cried, scrambling forward and jabbing the point of the rapier downward at the gloved hand that was attempting to pull Hannah from her perch.

"Ouch! What the devil?"

Anne lifted the rapier and jabbed it downward again. "Unhand her, I say!"

The hand released its hold with the second jab and attempted to grab the blade, but Anne pulled it up much too swiftly and it bit his hand, causing him to cry out again.

Hannah pulled her legs up, gained her feet with Anne's help and seized the fireplace poker. Together the girls bolted to the front of the belvedere and down its three shallow steps.

"I should not run out into the maze if I were you," declared a deep voice behind them. "Not only will you become completely lost, but I will find you, my darlings, and I will be frightfully angry when I do." Patrick McClane stood staring at them across the length of the belvedere as they turned to face him. They could only see him from the waist up, but that was quite enough of him to appear most intimidating.

"What makes you think we will get lost?" Anne queried, resisting the urge to cringe and giving McClane back as solid a stare as he was just then bestowing upon the two of them.

"Now let me think. Oh, I know. A little conversation I

overheard about a missing map," McClane responded, rubbing at the spots on his hand where the rapier had bitten him and blood was flowing in a most insignificant amount.

"Have you been under the belvedere listening to us the entire time?" Hannah asked. "What were you doing under there? Rolling around in the dirt like the dog you are?"

"Hannah!" hissed Anne, intensely aware of the hatred rising into the farm manager's face, of the viciousness of the sneer he sent in Hannah's direction.

"You are the man who murdered my papa," Hannah accused, ignoring Anne entirely. "You murdered him and Mr. Thistledown and the others like the poltroon you are, without giving them the least opportunity to defend themselves! Do not deny it, because I know it to be true. You are Harvey Lanton's ghost. It is you who donned the armor and frightened Papa's horses."

"And it was your father who murdered my father," McClane replied with a threatening calm. "And one of your ancestors who stole all that should belong to me."

"That is complete nonsense," Hannah declared. "We have never taken anything that belongs to you or to anyone else. The Thornes do not steal. No, and my papa never murdered anyone, either."

"Ask your mama," McClane hissed. "Ask your brother. Mention a gentleman named Dight."

"Anne, do you know how to use that rapier?" Hannah whispered, keeping her gaze fastened on McClane.

"No."

"Give it to me, then."

Before the shallow steps of the belvedere, the rapier and the fireplace poker changed hands.

"I rather think now would be a good time to call for help," Anne suggested under her breath.

"Yes," Hannah agreed. "Hurry into the maze, Annie, and cry out while I keep Mr. McClane in my sight."

* * *

There was no sign of McClane or anyone else in the north meadow. Berinwick looked about him, bewildered. He had ridden here directly from Mrs. Thistledown's cottage. So impressed was he with the simplicity of his mother's plan and so determined was he to abide by it, that he had not even protested the part where the Reverend Mr. Dempsey was to escort the Duchess of Berinwick safely back to Blackcastle without him.

"Where the deuce has everyone gone?" he muttered. "Damnable villain cannot have abducted each and every one of my haymakers. And even if he could have done, why would he?"

His mother's plan was firmly rooted in the assumption that McClane would even now be overseeing the haymaking, that the farm manager dared not deviate from his routine lest people became suspicious. Therefore, McClane would not have a moment to call his own until the haymaking ceased for the day. Then and only then would he have the opportunity to discover that she had escaped. It seemed reasonable that since he would not know she was free of him and had identified him as her abductor to her son, the villain would not be the least bit suspicious did Berinwick ride out into the meadow, pretend to have discovered Tom Hasty's dead body at last and, fearing for his mother's life, enlist McClane's aid in collecting and packing up the treasures demanded by her abductor.

When she had heard of the fire at the Tofars', the duchess had been both saddened and buoyed. Although she grieved for her neighbors' loss, the fire did provide Berinwick with the perfect excuse to beg McClane's aid in particular. The rest of his household staff, the duke could say, was either incapacitated or greatly distracted as a result of that fire, and he had no one else to turn to in his haste to collect and pay the villain's demand. McClane would believe him and accompany him willingly back to Blackcastle where the duchess, Mr. Dempsey, Harold Belowes, and Gaines would be waiting to confront the farm manager and capture him while one of the grooms rode into Barren Wycche to fetch Constable Lewis.

"It's a sound plan," Berinwick told himself again, "but where the devil *is* McClane? And where are my haymakers? Have they finished here and moved on to the next field? No, it's obvious they have not finished here as yet."

The sound of a horse's hooves galloping along the road behind him caused the duke to turn in his saddle. "What the devil?" he muttered as young John headed his mount straight at the nearest hedgerow. The horse and John came down in one piece on Berinwick's side of it and in a moment they were beside him.

"John? What are you doing here? Tom is not dead?"

"No, your grace. Tom be better and better. Mr. Langton sent me to find you. It were Mrs. Thistledown said you would be here. I stopped at her cottage to see she was safe before I went to seek you out in Hatter's field or follow you to wherever you had gone from there. It be Mr. McClane who shot Tom Hasty and took her grace!"

"Yes, I know," Berinwick replied.

"Aye. O' course you do. You know that. Mrs. Thistledown said as the duchess was rescued. The duchess will have told you."

"You're going on and on and saying nothing, John," Berinwick pointed out. "Is that the reason Langton sent you after me, to say that Tom was able to tell the name of his attacker?"

"That, your grace, and one thing more. Giles Pervis did come to see Miss Beth at the rectory. They be betrothed, you know. At any rate, he came to tell her and her ma and pa of the fire at Tofar Farm and how Mr. McClane did send him and all the haymakers over there this morning to help with the cleaning up."

"McClane is at Squire Tofar's?"

"No, your grace. That's just the thing. Mr. McClane did not go with them. He said as he were going back to Blackcastle to be of assistance to *you*. Well, we all knew that weren't true, your grace. And we reckoned Mr. McClane had plans of his own."

"When? When did McClane send them all off to Tofar's?" A ball of lead was beginning to form in Berinwick's stomach.

"Very first thing this morning, your grace. The villain has likely had a free hand at Blackcastle the entire morning."

"Was the Reverend Mr. Dempsey at the Widow Thistledown's when you stopped there? Dempsey *and* my mother? Did you tell them what you just told me, John?"

"No, your grace. They was already gone off to Blackcastle. I thought it would be best to come for you, them likely being in the dastard's clutches already."

The lead ball in Berinwick's stomach grew larger. He turned Triumph's head toward Grydwynn Wood and the shortcut to Blackcastle and urged the horse into a run. Young John was forced to ride neck-or-nothing to keep up with him.

Anne, fearing to leave Hannah and the villain alone too very long, but knowing if she were not decidedly out of McClane's reach he would come straight for her and prevent her from calling out, ran as far as the first turning in the maze. There she halted and began to shout for help. Someone must hear her. Surely the shepherds had come into the park by now. The sun was already straight up in the sky. Certainly they would hear her and come rushing into the maze at the sound of her cries. "Help! Help us!" she shouted. "Lady Hannah and I are at the center of the maze and there is a villain here attempting to kill us!" That last bit would increase the shepherds' speed and warn them to bring weapons as well. She cried out again and again. And then, as she paused for breath, she heard a pop and smelled gunpowder on the breeze. "Oh, my gawd!" she cried, startled. "The man has a pistol! He has shot Hannah! Help!" she shouted again. "Help us! Lady Hannah has been shot!" And then she turned right around and dashed back toward the center of the maze, the fireplace poker clutched tightly in her hand.

Inside Blackcastle, where no one could possibly hear Anne's cries, Harold Belowes was just then rushing into the duke's study with the tooled leather box that held Berinwick's dueling pistols. He was followed immediately by the duke's valet carrying the gunpowder and balls. "Nordstrom knew where they were, but not how to load the things," Belowes explained. "Gaines has gone off in search of Trewellyn or Overfield."

"Hand them here," Dempsey said, taking the box from the footman, setting it on the duke's desk, and opening it up. He leaned over the desk and studied the pistols for a moment, admiring them, then he took one from the box, took the powder and the balls from Nordstrom, sent the two men off to keep watch for McClane, and proceeded to load the gun.

"Where did you learn to do that, Richard?" the duchess queried, once the servants were beyond earshot. "Your father never had dueling pistols."

"No. But a parson who goes fiddling about in places he ought not to be, looking for things he ought not to know anything about, can find himself in need of a pistol from time to time."

"Richard!"

"Do not look at me with that particular light in your eye, Veronica. I did never actually shoot anyone. I doubt I could hit the side of a barn from two feet away with one of these things. It was merely often expedient to let it be known that I had one near me."

"Because of thieves?"

"Because of other avid antiquity hunters, and smugglers, and thieves, yes," he replied, setting the first pistol aside and beginning to load the second. "I know people think all preachers are dull, sanctimonious toads, but I have been anything but dull all these years, Veronica. Anything but dull."

"I never thought you dull, Richard," she said, stepping up behind him and putting her arms around his waist. "I certainly do not think you dull now. Nor are you sanctimonious or a toad. You are still filthy, however," she laughed. "Filthy and smelly."

"Do not be placing the blame on me for that stench,

Vernie," Dempsey protested, setting the second pistol aside. He turned within the circle of her arms and hugged her to him. "It is the smell from that torch of yours that has infiltrated my clothing. I could not fit into one of Mrs. Thistledown's gowns in order to rid myself of it as you did, you know."

Veronica giggled. "How I should like to have seen you make the attempt," she replied, nestling cozily against his chest. "You, attempting to stuff yourself into a woman's gown! Your face would have been red as a cherry and your ears even redder. And the gown, of course, would split wide at every seam."

"You find that humorous, do you? She finds that humorous, Theophilus," he informed the hound, who was stretched on the carpet enjoying the sunlight that shone through the window.

"Oh, yes, indeed! Most humorous," Veronica responded. "Richard? Once we have captured McClane and sent him off with Constable Lewis, there is something I should like to ask you."

"Is there? Ask me now."

"No, not now. I fear to ask you now when you have so much on your mind."

Dempsey kissed the arch of her left eyebrow tenderly. "There," he murmured. "With that one, simple but mystical action, all is wiped from my mind but you. Ask me now, Veronica."

"I—I—Richard?"

"Yes? I am listening, Vernie."

"I merely wish—when I left you with Dilys Thorne's diary, I found that I hoped with all my heart—I did not think it at all possible, but—"

"But you wished I could find . . ." he said. "Then you ceased to speak and hurried away."

"You remember?"

"I remember every word you have said to me since we met again on that little hill, Veronica, and almost every word you said to me in my youth, too. What is it that you wish I could find? I have spent practically my entire life finding things. I am very, very good at it. Only tell me what you seek and I will be pleased to find it and lay it at your feet."

"I wish," Veronica began again. The hope that had filled her heart when he had come to her in the cave and kissed her so thoroughly shimmered and shifted inside of her, lighting a fire in her soul. "I wish you could find it in your heart to love me, Richard. Not like an old friend, but—but—as a man loves the woman he wishes to marry, the woman he will marry. Can you do that, Richard? Do you think it possible? For I find that I love you with all my heart, you see."

"Can I love you as a man loves the woman he wishes to marry? Do I think it possible? Veronica, for weeks and weeks, I have been attempting to keep from telling you that I love you precisely in that manner. I expect I have loved you with every fiber of my being from the time I was seven without realizing what a marvelous and significant love it was. A child would not, you know. But now I am grown and have come to realize that I have never felt for any other woman what I felt for you then, Vernie, what I feel for you now. I merely did not think it possible that you could love me in that same fashion. And I thought, too, that it was incredibly arrogant of me to entertain the least hope that you would *ever* love me in such a way."

"Arrogant of you? Richard, no!"

"Well, but I am nothing but a clergyman, Veronica. I have no title, no fortune. I have monies enough on which to live a fairly decent life, but I could provide you with nothing like the life you live here at Blackcastle. It is not as though I am the Archbishop of Canterbury, after all. And let me assure you, I am never likely to be—the Archbishop of Canterbury, that is."

"Richard Dempsey, you are *such* an innocent! As though women love gentlemen because of such things as money and titles! Women who truly love, love a man for who he is, not what he has. I did not grow to love Julian because he held the title Duke of Berinwick and was possessed of a fortune. Truly, I did not. And I cannot help but love you, though you have neither. It is the sort of gentleman you are that makes me love you. You, sir, stir me to the very tips of my toes. You make love rise up inside of me as no man has ever done—not even my dearest Jules. There is something so special about you, Richard Dempsey—the way you look at life and help others to see it in a new fashion—the way you believe in people, in their strengths and goodness—your selflessness and your sense of humor—I could go on for days listing this and that, there are so many things that fill my heart with love for you."

"I did think that you had come to love me as more than an old friend—to love me truly, as a woman loves the man she will marry," Dempsey replied. "When you allowed me to kiss you in the cave this morning and then kissed me back in a manner so very different from the way you kissed me in the gatehouse, I thought to myself, this kiss, the love in this kiss, is true and real and intimate. But then I thought, no, it is merely her relief at escaping that dastard. Tomorrow all will be different."

"Tomorrow all *will* be different," Veronica murmured, pushing away from his chest just enough to look into his eyes. "Tomorrow I will love you even more than I do at this moment, Richard. And from day to day, forever, I will love you and desire you more than I did the day before."

Dempsey, his brilliant blue eyes afire with passion, tasted her lips teasingly with his tongue, placed his lips on hers.

"Your grace! Mr. Dempsey!" a voice rang out along the corridor, causing them to step apart on the instant. "Your grace! Mr. Dempsey! You must come at once!" It was Gaines, and he rushed into their presence without the least hint of but-lerish conservatism about him. "Miss Anne Tofar has screamed from the maze that she and Lady Hannah are at the center and being attacked by a villain. And there has been a gunshot. Harry Belowes and Nat Tine—he was checking on the sheep, Nat was, and heard her shout and came at once to tell us—they have just now gone charging to the rescue, but there is no telling what—"

The Reverend Mr. Dempsey was out the study door, his boots pounding down the corridor and Theophilus lunging after him before Gaines could finish his sentence.

"Richard!" the duchess shouted. "Richard, you have forgotten to take the pistols!" Hurriedly placing the guns back into their box, Veronica shoved them at Gaines. "Follow me," she commanded as she gathered the skirts of the gown she had borrowed from Mrs. Thistledown out of her way and dashed off in pursuit of the parson. Gaines, the box of pistols clasped against his chest, spun on his heel and darted off in pursuit of her.

"I daresay you missed me," Hannah observed, her voice cool and calm as she stepped out from behind one of the belvedere's columns to face McClane again. She was pretending to be Will. Will was excellent at role-playing. He pretended to be gruff and unconcerned all the time; surely she could do the same for this one moment when it was likely that Anne's life and her own depended upon it. "Should you like another try at me?" she asked in the nonchalant tone that Will often assumed when he was most fearful of what might be said or done to him. "Here I am, then. Fire away if you think you must."

"You think I will not? More fool you," McClane replied, pointing the multiple barrels of the little pistol at her again. "In case you are totally witless, Lady Hannah, I feel obliged to inform you that this particular pistol fires three times."

"At least you hope it does," Hannah replied.

"It is the latest thing. I had it made by the premier gunsmith of Paris."

"French. Useless, then," Hannah goaded. "Anne, stay back!" she shouted as Anne came bolting around the corner of the maze. Hannah leaped down from the belvedere, knocking Anne to the ground just as McClane fired the second time.

"I th-thought he shot you," Anne gasped from beneath Hannah.

"He didn't," Hannah replied, disentangling herself from her friend. "Stay down, Anne. He has one more shot to fire and then the gun will be useless."

"You are not going back up there?"

"Yes. He is a miserable shot, Annie. He tried to shoot Will and shot Triumph instead. Then he tried to shoot Mama and shot Mr. Dempsey instead. As long as he is attempting to shoot *me,* I will be perfectly safe. But I do not wish him to hit you by accident." Hannah popped to her feet and hurried back up the belvedere steps, the rapier held out before her. Mc-Clane had moved forward, to the middle of the building.

"I do beg your pardon, Mr. McClane, for that untimely interruption," Hannah drawled. "I see you have taken advantage of my absence to better your position. Step even closer, sir, do. Within range of my blade, if you will."

"I will kill you with my bare hands, you daughter of a she-devil."

"Will you? You admit that you cannot hit me with a shot from your pistol then?"

McClane pulled the trigger and the little pistol popped. Hannah heard the buzz of the ball as it whizzed past her and gave thanks she had not decided to dodge away.

McClane threw the pistol itself at her and followed it warily, watching to see what she intended to do with the rapier. Certainly he could seize the girl and rip the sword from her grip without the least effort, but it was prudent to remain clear of that sharp blade as he did so.

"Miss Tofar!" Harold Belowes shouted, running steadily behind Nat Tine, through and around the bushes of the maze—trusting in the old shepherd to know the way. "Sing out, Miss Tofar, if you can!"

Anne scrambled back into the maze. "Here!" she called. "At the very center! Hurry! Hannah is not shot, but the beast is like to kill her with his bare hands!" Then Anne hurried back into the center again and, seeing McClane closing on

Hannah, she hurried up the steps and stood beside her best friend, fireplace poker gripped tightly in both her hands.

Hannah held the rapier lightly in her right hand and waited for McClane as he approached. Her stance, the light in her eyes, and the grim determination on her face gave McClane pause. Perhaps the girl did know how to fence. Was she not the daughter of the same Julian Thorne who had run Mc-Clane's own father through in the Church of St. Milburga's of the Wood? Did Thorne men teach their daughters to fence as well as their sons?

Why not? Why not? McClane asked himself. Look what strength and cunning that blasted man instilled in his wife. Why should I doubt he would teach his daughter with equal abandon?

His doubts held him back. That and the second threat of the poker that now faced him. He would have to go about this thing carefully. Very carefully.

And then two men burst from the maze into the center. The footman, Belowes, and the shepherd, Tine. McClane recognized them at once. But they had no weapons. None at all. And though Belowes was large enough and young enough to be taken as a serious threat, even barehanded, Tine was not. He was a short, thin, old man. The two parted ways then, Belowes hurrying along one side of the belvedere, Tine along the other.

Going behind me, McClane thought. Preparing to attack from the rear, Belowes is. That will give him some advantage even if he cannot depend on much assistance from Tine.

His eyes still fastened on the girls, McClane took a step to the side, then turned and dashed across the wooden floor and leaped to the ground just as Tine and Belowes ascended the back of the belvedere. McClane waited until the two began to dash forward, to the girls, and then spun away toward the rear of the building. He would give them the girls and retreat for now, into the safety of the cave. He would return when the time was right. McClane broke into a run and dove to the ground at the entrance to the cavern. He rolled inside. A hand reached in after him and seized the lapel of his coat.

It cannot be the fool footman or that simpleton of a shepherd, he thought. Neither of them is as fast as that. McClane struggled to free himself from the hand, but it would not give up its hold and, with a strength McClane could not fathom, it began to pull him from beneath the belvedere like a terrier tugging a rat from its hole. A hound bayed, sending shivers up and down McClane's spine.

Veronica, who had burst into the center of the maze mere seconds after Dempsey, who himself had been only moments behind Belowes and the shepherd, dashed up the shallow steps and halted, amazed to see Hannah, Anne, Harold, and Nat at the rear of the building, doing nothing but gazing downward.

"Where is Mr. Dempsey, your grace?" Gaines asked breathlessly as he caught the duchess up, set the pistol box on the floor, and took the pistols out, one in each hand. Then he stood and followed the duchess's gaze. "Oh, thank the Lord," he said. "Lady Hannah and Miss Tofar are safe. But where is Mr. Dempsey?"

Together, the duchess and the butler hurried to join the other four people. Veronica gasped as she looked down to see a kneeling Dempsey pulling a squirming McClane steadily, inexorably, from beneath the belvedere.

McClane, coming to the conclusion that he could not pry himself from the man's grasp, ceased to struggle and allowed himself to be tugged into the open.

Dempsey dragged him clear of the floor above, stood, and hauled the man to an upright position. Then he loosed his grip on McClane's lapels.

Instantly the farm manager swung a fist at him.

The Reverend Mr. Dempsey ducked and landed a solid right to McClane's jaw and then sent a punishing left to his stomach. McClane groaned and doubled over.

Dempsey muttered angrily, seized the villain by the collar and the waistband of his breeches, spun him around, and cracked McClane's head against the floor of the belvedere.

The farm manager sank to the ground, senseless.

"Oh, I say," Hannah murmured.

Dempsey looked up to see the lot of them standing there, staring down at him. "I beg your pardon," he said. "This is not the manner in which I generally deal with troublesome people. Nor do I advise my parishioners to deal with each other in such a fashion. It is most inappropriate."

"Aye, Rector," mumbled Nat.

"Indeed, sir," Harold Belowes replied. "But Jupiter!"

Nat Tine led them from the maze, hugging Berinwick's box of dueling pistols to his chest. Harold Belowes and Gaines carried the unconscious McClane between them. Hannah and Anne, close behind, kept their weapons at the ready should the villain begin to twitch into wakefulness. The duchess and Mr. Dempsey, Theophilus cavorting around them, trailed slowly along, barely in sight of the others, holding hands behind the skirt of Mrs. Thistledown's old round gown. One would think, except for McClane's unconscious body, that they had all gone off for a summer stroll and nothing more as they emerged into the park. But then, one after the other, their eyes widened in awe.

"Who be all these blokes?" Nat asked quietly.

"It's everyone in Blackcastle and Barren Wycche, I think," Harold Belowes whispered.

The little park was filled with people. So filled with people that the sheep were becoming annoyed at the prospect of not having a blade of grass to call their own. So filled with people that Theophilus, when he emerged, began to wiggle his nose in ecstasy. There were boot smells everywhere. And sheep smells, too. And the lovely lady who walked beside his master was leaning down to twiddle his ears. How much better could life be?

"What the devil happened in there?" growled Berinwick, stomping up to them, seizing hold of Hannah and removing the rapier from her grasp. Just as abruptly, Squire Tofar tugged Anne into his arms and removed the fireplace poker from hers.

"Someone relieve Gaines and Belowes of that villain and carry him into my study," Berinwick commanded. "Tie him up with something strong and stand watch over him until I come."

Five gleeful Welshmen lifted McClane onto broad shoulders and hurried off with him. Gaines kept pace, intent on ushering them through the corridors to the room his grace had indicated.

"Hannah, are you all right?" Berinwick asked. "Tofar said you were in the maze and being attacked and I could not find one gardener or a single shepherd to lead me in when I arrived, so I was forced to waste time dashing into the house to get the map. And I could not find the map. What happened to the map?"

"We lost it, Will," Hannah confessed, staring down at her toes. "We looked everywhere for it and it was not to be—oh! Oh, my goodness!" Hannah covered her mouth with her hand and began to blush guiltily.

"Oh, my goodness?" said Berinwick.

"I remember where it is. I rolled it up and tucked it under my bonnet so I would be certain not to lose it!" With a flourish, Hannah untied the bow at her chin, swept the sweet little straw hat from her head, and handed Berinwick the map.

"Good girl," murmured Dempsey.

"No, she is not a good girl," Berinwick growled, glaring at the parson with his one dark eye. "She almost got Anne and herself killed."

"Well, I'm certain she didn't intend it, Will," Anne said at once in Hannah's defense. "And it was Hannah who faced the fiend down and saved both our lives."

"But it was Nat and Harry who frightened Mr. McClane back into his little hidey-hole at the last," Hannah added. "And the Reverend Mr. Dempsey who pulled him out again and beat him into submission."

Berinwick stared from one to the other, the relief he felt

in his heart only slowly transforming the features of his face into something near a smile.

"William? From where have all these people come?" his mother asked, in wonder. "It looks like the entire congregation of St. Milburga's of the Wood has assembled here on the lawn."

"From what I have been able to gather, Mother, when word of Anne shouting from the maze spread through Blackcastle, everyone inside poured outside," Berinwick replied. "I was already in the study, searching for the map, by then. And I am told that Giles Pervis, who has been helping with the haymaking, you know, and went to help at Tofar Farm today, went to visit his betrothed at the rectory to share a bit of luncheon with her. His betrothed—that will be the Langton's eldest daughter to you, Dempsey—his betrothed told him that Tom Hasty had been shot and you taken, Mother. And Tom was strong enough by then to say that it was McClane who did it. So Giles rode back to Tofar Farm and everyone there came here to do what they could to be of aid."

"Oh," Veronica said softly. "We shall have to do something for them, William. To repay them for such kindness."

"We be paid just to see you safe, your grace," called a voice from the crowd.

"Aye," called another. "But we be stayin' here for a bit, if you don't mind, your grace. Just to be sure that dastard goes directly off with Constable Lewis and don't cause you no more troubles. I reckon some of us be willing to ride along with Constable Lewis back to Barren Wycche."

"Indeed we be!" called out many more voices.

"And those of us what don't will be going back to Tofar Farm to finish up with what we started once McClane be on his way to jail. So ye need not worry about what to do with us."

Berinwick and Hannah, Veronica, and Dempsey gathered in the study and set the Welshmen on guard beyond the study door and outside the study windows once word came that McClane had regained his senses. The Welshmen were pleased to do it.

Bound tightly with leather strips from the stables, McClane sat upright in a straightbacked chair, so the others simply moved chairs close together before him.

"He said Papa murdered his father," Hannah began. "He said to ask you, Mama, or you, Will, about someone named Dight."

"You are Mr. Dight's son?" Veronica asked, shocked.

"Did you and your husband think Mr. Dight had no family?" McClane responded. "That none of the men your husband murdered in the church that day had families? Did you truly believe that there would be no one to hold you responsible?"

"How dare you!" the duchess sputtered. "How dare you to speak of responsibility when your father came here with the express purpose of murdering my husband, myself, and Will, stealing all we possessed of value and setting Blackcastle afire! There lies the responsibility for your father's death, in his own vile mind and the plans he made."

"Had he not come here, I rather think Father would not have gone to wherever you lived to search him out," Berinwick offered, "and he would be alive still. He and all his men with him."

"But it was not your father or one of those men who gave you my pendant, McClane," Veronica said. "It *was* you who hung that pendant on the tree for Hannah to find?"

"Indeed. And she took the bait as quick as any trout in the stream. I would have landed her and taken her away with me, too, had Lancaster not interfered."

"Who gave it to you—my pendant?"

"May as well say," Dempsey murmured, considering the stubborn look on McClane's face. "Certainly he is not here with you and I doubt anyone from Blackcastle will go in search of him. He was far from young at the time or he would have stood up with the rest of them."

"Do you mean to say that you *know* who gave him the pendant, Dempsey?" Berinwick asked, bemused.

"I can guess," Dempsey replied. "It will be the same person who filled his head with the lies about your father that he has just spouted. Likely passed on to him the history of the Poles and how they were wronged, too. I should like to hear that entire story someday, by the way. At any rate, I don't doubt for a moment that the fellow we are discussing provided Mr. McClane, here, with a copy of the catalogue of your father's collection, Berinwick, from which McClane decided which of the articles he would demand in ransom for your mother."

"You think he has a catalogue of my father's entire collection?"

"Yes. How else would he know what to demand? You didn't give your farm manager a key to that room in the tower, did you?"

"No, but—"

"It was Mr. Tweed, eh, McClane? The man Berinwick hired to catalogue his collection? It was Tweed filled your boyish mind with hate and greed and dreams of power, was it not?" Dempsey asked, giving Veronica's hand a supportive squeeze. *"Was* he a relative of yours?"

"A parson with a brain," McClane spat out angrily. "He was my uncle. He saw the boy drop the pendant on the church floor that morning, scooped it up, and brought it home with him when he left this place. It was magical, he told me, but it isn't."

"Not quite," murmured Dempsey.

"Is he dead, your uncle?" Berinwick asked.

"Dead."

"What was his real name?" Veronica queried a bit unsteadily, her hand fisting in Dempsey's. "What was Mr. Dight's real name? And what is yours?"

McClane glared at her and refused to answer.

"Tell me!" the duchess demanded.

"It is none of your business, witch," the man replied through tight lips.

"It *is* her business," Dempsey said in slow, measured tones. "You *will* tell her all she wishes to know," he added, his eyes narrowing. "You will answer her questions and Berinwick's and even Lady Hannah's or there will be hell to pay, McClane, I promise you that. I'm a parson. I know a great deal about hell and I shall be more than pleased to introduce you to it."

"It isn't Pole, if that's what she thinks," the villain replied grudgingly. "Ha! That is what she thinks! Fool woman! My name is Hurley, just as my father's was Hurley and my uncle's. But there is a drop or two of Pole blood in me, I've been told, and that golden bowl on the silver stand is mine. My father had a piece of it to prove it, too."

"Do you, perchance, have another piece of it?" Berinwick asked quietly. "A silver lion? Holding a crown? With a griffin rising?"

"No."

"Good. I should like to think that my father was wrong and that we now have all of the blessed things. You don't have any sons running about who are like to come and avenge you, eh, Hurley? I mean to say, once you are hanged, I should like to think it is the last we will see of anyone with any claim to a drop of Pole blood in them. I have grown to suspect that the Poles actually were the traitors my ancestors proclaimed them to be and they deserved to lose their titles and their wealth and be shipped off to France."

"William, hush. You cannot know that to be true."

"No, but only look at this one, Mother. He's a murderer and a thief and he has only a drop of their blood running through his veins. Wretched stuff, Pole blood, I think."

"Then you think wrong," the duchess proclaimed. She could not think why she did, but she felt obliged to do so. "I am reading the diaries and the journals of your father's ancestors even now, William, and if what one person in a family does must be considered representative of all, then you and Hannah, with a good deal more than a drop of Thorne blood running through your veins, are wretched, ruthless traitors. Which you are not, my darlings," she added at once.

"Not even Will?" Hannah asked, hoping that at last her mother could see clearly the facade behind which her brother hid his true self.

"What does *that* mean?" Berinwick grumbled. *"Not even Will?* I'll hack your ears off with a dull hatchet for that, you scamp."

"Oh, I am shivering in my shoes," Hannah replied. "Cannot you see? Why, I am almost as frightened of you, Will, as I am of that—that—dastard there."

"And she is not frightened of him in the least, Berinwick," Dempsey pointed out helpfully.

Gaines knocked on the study door and entered without waiting for an answer. "Constable Lewis," he announced, ushering that worthy into the room.

"You are lucky, Dempsey," Berinwick said quietly as he stood. "Saved in the nick of time from considerable retribution."

"Oh, did I address you improperly again, your grace?" the parson queried, his eyes twinkling with laughter. "How fortunate for me that the constable is here to save my skin, eh?"

Fourteen

The haymaking had been completed and the grain harvest was almost ready to begin. Patrick McClane was on no one's mind at all and Hannah's fifteenth birthday was rapidly approaching when one day, early in the afternoon, Veronica begged her son to go down with her into the cavern beneath the belvedere.

"I do not understand what we are doing under here, Mother," Berinwick said as he set his lantern down and sat beside her on one of the rocks. "I mean to say, I do understand that you wished to have the armor taken to the house and cleaned at last and given to Dempsey. And I expect he is the one person who ought to have it, considering his interest in antiquities and all. Though if it is actually Glyndwr's armor, he will become a frightfully rich sort of parson and we will have nothing from it."

"Do we need to have something from it, William?"

"No, not actually."

"Just so. I have requested that you accompany me down here one more time for very personal reasons. Do you realize that there is a diary written by the very first Duchess of Berinwick? And in it she mentions—"

"That will be my many-greated grandmother who built the maze, will it not?"

"Precisely. And in that diary, she wrote that she had ordered the belvedere to be built over Owain Glyndwr's grave."

"Surely you jest."

"No, I do not."

"Are you certain that you did not misread her penmanship, Mother? You ought to read it again, I think. For what she likely wrote is that she ordered the belvedere to be built over Owain Glyndwr's *cave*."

The Duchess of Berinwick smiled. "Perhaps you're correct, William, for I cannot see how there can be a grave beneath the belvedere when this wretched cavern seems to run the entire length and breadth of it. You do not suppose that there is a grave beneath the building but above the cave's ceiling?"

"No. But if there were, the only way to get to it would be to tear down the belvedere."

"It would be a great triumph," she said thoughtfully, "for a gentleman to discover the final resting place of Owain Glyndwr. If he were not already a Fellow of the Royal Society, the gentleman would most certainly become one almost instantly."

"I thought you said that Dempsey was a Fellow already."

"Yes, he is, and only think how exciting it would prove for him to be able to stand up before the others and describe the exact location of the grave of Owain Glyndwr and present them with artifacts from it. Mr. Dempsey's name would be engraved in their hallowed halls forever."

"Do they have hallowed halls? The Royal Society?"

"I am not certain. I have never taken an interest in such things before. Well, I did take an interest in your father's collection, of course, but never in where he went and what he did in London."

"You do not actually wish to tear down the belvedere, do you, Mother?" Berinwick gazed at her with the most quizzical look on his face.

"I would if Richard asked me to do so and it were in my power to do it. But it is no longer in my power to do it without your permission, William."

"Has he asked you to tear the belvedere down?"

"No, and I do not think he will. But I cannot say for certain. I only wish to know—if he should request it of me—would it be such a terrible thing in your eyes that you would forbid it?"

"I would forbid you nothing," Berinwick replied. "How could I? You're my mother, after all." He took one of her hands into both of his. "You must do as you think fit, Madam. This is the personal thing you wished to discuss with me? Tearing down the belvedere? I think you're merely leading up to the personal part, are you not? You are falling in love with that dratted parson."

"Have, William. I have fallen in love with that dratted parson. I think I have always loved him. Do you realize how blessed a woman I am, to have loved and been loved by your father, and now to discover that I have been given a second opportunity to love Richard Dempsey as he deserves to be loved?"

"No."

"No?"

"Somehow, Mother, I cannot quite see how being in love with the Reverend Mr. Dempsey can be called a blessing of any kind. I don't dislike the man, mind, but even you must confess he's an odd sort of fellow."

"Yes, I expect he is in some ways. But it is not only my thoughts of Richard that I wish to share with you. There is something else. Something I have put off mentioning," Veronica said, "because I wished to enjoy you, in the new way I have come to see you, William, for as long as I can."

She stood then, clasped her hands behind her back, and paced away from Berinwick to gaze off into utter darkness. "There is something I must tell you. It is most serious, so I hope you will say nothing droll in the midst of it. I—it—I shall not blame you if you never wish to see my face again. Or speak to me again, either. But it is time you know the truth."

Berinwick could tell how difficult it was for her to say the words. Even though she kept her back to him as she began to speak, he could see the tension in her shoulders, in the stiffness of her back, in the white-knuckled clasp of her hands behind her. But he could tell from the way she held her head that her chin was high, and from the tone of her voice that she was set on saying what she must say.

Berinwick fought hard to hold his tongue as she explained to him how she had grown selfish and ambitious and proud, for he thought her none of those things and could not think why she said them. Only when she told about THE ACCIDENT did he begin to understand why she had started by speaking of herself in such terms and in such a tone. And the more she continued with the story—continued to confess to him how she had not been able to bear the sight of him because of her own weakness, her inability to face what she had done—confessed to him that his father would have kept him at Blackcastle but for her—the heart he often pretended not to have rose up into his throat. He thought he would choke on it. But he forced it back down, listening patiently, silently, without a word of interruption.

When she ceased to speak and turned to him at last, her cheeks were wet with tears. They glistened in the lantern light like crystals growing on soft, white velvet. "And that is why— truly why—I asked you to come here with me, William. Because I could not bear to tell you all these things in the sunlight, to see the pain, the anger, the hatred in your face unshadowed—and the pity, too. I am coming at last to know the real you, you see, and I doubt not that there is pity for me in your heart. But I can see none of these things clearly in this place. They are hidden, disguised by the shadows the lantern throws, and so I am saved from them for a time. I am still weak, you see. I thought I had grown so very strong, but I am not yet as strong as I need to be to tell you straight out all the sins I have committed against you while the light of day shines down upon me."

Berinwick looked away from her. He stared down at the cave floor and said not one word. A great silence filled the chamber.

* * *

"She is *where?*" Dempsey asked as Hannah and he strolled toward the stables to check on Eloquent's foal.

"Under the belvedere with Will. Truly, she is. First, she said she required his assistance to see that the armor was removed and taken up to the house to be polished, and then she sent us all away but Will, and they went back down under the belvedere. They went into the cave, I should think."

"I see."

"Do you truly? Because I don't understand why she would do that at all. Not Mama. Not after having had to make her own way out virtually in the dark the way she did. If I were Mama, I should never wish to go down inside any cave ever again."

"But your mother found a great source of strength inside of her while in that cave, Lady Hannah. Perhaps she needed to call on that strength again, eh? Or perhaps she is even now attempting to find her way out of a different sort of darkness and into another sort of light—figuratively speaking, of course."

"Now you sound like a preacher," Hannah complained. "You do not in general sound like one."

"I do not?"

"No. Especially you did not in church last Sunday. I like the way the church is beginning to look now," she added, smiling up at him.

"Why did I not sound like a preacher in church last Sunday?" Dempsey queried with a cock of an eyebrow that made Hannah giggle. "It took me a goodly number of hours to write that particular sermon. I thought it turned out excellently well."

"Oh, I did not intend to say it was not an excellent sermon, but you kept making people snicker, you know. And when you compared the Fallen Dog to the Tower of Babel, Mr. Langton laughed aloud and Mrs. Langton hit him over the head with her new reticule to make him hush. And that set Tom Hasty off, chuckling behind his hand."

"How do you know these things? You were sitting in the Thorne family pew."

"Which is still missing half the back and both sides, Mr.

Dempsey. And I could not resist turning around when Mr. Langton guffawed. And then there was Theophilus, you know."

"Theo? What had Theo to do with my not sounding like a preacher?" Dempsey asked, grinning down at the happy hound trotting along beside him.

"He burped," Hannah said succinctly. "During the sermon. Any number of times. Even Will was having a difficult time keeping his frown in place. I wondered at the time. You will not think me forward do I ask you a question?"

"Think you forward? Never."

"Do rectors always bring their hounds right into the church on Sunday and let them lie in front of the pulpit? Because none of the itinerant preachers ever had any hounds, so I truly don't know. They never actually had a pulpit, either," Hannah added. "They just sort of stood in the middle of the village square, on the edge of the fountain, with a stack of wooden boxes piled up before them. Oh, there she is! There is the foal. I am going to purchase her, you know. For Will. For his birthday. And the squire is dropping the price a bit, too. He says it's because her lungs are damaged from the fire, but they are not so badly damaged as all that. She merely grows winded a bit sooner than other horses her age. He is doing it because he's grateful to Will for saving Anne's life and for all the help Will has given him since the fire. The house is nearly rebuilt, you know."

"Do you ever keep still?" Dempsey queried with a smile. "I cannot remember you speaking quite so constantly when first we met. You were shy then, I believe."

"Shy? That one?" asked Tom Hasty as he stepped out of the stable to shake the parson's hand. "I think not. Come to have a look at Hannah's Darling, have you, Mr. Dempsey?"

"Hannah's Darling? Is that the foal's name?"

"It's what we call her now. I reckon she'll keep it. His grace don't generally change a horse's name once he acquires it."

"That's so," Hannah giggled. "And we all thought what fun it would be to have Will galloping about and yelling, "Whoa, Darling. Faster, Darling. What the devil are you doing, Darling?"

* * *

"Well," Berinwick said quietly just as Veronica thought she would die from the lengthy silence. She had been staring down at him where he sat with his head bowed for the past five minutes, hoping, praying that he would not simply rise to his feet and leave the place—leave her—without a glance, without a word, with nothing.

"Well," he said again, raising his gaze to her, rubbing at his chin as he did so, "it's a far cry from what I thought happened, Madam. That is to say, at least I did not manage to poke my eye out all by myself."

"Oh, William!"

"That's what I always assumed. That I had done something purely stupid. No one ever spoke of it, you know. Not you. Not Father. Not even the staff."

"My fault," Veronica murmured.

"What is your fault?"

"That no one ever spoke of it. They feared to hurt *me* by speaking of it."

"I see. And it is your fault as well that I was plagued all the while I was at school by boys intent on making sport of me?"

"Yes."

"And that I spent so many holidays away from home?"

"Yes, William."

"So it is also your fault that I have a vile temper, a cutting wit, and have developed a glare that can intimidate a raging bull?"

"I—I—yes. All my fault."

"I don't think so, Mother."

"What?"

"I said, dearest mother, that I don't think so," Berinwick repeated, standing, taking Veronica's hands into his own. "I have put a considerable amount of planning and effort into developing my temper, my wit, and my glare over the years—not to mention the foul reputation I hold among the privileged lads in London—and I don't wish you to have *all* the credit for it. You mentioned the words Father said to me that day—that I would be the Duke of Berinwick one day and must learn to act like a Berinwick."

"It was cruel of him! He did it because of me, William. I know he did."

"Did what? Informed me of the truth of my life? I did grow up, Madam. I am a Duke of Berinwick. And I am a damnably good one, too. I think I ought to point that out to you, in case you haven't noticed. I am almost a perfect Duke of Berinwick."

"You are hiding your heart away, protecting it, even now," Veronica whispered.

"Yes, I am," Berinwick replied in a whisper of his own as he freed her hands, stepped behind her, and put his arms around her instead. "I am very good at it—hiding my heart away—Mama. And I cannot think but that learning to do it has saved me from terrible sorrow many times over."

"But kept you from finding a love of your own."

"Oh, Mama, of all things! I doubt there is any lady in all of England who would wish to love a one-eyed devil like me. But if there should be one kind enough to wish to do it, do you not believe she might also be wise enough to realize that I have a heart somewhere and brave enough to dig down inside the shell I have grown around it and pluck it out into the sunlight?"

"I thought I had destroyed the heart you once possessed," Veronica replied, thankful for the comfort of his arms around her, the feel of his chin resting atop her head. "It took Richard and Hannah to bring me to see you untainted by my own guilt. It was your sister and Richard who pointed out to me the real you I could not see. And then one day, I saw your heart all by myself just as clearly. And it is as kind and sweet and good as ever it was before I did you such great harm, Will."

"Well, of course it is. That particular thing *is* your fault, Mama. If you had come to me sooner and explained how you persisted in torturing yourself—and over such a thing as that—I should have been pleased to tell you that I have the same sort of heart and feelings as any other gentleman. It was a silly thing to worry about. You will not worry about it anymore, will you? Eh? No matter what I say or do?"

"No, William."

"Good. Because if you do, I will send you off to live under the Thistledowns' woodpile with Mrs. Quillbristle."

"M-Mrs. Quillbristle?"

"She's a hedgehog, Mother. Millie and Charlie's hedgehog. May we leave this place now? Please? I don't know about you, but I am not overly fond of caves and I am growing less and less fond of them the more time I spend underground. What?" he asked as he took his arms from around her, retrieved the lantern, and began to help her up the waiting ladder.

"You d-do not despise me, William? Not even a bit?"

"You will not be happy unless I do, will you? All right, then. I despised you, Mother, for—oh, let me think—one half of a half of a second? Will that make you feel better? What earthly reason have I to despise you? Have you not suffered enough already? I know you love me. I have always known it. I thought, perhaps, that you had a rather peculiar aversion to being touched when I was young, but it did never occur to me that my own mother might not love me. Return me the favor and never think that I don't love you. Never again. No matter what insensitive words pop out of my mouth. For now I have said aloud, over and over, that I do love you.

"What's past is past," he added in a gruff mumble, climbing up the ladder behind her. "There is nothing to be done about the past but smile at the best of it, learn what we can from the worst of it, and toss the rest of it onto the rubbish heap."

They gathered in the smallest of the drawing rooms after dinner two days later, Berinwick and Hannah, Veronica and Dempsey and Theophilus.

"Do you never go anywhere without that hound?" Berinwick queried, a glass of port in one hand, the other fiddling with a figurine on the fireplace mantel.

"Only when Mrs. Langton is at the rectory and baking," Dempsey replied. "Though I should like to go somewhere without him at the moment."

"You should?"

"Yes. I would be obliged, Berinwick, if you and Lady Hannah would watch over him for me for a mere quarter hour or so."

"Now?"

"Right now. You will, won't you? You do owe me a favor, after all."

"I do?"

"Both you and Lady Hannah. Do not look at me with such disbelief, Berinwick. Did I pray more than once over dinner? Did I bless every potato and pea? No, I did not. I might have done, but I was most considerate and did you the great favor of subduing my natural inclinations."

"Do not call me Berinwick, you audacious, *old,* parson."

"Beg your pardon. Slipped out. But you owe me a favor, nevertheless. Watch the hound. Your sister will help you. Your mother and I have something to discuss. Privately."

"We do?" Veronica asked, smiling at the insolent cock of Berinwick's eyebrow and the sparkle in Dempsey's eyes. "I cannot guess what it can be."

"Come with me, my dear, and you need not guess. I will tell you straight out," he said, taking her hand in his and escorting her from the room, down the hallway, and in through the next available door. "What the deuce is this?"

"It's a ballroom, Richard. At least, it was once. Now it is merely an empty room. I cannot think why Gaines should have lighted the chandelier. What an enormous amount of work."

"I asked him to do it."

"You what?"

"Well, I requested to have lighted whatever candles there were in the room immediately beyond the drawing room. Apparently the only candles were those in the chandelier. Just look how the floor glows, Veronica! I can see myself in it."

"Yes, indeed," Veronica replied with a giggle.

"I have never seen an actual ballroom—not one that isn't simply two drawing rooms combined with the rugs rolled up and put away. I should think it's a glorious thing when it is decorated and filled with people."

"Oh, yes, indeed. Most glorious. Richard? Why are we here?"

"Well, there is something I wish to say to you, Vernie. I must admit, I did rather think there would be chairs. There is not one chair. Not even a table. This room is as naked as can be except for the chandelier."

"Richard," she said, calling him to order with simply the tone of her voice. "You are babbling like the merest babe. Is there something wrong? Do tell me, Richard, if there is something wrong. If there is anything I can do . . ." She reached out to stroke his cheek, which was surprisingly red. "Why are you so flustered?"

"I am not flustered. It is simply that I—that I—"

The sound of a pianoforte—of lean, long fingers rippling softly over ivory keys—floated to them from the next room. Veronica noticed at once that it was not a melancholy song, but soft and tender and filled with quiet laughter. It was William, of course. All the household was pausing now, to listen. As was she. As was Richard. Pausing to let the music seep into the air around them, to allow it to entangle them in dreams.

Richard Randolph Dempsey put his arms around the Duchess of Berinwick. He placed his cheek against hers and began to sway sensuously to the melody. Veronica, so close against him that she could feel his heart beating in her own breast, closed her eyes and swayed with him—softly, slowly, safe in his arms—losing herself in the movement, in the music, in the tenderness of his touch. It felt to her like the most sinful thing she had ever done. Yet, she did not wish to cease doing it. Ever.

And then Richard whispered in her ear, "I loved you once,

Veronica, in the springtime of our lives. Now that autumn is closing in upon us, I find that I love you still. You know that. I have told you over and over how much I love you. And I wonder—I wonder if you will allow me to love you from one day to the next into the very dead of winter and for all eternity following that. I wonder if you will do me the honor to be my wife." He took his cheek from hers then, and gazed down at her, his unspeakably beautiful blue eyes brilliant with love, brimming with hope.

"How can I not?" Veronica answered quietly, raising her lips to meet his. "Oh, Richard, how can I not?"

When they returned, at last, to the drawing room, Berinwick was once again before the fireplace, fiddling with the figurine, and Hannah was ensconced in the largest of the padded armchairs.

"Hannah? Are you all right?" Veronica asked at once. "Your cheeks are flushed and you are gasping as though you are out of breath from running."

"She is," Berinwick said. "Out of breath from running. I bet her that she could not run out to the stables and back before I finished playing."

"William!"

"Do not frown at me, Mother. She won the wager. Did you like the song, Madam? It came to me out of the blue. A rather romantic sort of thing, I thought, but I played it anyway."

"It was lovely, William. If you are certain you are well, Hannah, there is something that Richard and I should like to say to you both."

"It worked," Hannah giggled, with a triumphant look at Berinwick.

"Of course it worked," he replied arrogantly. "And if that obnoxious hound had not kept trouncing all over the pedals trying to eat my boots while I played, it might well have worked even better. The two of them might not be here in this room yet, except for that."

"What are you saying, Will?" asked the duchess.

"Nothing. Hannah and I beg your pardon for interrupting. Do go on and say what you have to say, Mother."

"When I am out of mourning—" she said, glorying in the touch of Dempsey's hands on her shoulders as he stood behind her. "When I am out of mourning, Richard and I are going to be married."

"The old scoundrel never asked my permission to address you," Berinwick drawled.

"That particular nicety does not apply to mothers," Dempsey replied, as Veronica stared at her son with her lips parted and no words forthcoming. "Say you are happy for her, Berinwick."

"Since you are going to marry him, I expect I shall be forced to allow him to call me Berinwick, eh, Mother?"

"Unless you would prefer him to call you William. Well, you cannot truly insist on 'your grace,' Will," Veronica replied. "He barely ever manages to call you that now. He will not do it at all, I think, when he is your stepfather."

"Berinwick, then. But be clear on it, Dempsey. I am never going to call you Papa." He grinned then, most unexpectedly, and laughter sparkled in his eye just as truly as it had once sparkled in his father's. "I do wish you happy, Mother. You as well, Dempsey. Congratulations," he said, stepping forward to shake the parson's hand and give Veronica a kiss on the cheek.

"Yes, I wish you happy, too, Mama," Hannah added, though she did not rise from her chair. "And I will be pleased to have you as a stepfather, Mr. Dempsey. We did wonder, Will and I, if you were ever going to ask her. And then when the two of you left the room this evening, we *did* hope. Now, Will?" she asked.

Berinwick nodded and Hannah stood, taking something she had stuffed down into the chair behind her into her hands and carrying it carefully to the parson. "Will and I have been keeping this for you—for this precise occasion. I ran all the way out to the stable to get it after I peeked into the ballroom and saw you and Mama—welcome to our family, Mr. Dempsey."

"Thank you, my dear," he said, as Hannah placed the gift into his hands and, standing on tiptoe, kissed his cheek.

"Hannah, wherever did you find that?" Veronica asked, as Dempsey held the thing up before his eyes. He turned it 'round and 'round. His eyes widened with every turn.

"I'll be scuttled!" he exclaimed. "It cannot be, but it certainly matches the few descriptions we have of Glyndwr's cup."

"Does it?" Berinwick asked with a gleam in his eye. "And when Hurley demanded it as part of Mother's ransom, I thought the thing must be a silver chalice at the very least. Hurley learned of it from Father's letter to you, you know. Read the thing before it was sealed. Not a chalice at all. Just an old clay cup with odd markings on it."

"Yes, but the markings are everything," Dempsey replied.

"So Mother said when I asked her to describe it to me."

"Will has had it for a year and more," Hannah grinned.

"Exactly so. Found it in the north tower of St. Milburga's the day Langton fetched me to see how very unstable the tower had become. Dastardly bricks were going to powder before my eyes. And as a few of them did puff away, out popped this cup. So Langton and I propped up the tower as best we could and home I rode with the cup to clean it up and use it for mixing powders and ointments in the stables. It has been there ever since."

"Used it for mixing powders and ointments in the stables? By Jove, do you know what this is, Berinwick? If it should prove to be real, I mean?" asked Dempsey.

"I know it was supposedly given to Owain Glyndwr at Machynlleth by some old man."

"By a sorcerer, perhaps even Merlin himself, returned from the cave," Dempsey explained, escorting Veronica to the sofa and sitting down beside her. He set the cup on a low table before them. "Sit down, Hannah, Berinwick, and I will tell you one of the finest tales you have ever heard. It is about this cup and how it was given to King Arthur one evening in the greatest secrecy."

"King Arthur?" Hannah asked, surprised, settling once again into the armchair while Berinwick sat in the matching chair beside her.

"Indeed. King Arthur. He was warned to keep it with him always. One sip of water from this cup and it would heal even mortal wounds. One sip of water from this cup and even a man long dead—well, not any man, but Arthur—would rise from his grave to rule again. Oh, it's a deucedly good tale— who gave it to him and how it was stolen and who had it at the last."

"Apparently *you* have it at the last, Dempsey," Berinwick pointed out. "If it truly is the same cup. If there ever was such a cup. Personally, I shouldn't put much trust in it. I would be considerably more inclined to put my trust in—"

"This particular treasure here," Dempsey interrupted, placing his arm tenderly around Veronica's shoulders. "Another treasure which I have—at the last. And so I will, Berinwick, put my trust in her. You're a bright lad. A very bright lad. Bright enough to know when it's time to make yourself scarce, I think, and take Lady Hannah with you."

Whereupon, the Reverend Mr. Dempsey turned his back on the cup and the duke and Hannah, took the duchess in both arms, and began to kiss her with most unparsonlike abandon.

Thrilling Romance from Lisa Jackson

__Twice Kissed	0-8217-6038-6	$5.99US/$7.99CAN
__Wishes	0-8217-6309-1	$5.99US/$7.99CAN
__Whispers	0-8217-6377-6	$5.99US/$7.99CAN
__Unspoken	0-8217-6402-0	$6.50US/$8.50CAN
__If She Only Knew	0-8217-6708-9	$6.50US/$8.50CAN
__Intimacies	0-8217-7054-3	$5.99US/$7.99CAN
__Hot Blooded	0-8217-6841-7	$6.99US/$8.99CAN

Call toll free **1-888-345-BOOK** to order by phone or use this coupon to order by mail.

Name_____

Address_____

City_____ State _____ Zip _____

Please send me the books I have checked above.

I am enclosing $_____

Plus postage and handling* $_____

Sales tax (in New York and Tennessee) $_____

Total amount enclosed $_____

*Add $2.50 for the first book and $.50 for each additional book.

Send check or money order (no cash or CODs) to:

Kensington Publishing Corp., 850 Third Avenue, New York, NY 10022

Prices and Numbers subject to change without notice. All orders subject to availability.

Check out our website at **www.kensingtonbooks.com**.